THE
RIVER
GIRL

A compelling saga of love, loss and self-discovery

TANIA CROSSE

Devonshire Sagas Book 2

JOFFE
BOOKS

Revised edition 2021
Joffe Books, London
www.joffebooks.com

First published by Pan Books in Great Britain in 2006

Cover art by Jarmila Takač

Photograph by Paul Rendell

ISBN: 978-1-78931-802-9

For Pearlikins, who nurtured my interest in both medicine and plants.

And for my husband, who has been the rock of my life.

IMPORTANT AUTHOR'S NOTE

The herbal remedies referred to in this novel are used fictionally and are not a suggestion for use. You should never take any herbal remedy without consulting a qualified medical professional. The author and publisher are not recommending or advising anyone to use any of the remedies described.

PROLOGUE

Cornwall, 1854

The child did not shed a tear throughout.

She stood at the side of the deep, rectangular hole in the earth as motionless as a statue, looking for all the world like a little old lady, her pale skin almost translucent against the enormous black bonnet that framed her diminutive face. Only her eyes moved, gazing up solemnly at the adults, huge, soft eyes the colour of amber and fringed with long, silken lashes. She put him in mind of a young fawn, the vicar thought, with a grace and alertness not usual in a child who could be no more than four years old. But at this moment, he had a Christian duty to perform, and Hannah Thornton, the distraught, grief-stricken widow, to console.

The little girl watched, her brow gently furrowed, as the plain box was lowered into the ground. This game was going on too long. Why was her dear daddy, who always had a smile and a laugh for her even when he came home exhausted from the mine, still pretending to be asleep in the box? And why were her mother and all these people with long faces burying the box in the garden next to the church, surrounded by big stones with writing on them? Her mummy had said

1

that her daddy needed a long sleep, but it was three days now — she had counted them on her fingers — and surely that was long enough for anyone? And now her mother had thrown a clod down onto the box, and someone pressed a handful of earth into her own palm. Was she supposed to do the same? She glanced up for reassurance, and met a sea of faces all nodding at her with strained, encouraging smiles. She dutifully pitched the soil into the air. It landed, like splashes of heavy rain, on the thin wooden cladding. As the reverend pronounced some final words, two unknown workmen began shovelling a huge mound of earth into the hole. It clattered noisily at first, masking the swish of skirts and the creaking of worn boots as the feet around her turned and made their mournful way towards the gate. But once the box was covered with a layer of earth, each new spadeful simply produced a dull thud. One of the men hopped down into the pit to spread the soil more evenly and tread it down with his mud-covered boots.

''Ee'd best be following the others,' he nodded kindly at the grim-faced little soul, who stared down at him with an arresting, steady gaze.

She blinked at him with those troubled, velvet eyes and slowly turned away. Yet she did not run to catch up with her mother. Instead she walked with the restrained dignity of a nun, her hands clasped before her. When she reached the humble but clean cottage that was her home, she moved in silence among the people she was surprised to discover there. They spoke in whispers, patted her head sympathetically, and when they departed, the room seemed to echo with a strange emptiness.

Her mother's eyes moved regretfully about her, taking in their few possessions, lingering on the memories. Then she sighed weightily, and with a faint smile, took her little daughter's hand.

'Help me wash up these cups, Lizzie, my love,' she said fondly, but the child knew there was something odd in her voice. 'Then we must pack all we can into that wooden crate, and I want you to put all your clothes and other things into the carpet bag. And in the morning, we must be up early to tie all the bedding into a bundle. We must be ready when the carrier comes.' And when the girl raised her large, round, questioning eyes, her mother explained with forced brightness, 'We're going to live with my sister Margaret and her husband. Your aunt and uncle. They work a small farmstead on the edge of Dartmoor. You know. I've told you about it before. Aunt Margaret's just had a baby, a little girl. Nellie they're calling her. That'll be nice, won't it?'

'But I want to stay here.' Elizabeth Thornton spoke for the first time, her mouth puckered into a rosebud. 'And what about Daddy? We can't leave him behind!'

The breath caught in her mother's throat. 'Daddy . . . won't be coming with us. And . . . the cottage will be needed for another miner and his family. But you'll like it on your uncle's farm. With Nellie. And all the animals. And 'tis not so very far away.'

But for all Elizabeth knew — or cared — it might have been on the moon.

ONE

Western Dartmoor, October 1858

'Matthew.' Hannah Thornton's voice was grave as she addressed her brother-in-law. 'I really think 'tis time we fetched the doctor.'

Elizabeth felt uneasy as she sat beside her cousin Nellie on a rag rug in front of the smouldering peat fire. It was well into the afternoon, and Aunt Margaret's harrowing cries had been splitting the usual quiet of the isolated farmstead since dawn as she struggled to bring yet another child into the world. Nellie was playing happily with a play-worn rag doll, seemingly oblivious to her mother's agonies in the next room, but Elizabeth vaguely remembered when her other cousin, Nathaniel, had been born eighteen months before. As if to keep the fear trundling through her veins, another tortured howl wailed through the open door.

Elizabeth lifted her eyes to her Uncle Matthew, whose thickset form slouched on the rustic settle by the fireside, sucking on his clay pipe, apparently unconcerned.

'Us doesn't have no money fer no doctor,' he slurred in his slow Devonshire accent, and puffed a wispy lungful of tobacco smoke into the air.

4

'And if we don't get that babe out of her soon, you'll have no wife, neither!' Hannah's eyes snapped.

Elizabeth watched as her uncle glanced up indolently and spoke with his pipe still clenched between his large, square teeth. 'You'm the local wise woman,' he drawled accusingly.

'Which is precisely why I know when there's something wrong!' Hannah retorted from the door that led directly to the bedroom.

'Then I be certain you knows how fer put it right.' He tapped the spent tobacco from his pipe into the open hearth and hauled himself to his feet. 'Well, I've they wethers fer check on up on the leer, so I'll be off.'

'The sheep mean more to you than your wife, do they?' Hannah fumed. 'My God, our father would turn in his grave if he knew Margaret were married to a man like you!'

'Well, then.' Matthew hunched his burly shoulders. 'He shouldn't have left you both so poor as you had fer marry the first stupid sods as came along, should he? And you only found yersel a miner, as I do mind!'

'John was in line for mine-captain, as well you know. He worked damnably hard, and he *cared*, God rest his soul!'

'And are you saying as I doesn't?' Matthew barked. 'I've provided fer you and Lizzie fer the past four year, may I remind you. 'Tis not easy on my own with little help from you womenfolk. 'Tis only Lizzie as has any idea 'bout farming. Look how her raised they orphaned lambs last spring when I didn't have the time fer them!' The surge of red anger in his cheeks softened as his eyes rested on his niece. 'Farmer's darter her should've bin, not a miner's! Bloody natural, her be.'

'Watch your language, Matthew Halse. You mightn't mind what filth your children hear, but I care what Lizzie does!'

'I'll use whatever language I please in my own home, parson's darter!' he retorted with a triumphant snort. 'Now get yersel back in there and take care on my wife. An' p'raps Lizzie can do summat more towards her keep, eh, Twinkle?'

His teeth gleamed like tombstones in his weather-beaten face as he grinned down at Elizabeth before pulling on his old coat and opening the door that creaked on its protesting, rusty hinges. Elizabeth's eyes were wide with confusion as she heard him go out through the cross passage. She wasn't quite sure how to take her uncle's praise when it was so muddled into his bad temper. But that was typical of her Uncle Matthew, wasn't it, his bark far worse than his bite. As he allowed the outer door to slam shut behind him another desperate cry came from the bedroom. Hannah glanced anxiously over her shoulder as she wiped her hands on her blood-streaked apron.

'Lizzie, dear, could you make sure all the buckets are full of water, and then go down to the village and ask the reverend to go into Tavistock and fetch Dr Greenwood. Take Nellie with you. Nathaniel's having his afternoon nap, thank goodness, but he'll wake before long, so be as quick as you can, won't you?' Her agitated eyes darted towards the room behind her, but she paused long enough to cast a proud if fleeting smile at her daughter. Thank the dear Lord for the child, the only one of a series of pregnancies to last to term. She wasn't quite eight years old, yet had more sense in her head than most women accumulated in a lifetime. Certainly more than Margaret had shown when she'd married Matthew Halse! Not that he was really so bad when you saw past his pig-headed exterior. He just didn't like the way Hannah stood up to him but he had cared for herself and Lizzie since her dear John's death and it meant hard work and long hours for him, so no wonder he was apt to be surly. As for his attitude to his wife's extended labour, well, he was surrounded by birth, wasn't he? He was a good farmer when all was said and done, and rarely lost an animal through what was only a natural process. Hannah was considered a skilled midwife, so surely she could attend her own sister successfully!

But Hannah wasn't so sure. As with all her expectant mothers, she'd encouraged her sister to drink raspberry leaf tea in the last months of pregnancy to assist the birth. But Margaret's strength was failing with each contraction, and she was in unbearable pain, despite the meadowsweet Hannah had given her. William Greenwood could administer chloroform which would be far stronger against the pain. However, more than anything, Hannah was concerned about the bleeding, and the fact that still no baby's head was showing, even though the birth canal had been fully dilated for some time. If, as she suspected, the placenta had formed low down in the womb and was blocking the entrance to any degree, there was quite definitely need of the doctor, and the sooner Lizzie fetched him, the better!

Elizabeth had already collected the empty buckets and was standing in the doorway.

'Come along, Nellie. Put your shawl on.'

Nellie's moon-shaped face lifted slowly, her docile, bovine eyes widening with eagerness to obey her beloved cousin, and a minute later the two little girls were crossing the yard. The late October sun was starting its gradual descent, casting long shadows across the muddy ground, while the air was becoming cold and damp, as it would be all winter long here on the western fringe of Dartmoor. But when they reached the granite water trough, which was fed by a leat cut from a brook high on the hillside above the farmstead, Elizabeth and Nellie found it bathed in sunlight. Elizabeth could feel the sun's faint warmth on her back as she placed the first of the three buckets beneath the cascade of silvery water that tumbled over the end of the leat. She smiled at the younger child as she waited for the pail to fill, and then her pretty mouth spread into an impish grin as she scooped a handful of water from the trough and tossed it over her cousin. Nellie's dull face lit up with glee, and dipping her own chubby fist into the water she proceeded to chase Elizabeth around the yard on her short squat legs. Since the bucket was not yet full, Elizabeth abandoned herself wholeheartedly to the game, sending the hens squawking indignantly in every direction, and dodging fleet-footedly about the yard so that by the time Nellie finally launched the precious cargo of water at her, it had already trickled away through her fingers and they were breathless with laughter. But once they'd calmed down, Elizabeth felt mortified that she'd been playing when her aunt was in such dire pain. She loved Aunt Margaret, who was full of fun and always ready to play even though she was so busy with the innumerable tasks the women on a farm took care of — no matter what Uncle Matthew had said just now!

'Nellie, we must hurry.' Elizabeth's face was serious again as the merriment faded. 'You put this bucket inside and I'll bring the others,' she instructed as she heaved the full pail from the trough. 'Then we'll go down to the village.'

She turned back to her task, knowing it would take Nellie a little time to totter back to the house with the heavy bucket. They must hurry, and she suddenly felt very grown up, the importance of the errand gripping at her stalwart little heart. She struggled back across the yard with her own consignment of water as quickly as she could. Soon afterwards the two girls were scuttling down the steep stony track and onto the rutted lane that would take them the mile and a half into the village.

They came into Peter Tavy by the church, passing the turf building at the side of the old church poorhouse. Elizabeth had spent most of the day there, crammed amongst the seventy children of the village who learned what they could in the makeshift school that was still in use after nearly twenty years. But the rectory stood at the far side of the village, so they had to hurry onward, passing the couple of farms that were situated within the village itself. Smaller cottages were occupied by farm labourers, and some by miners who worked down the great copper mines of Wheal Friendship in nearby Mary Tavy. Many of the men here were both miner and farmer, working shifts below ground and supplementing their income by growing crops on the limited land that adjoined their cottages. Not *proper* farmers, Uncle Matthew would jeer, but forced to scrape a living in whatever way they could. Just along the way, Elizabeth could hear the clang of the blacksmith's heavy hammer, preparing a horse-shoe, perhaps, or attending to the metal parts of farm machinery that were endlessly brought to him for repair. But there was no time to stop and chat to him now.

'Lizzie, dear, what you'm doing yere?'

Dandling an infant on her hip, farmer's wife, Mrs Peters, emerged from the front room of her house which had been converted into a grocer's shop.

''Tis my Aunt Margaret. She's having the baby, but Mother wants Dr Greenwood to come, so we're going to the rectory.'

The woman frowned. 'Well, if your mother thinks there be summat *she* can't cope with, there must be summat amiss.'

'Yes, so can't stop, Mrs Peters. Come along, Nellie!' And grasping her young cousin by the hand, Elizabeth dragged her through the sleepy village. Mrs Peters watched them with a shrug of her shoulders. Sensible little soul was Lizzie Thornton, and bright as a button! She wished Margaret Halse well, for if her sister was worried, there must be something to worry about. Hannah Thornton had a reputation as a midwife second to none. Not one babby or mother lost in the four years she'd been in the village. What was more, her herbal remedies had helped so many when they couldn't afford the doctor's fees or the price of his medicines. Dr Greenwood was also the local mine-surgeon. The men who worked at Wheal Friendship received his services free of charge, of course, or at least in exchange for the shilling a week they paid into the fund. But the scheme didn't extend to the miners' families, and although the doctor's charges were nominal, as he made a reasonable living from his wealthier clients in Tavistock, Hannah Thornton's remedies were even cheaper!

Mrs Peters turned back into her shop while the two small girls continued on to the rectory. Elizabeth had never been to the substantial house before and found it a little overwhelming. But hadn't her own grandfather been a parson? And hadn't her mother often told stories of how their family had been as poor as church mice, because her grandfather gave all he had to the paupers of his parish? It was he who had studied nature's healing secrets under the guidance of an ancient countrywoman, not for his own edification, but to help his impoverished parishioners. And now Hannah was passing down that knowledge to Elizabeth. She'd never known her grandfather. Already widowed, he'd died relatively young, leaving his two unmarried daughters without a farthing to their names or a roof over their heads. So, Elizabeth's young brain reasoned, the vicar of St Peter's, whom she knew only from the kindly smile he offered her every Sunday after morning service, could be no different from the caring man her grandfather had been. So bracing her slim shoulders, she walked boldly up the drive.

They were shown into the parlour. A matter of life or death, she'd announced to the housekeeper who'd frowned in bemusement at the message entrusted to such a small visitor. The reverend appeared at once, and was out of the door again almost before Elizabeth had explained why she'd come. The room was cold and draughty, but the housekeeper ushered them into the kitchen where she fed them on hot muffins and mugs of steaming chocolate while the reverend galloped into town.

Their bellies full to bursting, the two little girls walked back into the village, the elder holding the other's hand, her head held high with pride at having accomplished her mission so successfully. She stopped by the church. She would love to slip down the alleyway and past the inn, taking the road that led down to the river. The level of the lively, boulder-strewn waters of the Tavy would still be low, the ford quite passable to horses and wagons. But she and Nellie could stand on the long wooden bridge that spanned the river and gaze down into the bubbling cascades of water that hurried between the moss-covered rocks. The bridge was called Mary Tavy clam if you lived in Peter Tavy or Peter Tavy clam if you lived in Mary Tavy. But a beautiful spot it was for everyone, and a perfect place to paddle on a hot summer's day. On the Dartmoor bank were the remains of Wheal Anne, abandoned a few years earlier after only a short life raising copper and black tin, but a little further down, the small mine of Wheal Rosalind thrived on land owned by the Pencarrow family. The Pencarrows were successful farmers and indeed, over the generations, had bought four other small farmsteads in addition to their own, one of which they now rented to Matthew Halse.

Elizabeth's mouth twitched. A few minutes playing on the riverbank would have been fun. It might be the last opportunity before the rains set in and the Tavy rose dangerously. In winter, the shallow gravel bed would disappear beneath a swirling torrent that foamed over the rocks as water poured off the moor high up in Tavy Cleave, and streams and brooks emptied into the river.

Elizabeth sighed with regret. This was no time for playing. She was about to have a new baby cousin to care for. Her mother would have her hands full, so Elizabeth would be needed to take care of Nathaniel who could be a demanding child at the best of times. So, with a wistful glance in the direction of the river, she struck out towards the moor with Nellie waddling along behind her.

TWO

'Be that all o' them, then?' Matthew asked early that evening as they worked in one of the fields next to the farmhouse.

''Twould seem so, Uncle.' Elizabeth straightened up from checking the last ewe, loose strands of her golden hair billowing about her heart-shaped face. 'They all have a yellow stain on their rumps.' And that was the object of the exercise, the dye on the ram's chest transferring onto each ewe to show it had been mounted and would produce a lamb, or maybe even twins, in the spring. Although quite why these antics ended in such a result, Elizabeth never thought to ask.

'Good! Then us must corner that aud ram and put 'en in the shed fer rest fer a few days, afore us puts the next set of ewes in to tup. What colour will't be next, little maid?'

'Blue, I think,' Elizabeth grinned, for the dye would remain on the ewes all winter, so that her uncle would know when each one was about to lamb and the process could be spread over several weeks.

'Then blue it shall be!' Matthew laughed throatily. He was in a good mood. That afternoon, Dr Greenwood had arrived none too soon to save both Matthew's wife and his new son, although it had taken every last vestige of the physician's skill to do so. And now Matthew would have another boy to work on the farm. The little lad wasn't robust like Nellie and Nathaniel had been at birth, tiny replicas of their father. Rather he was a sickly scrap with his mother's graceful looks. But he was a boy, nonetheless, who Matthew was sure, in time, would prove more use than a girl. With the exception of Lizzie, of course, who wasn't strong but had a way with the animals and a practical brain that could cope with anything. He put his big hand on her shoulder and drew her so sharply against him that she nearly lost her balance. 'Bloody good farmer you'd have made! Pity you'm not a lad. Or a brawny wench, even. But you'm nort but a skinny maid. Still, niver mind. Us've got this ram fer catch afore 'tis dark. Now if you keep they ewes over that side o' the field, Spot an' us'll drive the aud fellow into the corner by the gate. But if the bugger rushes at you, don't try fer catch 'en! He knows how fer use they horns!'

'I promise,' Elizabeth smiled, for this was the caring uncle she was fond of, and not the short-tempered bully who'd argued with her mother earlier that afternoon. She turned, arms spread wide, to the ewes which were huddling uneasily together, shifting nervously at the low whistles and commands Matthew gave to his faithful dog. Above them, the black silhouette of Dartmoor rose like the back of a sleeping lion in the gathering dusk. The moon was already high, and the clear sky that had given the fine autumn day promised the first frost. Elizabeth shivered in her worn coat, two sizes too small for her now, and glanced over her shoulder. Matthew had the ram securely by the horns as he straddled its back, and was manhandling it through the gate. Elizabeth could leave her post now, and ran across the field, scattering the startled sheep. She was hungry, and she knew there would be some tasty broth in the hot-pot her mother kept constantly over the open fire. A dim light glowed comfortingly from the tiny windows on one side of the farmhouse. On the other was the shippen where the cows would spend the long, harsh winter, and in the centre was the cross passage, used as the entrance by both humans and animals alike. Out in the yard was a separate barn, with stabling for the two sturdy farm ponies. Here Dr Greenwood's horse was idly waiting for its master while he attended to his patients. At one end of the barn, a rickety lean-to acted as a turf house to store the peat-faggots cut in summer, by Commoners' Right, on the ties high up on the moor; at the other end, the roof was extended to form an open linhay. Not visible, since it was deliberately placed on the north side of the farmhouse, stood a small dairy. All so familiar and reassuring after the drama of the day. Elizabeth had already glimpsed the tiny, snuffling bundle in the crude wooden box that had served as a crib for both Nellie and Nathaniel, and her heart had trembled for the frail life of her new cousin, Daniel. But most of all, she'd been shaken rigid by the deathly grey face of her aunt, more unconscious than asleep, and the blood-drenched sheets her mother had put to soak in the washing tub.

Elizabeth crept along the cross passage and opened the door quietly. Her mother was sitting by the fireside in a pose of utter exhaustion, the two small children playing at her feet. But Nathaniel chose that moment to snatch the rag doll from his sister's hold, sending Nellie into a fit of wailing tears.

'Now, now, Nathaniel, 'twasn't very nice.' Hannah was obliged to lean forward wearily. 'Give Nellie back her doll. You've your own toys.'

'No!' The toddler pouted fiercely, his face the image of his father's, as he clutched the sorry item even more jealously to his chest.

A ponderous sigh breathed from Hannah's lips. She'd been tending to her sister since five o'clock that morning, and the worry of it all had drained her. Elizabeth's young eyes appreciated at once how tired her mother looked, and hanging her coat on the hook behind the door, she skipped across the room and dropped on all fours.

'You give Nellie back her dolly, and I'll play horsey with you!'

The little boy instantly beamed as he recognized the word 'horsey' and, unceremoniously discarding the coveted doll, clambered onto his cousin's back. Elizabeth lifted her head to give an imitation of a horse's whinny, and caught the grateful look that emanated from her mother's warm, hazel eyes. With Nathaniel jigging up and down on her back, she proceeded to scramble about on the stone floor until her knees were sore and she had to stop.

'There! Let's play with your train now!'

She lay on the rug with him, pushing the wooden engine his father had whittled for him from a piece of fallen branch, and mimicked the exciting noises she imagined a train would make. She'd never seen one in her life except for a sketch in a book, the same that Matthew had copied in making the toy, as he'd never seen one either. Nathaniel soon became fully engrossed in the game, so that when Dr Greenwood emerged from the bedroom and carefully closed the door, Elizabeth was able to leap up and stand expectantly by her mother's side.

The doctor's expression was strained as he pushed his hand through his receding hair. 'They're both asleep now,' he announced wearily. 'I'll call again first thing in the morning.'

'Thank you so much.' Hannah rose to her feet, though her shoulders drooped with fatigue. 'Won't you have some tea before you ride home? There are some scones Lizzie made yesterday, and some butter she churned just the other day.'

William Greenwood raised an appreciative eyebrow. 'Quite the accomplished young lady! That sounds quite delicious, but I really must get back to my own family. And I have a couple of patients to visit on the way. But, before I forget,' he added a little hesitantly, 'I met Mrs Saunders as I came through the village. Her family are all down with dreadful sore throats, and I wondered if, well, I know it's a great deal to ask when you're so busy just now . . .'

But Hannah smiled in that accommodating way Elizabeth knew so well. 'Well, *I* might have my hands full, but I reckon as Lizzie can manage something.'

Elizabeth was convinced her heart gave a bound as her chest inflated with pride. Her mother would trust her . . .

But then she saw the misgiving on the doctor's face, and the glorious moment was gone.

'Lizzie, what would we give for a sore throat?' Hannah's encouraging voice reached Elizabeth through the veil of dejection that was curiously misting her eyes, and she swallowed hard.

'Chamomile, sage, rosemary and thyme,' she stated earnestly. ''Tis not difficult. You can gargle with it, or drink it or add it to a stew. And 'tis likely to turn into a cold, so some rosehip or elderberry syrup would be good.'

'And?' her mother prompted.

'Er . . . oh, a crushed clove of garlic in a spoon or two of honey, three or four times a day. Onions are good, too, but not so good as garlic.'

She had clasped her hands behind her back and was gazing up nervously at Dr Greenwood. His expression was inscrutable for a moment and Elizabeth's chin quivered. But then his jaw dropped open and his eyes stretched in amazement.

'Good Lord, I am impressed! You and your mother will do me out of my job between you! Tell me, Lizzie, just how old are you?'

'I'll be eight next month.'

'My word, well, I'd say you're a very clever girl for your age!'

'I want to be like Mother when I grow up.' Elizabeth's mouth set determinedly. 'Or like you. A physician.'

William Greenwood rubbed his jaw and frowned awkwardly. 'Well, yes, although it would be unusual, not to say difficult, for a woman. If I were you, I'd learn as much as you can from your mother and become a respected midwife. Then when you're older, perhaps I could train you myself and you might be able to make a proper profession of it, especially with a good knowledge of herbal remedies to boot.'

Elizabeth's face lit up like a beacon. Her mother was trusting her to make up her first remedy, and now Dr Greenwood was suggesting he might take her under his wing! She was so enthralled, she hardly noticed when Uncle Matthew burst in through the door, sending a pall of acrid smoke from the fire billowing chokingly into the room instead of wafting its way up the chimney.

'What you'm grinning at?' he demanded with a fierce scowl.

'Lizzie was just saying how she'd like to study medicine,' William told him, 'and I said—'

'The soft idjit!' Uncle Matthew roared derisively. 'Whoever yerd tell of a woman being a doctor!'

Elizabeth's mouth puckered into a tight knot. He wouldn't even listen to what Dr Greenwood had to say! She narrowed her eyes. When the time came, it wouldn't matter what her uncle thought. There was nothing on earth that would stop her!

The doctor coughed diplomatically. 'Mr Halse, I wonder if I could have a quiet word with you, please? About your wife. Perhaps we could step outside?'

Uncle Matthew's scowl deepened, but he obeyed with a dark glare. The two men went outside, Dr Greenwood slipping into his overcoat and picking up his medical bag as he went.

'Well then, shall we get some dinner on the table?' Hannah suggested. 'You children wash your hands now.'

They trooped over to the washbowl, their voices a hubbub of chatter. But scarcely were they seated at the old table, the pot on the trivet in the centre, than Matthew stormed back inside, slamming the door so violently the whole building shook.

'By God, who the bloody hell do he think he be?' he bellowed as he pushed his stocky frame across the threshold. 'Coming yere and telling us what I can or cas'n do wi' us own wife!'

Elizabeth froze, her little heart beating furiously. But her mother got to her feet and squared up to Matthew, her eyes like feline slits. 'Well, I can imagine what he said to you, and you know he's right!' Elizabeth heard her hiss. 'He told you

17

last time poor Margaret shouldn't have any more children, and there she was expecting again in no time!'

'So I cas'n sleep wi' us own missis now!' Matthew snarled, his face an alarming shade of purple. 'Well, he can whistle for 'is money! Us doesn't have none, and no doubt aud Pencarrow'll be sending that upstart son of his fer collect the rent agin afore too long!'

'Master Richard?' Hannah's voice was surprised at the unexpected change of subject. 'Why, a nice lad he always seems to me, polite-'

'Huh! Not when he be asking fer his money!'

'Well, 'tis several weeks overdue, so 'tis no wonder! Trouble is, his father was too lax with you. Since Master Richard finished at school and virtually took over the running of the place, he simply wants what's due to them.'

'Bah! Just throwin' his weight about as if *he* were the maister!' Matthew grumbled as he sat down in the chair with a thump. 'And what's he gwain fer do when that there mine closes, just like Wheal Anne did, eh? Yere! Make sure there's enough left fer me!' he snapped, poking his bulbous nose almost into the pot as Hannah began to serve out. 'I be mortal hungered!'

'You always are!' Hannah muttered under her breath.

Elizabeth sighed with relief. The storm, for the moment, appeared to be over. She hadn't understood what they'd been saying about her aunt, but she knew her mother was angry. Nevertheless, she attacked her food with gusto, for Uncle Matthew wasn't the only one whose stomach was rumbling. The meal was a noisy affair. Matthew had never quite managed the art of eating with his mouth closed and constantly smacked his lips, while Nathaniel complained vociferously the second his plate was empty, and banged his fists loudly on the table.

'Good day's work, then,' Matthew finally admitted when his belly was full.

'Not for Margaret it wasn't.'

Elizabeth caught her mother's mumbled, bitter words. But Uncle Matthew simply snorted. 'She's come through

18

fine. Now tomorrow, I gwain fer drive they ewes to the top field, and then Lizzie and me'll fetch anither load o' bracken for the cows' bedding whilst us still has the chance.'

Elizabeth caught Hannah's eye across the table. She knew precisely what her mother was going to say. 'Lizzie has school tomorrow, as well you know.'

'And us has a farm fer run, that do keep food in our bellies and the roof over our heads,' Matthew was quick to retort. 'What can that school larn a bright young thing like Lizzie that she don't know already? And what good'll larning do her, anyways, you? Farmer's wife wi' a swollen belly by the time she be sixteen, that one, pretty girl like her!'

Elizabeth gazed in puzzlement from her mother to her uncle and back again. She could see Hannah's lips were compressed into a thin line, for once, it seemed, unable to find a suitable response.

'Well, I be off to the inn fer wet the babby's head,' Matthew announced, getting to his feet so abruptly his chair rocked on its back legs. And a moment later the door banged shut behind him.

Hannah closed her eyes, regaining her sorely tried composure. ''Tis a wonder to me he ever finds his way back.' She breathed heavily through her nostrils before seeming to snap into action. 'Right, then. If I put the little ones to bed, will you clear up here, Lizzie, and then get on with the throat remedy? You can drop everything in to Mrs Saunders in the morning on your way to *school*!' she said pointedly. And Elizabeth wondered quite what battles the next day would bring.

* * *

Having tidied up and proudly mixed the remedy, Elizabeth sat down cross-legged on the rug in front of the fire. It was her favourite time of the day, when Nellie and the irksome Nathaniel were asleep. She was always allowed to stay up an extra hour, talking to her mother and aunt, or reading one of her grandfather's old books. At least it was her favourite time of the day if her uncle was in a good mood, content to sit and puff on his pipe, or, as that evening, had taken himself off to the inn. Tonight, though, had been different. Aunt Margaret had woken, as had baby Daniel, feebly mewing for his first feed. Hannah and Elizabeth had sat one on either side of them in the big bed, as the new mother, regaining her colour, smiled down on the pathetic fragment of life that was her son, his tiny wrinkled face peppered with the minuscule white spots of the newborn. At first he wasn't sure how to suckle, but both his mother and aunt were experts at persuading an infant to follow its instincts and soon had him sucking strongly. Elizabeth glowed from within as she shared in that moment of wonderment at the eternal miracle of new life. And that was where her future lay, especially after Dr Greenwood's promise, for he was a man of his word. To help the people of the valley with her knowledge and experience. She hugged the dream close to her heart, determined to become every bit as skilled as her mother.

But now Hannah was settling the baby back in his box as Aunt Margaret wouldn't be allowed out of bed, even to achieve such a small task, for some weeks. Elizabeth had hurried outside to the closet, the moon lighting her way, and then had washed her face and hands back indoors. Sitting alone now by the fire, she was brushing the bouncing tangle of her hair, loosened from its thick plait. The wind was getting up, whipping angrily about the farmhouse and rattling the small windows, so perhaps there wouldn't be a frost after all. When Uncle Matthew threw open the door, the blast of cooler air made Elizabeth shiver.

She cast a curious eye at him. An inane smile stretched his over-generous lips, his brown eyes a muddy glaze as he swayed across the small room. Elizabeth's brow puckered. She supposed he must be drunk, though she was always in bed before he returned from his drinking bouts and had never seen him like this before. He lurched sideways and somehow ended up opposite her on the rug in a precariously balanced heap.

'You bin reading agin, Lizzie?' he grinned as he picked up the book on the floor beside her. 'My, all they words! You'm a clever maid, you, Lizzie!'

Elizabeth frowned. He seemed, well, floppy was the word that came into her child's brain. It was actually quite funny and she wanted to laugh, not really understanding why her mother considered being drunk so bad.

'You've a birthday coming up soon, haven't you?' He winked at her mischievously, his contorted face making her giggle. 'I wonder what little summat us might be able fer find fer you. A new book, p'raps?' he chuckled deep in his throat.

Elizabeth's heart began to pump with excitement. A new book! That would be wonderful! 'Oh, yes please, Uncle!' she breathed, cradling the delicious thought in her head. She sat up straight, arching her back in a fluid, catlike stretch, her hair waving about her shoulders in a golden mantle.

'Let us do that fer you.' Her uncle's voice was oddly thick as he took the brush from her hand, but she thought nothing of it as he stroked the bristles down the length of her hair. He shuffled up close to her, and her nostrils flared at the bitter odour of stale pipe smoke and beer on his breath. She didn't like it, and turned her head away. 'You'm a pretty cheel, just like your aunt,' he murmured into her ear. 'You'd understand, wouldn't you, Lizzie?'

There was something strange in his voice, something that frightened her. 'Understand what?' she gulped, suddenly uneasy.

'You will when you'm auder. You see, Lizzie, some women doesn't understand a man's needs,' he rambled distantly. 'But your aunt do, and so will you, Lizzie. You'm so like her. Such a sweet maid.'

She turned to him, her heart knocking in her chest. She really didn't have a clue what he was talking about, and just wanted to get away from him. But in a trice, his hand in her hair pulled her towards him and he kissed her hard on the mouth. Of course, he'd kissed her before. On the cheek. He was her uncle, after all. But never like this. Bruising her delicate lips. She was stunned. Not daring to move. Hardly daring to breathe in the foul stench of him. Until revulsion rose from her stomach and she had to push him away.

His arms dropped to his sides, but he was still smiling at her. Stupidly. Not seeing the confusion in her eyes turn to offence as their amber warmth hardened to a cold yellow glint. She tossed her head with a haughty flourish, her chin held high as she deliberately drew the back of her hand fiercely across her lips. She scrambled to her feet, taking with supreme dignity the few strides to the open rustic staircase that led up within the room to the loft above. The door to the upper room opened directly at the top of the stairs, and once Elizabeth was inside she closed it silently behind her.

The room created in the loft space was so familiar it seemed to bring her some comfort. She slumped forward, her chin drooping on her chest as her head swam wildly. What on earth was that all about? She really didn't understand. But she'd heard her mother say often enough that Uncle Matthew didn't know what he was about when he was drunk. So that was it! That was why her mother considered that beer and cider and everything like it was evil. Well, she was right! But at least it *explained* her uncle's behaviour. He'd kissed her hard because he loved her and because he'd drunk too much at the inn. Certainly nothing to worry about, and nothing to bother her mother with. And what was there to tell, anyway?

She changed into her nightdress as quickly as she could for it was cold up here, and dived into bed beside Nellie and Nathaniel. Her cousins were as warm as toast next to her, and as she stretched downwards, her toes found the welcoming stone hot-water bottle her mother had placed there. Before too long, Hannah would be coming up to her own bed beneath the thatch, although no doubt she'd go down again in the night to help Aunt Margaret when baby Daniel awoke, as Uncle Matthew would be of no use. Feeling reassured, Elizabeth snuggled down to sleep, the incident with her uncle forgotten as she dreamed of her future and Dr Greenwood's promise.

THREE

Elizabeth drew in a trembling breath, her head tipped towards the smoke-grimed ceiling of the main room of the farmhouse as she choked down the ache that clawed at her throat. Nellie's tousled head was buried against her chest, the younger girl's chubby arms clasped in an agonizing grip around Elizabeth's slim waist. Being raised on a farm with animals all around her, she understood the meaning of death even at the tender age of five. Elizabeth's own eyes were pricking with searing tears, but she simply must not give in to them.

'There, there, my sweet,' she crooned into Nellie's hair. 'Your mummy wouldn't have wanted you to cry. And we must look after Daniel and Nathaniel while Aunt Hannah sees to your new baby brother. Don't you think he's beautiful?' she added with forced enthusiasm.

'No, I doesn't!' Nellie pulled away and glared up at her with anger on her tear-stained face. 'I've already got babby Daniel. He cas'n hardly walk yet, so I doesn't want anither brother, especially one what's killed my mammy!'

'No, Nellie! You mustn't say that!' Elizabeth was appalled. 'It does happen sometimes. 'Tis not the baby's fault. Your mummy would want you to love him!'

Nellie's lips screwed into a pout and she sniffed hard. 'Yes. You'm right, Lizzie. You always are.' But she looked dolefully over her shoulder and through the open bedroom door to where her father was crumpled on the floor beside the high bed, motionless for the past hour, his face resting against the slender white hand that lay, peacefully at last, on the edge of the quilt.

'Lizzie, go down to the village, would you?' Her mother's calm voice seemed to echo about the stillness of the farmhouse. 'Dr Greenwood was going to see the reverend on his way home, but would you tell Mrs Peters what's happened, and ask her to tell people as they come into the shop? Take Nellie and the boys with you. I'll need to . . . well . . . see to your aunt.'

Elizabeth nodded gravely. Not quite nine years old, but she knew what had to be done. And she needed to get outside. To breathe. And perhaps Nellie would feel better, too. It was October, but warm and the sun was shining. Which seemed wrong somehow, with poor Aunt Margaret lying still and cold in the bed.

* * *

No one came back to the farmhouse afterwards, but most of the village had packed into the church to say their final fare-well to the lovely maid Matthew Halse had returned home with back along twelve years now. No babby for seven summers, then four in quick succession, the last child exactly a year after the previous one, so 'twas no wonder the poor woman had died. And maybe she were well out of it, being married to Matthew Halse? After all, he were well known for his short temper. He'd been quite handsome in his youth, which was probably why she'd fallen for him; stockily built but attractive with large brown eyes and a merry smile — until too much weight and too much drink had ruined both his appearance and his personality. And now he was wid-owed, his grief showing itself not in tears but in a deep scowl as if he were angry that his wife had let him down.

As for the rest of the family, only the woman's sister and the two little girls attended, the boys being too young to understand what had happened. A neighbour had offered to keep an eye on them during the service, happy to look after the lovable Daniel but forgetting the exasperating ways of his elder brother. The new baby, David, had been temporarily farmed out to a local wet-nurse whose ample bosoms were producing more than enough milk for two eager mouths, and whose husband was pleased to receive the extra income. At the graveside Margaret's sister appeared gaunt and stood as stiff as a mine-rod, fighting to control her emotions. Didn't everyone know of the kindness and compassion that ema-nated from Hannah Thornton's heart for the human race in general, and for her light-headed sister in particular. She must have felt more acutely than anyone the loss of the lovely woman they were burying that fine autumn day. Little Nellie Halse trotted along awkwardly beside her cousin, not quite sure what to do and clearly following the older girl's every move. It seemed odd really, the dark, plump child looking the image of her father, while her cousin, well, anyone would be forgiven for thinking *she* was the deceased's daughter, the resemblance was so striking, far more like her dead aunt than her own mother. For though Hannah was not an unattractive woman, she lacked her daughter's elfin charm.

Just now, her slim, bony figure was grimly dignified as the villagers paid their respects to the bereaved family. She smiled wanly at their sympathetic words, while all Matthew managed was an ungracious grunt that sent his good neighbours scuttling away. Elizabeth, still holding Nellie's hand, kept her head bowed. She couldn't feel part of this adult ritual. All she wanted was to hide herself away in some secret place and cry until her tears ran dry.

'My father sends his condolences, Mr Halse, and his apologies for not attending the service, but he is indisposed at present. And please accept my own condolences at your sad loss.'

Elizabeth felt her curiosity aroused by the voice which, though it lilted with a Devonshire accent, was so different from any other she had ever heard, except perhaps for Dr Greenwood and the reverend. She looked up in time to see Uncle Matthew grudgingly shake the hand that was offered him by the slender, well-dressed youth who was already so tall that he towered over him.

'And Mrs Thornton, I'm so sorry,' the cultured voice continued, politely addressing her mother. 'I believe Mrs Halse was your sister?'

'She were indeed, sir.'

'And you will be staying on to look after Mrs Halse's children?'

'Oh, yes. This is Nellie, the eldest.' Hannah smiled encouragingly at the child who gazed, dumbstruck, at the stranger, with her plump thumb plugged firmly in her mouth. 'And this is my own daughter, Lizzie.'

Elizabeth lifted her searching velvet eyes to the stranger's face. She recognized by his height that he was a man, but he seemed to her a very young one. He had a kind face with wide-set, expressive eyes that scarcely glanced at Nellie, but held Elizabeth's gaze for some seconds with a smile that somehow warmed her heart. She was almost disappointed when he straightened up and turned to the grownups again.

'Please let me know if there's anything I can do.' He paused to smile again at Elizabeth and then turned to walk respectfully out of the churchyard gates. Elizabeth's eyes followed him, watching as he mounted a fine horse that was tethered outside, and trotted across the square and out of sight.

'Bah!' Matthew scoffed under his breath, his expression so thunderous that the remaining mourners paid their humble regards as swiftly as possible and made for home.

When it was finally over, the two small boys were collected and the grieving family turned its back on the village, trudging up the lonely track to their lowly farmstead on the edge of the moor. They went in single file, the man leading with his great shoulders hunched, the woman striding out behind him carrying the year-old baby, while the three older children followed in their wake, the gap between them ever widening. But it didn't matter. Elizabeth, although so slender a breath of wind might carry her away, was evidently in command, and would make sure they all got home safely.

All their hearts were heavy with sorrow but once they'd arrived back at the farm, there was no time for mourning. The cows needed milking and feeding. The ewes had been brought down from the moor for the winter to be built up ready to go to tup, and they, too, needed extra fodder. The hens had obligingly retired into their coop for the night, and Elizabeth shut the door securely against any marauding fox, then went to attend to the two pigs. She cleaned the sty, put down fresh bedding and emptied the swill into their trough. It was late. Nearly dark, and turning chilly. But she stayed with them for a few more minutes as their wide snouts rooted noisily among the leftovers and outer cabbage leaves. Friendly, intelligent creatures, giants now in comparison to when they'd arrived in the spring. But soon the slaughterman would be coming. You had to accept it. They'd be turned into bacon, salted, smoked, pickled, to last the winter through. But somehow, with Aunt Margaret sleeping her eternal slumber, the thought that the pigs would also soon be dead was unbearable. A tear rolled slowly down Elizabeth's cheek, not for the swine, but for the pale, beautiful woman who'd once laughed and sung and believed life was a frivolous game. Elizabeth simply couldn't believe she was gone.

Later, when Nellie and Nathaniel were well asleep, Elizabeth kissed her mother goodnight and padded up the steps to the attic above, leaving Hannah to settle little Daniel in the box that still served as his cot, and Uncle Matthew staring into the vacillating flames in the open hearth as he sucked on his empty pipe. By the glow of an oil lamp that had been turned down as low as it could go, Elizabeth wriggled into the bed. It was getting more and more cramped as they all grew, so that they now slept head to toe with Nathaniel at the other end. Elizabeth usually fell asleep the moment her head touched the pillow she was so tired, but tonight . . . Well, she'd only done the chores that were strictly necessary, and it had been a strange day, hadn't it? The funeral left you feeling . . . empty, she supposed. Or numb. Had Aunt Margaret really been in the box they'd buried that day? Aunt Margaret who was such fun when she was well? Naughty, really, not caring if she spoilt the butter, so long as she was enjoying churning it! So unlike her sister who was always so serious. But then, Hannah Thornton held the world together, didn't she? Everybody's world.

Elizabeth sighed as she realized she'd been staring up at the rafters above her head, and the thickly packed thatch between. There were a couple of places where the roof leaked when it rained, and the dampness gave off a musty frowstiness. It was Matthew's responsibility to have it repaired, but thatchers were scarce and reed expensive, so he hadn't bothered. With just one tiny window, it was stifling up here in summer, but as soon as the weather turned, as it was beginning to now, the unheated attic was as cold as — where was it — oh, yes, Siberia. And somehow, for the first time in her life, Elizabeth felt dissatisfied. Her mother had been brought up in a poor, draughty parsonage, but it would have been a deal better than this! And her mother worked so hard, for everyone but herself, and surely deserved more?

Elizabeth tossed and turned. She glared at Nellie beside her as the girl's plump frame spread itself in the bed, almost pushing Elizabeth off the edge, her steady breathing so heavy it was almost like snoring. And when Nathaniel stretched out a foot and scratched her shin with his toenail, Elizabeth slid out of bed in disgust. Perhaps if she went down for a glass of milk and sat quietly by the fire for a few minutes, she would start to feel sleepy.

She'd been aware of her mother and Uncle Matthew talking in low voices, but as she opened the door, she stopped, her hand holding the latch. As she caught their words, something told her she shouldn't interrupt.

'Well, you knew we'd have had to do something about it soon,' her mother was saying, her voice gentle. 'We can't move in that there attic. And Nathaniel's ready to leave his napkin off at night, and well, it wouldn't be very nice for the girls if he had an accident.'

'So what does you suggest then?' Uncle Matthew's words were strangely detached, Elizabeth reflected, as if he didn't much care.

'Well,' her mother hesitated slightly, ''twould be good to put Nathaniel on his own in my bed, especially with him being a boy.'

'And what about you?'

'Well, I thought . . . Daniel mostly sleeps through the night, bless him, but you're none too happy if he does waken. And when baby David comes back from the wet-nurse, your nights will be very disturbed. So, for your own sake, if you made yourself a good bed in the hayloft over the shippen, I could sleep in the bedroom and take care of the babies.'

'What!' Matthew's roar broke the stillness of the old farmhouse so that Elizabeth started and her heart bounced painfully for fear they'd heard the latch drop from her fingers. But they obviously hadn't as her uncle bellowed on, 'You'm throwing me out o' my own bed now, woman, and telling us to sleep wi' the cows!'

''Tis not an easy problem.' Hannah was trying to humour him, but Elizabeth recognized that quiet determination in her voice. 'But the hayloft is no worse than the attic the children and I have always shared, and probably a sight warmer in the winter with the cows below. 'Tis plenty a cowman lives his whole life over his cows.'

'But I be a tenant farmer, not a cowman!'

'Huh! When you pay the rent! Which reminds me, 'twas thoughtful of Richard Pencarrow to represent his father at the funeral, don't you think, when he's so young? Can't be more than eighteen. And he hasn't bothered you for his father's money since-'

'I doesn't see what be so decent 'bout that! A man should be allowed to bury his wife in peace, and the Pencarrows'll be arter the rent soon enough.'

'So when you do pay him, why don't you ask if he'd mind you building on a little room, and then you wouldn't have to sleep in the shippen.'

'Build!' Matthew exploded again so that a wave of fear rippled through Elizabeth's small form as she shivered at the top of the stairs. 'With what? Buttons? And who gwain fer help me? You've no idea 'bout building, you!'

'Come up with a better solution, and I'll be listening. But really, Matthew, 'tis your own fault. You just couldn't keep yourself away from poor Margaret, could you? Not even after what Dr Greenwood said to you. 'Tis your own fault you've so many children there's no room for them all to sleep!'

'And I suppose it be my fault she died, too!' Matthew's anger was so dangerous Elizabeth instinctively drew back into the shadows.

'Well, you said it, my man, you said it!' Hannah's fury was finally unleashed. 'She were a fool ever to have married a good-for-nothing monster like you, and yes! I do consider you killed her with your carnal lust!'

'And I suppose John niver came to you in bed? Well, he must've done once, or you wouldn't've had that girl o' yourn! And if I cuddn't go to my own wife, would you have rather I'd visited a whorehouse in Tavistock, eh? Or p'raps I should've gotten myself invited to Josiah Pencarrow's dos up at the Hall, you seem to think so much on them! They say he and his friends bring loose women back wi' them and get drunk and smoke heaven knows what through one o' they water contraptions! Or,' and his tone changed so horribly that Elizabeth felt sick, 'maybe *you* was thinking of obliging when your sister were unavailable!'

A dreadful silence settled over the room, followed by the unmistakable ring of a resounding slap. As Elizabeth leaned forward, she saw her uncle nursing his cheek. She snatched in her breath, and watched as he stormed out of the room. And then the outer door crashed shut, causing the whole building to rock as Matthew slammed it with some almighty force. Elizabeth reeled with confusion. Should she go down? If she did, she had the feeling her mother would send her straight back up again. Slowly, she inched her way back into the attic room, praying the floorboards wouldn't creak, and slipped into bed beside Nellie once more. Oddly the younger child's warm body was as comforting now as it had been irritating earlier, and Elizabeth snuggled down, her eyelids suddenly heavy with sleep as the strain of the long, sad day caught up with her.

* * *

Richard Pencarrow's dark eyes smouldered with anger. 'Really, Father, I felt terrible lying to them like that. Making excuses for you when you were really suffering from drinking too much last night and smoking God knows what in the hookah. I wish to God Uncle James had never brought the thing back with him.'

Seated by the blazing fire in the drawing room of Rosebank Hall, Josiah glanced up at his son from beneath the hooded lids of his piercing blue eyes. 'Don't talk ill of the dead. And anyway, you know I don't touch the stuff Maurice brings.'

'But you *were* four sheets to the wind,' the young man rounded on him, 'and you *knew* it was the funeral this afternoon. I just can't understand why you continue to allow Maurice Brett to use the Hall like this. He's turning the place into an opium den!'

'I owe him money, as well you know,' his father growled back.

'Oh, yes! Gambling debts!' Richard cried in exasperation, placing his hands on the arms of Josiah's chair and leaning accusingly over him. 'But why on earth don't you pay him off and be free of him and his partisans for good?'

Josiah's face hardened even further. 'My private affairs are none of your business, and I'll keep whatever company I choose!'

'Even if it brings our name into disrepute?' Richard argued, but his fired words didn't receive an answer. A commotion from the hallway and the loud, protesting tones of the butler had them both turning their heads; but before even the agile youth could spin on his heel, the door was pushed open and an impeccably dressed gentleman strode into the room as if he owned the place.

'Talk of the devil,' Richard muttered under his breath.

But the visitor had heard his bitter tone. 'Nice to know I'm welcome, Ritchie, lad,' he sneered.

'You're not. Not as far as I'm concerned.'

'Richard!'

'Well, as things stand,' Maurice Brett replied, ignoring Josiah and removing his fine kid gloves with deliberate care, 'I reckon I can come and go as I please. Until you decide to pay up, Josiah, my friend. Or until you persuade that pretty dairymaid that she'd make a better living as my mistress than as your servant.'

Richard threw up his head with a groan. 'You disgust me,' he grated. 'Father, how can you—'

'Come, come, my dear boy,' Maurice put in before Josiah could answer. 'At least I'd look after the girl. Treat her well. Which is a deal more than most men do for their mistresses. I do expect to pay for my pleasure.'

'So I've noticed. You're turning our home into a whorehouse.'

'Your father doesn't seem to mind too much—'

'Well, he's a damned fool!' And though Josiah's mouth dropped open in protest, Richard allowed him no time to retort as, his jaw set defiantly, he went on, 'And if *he* hasn't got the nerve to stand up to you, *I have*!'

Maurice Brett's face registered his disquiet for just an instant as he raised his eyes to the lad who topped him by at least two inches. And then he shook his head with a bellow of laughter. 'My, my, your boy's developing some spirit, Josiah! Perhaps next time we have one of our little parties, I should bring along a girl especially for him. We could all have some fun teaching the milksop what to do with a member of the fairer sex!'

He gave a forced chortle at his own jest. He knew it wasn't the least funny, but it had been meant to cut the boy down to size, to counter-attack. He hadn't expected what happened next. Josiah glowered up at him in disapproval, not joining in his mirth and for once, it would seem, siding with his son. Whether it was this which triggered it, Maurice Brett didn't get the chance to consider. He was still guffawing when Richard Pencarrow clenched his fist and with the force of youthful passion, smashed it across Maurice's face.

Maurice was too stunned and in too much pain to cry out. He staggered backwards and toppled into a chair, both his hands covering his face. Richard stood over him, his arm raised and poised for action again. It wasn't necessary. When Maurice moved his hands, they were scarlet and dripping with the blood that flowed from his nostrils and down his immaculate shirt front. His nose had already swollen like a ripe plum, with a deep gash where the youth's knuckles had split the skin, and the whole thing looked decidedly odd and twisted.

Josiah slowly raised his tall, broad figure from his chair. 'Good God, boy, what've you done?'

'Broken his nose, I hope!'

'For God's sake, go and get some towels or something! Oh, Maurice, I'm sorry!' Josiah postured, bending over his friend. 'That boy'll be the death of me!'

He glared at his son who hovered audaciously for a moment before striding from the room. When he returned some minutes later, his father had Maurice seated properly in the chair. The crimson stream was still dripping over his mouth and chin, and Richard threw the towels at him.

'Richard, apologize to our guest at once!' Josiah barked as he attempted to help Maurice staunch the bleeding.

'You call *him* a guest? And *he* should be apologizing to *me*, not the other way round!'

Josiah shook his head in vexation. He could deal with his son later, but just now he must turn his attention back to the injured man. 'Let me send for the doctor,' he said anxiously.

But Maurice staggered somewhat unsteadily to his feet, one of the towels clamped over his nose. 'No, it's all right, Josiah,' he mumbled, his voice sounding strange and nasal. 'I'd sooner get home and call out my own physician.'

Josiah hesitated as he supported Maurice by the elbow. 'You . . . you won't press charges?' he faltered.

'Of course he won't, Father! Just think about it!'

Maurice paused as he crossed the room, his steel-grey eyes narrowed venomously above the bloodied towel. 'No. I won't be pressing charges, but I won't forget this, you insolent pup! I promise you I won't!'

But Richard's fists were still clenched by his sides, his young face white and strained. 'Just get out of my house, you bastard,' he snarled. And when Josiah came back in from seeing Maurice away in his hired carriage, and tipping the driver to say nothing of the incident, he found his son tossing a glass of fine malt whisky down his throat.

'You bloody idiot!' he bawled. 'And may I remind you, Rosebank Hall is not *yours* until I'm dead and buried! And if I want to go on inviting Maurice and his friends, then 'it's none of your business, and you'll just have to put up with it!'

'Then I don't know who's the bigger idiot, you or me!' Richard hissed, and turning on his heel, he stormed out of the room, slamming the door behind him.

* * *

'You'll niver guess what!' Matthew chortled with delighted satisfaction as he lurched boisterously across to the table where Hannah and Elizabeth were serving out Sunday dinner. It was over a year since they'd buried Aunt Margaret, a year which had seen Matthew Halse stationed in his corner at the inn almost every night.

'Oh, yes, I will!' Hannah faced him defiantly with her hands firmly on her hips. 'You've been drinking again at the inn, and not just one, neither! 'Tis immoral the time you spend getting drunk there, and right next to where poor Margaret is hardly cold in her grave! And on a Sunday! You should be in church.'

'Well, you would say that, wouldn't you, parson's darter!'

'Very well, a Methodist meeting, then. At least 'tis better than the inn.'

'But the ale be not so good!' he guffawed, and Elizabeth jumped as he clapped her rumbustiously on the shoulder. 'And neither be the intertainment! There be a brave aud uproar! 'Tis all over the village, and you'll be so surprised as the rest on us.'

'Oh, stop your gossiping and get your hands washed.'

'Already done!' He waved his hands in front of Elizabeth's face, and her nose wrinkled as she caught the unpleasant odour of beer on his breath. 'Just give us my dinner and listen on this.' He sat down heavily in his chair and all but snatched the plate of meat from his sister-in-law.

'Grace, Matthew!' she chastised him.

'Hang bloody Grace! Just listen, you! Aud Pencarrow and that precious son of his were fighting over a dairymaid, would you believe. Yes, brawling on the dairy floor! Kicking and punching each ither! And yesterday morning, the boy be gone. And so be half the family silver!'

'What?' Hannah's voice was indeed so shocked that Elizabeth looked up sharply from chopping Daniel's food into tiny pieces. The child was gazing up at her with a sweet smile on his angelic face. He was a joy, with his mother's looks and Nellie's placid nature, but blessed with a sharp intelligence and none of his elder brother's belligerence. Elizabeth smiled back, but despite herself she was intrigued by the news her uncle was taking such delight in delivering.

'The aud chap sent someone arter 'en, and someone answering his description were seen getting on that there new train to Plymouth, and once there, well . . . He could get on a ship going anywhere. So what do you think on that, then?' he gloated smugly.

'Well, I never did!' Hannah wasn't the only one taken aback. Elizabeth's eyebrows had arched with deep curiosity as she stared into her uncle's grinning face. After all, it made quite a change not to have him and her mother arguing, and to have some outside matter to discuss instead. And something quite scandalous, too, it would seem! Elizabeth might have only just turned ten years old, but she was beginning to understand how the world worked. She knew that the Pencarrow family had been yeoman farmers for generations. They'd worked their own land, and by the sweat of their own brows had built up the small estate that included Uncle Matthew's farmstead. The mine, Wheal Rosalind, that they'd opened on land they already owned along the riverbank, had been a bonus. Wheal Anne, just by the clam, had been developed by a company of adventurers some fifteen years back. Being on the same vein, Wheal Rosalind had opened a year later. Wheal Anne had closed as not being financially viable in 1854, as it wasn't satisfying its London investors. But the Pencarrows had sought profit only for themselves, and *their* mine was still lucrative enough for their own purposes and was still productive. Being farmers, they'd always employed a mine-captain. It was rumoured, though, that Master Richard had been keen to go away to study mine-engineering when he left school. However, his uncle, a captain in the army, had got himself killed in the Crimea a few years back, and Josiah had broken with the family tradition by not being too enthused about farming. So young Richard had been forced into running the estate for him. Everyone knew the Pencarrows weren't aristocracy, but they held a certain position in local society. Even at her tender age, Elizabeth knew that for father and son to fight like common miners on pay day, and over a dairymaid . . . 'Twas hardly the done thing.

And for the son to steal from his father . . . well, 'twas a proper turn up!

"'Twould seem the boy be no more than a common thief,' Matthew pronounced with glee as he chomped noisily on the pork with his mouth half open so that the rich gravy dribbled down his chin. 'What should you expect, mind, wi' a father like that? I really doesn't comprehend why you thinks we should respect them so. Regular opium parties he has, they do say.'

Elizabeth turned her surprised eyes on her mother. 'I don't understand,' she frowned. 'Opium's akin to laudanum. To kill pain. So how can you have opium *parties?*'

She saw her mother exchange glances with Uncle Matthew, and even he looked somewhat awkward. 'Well, it makes you feel good,' Hannah explained hesitantly. 'As if you're floating, they say. So sometimes, if people have a lot to worry about, a little opium can help them. Some of Mr Pencarrow's friends are businessmen from Tavistock. It might not seem so to us, but they have a lot of responsibility, with folk relying on them for their livelihood. But you're quite right,' she added hastily. "'Tis not the right and proper use of opium at all.'

'Well, it seems to me they'd be better off with some of our chamomile tea!' Elizabeth declared with such innocent assertiveness that Uncle Matthew nearly fell off his chair with mirth.

FOUR

June 1862

'Good morning, Lizzie! Shouldn't you be at school?'

Elizabeth was sitting by the mill-pool in the sun-drenched combe above Higher Mill. She'd removed her old boots and pulled her skirt above her knees, allowing her slender legs to dangle in the cool water. She lifted her head at the familiar voice, and her sun-browned face stretched into a radiant smile. 'Good day, Dr Greenwood!' she greeted him cheerily, squinting up into the brilliant sunshine. 'I didn't hear you coming.'

The doctor slid from his horse and, allowing the animal to graze freely on the grass, sat down on the ground next to the young girl. 'You certainly seemed lost in thought. And this is a lovely spot, especially in such glorious weather. But I wouldn't have expected to find you here. I thought you'd be at school.'

'I don't go to school anymore,' she shrugged dejectedly. 'Uncle Matthew won't pay the pennies any longer, and besides, I'll be twelve come the autumn and even the teacher agrees I know as much as she does. Mother teaches me, though. Things like history and geography. And about plants, of course. But we don't have many books. Only a few that once belonged to my grandfather.'

William Greenwood sighed as he contemplated the girl's bowed head, and in an effort to raise her spirits, reached his hand into the pool and splashed an arc of glittering water over her sombre figure. She replied with a playful laugh, and her hair, which was tied simply in a blue ribbon, swung jauntily down her back. 'I suppose I ought to get back,' she told him. Retracting her legs from the water, she bent her feet up in turn so that she could dry them on the hem of her skirt before replacing her boots. 'Uncle Matthew was just mending a gate near the house, and then we're up to the peat ties to cut more turf.'

'In this heat?' the doctor queried.

'We must have plenty for the winter,' she informed him casually. 'We can't afford coal.'

'Well, make sure you take plenty of water to drink. It's a fair step.'

'Four miles, I reckon. But there's no need to worry about water. There's enough in the streams up there, and 'tis pure enough coming straight off the moor.'

Dr Greenwood shook his head in amusement tinged with not a little admiration. What was it about the child? She was so capable, so mature for her years, and always had been ever since he'd known her. But he could sense there was something in her, bursting to escape. She was edging ever nearer to young womanhood, so graceful and, there was no denying it, so beautiful. But what hope did she have for the future? Dependent on her uncle, she'd face a life of poverty and stultifying hard work. Even if she followed in her mother's footsteps, the prospects weren't dazzling. He had no doubt she had the brains and the stamina to study medicine, but a woman doctor was unheard of. With his own practice being in Tavistock and few connections now in London where he'd trained, he hardly had the wealth or influence to change the prejudice of years of tradition in one fell swoop! But as a nurse and midwife *par excellence*, whom he could recommend to colleagues in Tavistock and Plymouth, she could achieve the next best thing.

'I'll walk home with you, if I may,' he said curiously. 'I've just been to see your landlord, Josiah Pencarrow, and I'd like to have a word with your mother about him. And perhaps I can look out some of my early notes as a medical student for you. I wouldn't expect you to understand everything, but I'm sure you'd learn quite a lot. That is, if your mother agrees. Tell you what, would you like to ride on Rusty?'

Elizabeth's amber eyes gleamed like gold. 'Oh, yes, please!' she cried. 'I mean, not just Rusty. But about your notes. I really do want to learn, you know.'

'Yes, I can see that you do!' he said as he lifted her feather-light form onto the placid animal's back.

* * *

'Not over my dead body you doesn't!'

''Tis already arranged,' Hannah informed her brother-in-law, her matter-of-fact tone telling him there was no use his objecting. 'I start on Monday.'

'I'll not have you working in that den of iniquity!'

'Huh! That's grand coming from you, with you always drunk and blaspheming every two minutes! Besides, there's been none of those so-called parties since young Richard went away. 'Twas back along eighteen months now. Old Mr Pencarrow's a changed man. But 'tis true he still drinks too much — somewhat like yourself!—and it's given him gout. He's vastly overweight and has heart problems, too, which is what you'll get if you don't take care. And he needs someone to look after him.'

'He can take care on his bloody self!' Matthew roared again, trying to tower over her. But she simply exchanged the cooling flat iron in her hand for the other one which had been heating on the hearth. She spat delicately on its surface to see if it was hot enough, and as her spittle sizzled and instantly dried, Matthew instinctively backed away.

Elizabeth smothered a grin as she watched out of the corner of her eye. She'd learned to keep out of these arguments between her mother and uncle, but lately had begun to find some amusement in them, they were so predictable. 'And who gwain fer take care on the chiller while you'm away?'

'Lizzie's quite capable of looking after the boys.'

'Lizzie? But how be I supposed fer manage the farm wi'out her!'

Hannah was unperturbed by his fury and went on with the ironing. 'Spend less time drinking and more time working, and you'll manage, same as others roundabout here do. And you have a daughter of your own. I wouldn't expect her to cope with the little ones, but she can help you well enough.'

'Nellie be nort but a cheel.'

This time Hannah put down the iron and turned to face him squarely. 'She's the same age Lizzie was when she started working for you, and *she* coped with school *and* learning about my remedies as well. Now Nellie mightn't be so bright as Lizzie, but she's nearly as big and she's willing. And Nathaniel's turned five. If you'll not send either of them to school, then 'tis time they started to learn about farming.'

'But 'twon't be the same as having Lizzie.'

'Well, I'm sorry, Matthew, but that's how 'tis going to be. I'll be back by late afternoon, and Lizzie can still deal with the dairy and everything else she does about the farmyard. And I'll be paid three shilling and threepence a week.'

Elizabeth cocked an eyebrow. It was no surprise to her that the expression on her uncle's face softened.

'Hmm. Three and threepence, you say?' he considered, rubbing his chin. 'Well, I suppose . . . if Nellie helps wi' the milking in the morning, and then she and the boy come wi' us up to the peat ties, I cud see how things go. And us'll be checking on the sheep up on the leer. An extra pair o' hands be always useful catching sheep.'

'There! 'Tis settled, then.' And Hannah darted a surreptitious wink at her young daughter.

* * *

'Tell me all about it, then!' Elizabeth's eyes danced expectantly as she and her mother sat in the tiny garden at the front of the farmhouse. Nellie and Nathaniel, exhausted after a day's hard labour at their father's side, had gone to bed and the younger boys were already asleep. Uncle Matthew had departed, as usual, to the inn, and Hannah and Elizabeth were enjoying the evening sunlight that suffused the farmyard in golden shafts. Between the shippen and the barn they could see the lush, green fields rising to the high moor beyond, all so calm and beautiful in the still, warm air of summertime.

'Well,' Hannah began tantalizingly, 'the house is a lot bigger than this, of course, but 'tis not a mansion. There's a large drawing room where Mr Pencarrow spends most of his time, with full-length windows and a great Gothic-style overmantel, a hideous gurt thing, if you ask me!' She laughed and Elizabeth giggled with her. 'And then there's a dining room with a beautiful polished table. And a small study-cum-office with lots of books and papers and suchlike. My favourite room is a small parlour with a pretty bay window and green velvet curtains. 'Twas Mrs Pencarrow's afore she died. There's nice carpets everywhere, and good, solid furniture. Nothing ostentatious, mind.'

'Nothing what?'

'Ostentatious. Extravagant. Some lovely vases and paintings. Oh, and Mr Pencarrow's father had a fascination with clocks. There's lots of them about, quite valuable some of them, I shouldn't wonder. And the kitchen!' She threw up her hands in her enthusiasm. 'Well, 'tis almost as big as the whole of this farmhouse, with a proper range with a water boiler one side and two ovens. But my — 'twas so hot in there today! I didn't envy the cook one little bit!'

'Cook?'

'Oh, yes!' Hannah chuckled. 'And a dairymaid, although she makes enough butter and cheese to have a weekly stall at the market. And a housemaid and a manservant.'

'What? All those people to look after one man?'

'And now me, too! And there's a gardener. Not that they grow any flowers. But they do grow their own vegetables in a walled garden to the side. And,' she paused for effect, 'there's a herb garden. Mr Pencarrow says I can take whatever I like from it, and old Henry's to grow anything else I want, and I can still carry on my other work.'

'Oh, that's wonderful! So we can make even more medicines?'

'That's right! Mr Pencarrow . . . Oh!' Hannah stopped abruptly and drew a sharp breath through her teeth.

'Mother?' Elizabeth's voice quavered.

'Oh, 'tis nothing.' Hannah smiled at once. 'All today's excitement, I expect. And the rich food I was served at luncheon. Now, what was I saying?'

'About Mr Pencarrow,' Elizabeth prompted, all ears again.

'Well, he's not such a bad fellow. Cook warned me never to speak of his son, though. Letters have arrived in his handwriting from France, but he destroys them straight away without reading them. But all I have to do is stop him eating too much of the wrong things, keep him away from the bottle, which won't be easy, and persuade him to take his medicines. 'Twill be a battle of wills, but I'm used to that with your uncle!'

They laughed knowingly, but kept their merriment low so as not to break the spell of contentment that wreathed serenely about them. But then Hannah caught her daughter's hand and gazed intently into her eyes. 'Lizzie, dear, listen to me. When the children are older, there'll be no need for us to stay here. I brought you here when your father died because we had nowhere else to go, not to look after Aunt Margaret and her babies. I had my happiness with your father, short-lived though 'twas. But soon 'twill be your turn to live a life of your own. One day, we'll be free of this place. Maybe, with William's help, you can become an independent woman, mix with intelligent people, receive the recognition you deserve.' She broke off, and the light faded from her eyes. ''Tis always

43

worth holding on to a dream. And my dream is to get you out of this hovel if 'tis the last thing I do.'

Elizabeth forced a wan smile, but her forehead had folded into a frown; the magic of the moment had dissipated into the air like mist on a summer's dawn. The future — her future — seemed uncertain in the extreme.

FIVE

May 1864

'Oh, go on, Lizzie. Give us a kiss. My heart be mortal hurted when you won't even speak to us!'

'Oh, I'll talk to you all right, but 'twon't be to whisper sweet nothings! 'Tis a gurt lummox you are, Thomas Arkwright! But . . . oh dear.' She turned to face him, looking quite concerned. 'That could be nasty,' she said.

It was well known that Elizabeth Thornton was almost as quick at spotting ailments as the good Dr Greenwood, and the youth's eyes widened with fear. 'W-what is it?' he stammered.

'Looks like the start of impetigo,' she said gravely. 'Great big red blisters that'll burst out all over your face until the skin hangs off in shreds. Better get home to your mother while she can still recognize you.'

The terrified boy staggered backwards, almost tripping over little David and Daniel who were following their big cousin like two chicks behind a mother hen, and fled back up the path, stumbling as he went. Elizabeth gave a satisfied grunt, ushered her young charges across the narrow wooden bridge, and began the steep climb up the boulder-strewn track to join the lane that led back to the village. They'd been on their weekly visit to the nearby village of Horndon with butter and cheese for the mining families. The lead and silver mine Wheal Betsy had recently reopened under the name Prince Arthur Consols, providing employment for the entire hamlet, and so Elizabeth had thankfully sold every item, even though she was in competition against the farms in Horndon itself. But now, even empty, the two baskets weighed more heavily with each step as her feet slipped on the uncomfortably uneven stones, and David was moaning that he was tired. At least he didn't have a long skirt to battle with, or a silly bonnet on his head that made his brow clammy, and she told him so in no uncertain terms. The two little boys exchanged glances, and plodded on behind. You didn't cross Lizzie. She'd stand no nonsense, though she treated them with the utmost kindness and they loved her dearly.

The going was easier once they reached the lane, but they then had to trudge up the rough track onto the moor and Elizabeth was glad when they finally reached home. A new odour was coming from her warmed body, not exactly unpleasant like the way Uncle Matthew smelled after a day toiling in the sun, but she liked to give herself a stripped wash each morning nowadays. She supposed it was all part of the other things that were happening to her body, her chest beginning to swell like two small rosebuds, and other things 'down below'. Her mother said it was in preparation for having a baby. That idea had petrified her. She certainly didn't want a child yet! But then Hannah had explained that it would be some time before everything was in working order, and she wouldn't have a baby until she was married. That was a relief. Not that she saw herself ever being wed. Leastways, not to anyone around here. She didn't even *like* any of the boys she knew. Take Thomas Arkwright just now. Or the Grainger boys. To be blunt, they just had nothing between the ears, no manners, and they weren't much to look at either. When she was a proper nurse and midwife, though, recommended to good families and working with physicians, she'd be far more likely to meet someone suitable.

But that was a long way off and now she cut chunks of bread and cheese and poured some milk into enamel mugs for the boys, leaving them to consume it while she went out to the dairy. They were old enough to be left alone for ten minutes, and Daniel in particular was such a good little soul. Tomorrow was market day. Although Elizabeth wasn't going into Tavistock herself, a farmer's wife in the village regularly sold small amounts of dairy produce from other farms, like Matthew Halse's, that could only support half a dozen cows. Some butter she'd churned early that morning needed weighing into half-pound blocks, patted into shape and stamped, carefully wrapped and laid out on the cold marble shelves, ready to be taken to the village at the crack of dawn. There were probably some cheeses ready for consumption, and she wondered whether she might start a new batch after milking that evening. She had enough rennet, but it took some hours to warm the milk to blood-heat, separate the curd from the whey — which was then fed to the pigs — slice the curd into the lead bowl until the very last drop of liquid ran off, and finally crumble it into the vat for pressing. There was always so much to do! The elder bushes were putting forth their frothy sea of white blossoms which she must gather by the bucket-load for elderflower water and other remedies, and soon there would be coltsfoot flowers, nettles and tender dandelions. But at least it was something the boys could help with, and it kept them out of mischief.

She went out into the farmyard to draw a bucket of fresh water from the leat, then came back through the cross passage to the dairy. The drop in temperature as she entered it made her shiver. Rolling her sleeves over her elbows, she scrubbed her hands in the bucket. Everything was ready on the workbench, the utensils meticulously clean and covered with a boil-washed muslin, and the sheets of greaseproof paper carefully cut to size. Her dextrous fingers began their work, and she hummed softly to herself. She liked being in the dairy. It was quiet and peaceful, cut off from the familiar sounds of the farmyard, squawking hens and cats chasing after mice and rats. Uncle Matthew was ear-marking the new lambs, a month old now and ready to be released with their mothers onto the moor for the summer. Old Joe was there, too, the expert all the local farmers employed to neuter the males. It was a necessary process but one which Elizabeth detested, and she was glad to be out of the way. The sheep were penned in the barn so she wasn't the least surprised when Uncle Matthew appeared in the doorway.

'Don't you come in here with those dirty boots,' she told him with no more than a casual glance over her shoulder.

'You'm so bad as your mother,' he grumbled, unlacing his footwear.

'You know the dairy must be scrupulously clean. What d'you want anyway?'

'Some milk for old Joe.'

Elizabeth shrugged and went on with her work. With her head bent over the task in hand, she was hardly aware of Matthew padding over to the near empty churn from that morning, and the splashing of liquid as he upended what was left into a jug. She was deep in concentration, carefully pressing the stamp so as to leave a clear imprint of the clover leaf on the shining yellow block, and didn't hear him come up behind her. Suddenly his hand slipped under her arm and he began to stroke the small swelling of her budding breast.

A whimper of shock lodged in Elizabeth's throat. Her body froze, gripped in a vice-like pain. She didn't understand what was happening, but she knew instinctively that it was wrong. Horribly, unutterably wrong. And as she stood, unable to move, with every muscle screaming to escape from its paralysis, his other hand crept around her waist and, through her light summer skirt, sought out the secret place between her thighs.

Revulsion ripped through her like an explosion but still she couldn't move as his hard fingers rubbed against her with growing urgency, and he seemed to be gurgling somewhere at the back of his throat. Elizabeth wanted to cry out, to fight him off, but her entire being was locked in deep shock. Only her tense hands gripped the butter stamp so fiercely it sank deeper and deeper into the golden pat as she stood there, transfixed into stone and so numb she couldn't even tremble. Praying, not believing this was real. What in God's name was he doing? This *couldn't* be right! And yet . . . he was her *uncle*. Surely he wouldn't do anything that was so wrong? And he knew that Joe was only yards away. She only had to scream, but her voice refused to work. And so she stood there, mutely, until just as suddenly as it had begun, his great hands were no longer touching her. The relief was so overwhelming, her body nearly melted.

'I do have summat fer show you, Lizzie.'

She wasn't sure why, but she turned to look at him. His face was puce, his forehead wet with sweat as he fumbled with his trousers. And then she was shot through with horror as he held some terrifying, thick, throbbing thing in his great, grubby hands.

The foul sight galvanized Elizabeth into action. She stamped her foot, somehow all she could do to express her disgust and her anger. The shock, the bewilderment, was subsiding, and in its place, growing rage. And finding her feet, she fled past him and back into the farmhouse.

David and Daniel were climbing down from the table, each with a glistening moustache from the mugs of thick, creamy milk. She wiped their faces, sent them out to collect the eggs and cleared the table. Her movements were all mechanical, done without thought, her hands moving of their own accord, as if she wasn't really there. Her stunned brain struggled to put some order into what had happened. If it had happened. It was vile and shameful what Uncle Matthew had done, of that there was no doubt in her mind. But . . . but why? She didn't understand. But . . . the unknown sensation that had stung her body at Matthew's touch, cramping her stomach with such force . . . something . . . some instinct told her it was something to do with having babies. And somehow, from the hazy depths of her memory, she recalled her mother accusing Matthew of not being able to keep his hands off Aunt Margaret, which was why she'd given birth to another child. Daniel closely resembled his mother, but when you saw how Nellie and the two other boys looked so like their father, there must be some reason, some closeness, that meant Aunt Margaret had given birth to *his* children. Dear God! Had Uncle Matthew done to her whatever it was? Would *she* have a baby now? She began to shake, terror strangling her gullet. It was a sin to have a baby if you weren't married. It was some years ago, but she remembered how Annie Simpkin had been outcast by everyone, the Methodists in particular, until she'd run away never to be seen again. Was that to happen to *her*? Elizabeth sat down abruptly to stop herself from fainting. The shame of it sickened her. But what had she done? She . . . she must *know*! But how on earth could she tell her mother? She felt so humiliated, so . . . dirty, terrifying thoughts tumbling nauseatingly in her head. And yet . . . her mother had given birth to *her*, and her mother had never done anything that wasn't good and God-fearing, so . . . Somehow, she would have to find out, but without letting on what had happened. Oh, dear Lord, she prayed she would find the courage, but the very idea set her heart crashing against her ribcage. But until she knew, until she understood what her uncle had done to her, the very core of her soul would be shaking with dread.

* * *

Thomas Arkwright felt humiliation curl in his stomach as his friend pointed a jeering finger at him and fell about with laughter.

''Er's got one over on you this time!' Sam Grainger hooted with derision. 'There be nort wrong with your face! Having you on, 'er be! But I bet 'er wished 'er could see your face now!'

While Sam staggered about in mocking glee, Thomas scowled with piqued resentment. He'd run towards home, petrified that his face would be scarred for life, and quailing at the thought of looking in the mottled looking-glass in the tumbledown cottage where he lived. On the way, he'd run into his friend, and was so crushed by his fear that he'd revealed his terror to Sam at once. And now Sam was doubled up with delight at his expense. The little bitch! That stuck-up, self-righteous little bitch had played a trick on him! Had made him look a complete and utter fool in front of his friend! And no doubt it would be all over the village and the entire area by the evening.

Well, if she thought she could get away with it, she had another think coming! A smarting thirst for revenge rampaged in his immature breast as his angered fists clenched at his sides. He wouldn't let her get away with it! Nursing his injured pride, he turned and ran like a demon in the direction of Matthew Halse's farm. When he caught up with her, by God, he'd give her what for!

But he didn't catch sight of her until she arrived at the farmstead and went straight indoors with the two little boys. Damn her! Thomas pulled back and crouched behind the low stone wall that surrounded the small unkempt garden at the front of the house. He doubted she'd be alone at the farm. He didn't count the smaller children, of course, but Matthew Halse was known to be a force to be reckoned with. Perhaps if he bided his time . . .

He stole round to the back of the house where he'd be less likely to be seen. Just as he was about to peer in through the window, the rear door of the cross passage was flung open and Elizabeth bowled across to another smaller building, carrying a pail of water. Thomas's heart pounded as he ducked down again. She only had to turn . . . but she didn't. He waited for some minutes for his nerves to subside. Elizabeth hadn't come out, and he wondered what the outbuilding was and what she was doing there. Some unaccustomed caution made him consider he ought to find out before he went marching in to . . . Well, to be honest, he wasn't quite sure what he was going to do. But maybe his luck was in and she was stripping off for a good wash in the bucket she'd been carrying. In that case, he needn't do anything at all. He could watch her through a window, if there was one, and then reveal himself at the last moment, shaming her by announcing he'd seen everything and would relate every last detail to his pals in the village. That would teach her!

He hurried forward, keeping low. A window ran almost the entire side of the building, quite high up in the wall. But he was tall for his fourteen years. If he stretched up on tiptoe and held on to the sill with his fingertips, he might just about be able to see in. It took a little time for his avid eyes to adjust. Then he realized with disappointment that he was looking down into a small dairy and that Elizabeth was merely working at a marble bench. Damn! And now her uncle had come in, removing his boots. A minute later he was standing behind his niece, his burly shoulders and growing paunch making her dainty figure look like a fairy's by comparison. Thomas glowered with annoyance. He couldn't do anything with Matthew Halse around! And then his fingers nearly lost their grip as one of the farmer's hands started to fondle the girl's budding breast, while the other delved between her thighs.

Thomas Arkwright's sparrow-like eyes opened wide. He couldn't believe what he was seeing, and held his breath in astonishment. Lizzie Thornton, who was more righteous than thou, was standing there while her lecherous old uncle was working his hands over her luscious young body. Thomas had to lick in the saliva that dribbled from the corner of his mouth. His heartbeat had quickened, and inside his dirty corduroy trousers, his pencil-thin member was swelling unbearably. He'd never made use of it yet, though he boasted he had, and he fully intended to do so at the first available opportunity. But it would never be with Lizzie Thornton. He couldn't even get a harmless kiss out of her! And yet here she was, obviously enjoying her uncle's attentions, seeing as she seemed to be allowing the dirty bugger full range. Well,

Thomas would never forget it! He'd make the little trollop pay for it one day! The sweat was pouring down his face as he saw Matthew Halse get himself out, all ready and poised for action, and Lizzie turned round to face him.

What happened next, Thomas never knew for certain, though he had a bloody good idea! His fingers slipped and he fell backwards onto the ground, winding himself and landing painfully on his elbow. Bloody hell! What if his arm hurt so much he couldn't do his work down the mine on the early shift the next morning? His father would kill him! He'd only started working underground a few weeks back. And he could hardly say he'd hurt himself spying on Lizzie Thornton and her uncle when they were *at it* in the dairy! His father would beat the life out of him to hear him speak of such things! And something in his dull, ungifted brain warned him that he should keep the knowledge of what he'd seen buried deep in his memory. Perhaps for future use . . .

SIX

January 1865

The shrieks of their laughter echoed through the crisp and frosty air, breaking the strange silence only a heavy fall of snow can create. The white, muffling blanket had lain thick since New Year, the freezing temperatures preventing it from melting, but overnight, a fresh layer had floated softly from the sky, spreading a further magical carpet over the moor. Elizabeth and her mother, as always the first to rise, had been enchanted by the pure, clean surface, as yet undisturbed by tramping feet. But the working day was already beginning. Hannah left for Rosebank Hall via a longer but safer route in the snow, and Matthew had set off up to the leer, taking with him the elderly but faithful Spot, his shepherd's staff, and one of the ponies pulling a sled laden with hay for the wethers. He trudged off, all the time grumbling bitterly that he hoped the buggers — meaning his sheep — had followed their instinct to come further down, and that he didn't have to dig any of them out of a deep drift.

Elizabeth had set the four siblings to various duties as Matthew's tasks about the farmyard must still be completed in his absence. Not long after their frugal midday meal, however, a golden sun had emerged from behind the leaden clouds, sending gilded ripples across the twinkling snow. Even Elizabeth couldn't resist the desire to play. With coats buttoned and scarves wound about their necks, they cavorted in the crunchy white powder, screaming with glee as they chased each other in gay abandon and hurled badly aimed snowballs. The snow was so deep, David's little legs kept tripping him up, and Elizabeth and Nellie had to hold up their long skirts so that their red flannelette petticoats were on full view. They made the most enormous snowman, and Elizabeth surprised and delighted them by daring to stick Matthew's favourite pipe where its mouth should be.

'There!' she proclaimed, grinning broadly, her cheeks rosy and glowing from such exertion in the cold, her warm breath billowing about her head. They were all laughing, breathless and exhausted, and Elizabeth realized with horror that the sun was rapidly descending in the sky, and there were still chores to perform before Matthew returned.

'Come along, now. There still be work to do. Nellie, you and Nathaniel can muck out the cows, and you two little toads can get on with your lessons while I make the bread.'

There were long faces all round as they traipsed back towards the farmhouse. Within five minutes, wet gloves and boots were drying before the fire, and the cows were lowing in the shippen next door as the flagged floor was cleaned around them. The two smallest boys sat at the table while Elizabeth kneaded the dough for the four loaves the family devoured daily. The tranquillity didn't last long. As soon as her back was turned, Daniel and David had slid silently from their chairs, hoping she wouldn't notice, and were creeping towards the door again.

'Don't you think I haven't seen you,' Elizabeth rounded fondly on them, her flour-covered hands held in the air. 'If you don't settle down to copying those letters onto your slates, you'll have to help in the shippen. You've had some fun, so now 'tis time to work.'

Elizabeth glowered at the two boys who both pouted in protest but obeyed instantly. They knew that their cousin meant what she said, and anything was better than the unpleasant job of cleaning out the shippen.

Peace reigned again and Elizabeth was able to get on with the loaves which she had to bake on the open hearth. It would be so satisfying to have a proper range to cook on, like the one her mother had described in the kitchen at Rosebank Hall. It was two and a half years since Hannah had gone to work for Josiah Pencarrow on a daily basis. Although their landlord didn't live such an extravagant life these days, it was far above their own and Elizabeth never tired of her mother's anecdotes. The arrangement worked well, Hannah smiling that she was paid comfortably for doing nothing but making the old fellow behave himself.

There'd been a strangeness between Elizabeth and her mother for a few weeks at the beginning of the summer, after she'd plucked up courage to ask how babies were made. At first, she hadn't wanted to believe what her mother had told her. It was disgusting, and she found it hard to accept that she herself was the result of such an act between her revered parents. But it all made sense, and her mother would hardly invent such a thing, would she? Hannah insisted that one day she'd understand. That when she found a man she loved deeply, she'd not only be willing, but would yearn to give herself to him, body and soul. Elizabeth doubted it very much, and it certainly wouldn't be to the likes of anyone she'd met so far in her life!

She'd been so profoundly shocked that she'd all but forgotten the reason for her timorous questioning. Her relief that she wasn't about to have Matthew's child was obliterated by the terror of what he *might* have done to her, although she somehow doubted he'd have gone so far. He'd been the essence of the dutiful uncle ever since, and she was mature enough to realize it was his way of apologizing for his despicable behaviour. Nevertheless, she was always wary of his company, and made sure she was never alone with him. Just occasionally, when she was engrossed in some task as she was now, the memory of the horrific ordeal came flooding back to her, setting her heart thundering with a mixture of terror and bewilderment, and she slammed the dough of the last loaf savagely on the table.

The door to the cross passage opened just as Elizabeth was setting the four tins to prove before the smouldering peat fire. She hoped any draught of cold air wouldn't stop them from rising after all her hard work. But when she glanced up, it was her mother who slipped wearily into the room and sank down heavily on one of the straight-backed wooden chairs.

'You're back early, Mother.'

'It looks as though 'tis coming on to snow again,' Hannah explained with a sigh, 'and Mr Pencarrow said I should go whilst I could still get through. I reckon as the old devil's hoping I'll be snowed in here for a few days so as he can let Cook indulge him whilst I'm out of the way! She would, as well, even though she knows 'tis so bad for him. But to tell the truth,' she grimaced, stretching her stockinged feet towards the warmth of the fire, 'I wouldn't mind a little rest at home with my lovely daughter.'

Elizabeth's pretty mouth lifted into a glowing smile. 'Shall we have a cup of tea?'

'That'd be proper welcome. And I think just a little meadowsweet.'

Elizabeth turned her head sharply. 'Mother?'

'Oh, 'tis just a bit of a headache.'

'Wouldn't feverfew be better, then?'

'No, I think meadowsweet just now,' Hannah nodded decisively. But as Elizabeth crossed to the hearth to prepare the hot drinks, she didn't see her mother wince and rub her hand low down over her stomach.

* * *

July 1865

'What is it, Dr Greenwood? What's wrong with my mother?'

William Greenwood stopped in his tracks. He hadn't heard Elizabeth come across the yard behind him as he buckled his medical bag to Rusty's saddle. He turned to contemplate her, rubbing his chin thoughtfully. My, the child could be direct at times. Not that she was a child any more, and her maturity had always put her beyond her years.

'I know 'tis serious, so 'tis no use trying to tell me otherwise,' Elizabeth persisted. 'And I've seen her taking meadowsweet more and more over the past few months.'

The doctor chewed pensively on his lip. 'You know I can't discuss another patient, Lizzie, even if she is your mother. You must ask her yourself. But with you to look after her, I'm sure she'll be fine. If she can get some rest, and avoid tense situations . . .'

'Oh, what between my uncle and Mr Pencarrow?'

Dr Greenwood nodded his head knowingly. 'Old Josiah can be a cantankerous old devil, but it's more of a game between him and your mother. There's no malice in him, and she knows it. Your uncle, now I believe *he* can be a bit of a handful when he's drunk.'

'Huh! And when he's sober,' Elizabeth snorted. A tremor of fear rippled down her spine at the thought that Matthew might have overheard her. But it was high summer and he was out haymaking on another farm with the dubious assistance of his two elder children. The local farmers did that at haymaking, just as they did at shearing, helping each other and moving from one farm to the next. It was hard work, from dawn to dusk. Hay was a precious commodity especially on that side of the moor where it grew only on the lower slopes with the hardy crops of oats and rye. The weather was perfect for haymaking just now, and every farmer wanted to make the most of it while the good spell lasted.

Dr Greenwood gathered Rusty's reins in his hand. 'It can't be easy for him, supporting such a large family. And I'm sure he still misses your aunt a great deal.'

'He should've thought of that before he got her with child again, then, and she wouldn't have died.'

The bitter words were out before she could stop them, and the doctor's kindly eyes widened involuntarily. 'You shouldn't say such things, Lizzie.'

'Well, 'tis true.' And she lifted her chin imperiously.

William paused with his left foot in the stirrup before swinging himself onto the animal's back. 'I've learned in my time not to be judgemental of people's private affairs,' he said firmly. 'If you'll take my advice, you'll do the same. Human nature can be a queer thing. In his way, I believe your uncle loved your aunt very much, and still grieves for her.'

'Then why . . .' Elizabeth clamped her jaw resolutely shut, her heart thumping in her chest. Should she tell Dr Greenwood why she despised her uncle so much? But what good would it do other than admit to her own sense of shame? Besides, it was more than a year since the incident in the dairy, and perhaps it was best to let sleeping dogs lie.

'Lizzie?' William frowned down at her.

'Oh, 'tis nothing,' she answered quickly. 'I was just thinking he won't be too pleased to get your bill.'

'There won't be one. The eggs and cheese are payment enough.'

''Tis proper kind of you.'

'You just take care of your mother. And I'll be testing you on the heart and lungs next time I come, so make sure you study those notes I've given you.'

He clicked his tongue and Rusty obediently ambled out of the yard, his hooves treading with a muffled thud on the dried earth. William allowed the horse to go at its own pace while his own silent thoughts wandered elsewhere. Hannah Thornton had been a close friend for a good ten years now. Qualified as he was, William had learned from her, and now, when she really needed his help, there was little he could do for her. It might just be something harmless such as fibroids, but she was beginning to suffer too much discomfort for his liking, there were other symptoms now, and she was losing weight. If, God forbid, his suspicions were correct, it was already at an advanced stage, and there was nothing he could do.

* * *

October 1865

'Here you are, Lizzie! 'Tis a birthday present from Mr Pencarrow!'

Elizabeth, stirring the contents the pot suspended over the open fire, lifted her head. ''Tis not my birthday for six weeks. And why should *he* want to give me a present?' she demanded suspiciously. 'I've never met the man.'

'Well, he knows how proud I am of you, and how I'd like to be able to give you something more for your birthday than the trifle I can afford,' Hannah replied, dropping wearily into a chair, the sizeable parcel of brown paper, tied loosely with string, on her lap. 'And 'twill take some time to make it useable, shall we say? So come along and open it.'

Elizabeth stepped forward, the bright anticipation on her mother's drawn face sending a tingle of excitement down to her stomach. She knelt down on the stone floor, oblivious to its hardness, as her fingers patiently worked at the knots of string rather than cutting it into pieces, since nothing must be wasted in the constant battle to make ends meet. She glanced up, her eyes dancing with expectation, before finally unfolding the paper. A gasp of delight filled her lungs as her eyes fell upon the delicate greyish-blue material. She blinked at her mother, and when Hannah smiled back with an encouraging nod, her body trembled with pleasure as she shook the dress free of its packaging. She sprang to her feet and holding the collar up to her neck with one hand, and the waist against her stomach with the other, she twirled round twice, her feet scarcely touching the floor.

'Oh, Mother, 'tis beautiful! But I don't understand why Mr Pencarrow should want to give me something like this.'

''Twas his wife's,' Hannah told her, still smiling at her daughter's incredulity. 'And as he said, 'tis of no use to her, her being dead these twenty-five years. There's two whole wardrobes full of her clothes, and he told me to choose whatever I wanted. There were some lovely gowns. You'd have looked a picture in one of those, but what good would that have been to you? So I picked this one as I thought the style were more practical and could be brought up to date more easily. 'Tis the finest, softest wool I've ever seen. 'Twill take some work, mind, to alter it for you. I'm afraid you'll have to do it yourself. I . . . I'm not really up to it.'

Elizabeth was instantly stilled, the hem of the dress swaying about her ankles, and the gleeful grin slid from her face. 'Mother?' She dropped the garment over the back of a chair and bent to peer into Hannah's eyes. 'You oughtn't to be working, you know, when you're not well.'

'Working?' Hannah's features crinkled into a faint smile, with lines in her skin which Elizabeth was sure hadn't been there a week or two before. ''Tis hardly working what I do for Mr Pencarrow. I sit and talk to the old fellow most of the time. Well, argue, very often!' she laughed wryly. 'He wants to drink his wine and his brandy, and I won't let him. And Cook tries to slip him greasy lamb stew which he loves, and heavy suet puddings, and I have to take them away from him and take the full brunt of his moanings. And when his gout's bad, I have to rub his ugly toes! Look like bursting tomatoes, they do, on the end of his gurt long feet!' She was laughing aloud now, and Elizabeth smiled, feeling happier now her mother was more like her usual self. 'Might've been quite nice feet, once upon a time,' Hannah went on. 'In fact, I reckon as he must've been quite a handsome man in his youth before he started eating and drinking too much. But now, 'tis just a lonely old man he is.'

'Lonely? I thought as he were supposed to have had lots of friends at one time?' Elizabeth turned back to her task of preparing the evening meal. She could see through the tiny window that low clouds had ushered in an early dusk. Uncle Matthew was due back with Nellie and Nathaniel from driving the first-year lambs to the farm on the milder Bere Peninsula where they would spend the winter. The two younger boys were in the shippen supposedly milking the cows and, any minute now, the room would be crowded with hungry mouths, destroying the chance to talk peacefully with her mother.

'Oh, not real friends,' Hannah was saying now. 'Shallow types who took advantage of him. And when he lost to them at cards and owed them money, they forced him into hosting those shenanigans up at the Hall. Wanted to protect their reputations and thought no one would find out about them up on the moor like that. Disappeared into thin air when he put a stop to it all. To tell the truth,' and over her shoulder, Elizabeth saw her mother lean forward confidentially, 'I think he went off the rails, so to speak, when his wife died. Old Henry, the gardener, he reckons as Mr Pencarrow blamed his son for her death, and 'tis why they never got on.'

Elizabeth raised a surprised eyebrow as she set the table. 'How did she die, then?'

'In childbirth. Like Aunt Margaret.' Hannah sat back in the chair with a long sigh. 'Except that 'twas her first. And Henry reckons the drinking and what have you was Mr Pencarrow's way of forgetting. You know, others wouldn't, but I feel sorry for him. He rarely gets out of the house now, what with his heart and his gout, not even to the mine. And he ought to. Wheal Rosalind's been his main source of income for many a long year, but 'tisn't doing as well as it used to. Oooh.'

Hannah drew in a sharp breath as she moved in the chair, and her hand instinctively cradled her stomach. The sound made Elizabeth raise her head as she tested the potatoes baking on a speared rack in the open hearth, and her heart seemed to squeeze in her chest.

'Mother?' she managed to squeal.

'Oh, I'm all right.' Hannah flapped her hand in the air. ''Tis just a twinge. There! 'Tis gone!'

'Well, I don't think as you should be traipsing all the way over to Rosebank Hall in the morning. Sounds to me as if Mr Pencarrow can manage perfectly well without you!'

Hannah smiled gently, but the strain showed in her face. 'We'll see. Perhaps you're right. Just until I'm better.' But she hadn't yet told Elizabeth that she wasn't going to get better.

SEVEN

November 1865

Elizabeth paused with the needle speared through the soft woollen material, her lips drawn into a pensive rosebud. It hadn't exactly been the most enjoyable birthday ever. For a few more days after bringing home the lovely dress from Mr Pencarrow, Hannah had struggled back to the Hall and the tedious hours she spent caring for the old man. But the long walk over the moor really was becoming too much for her, and since then she'd stayed at home. Even there she seemed so weary, dropping asleep at any time of the day, the flesh falling from her bones. And since last Sunday, she'd taken to her bed, only shuffling out of the room to creep outside to the earth-closet. It was mid-November and the weather was rapidly deteriorating into its winter harshness. Elizabeth had begged her to use the chamber pot instead, but to no avail. Until this evening, when she was so fatigued, she could hardly drag herself out of bed.

Elizabeth finally lowered the sewing into her lap with a heart-wrenching sigh. How could she concentrate when her stomach was tumbling over and over like a butter churn? Her nerves were on edge, the silence of the farmhouse mercilessly taunting her anxiety. It was as if she was waiting for something dreadful to happen, and the anticipation of it was suffocating her. Outside, the clear frosty night was as silent as death, and the only sound in the room was the uneven hiss of the peat turfs in the open fire. It was warm enough, with her feet spread out towards the hearth, but somehow the core of her body was ice-cold.

'Lizzie!'

Her uncle's call as he stumbled in through the door cut into her unease, and she shuddered. She really could do without Matthew's drunken stupor, for no doubt he would have reached his usual state of intoxication, drinking at the quaint old inn in the village until he was thrown out. Most nights, she would already have retired, taking refuge in the bedroom she'd shared with her mother for some while, as Daniel and David were now considered old enough to sleep in the attic with their older brother and sister.

She looked up at the sharp influx of air, her heart lurching with dismay, as Matthew fell into the room, leaving the door wide open behind him. She tutted with exasperation as she got to her feet and pushed past him to close the offending door.

'Mind you take those dirty boots off!' she warned him as she glanced down at the trail of clods he'd left inside the door.

'A few clats o' dirt niver hurted no one,' he mumbled gloomily, staggering across the newly washed floor and crashing down in the rustic settle that groaned beneath his weight. 'If you wants them off, you'll have fer do it yersel, cuz us baint!'

Elizabeth had to grind her teeth to swallow down an angry retort. It would only lead to a futile argument and their raised voices could wake her mother who at long last had drifted to sleep. So with a resigned sigh, she got down on her knees on the hard floor and began to unlace the mud-caked boots. She had to hold her breath, for close to, the footwear reeked of the cow dung Matthew never attempted to avoid, and despite the clean socks she put out for him daily, his seldom-washed feet stank like putrefying cheese.

'You'm so like my dear departed Maggie, you knaws, Lizzie.'

A dart of apprehension stung into Elizabeth's chest and her hands hesitated for a moment as she pulled off the second boot. What was it in his voice — loneliness, self-pity brought on by the bout of heavy drinking, or something deeper and more dangerous? She picked up the boots and moved swiftly across to place them outside the door in the cross passage.

He was waiting for her as she went back in. She hadn't heard him steal across the floor in his stockinged feet, and a wave of shock pulsed through her limbs. She tried to sidestep him, but his thickset figure pinned her against the wall. Her heart began to pound with agonizing force and she turned her head away at the stench of his beer-laden breath. He brought his lips close to hers, and slipping one of his fumbling hands between their tightly pressed bodies, clawed at her young breast.

Bile rose to her throat as the familiar room seemed to spin in a giddy spiral. But within seconds, her senses snapped into action, her mind flooding with anger. Dear God, she knew what it all meant this time! Gone was the bewildered child who'd stood in the dairy paralysed with fear, and in her place, a young woman, burning with repugnance, was ready to defend herself.

'Get off me!'

She didn't know where she found the strength, but somehow she managed to push him away and spring across the room. But in her tearing madness, she collided with the settle, and throwing himself after her, Matthew caught her arm and spun her round to face him. He was panting hard, his eyebrows in a heavy scowl, but though his fingers were digging into her flesh, he made no further attempt to dominate her.

'I be sorry, Lizzie. I didn't mean fer frit you.' His frown deepened so intensely that his frizzled hairline came down low over his forehead. ''Tis just that you makes us mind Maggie so much. But no matter. A year today and you'll be sixteen. Aud enough fer marry us.'

Elizabeth's head rocked on her neck. She stared at him, her eyes stretched wide, as the horror and revulsion of the last moments trailed into incredulity.

'Marry you?'

'Yes!' Matthew poked his head towards her. 'A man can marry his niece if she baint a blood relation. I'll ask parson, but I be certain 'tis true. Think on it, Lizzie. I'll make you that happy, see if I doesn't!'

Elizabeth blinked at him, her jaw dangling open in disbelief. But as the shock subsided, she slowly shook her head, her lips clamped in a mocking sneer. 'You must be out of your tiny mind!' she hissed. 'I wouldn't marry you if you were the last person on earth! You're just a dirty old man!'

The earnest expression on Matthew's face instantly hardened. 'What d'you mean? You . . .' he gibbered, his cheeks flushing, 'you liked it well enough afore!'

'Liked it?' She scarcely managed to grate the words from between her clenched teeth, rage scalding her throat. 'I was petrified! But I know what you're up to now. If you lay a finger on me again, I'll tell the world and his dog!'

Matthew's lips flapped in confusion. 'But I love you, Lizzie! And arter all us've done fer you and your mother over the years!'

'Done for us? *You* couldn't have managed without *us*! We owe you nothing, and you'd do well to remember it!'

He merely raised a sarcastic eyebrow. 'I could always throw you out.'

But Elizabeth was ready for him. 'I don't think so. You just try, and I'll tell Dr Greenwood what you did to me. Or the magistrate in Tavistock. So,' she smiled with false sweetness, 'I think as we can stay on. Don't you?'

* * *

'I'm so sorry, Lizzie,' William Greenwood said gently. His heart wrung with sympathy for the ashen-faced girl who sat motionless at the table opposite him, her head bowed over her clasped hands. 'I was hoping I was wrong, but I'm quite sure now. I really am truly sorry.'

Elizabeth swallowed and slowly looked up. Her eyes were dry, but the pupils were huge and shining. The doctor recognized the signs of fear and shock, nature's instinct to defend itself with a surge of energy. But you couldn't run from something like this. And instead she began to tremble. Quietly. Controlled. 'And . . . there's nothing you can do?' she murmured almost inaudibly.

William bit his lip. 'You know there isn't, Lizzie. It's beyond us. All we can do . . .' and his own throat closed as he tried to speak, 'is to let her go peacefully and with dignity.'

Elizabeth met his gaze, her fine eyebrows arched at the ultimate question. 'How . . . how long?' she barely whispered.

He hesitated. He hated that question. But neither Elizabeth nor her mother were fools. 'A few weeks. Maybe months, but I doubt it. It seems to be spreading. I expect her to go downhill quickly now. I can give her willow bark and laudanum for any pain. Morphine injections if need be.'

Elizabeth rose to her feet. Unsteadily. Sick and faint from the grief that pulsed through her veins. 'Thank you for your honesty.'

'I'll call every day. Your . . . Hannah . . .' he gulped, cursing himself for his emotion, 'has been a good friend to me. I'll always be here for you, Lizzie, remember that. Now, you must look after yourself. You'll need to be strong for her. I've given her a sleeping draught. She'll sleep for some hours, so I suggest you have a rest, too.'

But she didn't. Nellie was at home that day and could fetch anything Hannah needed if she woke. So Elizabeth walked up to the river at Hillbridge with its salmon ladder and the weir head for the leat. The high moorland beckoned her aching spirit, and she followed the tumbling waters of the Tavy for mile upon mile, higher and higher until she reached the wild, desolate beauty of Tavy Cleave. On she went, far beyond the intake for the second hurrying leat in the shadow of Ger Tor, and up, up to the savage loneliness of the moor where only the mewing cry of the buzzard and the harsh bark of the raven could be heard above the howling wind.

EIGHT

'Happy Christmas, darling.' Hannah's eyes gleamed brightly from their deeply sunken sockets, two dark caverns in her emaciated face. Her grey, paper-thin skin was drawn tightly over her protruding cheekbones, her hair lank and lifeless, fanned out on the pillow. Forty-five years old. She might have been ninety.

Elizabeth forced a smile to her lips. It hardly seemed happy to her, but you had to pretend, didn't you? It was Christmas Eve, the younger children all in bed if not asleep, and Nellie, amiable and placid as ever, had just climbed the stairs to the attic above. Matthew had taken himself down to the village to fill his belly with ale. With luck, they wouldn't see him again that evening.

'Come and sit by me for a while.' Her mother's voice reached her with its now all too familiar frailty.

'I ought to be changing your sheets.'

'Never mind about that,' Hannah protested as forcibly as she could. 'They don't need changing. Just look at you. You're wearing yourself out. You haven't been to bed for days.'

'I've been sleeping well enough in the chair.'

Hannah blinked at her daughter, and felt her heart overflow. Elizabeth had been the rock of her life for so long, and now here she was, little more than a child, bearing so much on her young shoulders. Tears of pride pricked in Hannah's eyes, but she drove them back. There were things that needed to be said.

She inhaled with weary determination. 'I appreciate it, my love. But 'twon't be for much longer.'

Elizabeth lifted her eyes as a tearing ache tightened her gullet. There wasn't an ounce of flesh on her mother's bones, hadn't been for weeks. She was too weak to get out of bed or lift a spoon to her mouth and brought back every drop of nourishing soup Elizabeth persuaded her to swallow. So many times Elizabeth had thought she couldn't get any worse, and yet she had. But still she was alive, and somehow Elizabeth had convinced herself that, in spite of it all, her mother would go on for ever. Somewhere deep inside, she knew she was fooling herself, but her breaking heart could only cling to what she wanted to believe.

'Oh, Mother, don't say such things,' she croaked. But the words had come out in a rush, while she was still able to speak.

'Lizzie, I need to talk to you. Before 'tis too late.'

Elizabeth recognized the spark of strength in her mother's tone. She was right, as ever. What did a few drops of spilt broth on a sheet matter, when the time they had left was so precious? She perched on the edge of the bed and took Hannah's limp hand in hers. The skin felt strange, fragile, as if it might rub off as she stroked it.

'Now, I want you to listen carefully,' Hannah began in earnest. And then her mouth lifted in the hint of a mischievous smile. 'I'm afraid I have a confession to make. All this time, at Mr Pencarrow's, I didn't earn three shilling and threepence a week. I earned three and ninepence. Every week, I put sixpence aside for you. 'Tis hidden in a little hessian bag behind the fourth rafter on the left up in the attic. 'Twas always for you. For your future. Whatever that may be. To set yourself up as a nurse when the time comes. To get married. I'm sure you'll use it wisely.'

71

Elizabeth's chin quivered and she shook her head in confusion, the warring emotions inside her breast tearing her apart. It was good. Yes, the money was good, of course it was. And just like her dear, selfless, thoughtful mother to have done such a thing. But really, what did she care, when all the money in the world couldn't keep her mother alive? She tried to draw in a trembling breath, opening her mouth to say something, but her anguished mind was numbed. She turned her head away so that Hannah wouldn't see the tears that had suddenly collected in her eyes and slowly, one by one, were overflowing her lower lids and meandering down her cheeks like silver pearls.

'William will always be there to help and advise you.' Hannah's resolute voice reached her as if from some far, far away place. 'And there's something else much more important. When I'm gone . . .'

Elizabeth stirred with a tormented twist of her shoulders, and a strangled whimper caught at the back of her throat. Hannah's fingers tightened around hers in a feeble squeeze, and she felt guilty that her mother was having to comfort her.

'When I'm gone,' Hannah went on softly, her voice low and soothing, 'I want you to take my place at the Hall. Except that you'll be living in. Away from this place. 'Tis all arranged. William's been up and discussed it all with Mr Pencarrow. 'Tis quite settled. And William will go on teaching you. He wants you to start attending deliveries with him soon.'

Elizabeth swung her head to gaze at her mother, her brow puckered in an excruciating frown at the same time as her eyes were stretched with total bewilderment. Her heart was beating slow and hard, her lips twitching as she struggled to put some sense into her agonized thoughts. 'B-but I don't understand. I thought as Mr Pencarrow were nothing but a belligerent old lecher!'

An amused grunt was the nearest to a laugh Hannah could manage. 'Hardly. He walks with a stick, and on bad days, he can't put his feet to the floor. You'll have nothing to fear from him. He'll find you very pleasing on the eye, you can be sure of that,' she smiled lovingly, her gaze caressing her daughter's face, 'but his days of wandering hands are over. Which,' she hesitated only slightly, 'is more than can be said of your uncle.'

A trickle of ice shivered down Elizabeth's spine and she prayed her mother couldn't hear her heart, which had started to pound like a battering ram. The shame of what had passed between her uncle and herself clawed at her throat, and she felt her palms ooze with hot sweat.

'I've seen the way he looks at you. 'Tis only a matter of time before he . . . well, I think you know what I mean. With Mr Pencarrow you'll be safe. He's an intelligent man. Lazy and gruff, 'tis true, but not without his good points. So.' She closed her eyes with an exhausted sigh, and let her head drop back on the pillow. 'Promise me you'll do as I ask. Then I can go peacefully.'

Elizabeth's eyes rested on her mother's stricken face. A tranquil smile played almost imperceptibly on the dry lips, and the ravages of the disease that had sapped the lifeblood from her withered body seemed to melt away. Elizabeth's mind was bereft of thought, her brain stunned by grief and lack of sleep. But if that was what her mother wanted, then that was what she would do. She only thanked God Hannah didn't seem to realize that Matthew had already stepped a good way along the path she had feared. At least, she would never know.

'I promise, Mother,' she whispered.

She saw the smile deepen, then the muscles relaxed as Hannah drifted asleep, her chest rising and falling in shallow, laboured breaths. Elizabeth left her hand in her mother's, not moving, not wanting to move, for some time. Motionless, she sat watching the sepia shadows the lamp flickered about the dimly lit room, waiting . . .

* * *

She must have fallen asleep in the chair, as it was some time later when a groan from the bed snapped Elizabeth to her senses. It was cold. She must have dozed off without tucking the rug around herself as she normally did. She blinked her eyes awake, the lids itching and heavy, and she could feel them trying to close again. But another low moan catapulted her across to where her mother was moving restlessly beneath the thick blankets. The serenity had slipped from Hannah's face, and her eyes were dark and wild with suffering.

Elizabeth's pulse accelerated uneasily. 'Oh, Mother, why didn't you call me?' she demanded, the words bouncing back eerily from the solid stone walls.

'I didn't want to wake you.' Hannah's strained voice was no more than a thin trail, her breath punctuated with stifled grunts of agony. But a wan smile still flitted across her face for her beloved daughter. 'I'm mortal cold, and the pain . . . Fetch me some laudanum, would you, my darling?'

Elizabeth instinctively frowned. ''Tis not so long since you had some.'

'Lizzie.' In the dull glow from the oil lamp, Hannah's eyes fixed hers with calm resignation. 'I don't really think as that matters now,' she said meaningfully. 'And the pain's that bad.'

Elizabeth contemplated her mother, her heart twisting with anguish, and then slowly dragged herself across to the high shelf where she had put the dangerous medicines out of reach of the children. She carefully measured a dose of the brown liquid into a small glass of water and held it to Hannah's lips.

'Thank you, dear,' Hannah breathed when she'd swallowed it, and Elizabeth helped her to sink back on the pillows. A palpable stillness settled about them, hanging in the air like a fine mist. Strange. Unreal. 'You will . . . remember what I said just now? About Mr Pencarrow?'

Elizabeth swallowed hard and nodded, for somehow her voice had become stuck in her throat. Hannah was clearly speaking only with some effort now, even her thoughts laboured as the powerful drug began to take effect.

'Good.' Silence again. For a few minutes. It might have been hours. 'What time is it?'

'Gone midnight, I should think.' Before she'd dozed off, Elizabeth had heard Matthew return, singing his drunken head off as he staggered across to his bed above the shippen, so it must have been late even then.

'Christmas Day, then.' Another pause. 'I'm not afeared to go, you know. Just sorry to leave you. And the Lord will take care of you.'

'And so will Mr Pencarrow.'

'Yes.' Hannah gave a little snort of amusement. 'And so will Mr Pencarrow.'

'Are you still cold?' Elizabeth clung to practicalities as the night air wrapped itself about her own shivering form.

'A little.'

'I'll go and stoke up the fire and put some water on for a bottle.'

'That would be good. My dearest child.'

Elizabeth hurried out to the smoke-blackened chimney in the other room. She'd forgotten to bank up the fire earlier, and it would take some skill and a little time to coax the glowing ash back into life. Once or twice, as she waited for the tinder-dry firewood to catch and give sufficient substance to the fire to add some finely broken turf, she popped back to the bedroom door. Hannah had turned her head on the pillow so that she could watch the daughter she loved so deeply, and smiled at her across the room before she returned to the fire. At last, the flames were dancing merrily in the hearth, and Elizabeth wedged the kettle among the sizzling peat.

'There.'

She got to her feet and went back to Hannah, who was still watching the door with wide-open eyes. And then something in Elizabeth's heart lurched. Those adoring eyes were too still, hadn't moved, hadn't blinked. The young girl halted in her tracks as numbness deadened her senses. Oh, no. Surely . . . She floated forward in some twilight world. A hand, not hers, and yet it was, reached out and felt Hannah's neck where there should have been a pulse.

So quiet. So alone, in the dead of night. The fight was over. And yet . . . Hannah's eye twitched and a barb of confused hope tore at Elizabeth's breast. But it was no more than a final impulse as the nerves shut down for ever. Already Hannah was growing cold, her face setting like marble. Elizabeth lowered herself onto the bed, staring, as motionless as the corpse beside her. For ten minutes. An hour. Maybe two. Until her aching back screamed at her to stir herself.

Goodbye, Mother.

She stood up. Somehow found herself in the other room. The fire was nearly extinguished again. As she was suddenly aware of the violent paroxysms that had begun to shake her entire being, she became desperate for the comforting warmth of incandescent flames. She moved mechanically, like one of the automatons that had enthralled her at the Tavistock Goose Fair. She wanted this to be just as unreal. It certainly felt as if it wasn't happening. But the shivering that had set her teeth chattering told her that it was no dream. She could feel the blood racing inside her frozen body, the stillness of the night searing into her brain. The isolation of the farmstead, the quiet she loved and revered, just now was making her feel so alone.

There would be things to do come the morning. Dr Greenwood and the reverend would have to be called, difficult on Christmas Day. And then she'd have to explain to the children that they couldn't have Christmas this year. Or at least, not the one they were expecting. The cows would still need milking, the animals feeding, meals cooking. The others would still want to eat even if she didn't. But perhaps she should take a cup of tea, not Indian, but soothing chamomile. With plenty of honey to mask the taste she disliked.

She made the infusion, left it to draw for a few minutes, opened the shutters of the small window, looked eastwards towards the high ridge of land that was her beloved Dartmoor, and waited for dawn.

NINE

'Where the devil do you be going?'

Elizabeth paused as she fastened Hannah's worn cloak about her shoulders, but more at the strange mixture of grief and gratitude she felt at donning her mother's clothes, than at any fear of Matthew's tirade. She glanced down at the neatly packed carpet bag by her feet, the very same that had been brought with them to the farmstead more than ten years earlier. Her heart leapt at the thought that her uncle might open it in a fit of rage and scatter the contents across the room, discovering the hessian bag containing Hannah's secret nest egg hidden at the bottom. Elizabeth lifted her chin disdainfully to disguise the twinge of alarm as she wriggled her fingers into the woollen gloves she herself had knitted for Hannah the previous winter.

'I told you before,' she answered, boldly meeting Matthew's glowering gaze. 'I'm taking up Mother's position as nurse to Mr Pencarrow, only now 'tis a live-in position.'

'Not over my dead body you doesn't!'

'Oh, Lizzie, please don't!'

Elizabeth's eyes whipped across to where Nellie was standing by the hearth, arms dangling gormlessly either side of her wide hips. For just a second, Elizabeth experienced a pang of guilt, but the words that were stinging the tip of her tongue were already tripping out of her mouth.

'I wouldn't tempt fate if I were you!' she warned Matthew, her amber eyes glinting like burnished gold. ''Twas all arranged through Dr Greenwood before Mother died.'

'Us might've knawed that varmint had a finger in it!' Matthew thrust his face so close to her, she could see the hairs up his flared nostrils. 'You'll not go, and that be final. How's us gwain fer manage wi'out you?'

Elizabeth flicked up her head. Anger was bubbling inside her, the sorrow that had ripped her apart sapping the last vestige of patience from her wearied mind. ''Tis all you're interested in, isn't it? Well, Nellie can run the house and the dairy now, because I'm off, and I'll thank you to get out of my way.'

'Nellie? Her be nort but a cheel!'

'I've trained her well. She'll be eleven next week, same age I was when I had to do it, and I had David and Daniel no more than babies to look out for as well! So, if you don't mind,' and as her fingers closed around the handles of the bag, she straightened up and squared her shoulders defiantly, 'I'll be off.'

But Matthew showed no sign of moving, his sizeable bulk blocking the doorway and his face folded in a hideous scowl. 'And if Nellie's in the house, who gwain fer help on the farm?' he bellowed.

Elizabeth had had enough. The wretched misery that had tormented her since the early hours of Christmas morning had left her void of any other emotion. She was certainly numb to any fear that Matthew was trying to instil in her. All she knew was that she had to get away from the place where her mother had died.

'You still have Nathaniel,' she retorted. 'And Daniel and David are quite old enough to help as well. As I'll be living in, I'll only earn a shilling and sixpence a week, which will be mine to keep. However, come Lady Day, your rent is to be reduced on account of my working for Mr Pencarrow, if

I prove suitable. And don't forget, you've two less mouths to feed, too!'

For no more than a second, Matthew's face slackened with shock that the quiet, compliant niece he had always . . . well, loved, there was no doubt in his mind . . . was turning out to be as sharp and strong-willed as her mother. But if she left, what hope would he have of persuading her to marry him? 'I be your guardian, and I forbid you fer go!' he barked, grasping her arm in an iron grip.

'Well, I wonder what a lawyer would have to say about that!' she spat, and glanced with caustic disapproval at his hand on her arm.

From across the room, Nellie, too frightened to move a muscle, watched as Elizabeth raised herself on tiptoe and whispered something in Matthew's ear. What it was she said, Nellie never knew, but her father moved aside as meek as a lamb, and Nellie's heart sank as her beloved cousin walked calmly out of the door.

* * *

The ground was frozen solid, and the lush, rough grass, encrusted with heavy frost, snapped and crunched beneath Elizabeth's feet as she trudged across the moor. Her toes were numb with cold, and even inside the woollen gloves, her fingers had turned blue. A lacerating northerly wind whipped up towards the snow-peppered heights of Dartmoor and a visible cloud wreathed about her head as her warm breath collided with the glacial air. Even with the added effort of carrying the carpet bag, the exertion of the long walk did little to relieve the piercing cold. Her legs moved mechanically, her mind insensible to thought. All that existed inside her was a deep, fathomless void, a despairing emptiness that could never be filled. Her dear mother was dead. Her mother, yes, but also her teacher, her friend, her soul mate. She knew it was true, and yet she still couldn't believe it, even though she had watched as the coffin had been lowered into the ground the previous day. She felt so alone, trapped inside a glass ball, able to see the world carrying on all about her, yet not be part of it. No matter how she wanted to fight her way back to reality, she was powerless against the invisible force that kept her incarcerated in misery. She hardly knew why she was continuing to exist, why she was walking away from one life into a new one. She couldn't think why she was going to Rosebank Hall. At that moment, she really couldn't think of anything at all; it was simply what she had to do. Really she would as soon have wandered up to the high moorland and given herself up to the blissful oblivion of eternal slumber amongst the treacherous peat mires, but her fate had been ordained by her mother's last wish.

It was only as the farmhouse finally came into view that her thoughts began to focus in any way upon her future. As isolated as the humble farmstead that had been her home for as long as she could remember, the grey stone walls of Rosebank Hall melted into the purple shadows of the moorland behind, the feeble winter sun not yet having cleared the high ridge that formed the western rim of the moor. Elizabeth had seen the large, square building before and paid it little attention, although she'd never been this close. As she tramped along the seemingly endless track, she noticed that the Hall was constructed of dressed granite and must have been built in relatively recent years. There were two storeys, and even a couple of windows peeping out from the roof above. Instead of a shippen extending from the main house as in many of the poorer farmsteads, the farm buildings here were quite separate from the house across a wide yard to the rear. Her curiosity stirred, Elizabeth couldn't help thinking, though, that it seemed somewhat pretentious to call the place a hall. It hardly matched up to some of the massive, elegant houses to be found in nearby Tavistock, though she had to admit it was far more impressive than the lowly tenant farmsteads built of rubblestone that were dotted over the wild moorland.

The track veered to the left, but a sweeping gravel drive continued on to what appeared to be a level grassed area.

It dawned on Elizabeth that you came to the back of the house first, and then had to follow the driveway in order to reach the front. Her mind slipped back into action. Which door should she knock at? As nurse, did she count as a mere servant, or did she hold a privileged rank? Dr Greenwood, now he would surely go to the front. And so would she, she decided. Perhaps she would be reprimanded, but at this moment, she really didn't care.

The driveway, she discovered, swept across a neat lawn at the front of the house. On the opposite side of the grass, the ground fell away several feet, and over the drop grew a tangled hedge of wild roses. Of course! The revelation brought a smile to her mournful face. A rose-covered bank, incongruous amongst the open moorland, but quite enchanting. And clearly how the farmhouse got its name of Rosebank Hall. To the side of the house, a high wall ran at a right angle across the end of the lawn. It crossed Elizabeth's mind that behind it must lie the protected vegetable and herb garden her mother had spoken of. The thought made her feel her first hint of pleasure for some time, and she turned towards the massive, studded front door. She rang the enormous, clanging bell. Soon afterwards, she heard what sounded like heavy bolts being coaxed across, and the door groaned open.

'Yes? What do you want?'

The demanding tone pitched her back to reality. The man was dressed in a smart dark suit, his grey hair sleeked aside with macassar. He was short, but seemed to make up for his lack of height by standing erect with his shoulders braced so far back that his chest domed out in front of him like a turkey's. Although only a few inches taller than Elizabeth, he managed to give the impression of peering disdainfully down his nose, and scrutinizing her with eyes like shiny black beads.

Elizabeth stared at him, suddenly feeling nervous. 'Please, Mr Pencarrow, sir,' she stammered, 'I . . . I'm Elizabeth Thornton.'

The fellow lifted his chin and frowned at her, and she felt herself shrinking away. But then his expression softened and he wriggled his neck as if preening himself. 'I'm Mr Armitage, the butler, Miss Thornton,' he told her. And then, looking somewhat pleased with himself, stood back. 'Come in, and make sure you wipe your feet thoroughly on the mat. Wait here in the vestibule, and I'll tell the master you're here.'

Elizabeth obediently stepped inside, waiting while the front door was secured behind her. The butler disappeared through one of several heavily panelled inner doors, strutting with short, efficient steps. If there was an exchange of voices, Elizabeth couldn't hear it, the silence of the house setting her pulse racing. The vestibule, as the butler had so grandly named the hall, was indeed more than half the size of the whole of Uncle Matthew's ancient farmhouse. A narrow staircase, encased by a polished wooden banister with pleasantly turned spindles, led upwards at one end of the room. Against one wall stood a dresser with two ornate clocks on it, much as Hannah had described on her first day at the Hall.

Elizabeth's heart contracted at the memory of that balmy summer's evening, but then the door opened again and the butler ushered her into what was clearly the drawing room. A fleeting image of her mother's gaunt face forced itself into her head, mingling with the tension of meeting the formidable Josiah Pencarrow until she felt giddy.

'Come here then, girl. I can't see you if you dither by the doorway.'

Elizabeth gritted her teeth as she inched forward, sniffing back the unwelcome tears that were making her throat ache. The morning sun was filtering through the extensive casement windows at the far end of the vast room, and all she could distinguish was the silhouette of an enormous high-backed chair drawn up beside a roaring blaze in a huge open fireplace.

'Put down that wretched bag, girl, and take off that cloak so as I can have a good look at you.'

The voice was gruff. Deep. Demanding. Elizabeth knew she was trembling as she meekly obeyed. Her fingers fumbled with the fastenings of the cloak as she finally stood with downcast eyes before her new master, her mind unconsciously studying the carpet which had clearly seen better days.

'Why are you wearing your mother's clothes?'

As she tried to answer him, the words stuck in Elizabeth's throat. 'Pl-please, sir,' she managed to force a whisper from her lips. 'I . . . I don't have any black clothes of my own.'

What seemed like an interminable silence followed before Josiah Pencarrow replied, and then it was with a disapproving grunt. 'Hmm. Well, I suppose you must wear mourning,' he conceded. 'But I want you to wear something brighter when we have dinner in the evenings. A pretty girl like you shouldn't wear black all the time. And I don't expect to see that lovely hair hidden beneath that silly cap, either.'

Surprise cut through Elizabeth's nervousness. She looked up, moving out of the blinding shaft of light so that she could see the figure in the chair and come face to face with the man who would be in charge of her life from now on. He was . . . voluminous was the word that sprang to mind. Dressed in a padded silk smoking jacket that reached to his slippered feet, and with a matching pillbox hat above a rotund, florid face, he made a somewhat comic picture. He was tall, though, and broad shouldered, carrying his weight well. Although the whites were tinged with yellow, his faded blue eyes were sharp and intelligent. It was difficult to judge, but she would have put him in his late sixties.

'I . . . I expected to eat with the servants, sir,' she stammered.

Mr Pencarrow shifted forward in the chair. 'If I'm keeping a pretty girl under my roof, I shall expect her company at dinner. And you're a clever little thing, so I understood from your mother, so I'll expect some decent conversation, and nothing to do with mines or business, I hope. You don't play the piano, I suppose?'

Elizabeth lifted her eyebrows in astonishment. Josiah Pencarrow cut quite a redoubtable figure, it was true, but just as her mother had intimated, he appeared to be a man of many facets. 'No, sir. But I can sing a little,' she suggested timidly. 'I know a good number of hymns.'

'Bah! That's no good to me!' he barked so fiercely that Elizabeth inwardly recoiled. 'You can read, though, I take it?'

'Yes, sir,' she murmured. 'I love to read.'

'Good!' he bellowed so that she visibly started. 'You can read the newspapers to me, then. The print's so small these days my old eyes can't see it properly. And,' he waved a gnarled, swollen hand at her, 'you can help yourself to any of my books.'

Elizabeth felt as if she were being tossed about in a rough sea, lifted high on an exhilarating wave one moment, and dropped into a despondent trough the next. 'Thank you, sir.'

'It'll give you something to do in between looking after me, won't it?' he roared, seemingly finding something outrageously amusing in what he said. He had a wide, attractive mouth when he laughed, Elizabeth was surprised to notice, with good even teeth and a strong jawline when he lifted his head out of his double chin. 'The gout's been quite bad recently, so once you're settled into your room, your first job can be to do summat with my poor feet. I could hardly get down those damnable stairs this morning.'

The single word of dialect among what was otherwise the Queen's English somehow jolted Elizabeth out of her awe for Mr Pencarrow, at the same time as she realized that although not broad, he spoke with a definite Devonshire accent. It made her feel more at ease as she dared to address him.

'Have you been taking any of the remedies my . . . my mother left you?' she asked warily.

Josiah Pencarrow looked oddly sheepish. 'Well . . . er . . . Mrs Elliot wasn't sure how to prepare them.'

Elizabeth frowned as she remembered what her mother had said about the battle of wills she had with Mr Pencarrow over his treatment, and she tried to sound confident. ''Tis not exactly difficult. They're only leaf infusions or things to be added to your food. So, you've had no treatment for three months?'

'Only whatever it is that damned physician gives me for my heart. Visits me once a fortnight to monitor it, he calls it.'

'Is it digitalis he gives you? I can check your pulse daily for that, if you've a good pocket watch. 'Tis vital to keep the dose right. 'Twill help prevent another attack. You might not be so lucky next time.'

Josiah's deep chuckle startled her once again. 'You sound just like your mother, you know. So I think we'll rub along well enough.' He nodded with satisfaction. 'And I don't mind people coming to the back door for your remedies. Old Henry will continue to grow whatever it is you want in the kitchen garden, just as he did for your mother.' His voice suddenly softened and he shook his head sadly. 'She was a fine woman. It doesn't seem possible . . . I was deeply shocked. And so sorry these blasted feet wouldn't allow me to attend the funeral. I shall miss her dearly.'

Josiah's words trailed away on a sigh, and he turned his head to stare silently into the dancing flames in the grate, forgetting, it would seem, the presence of his new servant. The large, high-ceilinged room echoed coldly, and a pang of torment tore at Elizabeth's heart as she felt her mother's shadow flutter against her shoulder. For this was what Hannah had wanted for her, the company of a cantankerous old man with a dubious past to whom, nevertheless, she'd grown quite close. Hannah's spirit was so strong in the room just now, almost tangible, that Elizabeth thought she could see her standing there. She couldn't, of course. It was impossible. Just her mind playing tricks. Grief washed over her, and just as had happened so many times during the past week, her vision misted and soundless tears began to trickle down her pale cheeks.

It wasn't until Josiah spoke that she realized she was crying. 'Oh, stop blubbering, girl, and do summat useful. Pour us both a brandy. I think we could do with it.'

'Brandy, sir?' Elizabeth ventured, swallowing her sadness. 'But . . . you're not supposed . . .'

'I know I'm not. But if I want to drink a toast to your dear mother, then I shall do so. And tomorrow you can start bossing me about. It'll be New Year's Day, so a new start for both of us.'

Elizabeth nodded. He was right. What did one day matter? She had a whole lifetime of loneliness in front of her. And perhaps caring for this strange, unfathomable man might help her to face it. She crossed to where he had indicated. On a silver tray on a heavy oak sideboard was set a cut-glass decanter with matching glasses, so beautiful as they caught the light that she hardly dared to touch them. The decanter contained a deep amber fluid, and Elizabeth half filled two of the balloon-shaped glasses.

Josiah lifted an eyebrow at the glass as she presented it to him, and his lips curled into the hint of a smile. 'Don't know much about drink, do you?'

Elizabeth frowned. 'My uncle always drinks ale and I hate the smell of it on him, but this smells altogether different.'

'And so it should, my dear!' Josiah guffawed. 'Now you sit on the rug in front of the fire and enjoy your drink. You look half frozen. And I can study the prettiest little thing that's come my way for a long time. And . . . here's to your dear mother. God must be feeling very pleased with himself just now to have her by his side. Just as I am with you. So drink up, girl, and we can talk about your duties.'

Elizabeth obediently knelt down by the fire and sat back on her heels. The warmth thrown out by the vibrant flames was certainly welcome and her fingers began to tingle as feeling slowly returned to them. She brought the glass to her lips, aware of Josiah's eyes intently upon her. The fumes from the strong liquor made her eyes smart, but Josiah nodded encouragingly, his eyebrows arched in expectation, and she felt obliged to drink. She quickly took a mouthful and swallowed, but before she could even move the glass away from her mouth, a raging fire scalded the back of her throat and burned its way down inside her chest. The glass nearly slid from her grasp as she coughed and wheezed. Her eyes were watering freely by the time she managed to bring the spluttering under control, and even then, the irritation in her airways threatened to break out anew.

It was only then she realized Josiah was chortling wickedly. 'Never had brandy before, have we?' he chuckled.

'Mother said . . . alcohol is sinful,' Elizabeth gasped, still struggling against the rasping at the back of her throat.

'Well, your dear mother was right about most things, but not about that. It's what you *do* with alcohol that can be sinful. I should know.' Josiah sat back in his chair and Elizabeth, calmer now, noted with curiosity the wistful catch in his voice. 'I've done more than my fair share of doing what I shouldn't under its influence, and I regret it. But that doesn't mean to say that a little alcohol isn't good for the spirit. Just like now.' He gave a slight shake of his head and his folded jowls wobbled. 'So drink up, but you *sip* brandy slowly.'

Elizabeth contemplated the golden liquid in the sparkling glass and gingerly took another taste. This time, the tiny amount she consumed appeared, oddly enough, to soothe the pain it had previously caused, and a pleasing sensation gradually spread through her limbs making her feel calm and relaxed as she discussed her future life with this unpredictable old man. They would have battles, of that she was convinced, and she would have to stand up to him. That was what she was there for, after all, but, yes, as her mother had said, despite his strange personality, she couldn't help liking him.

* * *

'That was a truly delicious meal, Mrs Elliot.' As the staff all ate their supper in the kitchen that evening, Elizabeth thought it best to begin by praising the cook, but she was inwardly quaking at what she had to say next. 'But please, in future, if you could send to the table only sufficient for one portion of meat each. To send the whole joint is far too tempting for Mr Pencarrow, and he really must lose some weight. 'Tis extremely bad for both his gout and his heart.' She saw with horror that Mrs Elliot's eyes had grown wide and her cheeks were flushed and puffed out in an expression of scarcely contained outrage. Elizabeth's pulse galloped even faster, and her brain struggled to find a quick reply. 'After all, if he were to have another heart attack and die, we'd all be out of a job, and no one would want that, would they?'

She glanced hopefully from Mrs Elliot to Mr Armitage, who was daintily eating his own meal at the kitchen table. The two of them exchanged glances which seemed, reluctantly, to accept the sense of her words, and she took courage from the slow grin of old Henry, the gardener, as he looked up silently from his plate.

'Right, then,' Elizabeth sighed thankfully. 'From now on, we must reinstate all the rules I'm sure my mother had in place. Meat must have all the fat trimmed off, and 'tis better to cook it on a grill or a spit,' she said, dipping her head towards the well-equipped range, the likes of which she'd never seen before. 'That way, much of the fat is cooked out of it.'

'But fat do stick to the ribs and keep thee warm this snipey weather!' Mrs Elliot protested with bubbling indignation.

'And many physicians believe it also sticks to the inside of the arteries and can cause a heart attack or a stroke. Ask Dr Greenwood on his next visit.' She waited while Mrs Elliot pouted awkwardly, and out of the corner of her eye, she saw Henry wink at her. She wet her lips and took a deep breath. 'I'm sure you remember that liver and kidneys should not be given to anyone with gout, and neither should pulse vegetables. And no salt whatsoever, either in cooking or on the table. There's plenty of other things to give flavour,' she added hastily as Mrs Elliot went to open her mouth again, 'things which will actually be advantageous for his condition — fennel, sage, thyme, spices like cayenne and ginger. And garlic is wonderful. And I should prefer desserts to be replaced by fruit most days. Now, Mr . . . ?' she addressed the quiet, wizened fellow at the far end of the table who tapped his forehead in deference. 'I'm afraid I don't know your surname.'

'I'm just Henry, miss,' he answered in a friendly tone.

'Oh, right, thank you, Henry.' She smiled back easily. 'Now I understand you grew all manner of herbs and plants for my mother in the vegetable garden?'

'I did. 'Bout twenty different 'erbs an' other plants I takes seeds of fer the next year.' Henry nodded his nearly bald pate with enthusiasm. 'Kept everything going when thy mother left, God bless 'er. I'll show thee come morning.' He smiled good-naturedly, revealing clean but broken old teeth, and Elizabeth felt she had a friend in him, at least.

'Thank you, Henry. I shall look forward to it. And I see my mother had a shelf full of jars up there. I'd like to go through them tomorrow, if I won't be in your way, Mrs Elliot. I've given the master the medicine the doctor prescribed for his gout, but I want to rub his fingers and toes with sage unguent. But if there isn't any there, I shall have to make some. But we must *all* take care of Mr Pencarrow.' She looked from one pair of eyes to the next, including the dairymaid and the housemaid who she'd learned was Mrs Elliot's daughter. 'Which brings me to my last point. Mr Pencarrow is not to have another drop of alcoholic drink until his gout is under control again, and then only under my supervision. You may think 'tis only gout, but gout can damage the kidneys, which can lead to oedema, which in turn strains the heart, so 'tis all important. So, you do *see*?'

Four heads nodded, some more grudging than others, while Henry's face was split in a mischievous grin. 'Well, thank you, everyone,' Elizabeth concluded, deeply relieved the conversation was over. She smiled politely at them, and then swiftly escaped the room. Behind her she left the cook-cum-housekeeper and butler, as Mr Armitage liked to call himself, with their mouths dangling open. They both stared after her, glowering at the closed door for several moments until their eyes finally met.

'Well!' Mrs Elliot, her face flushed to a thunderous purple, folded her plump arms over her ample bosom. 'Who do she think she be? No more than a cheel, an' waltzing in yer as if she owned the place! Telling us how fer cook! *And* she's to have the room next to the maister's! Why cas'n she sleep in the servants' quarters in the attic like the rest on us!'

'Mrs Elliot.' Mr Armitage inflated his small chest indignantly. 'I am no more enamoured of the situation than you are. But Mr Pencarrow has employed the girl as his nurse, and we ought to do as she asks. And as for sleeping in the guest room, well, she'll hear him if he's unwell in the night. And as far as I'm concerned, she's welcome to it!'

The cook replied with a complacent nod. What happened to the cocksure young miss in the night was of no consequence to her! She could always say, 'I told you so,' with some sort of inverted pride. He had a past, did Mr Pencarrow, and if that little upstart thought she could benefit from a privileged position in the household, she had another think coming. Now, *she*, Mrs Elliot, she knew what the master was really like. She it was who had, on more than one occasion, secretly rescued from the waste-paper bin the unopened letters from France, and later read them in the privacy of her bedroom. It provided her with a kind of moral satisfaction to think that, despite his position, the master was really no better than she was. The letters were from his son. Although she'd never known the boy, she'd heard the same rumours as everyone else, that they'd physically fought over a dairymaid. It was only because she'd been widowed and was desperate for employment for herself and her daughter that she'd accepted the position at Rosebank Hall so readily.

The last letter had arrived a few weeks before Christmas, and it gave Mrs Elliot some sense of superiority that she knew far more about his son than did Mr Pencarrow himself. It might even have been quite sad had the animosity between them not been so evident in the letter. She had read it, peering in the candlelight of her attic room.

Dear Father,
I know you have little interest in me, seeing as you have never once replied to any of my letters since I left home in such

*unfortunate circumstances. I realize now that my behaviour
towards you was immature, but I was only a boy then, and
now I am a man. I beg your forgiveness, as I have done in so
many letters since.*

*It saddened me that you never acknowledged my mar-
riage or the birth of your granddaughter, so I will not expect
an answer to the news that my darling wife died last week
as a result of the debility caused in childbirth. You may
sympathize or not, as you choose, but I thought you should
know. Chantal is a little angel and I cannot blame her for
Madeleine's death as you seem to blame me for my mother's.
Rather Chantal is a joy and a great comfort to me.*

*If you have read my letters, you will know that we lived
with her parents on their farm. They are tenants and not
landowners like ourselves, but wonderful people. They are broken-hearted at Madeleine's death, and I will remain here to
care for them and work the farm for them. My own grief is
unbearable, and working hard helps to bury that grief. I miss
Dartmoor and the Hall, but France is my home now. I beg
you to write to me, though, and let me know you are all right.*

*Your son,
Richard*

Mrs Elliot sighed. Although she'd never met him, she felt
sorry for the young man, losing his wife like that. But it really
wouldn't do if it was discovered that she'd been reading the
master's private correspondence. She placed the letter in her
apron pocket. In the morning, she must remember to burn
it on the range when no one was looking. She blew out the
candle, snuggled down in the bed, and was soon dreaming of
a nice greasy roast goose and pigeon pie.

TEN

'So, my dear, it would seem I must close down the mine.'

Josiah Pencarrow was standing with his back to her, gazing out of the window, as Elizabeth entered the study. His voice sounded unfamiliar, frail almost, and certainly without its usual bombastic delivery that had, indeed, reverberated throughout the entire house for the past hour during his deliberations with the two gentlemen whom Mr Armitage had just seen out of the front door. The bank manager and the mine-captain of Wheal Rosalind had become frequent visitors over the five weeks Elizabeth had been at Rosebank Hall, and each time they arrived with increasingly grim faces.

Elizabeth instinctively knew she should tread carefully. 'Oh, sir, I'm so sorry,' she said quietly. 'Can I . . . can I get you some soothing tea, chamomile with valerian and mint would be good.'

Josiah turned to her with a hint of his normal humour. 'A brandy would be better,' he answered gruffly. 'But since I don't imagine you'll allow it, you can make me one of your concoctions in just a minute. Well,' he sighed wearily and came towards her, moving slowly but unaided, 'at least I have my little Lizzie to talk to now, rather than that pokerfaced midget who calls himself a butler. Just having you here has made a big difference to me, and look how much better I am, even if you do half starve me,' he grumbled. 'We'll leave those damned papers on the desk for now and go back to the drawing room. Which I can manage without a stick now, thanks to you.' Nevertheless, he shuffled rather than walked to the principal room of the house and sank gratefully into his chair beside the roaring fire. He undoubtedly had improved, and had lost more than a little weight, although not without hard-won battles between Elizabeth and Mrs Elliot, to say nothing of Josiah himself! Elizabeth was pleased, for she'd achieved almost as much success with him as Hannah had.

Ah, her dear mother. The pain was still like a dagger twisting beneath her ribs, an aching void somewhere deep inside her. Sometimes she felt as if she wasn't really here, as if her new life with Mr Pencarrow was actually happening to someone else. And yet it gave her something to do, to think about, distracting her from her grief for at least some of her waking hours. It was the nights she hated, when her mother's shadow brushed by her constantly in the darkness. Her room was warm and cosy, with coals glowing in the small grate and, behind the heavy curtains, sturdy shutters protected the window from the onslaught of the blustering wind. A luxurious carpet covered most of the polished floorboards and the bed was so comfortable Elizabeth still couldn't believe it. And yet she dreaded snuggling down between the soft sheets each night, for it was then that she would be engulfed in consuming sorrow.

But for now she had her job to do. She lowered herself onto the edge of the chair opposite Josiah, since he'd impressed upon her that she was not to consider herself subject to the usual rules of a servant. ''Tis definite then? The mine, I mean,' she ventured.

Josiah nodded with such vehemence that a lock of his iron-grey hair, of which he still possessed an abundance, fell over his forehead. 'Sadly, yes. The good lodes were exhausted some time ago, and now the poorer ones aren't yielding much either. Quite simply, it's costing me a great deal to keep the mine open. That damned fool of a mine-captain should have known months ago if he was any bloody good. Should have advised me to close it down then, before it got so deep in debt!'

His florid cheeks had flushed to a frightening vermilion, and Elizabeth experienced a moment of anxiety. 'Is there no possibility of investigating further?' she suggested eagerly, hoping with some desperation she might diffuse his agitation. 'Some mines have sunk extra shafts and found—'

'No. It'd be throwing good money after bad. We've just been looking at all the known veins. That's what all those bloody maps are! We've exhausted all those that run through my land. So, it's a case of salvaging any saleable machinery, sealing off the entrances and selling the poor quality ore already excavated. If anyone will buy it!'

His brow had pleated into a scowl, his lips puckered into a dangerous knot. But then the muscles relaxed and he smiled faintly. 'The mine was something none of my ancestors had — those who built up this farm and the land we own. It was only opened twenty years ago, named after my dear departed wife.' His voice trailed away for just a second or two before he shook his head as if throwing some unwanted thought from his mind. 'It's paid for many of the luxuries you see around you, but I dare say we can manage without it. I still have my own farm, and the rent from the tenant farms — one of which your uncle has, of course,' he added, gazing at her unnervingly from beneath heavy eyebrows.

'And for which you'll soon receive a lower rent because of me,' she whispered guiltily.

'And a bloody good bargain at half the price!' he suddenly boomed raucously, at once bouncing back to his normal self. 'And no one's wanted to rent Moor Top from me for some time, but never mind. You go and make me that foul-tasting brew you suggested, and make sure you put plenty of sugar in it. Oh, what the blazes does he want now?' he roared at the sharp, efficient knock on the door. 'Come in, Armitage!' Josiah bellowed irritably. 'What is it, man, what is it?'

'A letter for you, sir.' Mr Armitage strutted forward in his black suit and white starched shirt, reminding Elizabeth of a penguin she'd once seen in a book. 'Looks like it comes from abroad, sir. France, to be precise. I believe it's from—'

'No!' Josiah's unexpected explosion of rage was so violent that Elizabeth froze. Josiah had, amazingly, sprung to his feet and, furiously ripping the unopened letter into shreds, was hurling the scraps into the fire. 'I know no one in France!' he was shrieking like a madman. 'And how dare you suggest . . . ! Now, get out! Go on! Get out, both of you!'

For a moment, Elizabeth could only stare, the pupils huge and dark in her amber eyes, as she saw spittle flying from her master's lips. And then Mr Armitage hurtled past her, grasping her arm and forcibly dragging her with him. Before she realized what had happened, she was standing in the hallway and Mr Armitage slammed the door shut just as something crashed against the other side of it, and whatever it was smashed onto the floor in pieces.

* * *

June 1866

'Seven shillings and threepence. Put your usual cross, would you?'

'Oh.' The voice of the labourer who stood before the farm manager echoed with heartfelt disappointment. He was by no means a young man, his face crinkled and weather-beaten above his ragged, mud-spattered smock, and his callused, work-worn hands trembled a little as he picked up the handful of coins. ''Tis less again this week. An' what about the young folk wi' littl'uns fer feed?' he added more boldly at the chorus of discontent behind him.

'I'm sorry,' the better-attired fellow seated at the kitchen table replied sympathetically. 'The price of fleeces fell again this year. We've just lost those two cows with milk-fever, and you know we had so many male lambs born this spring.'

"Tiddn my fault,' the old chap grumbled. 'I bet the maister doesn't 'ave fer survive on nort but potatoes.'

'Mr Pencarrow's personal affairs are none of your business. The closure of the mine has put a strain on the estate. Be thankful you still have a job at all, unlike the miners at Wheal Rosalind.'

'Gwain abroad if they's any sense. Earn more there'n under this tight-fisted divil!'

'If they're lucky! And *you* have a free roof over your head, George.'

'A leaky one! An' I wanted some o' whatever it be that '*er* gives my missis.' George jerked his head towards Elizabeth. 'Now I cas'n afford it.'

Elizabeth had been waiting by the dresser where she stored her various concoctions as she'd done every Friday since she'd come to the Hall six months previously. When the men who worked Josiah's land came to collect their weekly wages, they often came seeking help for their extensive families. She'd witnessed the argument with concern. No one was more aware than she of the poor conditions the local people lived in, or the financial vagaries of farming for all who made their living from it.

'Well, I'm sure I can give you some for free,' she said, tentatively glancing at the farm manager who shrugged dismissively. 'That is, if 'tis helping your wife.'

'Oh, yes! The night sweats be much better, and they hot flushes . . .' George stopped abruptly and his own sun-browned face flushed as crimson as his wife's did several times a day, as he realized that in his enthusiasm, he'd spoken of her personal problems in front of the other men. He lowered his voice then, and whispered confidentially, 'Well, 'er do feel 'er can cope now.'

Elizabeth gave an understanding smile. 'I'm so pleased. It must be so uncomfortable, but it comes to most of we ladies in time.'

The man broke into a grin, not so much at the integrity of this young cheel, as at the way she referred to his Kate as a lady. He would have to mind to tell her, and could just see her round cheeks wobbling with laughter.

''Tis mortal kind of thee,' he nodded gratefully.

Elizabeth smiled again as she measured out the powders into some brown paper and carefully folded it so that nothing would escape. It was only sage leaf and chasteberry after all, which had cost her nothing to prepare. 'Oh, and Henry, I believe you said there were some vegetables going to waste in the garden. I'm sure Mr Pencarrow wouldn't mind if we were to give them to the men here for their children.'

Old Henry, supping his mid-morning tea in the corner, fairly jumped to attention. 'Yes, Miss Lizzie. I'll gwain fetch them right away.'

There were murmured thanks all round, and as each of the remaining workers stepped forward to receive his meagre pay, he nodded amicably at Elizabeth as she dispensed remedies for their families free of charge. They were lucky in that, at least. Everyone was happy. Apart from Mrs Elliot, who looked on in silent disapproval.

* * *

Elizabeth bit her lip to contain her exasperation. The summer had passed and the autumn too. She'd been at the Hall approaching a year, and she had no intention of allowing Josiah's health to slip back after all her hard-won battles. 'Mr Armitage, please be so kind as to take this back to the kitchen and ask Mrs Elliot to replace it with something cooked as I instructed. Mr Pencarrow's health has improved considerably since I've been here, and I'm not prepared to allow it to deteriorate again.'

It was absolutely true. Josiah's gout was now more of a grumbling nuisance than the crippling disability that had afflicted him when Elizabeth had arrived, although certain of his joints were permanently deformed. He'd shed a stone in weight, and the strength of his heartbeat and his general condition had so improved that Dr Greenwood had been able to reduce his intake of prescribed medicines. Instead of having difficulty moving about the house, during the summer Josiah had been able to take a little exercise in the garden. He'd even taken several excursions in the pony and trap down to the village, where he'd visited his wife's grave in the churchyard — something he'd been incapable of for some years. But with autumn deepening into winter, the master had been retreating into immobility again, and Elizabeth was determined not to be defeated.

'Indeed, Miss Lizzie.'

Mr Armitage's face, like his voice, was totally devoid of any expression as he placed the laden serving dishes back on the tray and glided out of the room. Josiah's eyes were bulging furiously as he watched his dinner being spirited away, and his mouth gaped open once more in disbelief that the lovely, fairylike creature could have the courage to affront just about everyone under his roof.

'What do you think you're doing?' he snarled. 'I haven't eaten all day, and I'm starving.'

'No, you're not,' she retorted bravely. 'You had lunch, and then you ate two apples and a wedge of cheese this afternoon, and 'tis only six o'clock. 'Twon't hurt you to wait ten minutes.'

Josiah's cheeks were puffed out like two melons, and Elizabeth felt her stomach grip tightly as she expected to have to bear the brunt of his wrath. But before either of them had a chance to utter another word, Mrs Elliot burst into the dining room as if the devil himself were at her heels. Josiah glared at her in astonishment, drawing his head back on his shoulders with intimidating presence, and Mrs Elliot visibly shrank away.

'I . . . I be sorry fer come in like this, sir,' she stuttered, but the hostility that gleamed in her eyes as she glanced at Elizabeth clearly gave her courage. 'But I won't be told how fer cook by that slip of a cheel who thinks 'er knaws everything!'

The hairs bristled indignantly down the back of Elizabeth's neck, and she felt the heat rise to her face. 'Please, Mrs Elliot, I'm here to take care of Mr Pencarrow's health. I expressly forbade salt in his food, but I can taste that you've been adding more and more recently. The sauce you served the meat in is thick with cream, and you've served lentils when I must have told you a thousand times that pulse vegetables will aggravate the master's condition.'

'That be perfectly good food,' Mrs Elliot insisted, crossing her arms reproachfully over her bosom and glowering vindictively at Elizabeth. 'I've just about 'ad enough of 'er! Either . . . either she goes, or I goes!' she flounced triumphantly.

Elizabeth drew in a sharp breath. Dear Lord, she hadn't expected that! She was only doing her job, and had been doing it well. She hadn't wanted to upset anyone. A horrible, ugly feeling cramped the pit of her stomach. What if . . . what if she were dismissed? She suddenly felt sick and her head began to spin. What if she had to go back to living with Uncle Matthew? The idea filled her with horror.

Josiah sat back from the table and, pressing together the palms of his stout hands, tapped his joined forefingers against his thrust-out chin. The silence was almost palpable as his hooded eyes considered the situation. Then he turned to Elizabeth and fixed his arresting gaze on her. 'Can you cook, Lizzie?' he demanded levelly.

Elizabeth gazed at him in confusion. 'I-I cooked for my family for years,' she stammered. 'Simple food on an open fire. Not the sort of quality ingredients Mrs Elliot has, but with 'twas mostly tasty.'

'Hmm.' Josiah breathed out heavily through his nostrils. 'Now then, Mrs Elliot, what would you do in my position, eh? Here I have a beautiful, intelligent young girl who can no doubt produce a presentable meal as well as care for my health. She reads the newspapers and books to me, can discuss what's going on out there, and knows all about farming.' He drew his hands apart then, turning the palms upwards as if in submission. 'You, on the other hand, Mrs Elliot, cook me meals which, delicious as they are, are shortening my life. And, please forgive me, but you have a face like a cow's backside. Now, you're mighty welcome to stay on in my employment, but whether or not you like it, Lizzie stays.'

Elizabeth was convinced her heart was bouncing about inside her like an India-rubber ball. Her mouth had dropped open and she stared, first at Josiah, and then at Mrs Elliot. Her slight frame almost shrivelled with shame, even though it was hardly her fault what Josiah had said. Mrs Elliot, however, evidently considered it was, and looked daggers at her.

'I'll be taking Emma wi' us, so thee'll have fer find an 'ousemaid an' all,' she spat viciously. 'I bet *'er* cuddn't do the 'ousework besides!'

'I bet her . . . I mean, *she* could!' Josiah came back quite unperturbed. 'If you really want to leave, Mrs Elliot, I'll not stop you. I need to make some economies, and Armitage can do more for his wages, too. I'll give you a good character, Mrs Elliot, you and Emma. I'm sure you'll find good positions elsewhere.'

'Well!' Mrs Elliot truly looked as if she were about to explode, her raging eyes ready to pop out of her head. 'We'll be leaving first thing in the morning! And if 'er wants thee fer eat summat different, 'er can prepare it 'ersel!' And with that, she swept majestically out of the room and let the door bang noisily behind her.

Every muscle in Elizabeth's body was stilled with shock. Only her eyes moved in her blenched face, gazing from the closed door and back to Josiah who, to her surprise, was looking very pleased with himself.

'Well, that were a good day's work,' he declared with satisfaction.

'But . . . but she's been your cook for years, sir! Oh . . . oh, this is all my fault!'

It was all Elizabeth could do to stop herself from bursting into tears, but Josiah was having none of it. 'Well, you've often said you haven't enough to do,' he answered sharply.

'Oh, I'm not afraid of hard work, sir, but . . . 'Twould seem a little hard on Mrs Elliot and Emma. And if I've to cook *and* clean this big house, and do all the washing and ironing, and fetch the shopping and all the other things they usually do, on top of my own duties . . .'

'You will manage,' Josiah finished confidently. 'I'm not a proud man. I don't expect the place to be kept like a palace. It's not as if I ever have any visitors. You'll have to cut corners, I realize that. But . . .' his face twisted as he said awkwardly, 'I need you, Lizzie. Your mother were a remarkable woman, but *you* . . . And I promised her I'd take care of you till the day I die. I've been a lot of things in my time, Lizzie, but I'll never break that promise. Now, this great belly of mine's complaining again, so go and do whatever it is you want with my dinner, and hurry up about it!'

Elizabeth stood up shakily and made her way on uncertain legs to the door. She paused with her fingers tightly grasping the handle, bracing herself to invade Mrs Elliot's territory of the kitchen. Good God, what *had* Josiah let her in for?

ELEVEN

Fontaine-lès-Croisilles, North-East France, October 1870

Richard Pencarrow stared down the barrel of the Prussian rifle, fists clenched at his sides. It was almost six weeks since the disastrous battle at Sedan when the French forces had been decimated by the Prussian army in a horrific bloodbath, and most of the surviving French had been taken prisoner. Sedan was hardly on the doorstep of Fontaine-lès-Croisilles, but it was near enough for the now occupying Prussians to be patrolling the area in high numbers. They were searching ruthlessly for French soldiers, including any of those who either had evaded capture at Sedan, or, having been taken prisoner, had managed to escape. This was already the third time since the battle that a Prussian soldier had forced his way into the farmhouse demanding money and food when the occupants had little enough to survive on themselves, and Richard seethed with anger. The soldier threatening his in-laws with the gun, terrifying the elderly couple and his own small daughter, made his blood boil. He must have made some small gesture of defiance, as he felt Xavier place a restraining hand on his arm.

'*Richard, ça ne vaut pas la peine,*' the old fellow hissed in his ear.

Richard's eyes narrowed as he glowered at the Prussian. He was taller than the soldier and without a doubt would be far stronger. The fool was wielding the rifle so close, he could easily grasp it from him in one swift movement and knock him to the floor. But Xavier was right. It wasn't worth it. The soldier wasn't alone. There would be others crawling over the village. Richard couldn't fight them all. He would be overpowered, taken to the village centre trussed up like a chicken, and shot for all to see. It had already happened once, two weeks ago. A middle-aged couple, born and bred in the village and suspected of having assisted a French army captain, had been dragged from their house and publicly executed as an example. By chance, Richard had witnessed it and been sickened at the barbarism of it. What the hell did the Prussians expect? That the French civilians would sit back and let their country be overrun by an invading force? Not that the majority of them had supported their government's goading of Prussia, even if they'd been aware of it before events overtook the whole country. Several patriotic young men from the village had left to join the defending army, their fate still unknown. But Richard wasn't French. Though France was his adopted home, part of his heart still yearned for the dramatic heights of Dartmoor. But there were reasons why he couldn't return, not least his French family and the grave of his beloved wife. So he'd sat tight, wanting only to work the land for his in-laws and protect them and his child.

But at such a moment as this, his heart hammered with rage, and it took every ounce of his resolve to stop himself from lashing out in retaliation. The thought flashed through his mind that his quick temper had landed him in trouble before, with Maurice Brett and with his father. It wasn't that he was afraid. Fear wasn't something Richard Pencarrow experienced very often. But he wasn't anxious to die, and he wouldn't be of much use to Xavier and Marie and his daughter if he was six feet under. There were times when discretion was the better part of valour, and this was one of them.

So he stood, scowling at the soldier at the other end of the rifle, while Xavier surrendered to the Prussian his meagre savings, and Marie shuffled around the kitchen, gathering into a tea towel all she could find in the way of portable food. The soldier held the gun somewhat precariously while he used one hand to slurp down the bowl of broth that was to be the main meal of the day, and Richard cursed himself, as it would have been the ideal moment to overpower him. But self-will prevailed, and a few minutes later the intruder had left, carrying his spoils and leering tauntingly at Richard who all but lost control and flew at him.

The door slammed shut behind him, and for several seconds, no one moved. Then Richard sank down onto one of the crude, rustic chairs, his head in his hands. Dear Christ, he felt such a coward. What had he done to defend his family? Precisely nothing.

'Il le faut, mon fils. Il le faut.'

Slowly he lifted his head and gazed up at his mother-in-law's worn and wrinkled face. It was necessary. It didn't translate very well. In French, it somehow held a world of meaning. And here was the old lady, whose lovely daughter would still have been alive if he hadn't married her and got her with child, offering *him* comfort, when it should have been the other way round.

It made him feel ashamed. But then his little girl was crying with fear, and he drew her up onto his knee and rocked her in his strong arms. Here was treasure indeed. And though it galled him unbearably, he knew he had done the right thing.

But next time . . . ?

* * *

There! A bunch of carrots, a couple of onions and a handful of early sprouts: not a bad first picking, Elizabeth considered, from her initial attempts at autumn vegetables. Since dear old Henry had been taken by pneumonia last spring, she'd tried to keep the vegetable garden in production. The summer crop had already been established when he'd died, and all she needed to do was thin out the seedlings and keep them watered when the Devonshire rainfall was insufficient, which wasn't often. She'd been more than fond of the wizened old man who'd also cultivated the herbs she used. She'd learned so much from him, and smiled now at his memory. He would have been proud, she was sure, of what she'd achieved. Henry had been an integral part of her life at Rosebank Hall all these years. Though unbelievably hard work with never a moment to spare, it was a life she loved. Her services as midwife were called upon when the occasion arose, and William Greenwood would have set her up in Tavistock had she desired. But while Josiah lived, she felt her place was by his side, and she was content.

'You'm there, Lizzie? Thank the Lord! I brung Tom fer see thee. He be mortal poorly, you!'

Elizabeth straightened up, the battered wicker basket containing the vegetables hanging from the crook of her elbow. Samuel Grainger, the elder brother in a mining family from Horndon, and known to be Thomas Arkwright's partner in mischief, was standing by the gate in the high wall, looking suitably anxious.

'What's supposed to be the matter with him this time, Sam?' she demanded, for it wouldn't be the first time Thomas Arkwright had sought her assistance for some trumped-up ailment. It was just an excuse to see her — and inevitably to tease her about her spinster status and offer to rectify the matter. He knew she'd never accept. Despite what he'd seen in the dairy years before, she kept herself prim and proper, and his secret irked him deeply. Why did she refuse *him* when she'd given her uncle what he'd wanted? As far as Sam was concerned, this mocking was just a game from which they derived some pleasure, but for Thomas it held some darker hidden meaning. For her part, Elizabeth supposed she deserved it from the time when she'd deliberately terrified Thomas about the condition of his face. He could genuinely need her help now, of course, but she sincerely doubted it. 'Why didn't you go to Dr Greenwood?' she frowned sceptically. 'You work down Wheal Friendship and belong to the miners' club. 'Twouldn't cost you anything.'

'Oh.' Sam's face fell for an instant before brightening with satisfaction. 'He bain't there. Bain called out. An' Tom's had this mighty pain all shift.'

'So you traipsed all the way up here instead?'

'He wouldn't've, only he be desprit,' Sam came back readily, his expression begging her to believe him.

Elizabeth sighed as she briskly pushed past him. 'In the kitchen, is he?'

'Yes. You'm a good 'un, Lizzie.'

'I wouldn't be too certain of that if I were you, Sam Grainger.'

She hurried indoors, Sam trotting along behind her. As she entered the kitchen, she was sure she saw Thomas clasp his stomach and double up for her benefit. She threw him a wary glance and, setting down the basket, pumped some water into the sink to wash the earth from her hands. It was one of the small luxuries she'd grown used to at the Hall, a pump actually inside the kitchen, so that she didn't have to go outside in all weathers and lug in a heavy bucket every time she needed some water.

'So, what's the matter then, Tom?' she asked accusingly as she dried her hands.

'Oh, 'tis my belly, right down low,' the youth rasped, bringing his knees up to his chest to emphasize the point.

'You'd better lie on the table then, but keep those dirty boots off the end, if you don't mind. Now, let's see, shall we?'

Thomas groaned convincingly as he climbed onto the table. He was a talented actor, was Thomas, but not so his accomplice. The ribald snigger from Sam's direction hadn't gone unnoticed. Elizabeth had a good mind to send them packing, but perhaps she could teach them a lesson once and for all. Quite efficiently and with ultimate calm, she began unbuttoning his trousers as far as they would go, and then proceeded to unfasten his drawers. Despite his earlier bravado, Thomas squirmed uncomfortably, and Elizabeth had to conceal the smirk on her lips.

'Low down, you said?' She watched, one eyebrow raised, as he gulped hard and nodded, unable for once to find a witty response. Elizabeth moved her hands deftly over his abdomen and then pressed harder where she knew his appendix would be. 'Did that hurt?'

'Er, no,' he managed to reply.

'And that?'

Thomas's expression altered to one of complete surprise. 'Oh, yes. 'Tiddn bad, mind.'

'Constipation,' she announced wearily. 'Been breaking wind a lot, I shouldn't wonder. Could lead to piles, and they can be painful as well as embarrassing.' She paused to enjoy the glow of satisfaction as he flushed to the roots of his hair. 'And what about you, Sam? Are you suffering from the same condition?'

'Ah, yes,' he declared after only a second's hesitation, and eagerly unbuckling his own belt, almost pushed Thomas off the table in his desire to scramble on it himself.

Elizabeth waited until he'd pulled his trousers down to his knees before she shook her head. 'No need for that. Unless you want me to give you an enema, of course. I can give you some medicine. 'Tis very effective. 'Twill be sixpence each, please. But since 'tis so nice to see you both again, make it threepence.'

Somehow she succeeded in keeping a straight face as they paid up without question, each with the smile wiped off his lips and looking quite worried. Neither had noticed the wicked glint in Elizabeth's beautiful eyes. There were plenty of other remedies she could have given them which would have done the trick gently, but she'd given them something an awful lot stronger. It would cure Thomas's constipation with violent diarrhoea, but was also likely to make him as sick as a dog into the bargain!

* * *

Richard straightened up sharply at the distinctive report of a gunshot, followed a few moments later by a second. A few months back, he'd have thought nothing of it. With Prussian troops still swarming over the area and ambushes by rebel French partisans not uncommon, the sound of distant gunfire had become familiar. But the situation in Paris was reaching a climax and most of the invading forces had been summoned to assist in the siege of the capital, leaving the countryside to breathe again. Richard had been planting out endless rows of seedlings in the flat extensive fields, leaving his in-laws, too frail to work now, in the farmhouse with the young girl from the village who helped Marie with the domestic chores.

Richard frowned. The shots had sounded close, but he went on working uneasily for a few minutes, trying to convince himself it was nothing unusual. His thoughts instinctively went to his own daughter who was playing with a little friend in the village, and he found himself walking across the field. Then his stride lengthened as he broke into a run, flinging aside the trowel as he went. The gunfire had come — oh, sweet Jesus — he realized it now, from the farmhouse. A crucifying fear gripped his heart, setting it pounding in his chest, as he raced across the field.

* * *

'Lizzie!'

Elizabeth had been to visit Susan Penrose who, little more than a child herself, was due her first baby in a few weeks. She lived with her young husband's family in a cramped hovel on the far side of the clam. On her way back, Elizabeth had decided to visit Hannah's grave. It was one of those warm late spring days that eased her grief, and she'd been contemplating some of the many happy memories still so vivid in her head. It was more than five years since her mother had gone, but on bad days, the pain could be just as sharp.

But today she felt relatively content as she looked up at the sturdy girl who'd appeared before her.

'Why, Nellie!' Elizabeth sprang to her feet and the two cousins embraced tightly, Nellie almost crushing her with her natural bovine strength. 'Oh, Nellie, 'tis so good to see you! We haven't met for ages! You don't come to church anymore.'

Nellie shrugged as they drew apart. 'Don't see much point. They'm only asking fer money fer repair the church, and Father don't care much. I'm only come fer put these on Mother's grave.'

Elizabeth smiled fondly and waited while Nellie placed the few wild flowers on the grass in front of the simple headstone next to Hannah's, and then the two girls linked arms and went to sit side by side on the wooden bench. It was quiet and peaceful in the churchyard, the lime trees that enclosed it coming into leaf and shutting out the trials and tribulations of the world beyond.

'How are you?' Elizabeth wanted to know, her eyes shining above her grinning mouth. 'And how are the boys?'

'Oh, they'm proper clever,' the younger girl nodded. 'Nat's taller and stronger than Father now. And Danny's got hissel took on at Wheal Friendship.'

'What?' Elizabeth gasped, and her heart dropped like a stone. The thought of Daniel, by far the gentlest of the three brothers, working down a mine horrified her. 'Oh, no! Not Daniel! Oh, I'm really sorry to hear that. I've seen so many miners die young from lung disease, or be hurt in accidents.'

'Did it fer get away from Father, I reckons. Still rants and raves like a madman, he do.' Nellie grimaced.

'When he's drunk, or when he's sober?'

Their eyes met, but as each recognized the bitter resignation on the other's face, they both fell about laughing. Nellie's round, pink cheeks were wet with tears of mirth when she finally leaned back on the bench.

'Oh, dear,' Elizabeth gasped, fighting to catch her breath, 'we shouldn't be laughing like this, not in a churchyard.'

'Oh, I be certain they'll not mind.' Nellie nodded cheerfully towards the graves. ''Twill chuff them up a bit.'

'Perhaps,' Elizabeth agreed, and then fixed Nellie with serious eyes. She suddenly felt hot, the collar of her day dress uncomfortable about her neck. 'Nellie . . .' she hesitated awkwardly, 'you don't get any . . . trouble from your father, do you? I mean . . . at night . . . when he's drunk?'

Nellie turned to her, her frank, honest face frowning in confusion. 'Well, yer do have fer mind his fists. He lashes out a bit. Not actually trying fer hit anyone, but yer cud get hurted if yer got in the way. He do have a brave aud temper on him, usually about you, Lizzie, but he always falls asleep afore a minute be gone by!'

Relief gladdening Elizabeth's spirits. The sickening thought had been eating away at the back of her mind for some time now. But as dear, slow, dependable Nellie quite obviously didn't have a clue what she was talking about, and wouldn't have had the wherewithal to hide it if she had, Elizabeth felt satisfied. 'And what about you, Nellie? Any young man in your life?'

'Me?' Nellie's large dark eyes opened like saucers. 'Now, who'd want a gurt lummox like me? *You*, now, Lizzie! Every boy on Dartmoor'd be arter you!'

'Well, they wouldn't get very far. I'm just not interested.' Elizabeth spoke so adamantly that she saw Nellie squint at her strangely. 'Besides, I'm really happy at Rosebank Hall,' she put in quickly. 'I work really hard, but I can do as I please. I wouldn't change my life for anything.'

'Even aud Mr Pencarrow? Gruff aud so-and-so, they say, whenever he ventures out. Not that anyone's seen 'en fer some while.'

'No, they won't have.' Elizabeth sighed wistfully and pulled a sad face. 'He's getting worse again. Sometimes, no matter what you do, things can go wrong, Dr Greenwood says. 'Tis all the years of drinking and so on catching up on him. And his age, of course. He's well past seventy. I'd like to get him out, mind. It used to do him good to come down here to Mrs Pencarrow's grave. He was devoted to her, you know. But anyway, the pony and trap had to be sold last year.'

'Hmm.' Nellie's lips pursed and she pulled in her chin so that it folded into her neck. 'I've yerd tell things d'not be good at the Hall.'

'They're not.' Elizabeth drew in a rueful breath. 'When the mine closed, it left Mr Pencarrow with a lot of debts. I shouldn't really be telling you, but there's always problems over bills like the coal merchant's. The farm's falling apart. The manager and all the labourers have gone — apart from old George, and that's only because he's so old, he'd not get work elsewhere. He just keeps on a small flock of sheep. All the cattle have gone. We've just a couple of house cows, so the dairymaid's gone, too. And Mr Armitage, because he wasn't being paid either.'

'So, you'm all alone up there wi' the aud man?' Nellie's eyes were so huge in her shocked face that Elizabeth laughed softly.

'An old man with a bad heart who can hardly move from one room to another. He can't even get in the tub anymore, so I have to wash him every day.'

'Oh, Lizzie!' Nellie cried in disgust.

'Well, I *am* his nurse. And we get on well enough. I'm used to his temper, and we're quite fond of each other really. I always read the papers to him. We've been following all the events in France.'

'Events in France?' Nellie frowned vaguely.

'Why, don't you know? The Prussians invaded. There was a terrible battle last September. Thousands of French soldiers massacred or taken prisoner. Paris is under siege, though it looks as though 'twill fall soon, and the French are fighting amongst themselves over it all. 'Tis dreadful.'

Nellie's jaw dangled open, her expression quite blank. 'Oh, I doesn't knaw nort about what goes on in other places.

111

'Tiddn nort fer do wi' me. Father wuddn't waste money on a newspaper. None on us can read proper, not like you, Lizzie.'

Elizabeth smiled affectionately. Poor Nellie had wanted to learn to read and write properly. If she'd gone to the old school in the turf house, finally replaced a few years ago by a new school built on land in the village donated by the Duke of Bedford, she might have stood a chance. But Uncle Matthew had always refused to pay for his daughter to learn skills he considered to be of no use. Elizabeth was eternally grateful that her mother had insisted *she* had attended, or she wouldn't be working for Mr Pencarrow now.

'Well, I must get back.' She smiled gently at Nellie as she got to her feet. 'It's been lovely to see you. Send my love to the boys. And take care of yourself, won't you?'

'I think as I can,' Nellie assured her as they passed through the gate.

They hugged again, and departed in different directions, Elizabeth lost in thought as she pondered their conversation. It was quite true that she wasn't interested in any of the local boys, but even if she had been, she knew what it ultimately led to. What her uncle had done to her had scared her witless, and she would *never* have anything to do with that sort of thing! She shivered as the feeble spring sun sank rapidly over the Cornish hills in the west, and hurried back to the sanctuary of the Hall, the place she genuinely thought of as home.

TWELVE

September 1871

Elizabeth hummed softly to herself as she prepared supper in the kitchen of Rosebank Hall. The summer had come and gone so quickly. She'd been rushed off her feet, tending the vegetables upon which they relied quite heavily now, and also her herb garden, as well as collecting and storing so many of the fresh leaves and flowers of the various plants she used in her remedies. It was September now, and time to harvest berries such as the deep-purple elder, so good for coughs and colds in the hard winter to come. She'd been out gathering them that afternoon, but now Josiah was complaining vociferously that he'd been kept waiting for his supper. Elizabeth decided she'd soften his vexation with some freshly baked scones, lightly spread with butter and some of the strawberry jam she'd made in July from spoilt fruit grown the other side of Tavistock and sold off cheaply at the market.

She picked up the tray and carried it out into the hall. Josiah was in the parlour, and Elizabeth had lit a fire in the small grate, as the evening was cool and Josiah felt the cold. Last winter, they'd abandoned the vast drawing room because, not to put too fine a point on it, Josiah couldn't afford the fuel needed to heat such a large space. Elizabeth had suggested tactfully that they'd be much cosier in the smaller room, and Josiah had readily agreed. Most of the house remained shut off, and only the rooms they actually used were kept clean and warm. In many ways this was a good thing, since Elizabeth could really only cope with a certain amount of housework given all her other daily tasks.

Just as she was crossing the hall, a thunderous assault sounded at the front door, so sudden that Elizabeth literally jumped and nearly dropped the supper tray. The house was normally so quiet that it echoed with silence. All visitors came to the back door, even Dr Greenwood, who was now such a friend it seemed ridiculous to stand on ceremony. After only a few seconds, whoever it was started knocking violently again, and a dart of dread sparked down Elizabeth's spine. Someone needed her help, desperately by the sound of things. An accident down one of the mines? A sick child? She quickly placed the tray on the dresser, and flew to the door. The banging had ceased, and her small fingers struggled with the heavy bolts which were rarely moved. As she finally turned the giant key in its lock, the great door groaned open.

A gasp lodged in her throat as she stared up at the man before her. He was tall and the greatcoat he wore made his shoulders appear even broader, his silhouette filling the doorway. One arm was raised and leaned heavily against the massive timber frame, the fellow's head resting on the bent elbow so that his face was half turned away, and all she could see was a mass of dark tangled hair. The rest of his body seemed somehow to be dragging towards the floor as if it was having difficulty staying attached to his head and shoulders, and the stranger appeared for all the world to be a common tramp.

Elizabeth stood stock-still with astonishment. The vagabond didn't seem to have noticed that the door had been opened, and was as motionless as she was. And when he did move, he scarcely paid her any attention, but roughly pushed past her and lurched across the hall to the drawing room.

Elizabeth was so stunned that the man had already flung open the door, glanced around and come out again, before her muscles came back to life. She sprang after him, her heart hammering in her chest.

'Who on earth do you think . . . ?' she began indignantly. But he was too quick for her, despite the way he was staggering, and before she knew it, had checked the dining room as well. His hand was on the study door now, and Elizabeth was quaking with fear, too terrified to try to stop him. Dear God, who was he? And what in heaven's name was happening?

As he came back into the hall, he suddenly pitched forward, his upper body falling across the dresser where Elizabeth had left the supper tray. Everything went flying, the crockery smashing on the floor, tea and scones splattering in all directions. The fellow remained for some moments supporting himself on his forearms, his head drooping down from his shoulders and almost touching his hands. The lid of the silver teapot still clattered as it rolled across the floor, and when it came to rest, the only sound was the man's heavy, laboured breathing. When he finally spoke, it was on a snatched gasp.

'Where is he?' he mumbled without lifting his head, so quietly that Elizabeth hardly caught what he said. She heard him swallow, almost choking, and then he repeated, more deliberately, but with his head still bowed, 'Where is he?'

But those few seconds had given Elizabeth's brain the chance to snap into action. This . . . this savage ruffian who'd forced his way into the house, wanted to see her master with the intention of . . . well, from the looks of the scoundrel, of murdering him. Elizabeth was petrified, her stomach tying itself in knots. But she wouldn't let anyone harm Josiah, and her outrage at the blackguard's threatening behaviour suddenly filled her with courage. He straightened up and took a swaying step towards the parlour. But with her heart trying to escape her ribcage, Elizabeth blocked his path and valiantly braced her slender shoulders.

'You can't go—'

'Just get out of my way, girl.'

Somehow it registered at the back of her mind that his diction was clear and sharp, his words betraying the merest trace of a Devonshire accent. But she hardly had time to ponder on it as he swiftly grasped her upper arms and thrust her to one side. But as he did so, he lost his balance and, dragging her with him, nearly sprawled on the floor. It was only Elizabeth's back slamming into the wall behind that saved them. The shock of it winded her as she gazed into his wild, flashing eyes, and then he turned and disappeared into the parlour.

It only took an instant for her senses to recover and then she hurtled after him, dreading what she'd find. But the scene in the parlour was very different from what she'd expected. With the aid of his two walking sticks, Josiah had heaved himself to his feet from his chair at the opposite side of the room, something he normally required her assistance with nowadays. But instead of attacking him, the stranger was standing lopsidedly just inside the door. His weight appeared to be on one slightly bent knee, the other leg trailing out to the side. His shoulders were slumped forward, and one arm was reaching down towards the dragging leg, his whole body in an attitude of exhaustion and, incredibly enough, submission.

Elizabeth easily slid past him and went to defend Josiah, but then she halted somewhere between them. The two men both stood rigid, eyes locked across the room, but Josiah's glacial expression made Elizabeth shiver. She turned to the intruder, and saw his face clearly for the first time. His long, matted hair tumbled about his excruciatingly furrowed brow, and above his stubbled jawline, his eyes were strained with pleading. Elizabeth could hardly believe he was the same barbarian who'd bludgeoned his way about the house only moments earlier.

'Father?'

The word was scarcely a croaked whisper, frightened and despairing. Elizabeth held her breath as she stared from one man to the other. And then the stranger's eyes flickered and rolled upwards. With a stifled groan, his legs buckled beneath him and he dissolved into a heap on the floor and remained there without moving.

Elizabeth was transfixed, and several moments passed before she was able to move. She glanced towards Josiah. The coldness still glinted in his eyes, chilling her to the bone.

'Is . . . this your son?' she breathed.

Josiah's gaze didn't move from the prostrate figure before him. 'I have no son,' he grated between clenched teeth, the veins standing out thickly in his neck.

Elizabeth's head was spinning. Everything her mother had told her about Josiah's relationship with his son came flooding back. She remembered the letter from France, destroyed unopened, and the macabre interest Josiah had taken in the Franco-Prussian war. Elizabeth scoured her memory for the one time she'd seen Josiah's son up close, at Aunt Margaret's funeral. They'd both been so much younger then, but she remembered those dark, troubled eyes. And she knew that the villain collapsed at her feet was none other than Richard Pencarrow.

She automatically went towards him, but Josiah's harsh tone brought her up short. 'Leave the drunken sod alone and get me my supper,' he barked.

But Elizabeth narrowed her eyes keenly. So often she'd seen her uncle fall down in a drunken stupor, sinking at once into a leaden sleep, his breathing deep and heavy. But the breath was trembling erratically in and out of Richard Pencarrow's lungs, his body quivering in jerky spasms, and there'd been no reek of alcohol on his breath when they'd fought in the hall. He smelled unpleasant, yes, but from the state of him, she imagined he'd been sleeping rough, so it was no wonder.

'I don't think he's drunk, sir,' she told Josiah crisply. 'I think he's ill.'

Ignoring Josiah's growl of protest, she knelt down beside his son. He was lying face down, and she turned his head so that she could lay her hand on his forehead. Her fingers recoiled at the dry, searing heat, and when she felt the pulse at his neck, it was weak and racing. His skin was ashen, his long dark eyelashes fanned out on deeply shadowed sockets.

''Tis a fever,' she said, glancing up at Josiah and wondering quite how to pacify him. 'Why don't you sit down,' she suggested tentatively, 'and I'll make a fresh pot of tea? I'm afraid I dropped the last one,' she lied, not knowing why she was defending the stranger who'd frightened the life out of her.

Josiah grunted disapprovingly and Elizabeth went to help him settle back in his chair. She was still arranging the cushions at his back, when a movement by the door caught her eye. She fleetingly met Josiah's gaze before they both turned to look in the same direction. A small girl, no more than six years old, was sidling across the threshold, pressing herself into the wall as if trying to become invisible. Her eyes were enormous in her pinched little face as she cowered in the corner. But the instant she saw the man lying unconscious where he'd collapsed on the floor, she gave a muffled cry and threw herself onto her knees beside him, her small hands shaking him vigorously by the shoulders.

'Papa! Papa!'

Her voice squealed with despair and she began to whimper brokenly. Elizabeth clamped her hand over her mouth. Everything had happened so quickly, in a matter of minutes, and now here was this pitiable little girl weeping inconsolably. Elizabeth bit her lip. She mustn't frighten the child further, and approaching her slowly, she held out her hand.

''Tis all right,' she said softly.

But the child turned distraught eyes on her. *Il a reçu une balle dans la jambe!*' she wailed, tears staining her dirty cheeks.

Elizabeth frowned at her. The poor demented creature was gibbering! Or was she? It all became clear in a flash. The child must be speaking French! But Elizabeth didn't have a clue what she was saying.

'I don't understand,' she answered compassionately.

'*Une balle! Dans la jambe!*' the girl repeated, and when Elizabeth still shook her head, the child's eyes rolled frantically. But then her face lit up with inspiration. She stretched her left arm in front of her, and bringing her right hand in front of her nose, curled three fingers into her palm before snapping in her straightened forefinger to join them and then releasing it.

Elizabeth drew in a sharp breath as she realized the girl was pretending she was holding some kind of gun, and had pulled an imaginary trigger. Good God! Had Richard Pencarrow been *shot*? Was that possible? But . . . he hadn't just staggered into the house, had he? He had *limped*. And he was running a high temperature. Could it be the result of an infected gunshot wound? The thoughts whipped through Elizabeth's brain in a second. Who had shot him? Where had he been? And . . . dear Christ . . . *why*? Was he . . . some sort of dangerous criminal? A wanted man?

Alarm had scarcely shot through her when a feeble moan uttered from the man's grey lips and his eyes half opened. His face contorted with agony and his hand went down to his thigh. Of course. It all made sense now as Elizabeth watched him take several desperate breaths.

She dropped on her knees beside him, shaking like a leaf, but driven on by her instinct to help. 'Your . . . your daughter,' she faltered, for presumably that was who the child was, 'says you were shot in the leg?'

He barely nodded, his eyes screwed shut, then struggled to prop himself on his elbows. Seizing her chance, the child wrapped her arms around his neck, and in a gesture that was so natural, he managed to free one hand and pat her shoulder.

'So, you've come running back after all these years when you need something, have you, you blackguard? I suppose you're in some sort of trouble.'

In all the confusion, Elizabeth had almost forgotten Josiah was still sitting in his chair awaiting supper. Her eyes swept towards him, appalled at the vicious animosity in his

voice. Whatever had occurred between them in the past —
and who was she to judge which of them was to blame? — his
son was seriously ill just now and could do without a verbal
assault.

But Richard opened his eyes fully and looked directly at
his father. 'Not of any sort *you* might imagine,' he croaked.
'And don't think I'd have come back if I hadn't been forced
to. For Chantal's sake.'

'Oh, I'm to assume this urchin is your daughter, am I?
A bastard, no doubt!'

'What!' Beneath his shock of unkempt hair, Elizabeth
saw Richard Pencarrow's forehead corrugate with anguish.
'No! You know she isn't! I wrote to you. Letter after letter!
Not that you ever replied.'

'And why should I after what you did?' Josiah spat.

'What *I* did! *You* were the one who was behaving so
badly!' But as he exhaled sharply, Richard swung his head
from side to side. 'For God's sake, this is hardly the time.
Surely we can put that behind us? *Please*, Father!' he begged,
and wetting his lips, he swallowed hard. 'I wrote to you twice
just after I lost my wife and I thought you might have replied
then. She never recovered after Chantal was born. It took
her six months to die. You . . . you knew what it was to
lose your wife in childbirth,' he muttered. 'I thought you'd
understand.'

Witnessing the fierce exchange between father and son,
Elizabeth felt sickened by the vehemence of the argument
which had been carried on as if neither she nor the little girl
existed. She suddenly felt she hardly knew the man she'd lived
beside for the past six years, and with whom she *thought* she'd
developed a close relationship. Josiah had a mercurial temper,
but he'd mellowed in his dotage. And now everything that
had formed the foundation of Elizabeth's life since her mother's death seemed to have been swept away from under her
feet. And as if to plunge the dagger in further, a savage roar
from Josiah turned her head. Driven by his rage, it would
seem, he'd hauled himself upright once again, and taking

three steps towards them, raised one of his heavy walking sticks above his head.

Elizabeth couldn't believe the ruthless cruelty in his eyes. He wouldn't mean to do it. It was just the heat of the moment — the shock of his son's return. But if Elizabeth didn't do something quickly, he could strike not only his son, but the child or herself as well. She leapt up to stay his arm, but his face suddenly turned to marble, his eyes bulging out of their sockets. The hysterical breath he drew into his lungs was more like a howl, and instead of bringing the stick down on his son, the weight of it dragged his raised arm backwards over his head. His body seemed out of control, and with an almighty crash, he toppled backwards and landed on the edge of the chair, his torso slumped on the seat and his legs draped across the carpet.

Elizabeth didn't waste a second as her hand flew to Josiah's neck. It was slow and very faint, but there was a pulse. His breathing was sluggish, his closed eyes, but he was still alive.

'I think 'tis a stroke,' she said quickly over her shoulder.

The horror on Richard Pencarrow's face was torturing. 'Christ, what have I done?' she heard him murmur wretchedly, as she dragged Josiah's weighty upper body forward by the arms and propped him in an upright position.

'He could choke,' she told his son with a calmness she didn't feel. 'If he vomits, tip him forward and, well, do whatever you can to keep his airways clear. And tell your daughter to go upstairs and find some blankets. I'll go and send for the doctor as quickly as I can.'

'Well, for God's sake, hurry, girl!' he snarled.

'I hardly need to be told *that*!' she retorted tartly.

THIRTEEN

'Well, Master Richard, let's have you undressed and I can have a look at what you've been doing to yourself,' the doctor instructed.

Richard Pencarrow shot a dark look in Elizabeth's direction. 'Does *she* have to be here?' he said curtly.

Elizabeth drew in an irritated breath. The man was ill and in pain, but did he have to be so rude? In a few short hours, he'd turned her world upside down. She'd run like the wind down to the village, breathless, and stumbling on the uneven track. She'd gone straight to the rectory where the reverend had immediately saddled his horse and set off at a gallop towards Tavistock to find William Greenwood. On her way back through the village, Elizabeth had bumped into Mr Peters and asked for his help, and he and his farmhand had come back to the Hall with her. In her absence, Richard Pencarrow had dragged himself across to where his father still sprawled, unconscious, in the chair. The child had curled up and fallen into an exhausted sleep in front of the fire. As luck would have it, William had been at home and had arrived on his speedy new mare only an hour later, by which time the two men from the village had succeeded in carrying Josiah's gigantic form to his bed. It was a severe stroke, and there was nothing much William could do but wait and see how the old man came out of it. Meanwhile, he'd helped the son to hobble upstairs to his old room where Elizabeth had already lit a fire and made up the bed with freshly aired sheets.

William fixed his patient with reproachful eyes. 'You should consider yourself extremely lucky to have young Lizzie here to care for you. Miss Nightingale herself couldn't produce a finer nurse from that special school of hers.'

Richard didn't reply, but glared harshly at Elizabeth as he undressed down to his undervest. But when he stood up to remove his trousers, he swayed precariously, and William caught him as he passed out yet again.

'Right,' William said urgently. 'Let's get him into bed and stripped off whilst he's out cold. Spare his blushes, anyway. A little daunting for the best of us to have to undress in front of a pretty young girl.'

Elizabeth arched an eyebrow. She doubted Richard Pencarrow had any blushes to be spared! But she supposed by the time they had him laid out stark naked on the bed, it was perhaps as well he was unconscious, and she quickly tucked the blankets around his shivering body. His thigh was swathed in a thick, stained bandage that William now began to unravel with her help, but the entire upper limb was swollen and inflamed, and she knew from William's expression that he was deeply concerned.

He looked up as his patient moaned and his eyelids flickered open. 'Ah, good. With us again, I see. Now perhaps you can tell me when this happened?'

'Oh . . . er . . .' Richard muttered, frowning hard as if he really was having difficulty thinking straight. 'Six . . . maybe seven days.'

'And you've travelled all the way from France in this state? I'm putting two and two together, but I assume that's what happened?'

Richard's eyes moved warily from William to Elizabeth, but then he nodded briefly. 'I had to get home. Make sure Chantal was safe.'

'Well, you were a damned fool, even if you did have your reasons.'

'Oh, it wasn't like this when we left.' Richard rubbed a shaking hand over his forehead and swallowed hard. 'It was only when we got off the ship yesterday, I realized how bad it was getting. But I just *had* to get here. You've no . . .'

His words ended in a sharp wince, his lips curled in a tormented grimace, as William gently removed the last of the crude dressing from the wound. A jagged laceration deep in the flesh either side of a clear bullet hole oozed putrid matter. Elizabeth had never seen anything quite as horrific. The man must be in agony.

'Good God! Was it a doctor or a butcher who did this?' William exclaimed bitterly.

'Well, it wasn't a doctor.' Richard's voice was a strange mixture of irony and fatigue. 'I couldn't take the risk. There might have been questions asked.'

'Questions you don't expect from me, I assume?'

'What?' Richard's attention seemed to have wandered again, and he blinked his eyes wide to bring himself back. 'No, I don't. It's none of your damned business how I— Oh, Christ!' He threw his head back with a cry as William lightly probed the wound, and despite herself, Elizabeth bit down hard on her lip.

'Sorry, but I need to have a good look,' William apologized, puffing out his cheeks thoughtfully. 'I assume if it wasn't a doctor, there were no proper antiseptics?'

Richard replied with a wry grunt. 'Not unless you count brandy. But I had no choice. I needed the bullet out so I could get back here.'

Elizabeth couldn't help but shudder. There wouldn't have been any anaesthetic either.

'Well, whoever it was made a right old mess,' William said. 'And now *I've* got to decide what to do about it.'

Richard turned his head away, his eyes downcast. 'You're going to have to amputate, aren't you?' he barely muttered.

Elizabeth stifled a gasp of horror. However she felt about the way Richard Pencarrow had barged into what was, after all, his own home and destroyed his father's life, she was appalled at the idea of him losing his leg.

But William's reply at least brought some hope. 'Not if I can help it. Not yet, anyway. You were lucky. Another half inch, and the bone would have shattered, and you certainly wouldn't have been doing any travelling then! And being on the outer thigh, it missed the femoral artery, otherwise you'd have bled to death in minutes.'

'I do know that,' Richard snapped irritably. 'And I also know I could still die from gangrene or blood-poisoning. Or lockjaw, even. All I want just now,' and he dropped his head back with an exhausted sigh, his breath ragged again, 'is to have five minutes' respite from the pain.'

Elizabeth reared away from the sympathy she couldn't help but feel for him. Richard Pencarrow was arrogant and obnoxious. She only had to think of Josiah lying half paralysed and inarticulate in the room across the passage, to know his son wasn't deserving of her sympathies. She'd care for Richard as a member of the family she served, but she didn't have to like him after what he'd done.

'I just want a quick listen to your heart and lungs,' William was telling him, 'and then I'm going to put you to sleep. I'll clean out the wound, but I won't suture it yet. Tetanus likes deep puncture wounds, so by conjecture, it *dis*likes air. So I'm going to pack it loosely with an antiseptic dressing to allow the air to circulate, and hopefully it'll heal from the inside. But,' and he frowned grimly, 'it will need changing every day. It'll be tough going, I'm afraid.'

'If I don't die in the meantime.'

William drew in his chin, but said nothing as he gazed levelly at his patient. There was no point lying, and he cleared his throat as he turned down the blankets and peered at Richard's bared torso. Elizabeth knew he'd be looking for the telltale rash of blood-poisoning and joined in the search. For a split second the unpleasant odour that came from Richard's body reminded her of the offensive reek of her uncle when he'd molested her and she gritted her teeth. Richard's eyes were riveted on her, scornful and accusing. Did he think she was admiring his strong physique? The thought made her shudder, and she shrank away in disgust.

'So far, so good,' William muttered almost to himself. 'Now, before we start, could you find a nightshirt for our patient, Lizzie?'

'Of course.'

She hurried away to Josiah's room, her head reeling, and glad of something practical to do. The old man looked peacefully, but one side of his face was distorted and somehow seemed to be lower than the other. She stood at the foot of his bed, the clean nightshirt folded over her arm, gagging on the lump in her throat. Formidable, unpredictable Josiah had been her close friend as well as her master. And now . . . ?

She sighed deeply and stepped back across the passage. The nightshirt, made for Josiah's colossal figure, hung in voluminous folds from Richard's broad shoulders. But he seemed happier to have regained his modesty, and to Elizabeth's surprise, even mumbled a word of thanks.

'Right. I want you lying down with your head tipped back,' William instructed him. 'Then I'm just going to put this mask over your face and drip some chloroform onto it. Once you're asleep, Lizzie will take over while I see to your leg. Don't worry. She's done it a hundred times before. All right? Now just try to relax and don't fight it.'

Elizabeth stood to the side as she always did when assisting William, and took their patient's hand in hers. Above the mask, Richard's dark eyes rested nervously on her face. She saw the panic set in at that precise second when his brain made its last stand against the chloroform, and his body writhed in desperation. But she smiled reassuringly, her fingers tightening about his, and her other hand stroking his forearm. The moment of fear was over and his eyes slowly closed.

Assisting William was a nerve-racking experience. Although the bullet had already been removed, its entry had brought with it fragments of material that were still lodged deep in the flesh and William needed to extract them with painstaking precision. Despite his apparent composure, small beads of sweat bedewed his brow. He waited until Richard had woken from the chloroform and then gave him an injection of morphine, before setting off home in the dark, and leaving Elizabeth in charge of the two sick men and the small child. And now, at last, Elizabeth could enjoy a few moments of rest.

'*Papa! Papa! Où est mon père?*'

The child's high voice was hysterical as she raised herself from her exhausted sleep on the rug by the fire. Only minutes earlier, Elizabeth had sat down with a cup of her own soothing herbal tea, and her eyes were drooping. Now she snapped wide awake, and slipping onto her knees in front of the little girl, took her small, filthy hands in her own.

''Tis all right, my sweet.' She smiled encouragingly, staring hard into the girl's face. 'Your papa is asleep.'

It was easy to mime, and the girl's face, half hidden by a wild shock of springing curls, melted with relief. '*Alors, il ne va pas mourir, Papa?*'

Elizabeth shook her head. Oh, dear! The poor child was instantly looking so distressed again, it was heartbreaking. 'Papa . . . is good,' she said hopefully.

'Good? *Ah, oui! Je comprends.* Good!' She made a thumbs-up sign and Elizabeth nodded vigorously, copying the gesture.

'Yes, good!'

'Good!' Somehow, perhaps as a reaction to all that she'd been through, the little girl laughed, and Elizabeth found herself laughing back. It was a warm feeling, helping the child who . . . well, God knew quite what had happened! Her father obviously wasn't going to reveal how he'd been hurt. It was quite possible he was dangerous or a criminal, but his daughter quite clearly adored him. Elizabeth had to push to the back of her mind the thought that his life would be hanging by a thread for the next few weeks and that he could well die. But she couldn't have explained it to this little girl even if she'd wanted to and just now, she must offer as much support to her as she possibly could. All of a sudden it was incredibly important to her that Richard Pencarrow survived.

'Now then, what's your name?' she asked cheerfully, since she couldn't for the life of her remember what Richard had called her. But the child only cocked her head to the side and frowned. Elizabeth thought for a moment, then prodded herself in the chest with her forefinger. 'I'm . . . Elizabeth,' she pronounced slowly.

The child's face lit up with comprehension. 'Eleezabett,' she repeated, enchanting her new friend with her pronunciation.

'That's right! Or just . . . Lizzie.'

'Leezee. *Et moi, je m'appelle Chantal.*'

'Chantal.' Of course. She remembered now. ''Tis very pretty. Like you.' She smiled again at the child's quizzical expression. 'Oh, never mind. You must be hungry. And thirsty.'

It was easy to act out the meaning of her words, and Chantal grinned, revealing her small white teeth. She evidently felt safe now, and Elizabeth's heart glowed with gratification. 'Come along to the kitchen. We can have some supper. I suddenly feel quite peckish myself.'

She held out her hand. Chantal took it eagerly. She trotted along beside her, turning her ebony head this way and that, her lovely dark eyes taking in every detail of the house. Elizabeth pointed her in the direction of the sink, for her face and hands looked as if they hadn't seen water for a week. She had the impression Richard Pencarrow and his daughter hadn't slept in a bed since they'd set out on their journey either, and a bath would do the child a world of good. But weariness clawed at every muscle in Elizabeth's body, the events of the past few hours having tested her spirits to the limit. It was already nearly midnight and a bath could wait until morning. Elizabeth felt empty, ready to drop, and yet she was so on edge, she doubted she would sleep. Just as well. She had the feeling it was going to be a long night.

'Here we are then,' she declared brightly for Chantal's sake. 'Bread. Ham. Cheese.' She pointed as she put each item on the table. 'And scones to finish.'

''Am?' Chantal tilted her head. '*J'aime bien ça*, 'am!' she giggled.

Elizabeth smiled delightedly. The girl appeared intelligent and remarkably resilient. Perhaps she'd have been less enthusiastic if she'd known just how ill her father really was. Chantal waited politely to be served, then tucked in voraciously. Elizabeth ate more pensively. Although her stomach felt hungry, the apprehension that churned within it was nauseating her. When the child had taken her fill with a profuse '*Merci, madame*', she happily peeled off her dirty clothes and put on the blouse of Elizabeth's that, with the sleeves rolled up, would have to serve as a nightgown. Then Elizabeth opened the firebox of the range and they relaxed in front of the glowing coals, sipping warm, honey-sweetened milk into which she had stirred valerian root and lemon balm.

It was when they reached the top of the stairs together that Chantal tugged at her sleeve. '*Papa*,' she said insistently. '*Je voudrais revoir Papa.*'

'All right,' Elizabeth whispered, guessing her meaning. 'But you must be quiet,' she added, putting a finger to her lips. 'We mustn't wake him.'

They crept up to the open door of the room. Richard Pencarrow was lying exactly as they'd left him, his face the colour of wet clay in the lamplight. But Chantal was satisfied that her father was safe and followed Elizabeth contentedly into the room she'd prepared for her. But the minute she realized she was to sleep alone in a strange house in a country miles away from her home, the fortitude in her little breast dissipated into thin air, and she clung in panic to Elizabeth's arm.

'*Ne me laissez pas seule, madame!*' she wailed hysterically, her round eyes brimming over with tears.

Elizabeth's heart melted as she guessed Chantal's meaning, and picking the child up, she hugged her tightly, taking an unfamiliar comfort herself from the closeness of the small body. 'All right. You can sleep with me tonight,' she soothed, carrying her into her own room.

Chantal looked about her, and seeing signs of occupation — a hairbrush and soap on the washstand, a camisole thrown carelessly over a chair — she seemed to relax, and snuggled down in the big bed. Elizabeth left her and went to check on Josiah and then she would come to bed herself.

She entered his room with her heart fluttering in her chest. The old man was propped up amongst a sea of pillows in case his swallowing mechanism had been affected by the stroke and he choked on his own saliva. He stirred as Elizabeth came up to the bedside and his eyes opened to stare at her, one of them protruding grotesquely from a dragging socket. He tried to utter something to her, but only succeeded in producing a garbled grunt.

''Tis all right, sir,' she answered softly. 'Do you need anything? A bottle, perhaps?'

He managed to wring a guttural cluck from his throat, and his head bobbed in an uncontrolled nod. She had to help him, of course, for his left side was totally paralysed. She had to hold the bottle while he filled it, her heart torn by grappling emotions, part revulsion at the stinking stream of concentrated urine, part biting sorrow that her dominant, imposing master should be reduced to such indignity. Emptying the urinal into the chamber pot, she rinsed it out and then washed her hands in fresh water from the jug before moistening Josiah's lips. He was muttering fretfully again, and with heavy heart, she explained to him that she couldn't give him a drink. Tucking the blankets cosily about him, she went to empty the chamber pot in the water-closet at the end of the corridor. When she returned, he was sleeping soundly again.

The silence of the isolated farmhouse hit her like a sledgehammer as she watched over his still figure. His condition might improve over the next weeks and months, but the chances were he'd remain as he was. If, heavens forbid, he took a turn for the worse in the middle of the night, what could she do, all alone and miles from help? She also had to nurse his son who was very likely to knock on death's door in the next few days. And then there was the little French girl who, although quite mettlesome, was clearly deeply traumatized. Damn Richard Pencarrow! How dare he come bursting into their lives, destroying the calm of his father's dotage and causing the old man to end his days as a gibbering idiot! Why in God's name hadn't he stayed in France where he belonged? As Elizabeth finally changed into her nightdress and climbed into bed beside the slumbering child, her lips were compressed into a knot of anger and consternation.

FOURTEEN

Three o'clock in the morning. At least, that was what the grandfather clock in the hallway had just chimed as she made her way along the landing. Josiah always wound it every night before climbing the stairs, but tonight Elizabeth had had to pull on the different chains for the first time, trying to remember exactly what her master did. She'd stood by his side watching him so many times, but doing it herself was another matter. She prayed she hadn't made a mistake and damaged the mechanics of the thing.

Elizabeth had woken five minutes earlier with a violent start. For a moment, she'd wondered who on earth the small girl asleep beside her was and thought she must still be dreaming, but then the shattering events of the previous evening leapt back into her mind. She must check on Josiah and so, throwing a shawl about her shoulders, she lit the small oil lamp on the table and tiptoed along to his room. He was slumped awkwardly to one side, and for one heart-stopping second, she thought he was dead, but he'd simply slipped sideways in his sleep. He smacked his lips in response when she propped him back up again, his tongue lolling out of his now lopsided mouth. But he didn't wake up fully and was soon breathing heavily again in a semi-comatose slumber. It was as Elizabeth padded back along the passage that she heard the low moaning from Richard's room, and her spirits sank to her bare feet. All she wanted was to crawl back to bed and drift into sleep. But it was her duty to care for Richard Pencarrow no matter what she thought of him. As she entered his room, the muffled utterances became more distinct. She crossed to the foot of the bed and stood watching him, biting on her fingernail as she considered what she should do. He was muttering incoherently, his brow puckered into an anguished frown beneath the shock of tousled hair. His head moved restlessly, his breathing hard and irregular, his hand pulling subconsciously at the neck of the nightshirt. All of a sudden, he threw his head to one side, shouted vehemently the words, 'Go to hell!' and lifted his shoulders from the pillows. His eyes half opened and wandered vacantly as they tried to focus, then blinked in confusion as he peered fearfully into the shadows. He attempted to sit up, but the effort obviously caused him to move his leg, and he fell back with a tortured cry.

'What the hell are you doing, standing there like a bloody little ghost?'

The words were ground out with acid sharpness, but as his eyes closed again and his head rolled sideways, his voice petered out in a thin trail. Elizabeth stood motionless, tongue-tied with indignation. What right did he think he had to talk to her like that, especially after what he'd done to Josiah? And yet she couldn't help but feel some sympathy. The man was suffering physical agony, his pain and exhaustion etched deep into what she could see would otherwise be a strikingly handsome face. And although she couldn't even begin to guess the reason for the gunshot wound or why he'd felt it necessary to travel hundreds of miles in such a state, it must have been some horrific trauma he'd been through.

'I was just checking on your father and I heard you moaning,' she answered frostily. 'I thought you were delirious with the fever. But I see 'twas just a nightmare.'

His chest lifted and then fell heavily in a profound, ironic sigh. 'If only,' he murmured under his breath, his eyes tightly shut. Elizabeth had turned her back to place the lamp on the table, and only half caught what he said. She shrugged. As he'd pointed out so curtly the previous evening, it was none of her business, and really, why should she care?

'How are you feeling now, sir?' she asked flatly.

As he turned his head to look at her, his eyes seemed to stretch with surprise, then narrowed again as they rested on her face. 'That's a damned stupid question, isn't it?'

Elizabeth's nostrils flared with resentment. 'No, sir, 'tis not,' she bristled with prickly restraint. 'I can't help you if I don't know how you are.'

'What are you then, some sort of wise woman?' he grunted scornfully.

'As it happens, yes, I am!' she retorted.

'But . . . you're too young.'

Elizabeth lifted her head, her chin thrust forward in defiance. 'I'll be twenty-one in November,' she told him tartly. 'I'm the local midwife, and people come to me for traditional remedies from all over. There's a place near London where they study scientifically . . . Well, I'm sure you're not interested in that. But I've been working alongside Dr Greenwood for years, as you might have gathered.'

She was glaring at him with open hostility, her jaw clamped as she fought the raging desire to tell him just what she thought of him. He stared back at her steadily, then lowered his deep brown eyes as he shook his head.

'I'm sorry,' he mumbled. 'I didn't mean . . .' He paused, his eyes closed wearily again. 'I feel so bloody awful, I don't know what I'm saying.'

Elizabeth sucked in her cheeks, and reluctantly placed her hand on his forehead. ''Tis the fever. You're burning. And the leg?'

'It hurts like hell.'

He ran his tongue over his dry lips, his eyebrows knitted in distress, and a mild pang of remorse pricked Elizabeth's heart.

'I expect the morphine's worn off, but I can give you some laudanum. 'Twill help you get through the rest of the night.'

She carefully measured the standard quarter drachm into some water. But when she handed him the glass, she could see he was struggling to find the strength to take it from her, let alone lift his head sufficiently to drink it. Unwillingly, she slipped her arm behind his neck to raise him slightly, and held the tumbler to his lips.

'You must *sip* it, sir,' she told him. 'If you drink too quickly after the morphine, 'tis like to make you sick.'

He gave the merest hint of a nod and swallowed the liquid a little at a time. Elizabeth almost wished she'd left him to his own devices as she hardly relished being so close to him. When he'd finally taken the medicine, she lowered his head back onto the pillow. He groaned and shifted restlessly in the bed, wincing as he moved his leg and gagging on what sounded like a stifled sob at the back of his throat. Elizabeth rinsed the flannel on the washstand in some cool water, and began to swab his feverish forehead.

'Chantal!' His eyes flew open, his shoulders stiffening in alarm.

'Asleep in my bed,' Elizabeth reassured him. 'She didn't want to sleep alone. I hope you don't mind her being in with me.'

'No,' he sighed with relief. 'That's very good of you. Thank you.'

Elizabeth raised an eyebrow. It was almost the first civil word he'd spoken. 'She's had a good wash and some supper.'

Once again, he thanked her, but then took her by surprise by taking her arm in a strong grip. 'I'm not stupid. I'm well aware there's a good chance I won't get through this. If anything . . . Will you promise me you'll take care of her? I mean . . . her grandfather can't now, and that's the only reason I came.'

'He could have done if you hadn't given him a stroke,' she answered testily.

'I hardly meant to. How . . . how is he?'

'Paralysed down one side, can't speak and Dr Greenwood thinks he might have lost the sight in one eye.' Her voice was cold. Icy. For she couldn't expel from her mind the image of Josiah lying so helplessly in his bed across the hallway.

'Oh, God,' Richard muttered, and she saw his prominent Adam's apple rise and fall as he swallowed. He released her arm and his hand flopped back onto the bed. 'You obviously consider I've spoilt your cosy life here,' he said bitterly, 'and I'm sorry. But *I* don't exactly see the situation as a tea party, myself.'

'I don't suppose your father does either,' she replied, knowing she was being ungracious, but unable to help herself. 'Now if you don't need anything else, I'd like to get back to my own bed, if you don't mind.'

'Well, I know I can't, but what I'd really like is a long soak in a nice hot bath,' he confessed with feeling. 'I stink like a pig.'

'No, sir.' She couldn't stop the razor-sharp edge to her tongue. 'Pigs are actually quite clean animals.'

'What?' He stared at her, his face expressionless as the meaning of her words sank in. 'I could have you dismissed for that!' he growled, but there was a curl to his lip, and a spark of — what was it? Mischief? — in his eyes that caught her off guard. Dear Lord, was he teasing her?

'No, I don't think so,' she rounded on him, wanting to hit back. 'You wouldn't find anyone else prepared to look after your father like I do. Especially now. So I'm afraid you're stuck with me whether you like it or not. But if you can keep a civil tongue in your head, I might give you a bed-bath tomorrow.'

And with that, she swept out of the room without giving him the chance to reply. Weary and infuriated, she climbed back into bed, but her sleep was fitful and restless. Richard Pencarrow's unwanted arrival in her life had upset her so profoundly she felt as if her whole world had been turned topsy-turvy. She just wished to God he'd stayed in France!

* * *

Richard had watched her go, his eyes wide with surprise at her riposte. He snatched in his breath, wanting to call her back, to apologize. But quite frankly, he didn't have the energy, and so he let his head sink back into the pillow. Good God, what was the matter with him? It wasn't like him to behave like this, but the pain in his leg was swamping his mind, obliterating all else but the agony he was so desperate to escape. It had gone on for so long, he was at the end of his tether and he couldn't control the words that came out of his mouth. But he must! He was in a damned precarious situation, and he mustn't let slip what had really happened! The girl — whoever she was — was somehow too comforting, despite her sharp tongue. It would be so easy to give in, to break down and tell her everything. But she was a complete stranger and so young, although she seemed to be blessed with a wisdom beyond her years. And she clearly didn't think much of him, so how could he possibly trust her with such a dreadful secret? He could hardly believe himself what had happened! No. He mustn't give in to the burning desire to unburden himself. And if that meant keeping the girl at arm's length, then that was what he would have to do. Oh, Jesus, he could feel the laudanum starting to work, numbing his brain. He should be thankful that he could feel himself beginning to float above the pain and he'd soon fall back to sleep. But if only he could find some moments between the pain and the powerful drug when he could think straight and decide what the hell he should do.

FIFTEEN

'*Alors*, egg!' Chantal pronounced solemnly, contemplating the clutch she'd gathered from the hen coop. 'One egg, *mais* two eggz. One, two, zree, four, five. Good, *oui? Je veux dire*, yes?'

'Yes, very good!' Elizabeth chuckled as she stirred the onions in the large pot on the range. The child had slept like a top until mid-morning, long after William Greenwood had called to check on his two patients. Under his supervision, Josiah had been able to sip from the spout of a feeding cup, and the doctor had been happy for Elizabeth to administer her calming herbal teas. What the old man needed now was complete rest to allow his body to recover as best it could, but the stroke had been severe and William doubted there would ever be much improvement. He remained continent, though, which was a blessing. As for his son, the doctor had insisted on a further injection of morphine while he changed the dressings, and Richard was sleeping off its effects once again. The deep wound was still suppurating profusely, the leg horribly swollen, but so far, he seemed to be holding his own against the infection. But it was early days, his temperature worryingly high, and there were no guarantees he would survive.

Elizabeth smiled at his little daughter now as she counted the eggs out loud once more. 'Chantal, could you pass me the chopped *garlic*, please?'

Chantal's little face puckered as she gazed at the vegetables she'd helped prepare earlier. Refreshed and quite at ease now, it had given her something to do, and she was a willing helper.

'Yes, that one!' Elizabeth encouraged her as she pointed to the garlic ready crushed in a small saucer.

'*Ah, oui! L'ail.*'

'Lie! Oh, goodness, what a funny language! Fancy garlic being called a lie!' She laughed aloud as she scraped the pungent relish into the pot, and Chantal grinned back.

'Gar . . . ? *Vous pouvez l'écrire, madame, s'il vous plaît?*' she gestured, and drawing the pot from the heat so that it wouldn't spoil, Elizabeth went to fetch pencil and paper. Chantal could evidently read and write well for her age, so Richard Pencarrow must have done *something* right for his daughter.

'Madame, no,' Elizabeth said, wagging her finger emphatically. 'Lizzie.'

'Oh, yes, Eleezabett! *Mmm, ça sent bon!*' She wrinkled her nose over the pot as Elizabeth stirred in a cupful of herbs. '*Comment on dit ça?*'

Elizabeth wiggled her own nose and sniffed hard. 'Smell.'

'Zmell? *Écrivez, s'il vous plaît. Et dessinez un nez,*' she added, tapping her nose.

Oh, dear, Elizabeth would never get the casserole cooked at this rate! But surely the child's well-being must be the most important issue at the moment. So she stopped to write the words 'nose' and 'smell', and drew what looked more like an upturned parsnip with two eyes for nostrils. Chantal hooted with glee and then settled down to some drawing of her own, a smiling sun, some flowers, all in a row, like soldiers.

'That's very good,' Elizabeth commented over her shoulder as she went to fetch some carrots. '*Bon!*'

'*C'est l'Angleterre, pas la France,*' Chantal said grimly, her thin shoulders suddenly stiffening. '*En France, on a peur. Les*

Prussiens sont partis, mais ils ont laissé la guerre partout. Je sais bien, moi. Mais ici, on est sauf. On ne tuera pas Papa ici.'

Elizabeth's heart gave a heavy thud. She hadn't understood a word Chantal had said, but from the girl's grave expression, it was something to do with the war. But now she was drawing happy pictures, and Elizabeth prayed the future would bring the child some hope.

* * *

'You do feel up to it, sir?'

Richard shook his head lifelessly on the pillow. 'No. But I can't go on smelling worse than a *pig*, can I?'

He shot her a dark glance, but that spark flashed in his eyes again. Elizabeth smarted as she realized it was his way of reprimanding her. Mocking her almost, and making her feel small. But when all was said and done, she was only a servant, so though it rankled, it was probably best to ignore his comment and get on with the task she was there for.

'Well, let's have that nightshirt off, shall we?'

It was quite a struggle. He hardly had the strength to sit up, and fell back onto the pillows like a rag doll. Elizabeth folded the covers down about his hips and then hesitated a moment as she wondered if he was capable of doing anything for himself. She rinsed out the flannel for him to wipe his face, and then exchanged it for the towel. But when she gave him the soaped flannel to wash his torso, she could see he was genuinely fighting to find the energy to do so, and found herself taking the flannel from his hand and doing it for him. He turned his head away with a groan of dismay.

'I'm sorry,' he muttered under his breath. But when Elizabeth caught his eye, he answered her with an embarrassed smile. Elizabeth was taken aback. His sombre face really did look so different when he smiled, his strong, even teeth a white slash in the thickening stubble on his chin. He had the same wide, pleasing jawline as Josiah, but it was his eyes that were different, large and expressive and a rich mahogany, rather than Josiah's hooded, penetrating blue orbs. His mother's presumably, and he'd passed them on to Chantal.

Elizabeth couldn't help but smile back, reluctantly, and wishing her lips hadn't responded of their own accord. 'Let's get this done before you start shivering again,' she said, annoyed that she, too, was feeling somewhat awkward.

She worked as swiftly as she could, glad of something to concentrate on. His handsome smile had totally unsettled her. She was aware of his eyes following her every movement, and she fought to appear efficient and unruffled when inside she was quaking. She'd washed Josiah's white, blubbery body often enough, but his son's was so different — hard, with not an inch of flesh to spare, and finely muscled, although at the moment without the physical power of even a kitten. It stirred something within her she couldn't define, and wasn't sure she liked.

'Where's Chantal?'

'I left her playing with some pastry in the kitchen. She's a lovely child. You must be so proud of her.'

'I wouldn't have made it here without her.' His face was strained again, the shadows beneath his eyes tainted with a tinge of blue. 'I just hope I'll be around to share her new life with her.'

Elizabeth paused as she finished drying his chest. 'We'll get you well, sir. Now, let's have you in this clean nightshirt, and we're nearly done.'

It was a tussle to dress him again. The exertion had drained him, and he collapsed back in the bed, his eyes closing immediately.

'I just can't believe how weak I feel,' he muttered as if to himself.

''Tis hardly surprising, travelling all that way when you should've been in bed. You pushed yourself too far, and now you're paying for it, so 'tis your own fault.'

He gave an ironic snort. 'Unfortunately I didn't have much choice.'

'Well, 'tis no business of mine. Now then, how's the leg feeling?'

'Throbbing like hell,' he murmured feebly.

Elizabeth pulled on her lip. ''Tis a little soon for any more laudanum. Can you wait another hour?'

He looked at her sideways. 'I'll have to, won't I?'

'I'm afraid so, sir. But is there anything else I can get you?'

'Toothbrush and powder? My mouth feels like a sewer.'

'I think I can manage that. And a mouthwash with mint and fennel. 'Twill make you feel nice and fresh again.'

'That sounds good. Thank you, er . . . I'm sorry,' he said, his face stretching in an effort to keep himself awake. 'My brain's so muddled, I've forgotten your name.'

'Elizabeth, sir. But everyone calls me Lizzie.'

'Elizabeth. I'll try to remember.' But he was already drifting asleep again, and she crept out of the room, wishing fervently he hadn't aroused her sympathies.

* * *

She eyed the newspaper on the hall dresser with hostility. There was so much she should be doing, but she knew Josiah would love her to read to him about events beyond the four walls that now incarcerated him. At least, she imagined he would. Three days now, and he'd managed nothing beyond a senseless cackle, although he was obviously trying to speak. Words trapped inside his head. It must be so dreadful for him, she could scarcely begin to imagine. She'd tried giving him paper and pencil, as his right side was unaffected, but his brain had lost the power to convert the shape of the letters to his hand, and his writing was a mere scrawl. Poor Josiah. And all his son's fault.

When Elizabeth reached the top of the stairs, she heard Chantal's laughter and assumed it was coming from Richard's room. So she was startled to find the child by her grandfather's bed, chatting away to him with animated hand gestures as if she'd known him all her life. Josiah's eyes were riveted on her and his distorted mouth appeared to be smiling, although Elizabeth couldn't be sure. He no more understood a word of what Chantal was saying than Elizabeth did, but it was quite clear he was entranced by his granddaughter's engaging personality. His stubby, gout-deformed hand reached out and stroked her cheek, and she stretched up on tiptoe to kiss his whiskery jaw.

'*Je vais revoir Papa maintenant*,' she announced, and skipped happily away.

Josiah watched her go, his pale eyes misting forlornly. Elizabeth caught her lip. It was so unlike him to display any sentiment. He looked so old, frail, despite his size. She felt tears rise in her throat, and had to swallow them down.

'She's such a sweet little thing, isn't she, sir?' she said softly. 'And she's so quick to learn. She's picking up English that easily! And she's such a help. Now then, let me read the paper to you. The main stories, anyway.'

She pulled the chair up to his bedside and opened the *Tavistock Gazette*. It was evening and the light was fading. She'd managed so little sleep these last few days that her eyes were pricking and the print was dancing up and down on the page. She knew she was reading badly, stumbling over the sentences, her brain not making any sense of them. She was so busy concentrating that at first she didn't notice Josiah touch her hand. It wasn't until he began clumsily to caress her skin that she looked up at his twisted face. She felt her throat tighten again, and she had to grit her teeth against it.

'You've been so good to me, sir,' she croaked, and then stood up abruptly. She had to get out. She wanted to stay and comfort the old man who'd become almost like a father to her, but she was suffocating. 'I'll be back again soon.'

She hurriedly stepped outside. The cooler air in the corridor was calming, and she leaned back against the wall, her eyes shut as she breathed in deeply. Come on, girl. Take a hold on yourself. You can cope with this. You have to.

The sound of Chantal's insistent voice broke into her preoccupied mind. The child needed her father, but Elizabeth was concerned she was overtiring him, and she dragged her feet into the other bedroom.

'*Est-ce que grand-père Pairncarrov va aller au ciel avec grand-père et grand-mère Mélun?*' the small girl was demanding, the smooth young skin of her forehead wrinkled into a perplexed frown.

Richard couldn't even open his eyes, his face like putty and his lips barely moving as he spoke. '*J'espère que non,*' he mumbled almost inaudibly.

'Chantal, your father needs to rest,' Elizabeth told the child gently, miming out her meaning. 'And 'tis time you were in bed, too.'

'*Oui, au lit, ma petite,*' Richard added wearily.

But Chantal pouted her lips stubbornly and pulled a long, petulant face. '*Ah, non, Papa!*' she whined. '*Je veux rester ici.*'

'*Non!*' Her father forced open his eyes and glowered at her, his voice raised. '*Au lit! Allez, va!*'

Chantal's expression crumpled, her little chin quivering, and she shot out of the room with a fretful wail as Richard released a long, exasperated sigh. Elizabeth scowled as she thrust the thermometer under his tongue and roughly grasped his wrist to take his pulse. His brow was on fire but as dry as a bone, and she was sure the fever was soaring again as the evening wore on. But she couldn't forgive the way he'd spoken to little Chantal.

'You shouldn't shout at her like that,' she reproached him crossly.

'Who the hell do you think you are, telling me how to treat my own daughter?' he instantly barked, taking the thermometer from his mouth.

Elizabeth had to smother a desire to give Richard Pencarrow a piece of her mind. Instead, rather than lower his hand back onto the covers, she released it with a jerk and let it fall with a gentle thud. 'Well, I think you should treat her with more consideration after what she's been through.'

'What she's been through?' he hissed at her. 'You haven't a bloody clue what she's been through! Now . . .' He shook his head as if he couldn't find the means to express his rage. 'Just do what you have to, and then get out!'

Elizabeth felt cut to the quick. After all she'd done for him, a total stranger, over the last few days, and she was only offering her support to *his* daughter! The man was a chip off the old block, all right, except that his temper was even shorter than his father's! She raised her chin defiantly. 'If that's what you want,' she snapped. Snatching the thermometer from him and putting it on the tray without stopping to read it, she flounced out of the room, slamming the door behind her.

She paused in the hallway, waiting for her flush of wrath to subside. Yet her outrage at the injustice of his verbal attack was tempered with a desire to burst into tears. Why was it that she felt so upset? Was it because she felt he'd betrayed the thread of understanding that had seemed to develop between them that morning? But really, why should she care? She'd been about to give him a decoction of meadowsweet, feverfew and other fever-reducing herbs, and to administer a dose of laudanum. His leg was still hugely swollen and inflamed, and must be excruciatingly painful. Well, let him suffer. He deserved it! If he wanted anything, he'd have to shout for it, and she'd make sure he begged her forgiveness for his rudeness before she fetched it!

She sniffed hard, setting her jaw, and then tipped her head to listen. Oh, dear. Chantal was sobbing her little heart out in the room they'd been sharing. Poor child! And now it would be up to Elizabeth to comfort her. Damned Richard Pencarrow. How could he be so cruel to his own flesh and blood, first his father — with disastrous consequences — and now his daughter!

'Oh, don't cry, sweetheart,' she crooned as she wrapped her arms around the girl. 'Your Papa's mortal sick and he's in a lot of pain. He doesn't know what he's saying.'

It flickered across her mind that what she said was probably true and that she, too, shouldn't heed Richard's ill temper. But her hurt pride drove any sympathy aside. Chantal couldn't understand her anyway, and pulled back from her embrace, her lips compressed bravely in her tear-washed face. *'Je vais dormir dans ma propre chambre,'* she announced with feigned aloofness, and took herself off to the bedroom Elizabeth had prepared for her on the day of her arrival.

Elizabeth didn't attempt to stop her, sensing the child's need for solitude. Still seething, she went down to the kitchen and picked up her sewing, grateful for some task to immerse herself in. Chantal and her father had arrived with nothing but the clothes on their backs, but while Richard was confined to bed and could use Josiah's nightshirts, his daughter had no other garments to wear. Elizabeth had taken it upon herself to raid Rosalind Pencarrow's wardrobe and was sewing her some new attire, beginning with a change of underwear. She was sure the dead woman wouldn't have minded. Chantal was her granddaughter, after all. And as Elizabeth plied her needle, her vexation with Richard softened.

Her eyes were smarting with tiredness before she finally gave in and climbed the stairs to bed. She'd looked in on Josiah earlier, but checked him once again. He was snoring, saliva dribbling from his gaping mouth. Richard's door was still shut, of course. She hadn't heard another peep from him for the remainder of the evening, and released a sigh of resignation. She supposed she'd better see if he needed anything, and braced herself against his lashing tongue.

She opened the door quietly. A faint muttering whispered across at her, urgent and distraught. He must be dreaming again, so at least he was asleep. But there was something desperate in his breathing as he tossed his head from side to side. His shoulders were lifting from the pillow, his whole body writhing. He must have moved his leg then, for he cried out, every muscle rigid and his head thrown back in pain.

Dear God! She'd deliberately not given him the remedies to combat the fever, and now his temperature had risen so high, he'd become delirious. She snatched the thermometer and turned it in the lamplight to read it. A hundred and four. And that was hours ago! Oh, sweet Jesus! It was all her fault! If she hadn't been so stubborn, so pig-headed . . . He could die if she couldn't bring down his temperature. If only William

Greenwood were there, but it was the middle of the night and she needed to do something *now*! Even as she danced on the spot, a choking rasp came from Richard's throat. He was tossing wildly, and when she laid her hand across his burning forehead, the skin was almost too hot to touch. And then suddenly, he went limp and lay lifeless as a stone.

Oh, no. Oh, please God, no! Elizabeth's heart raced. Shakily, she searched for the pulse beneath the angle of his jaw. At first, she couldn't find it, and then . . . oh, thank God. It was feeble, and flying along so fast she could hardly count it. But it was there.

The knowledge she'd gained over the years kicked into action. Tepid water from the kitchen, for cold could cause a fatal shock. She whisked the bedcovers from him. His skin was on fire, but without a hint of moisture. She struggled to pull the nightshirt from him, but it was useless. Lean though he was, he was too heavy for her. So she quickly cut the garment straight up the front, running down to the kitchen again to fetch the large sewing scissors. Taking the stairs two at a time, she raced back. She *had* to save him. She'd never forgive herself if he died.

She worked as quickly as she could, the oppressive stillness of the night bearing down on her. Every minute slowed to an hour, and still her efforts appeared to be having no effect. He was thrashing again, his bare flesh still sweltering as she swabbed him liberally with the warm water. Two o'clock. Three o'clock in the morning. Jesus Christ, please let him live. She was so tired, desperate now, tears pricking her eyes. Please, *please*, sir! Come *on*! She shook him by the shoulders, trying to wake him, but his head just lolled backwards. Oh, God. She really couldn't carry on. But then she began to think . . . to notice . . . He'd started to sweat of his own accord. Just lightly at first, on his brow and upper lip. Was the fever breaking at last? Hope renewed her strength. Within half an hour, his hair was plastered to his forehead, the perspiration beginning to trickle around his neck, glisten on his broad chest. And when she felt his forehead, was it

147

her imagination, or did he seem a little cooler? The sweat on his skin would have the same effect as her swabbing him She was so exhausted, so could she stop now? Drawing up a chair, she rested her arm on the bed; she'd shut her eyes for just a few minutes. Elizabeth lowered her head onto her forearm, drained, praying . . .

* * *

Daylight was filtering through the gap in the curtains as her eyelids flickered open. Someone was stroking her hair, or was she imagining it?

'Maddy? Maddy, c'est toi?'

The voice was frail, scarcely audible. Elizabeth raised her head, her shoulders angrily protesting. It was Richard touching her hair and he was gazing at her through confused, wandering eyes.

'Sir?' She held her breath, relief creeping through her aching limbs as his eyes closed again.

'I'm sorry,' he breathed. 'I thought for a minute . . .'

His words faded away on a wave of sadness, but Elizabeth was only aware of her own growing joy. 'Sir? Sir, how do you feel now?'

He didn't open his eyes, but slowly inhaled a shallow breath. 'Strange,' he faltered, his voice slurred with fatigue. 'I can't explain . . .'

'And cooler?' she suggested eagerly.

'Yes. I think so. But . . .' He looked up at her from beneath heavy eyelids. 'Were you asleep just then?'

She lowered her eyes sheepishly. 'I'm sorry, sir, but yes. You've been delirious all night. Do you not remember?'

He frowned bewilderedly and brought his hand weakly over his forehead. 'No. Not a thing. Does that mean you've been up all night?'

'Yes, of course. I was afraid—' She broke off. She could hardly tell him she'd been afraid the fever would kill him before the night was out.

148

'Well, it's nice to know you care,' he murmured.

Was his tone mildly scathing? She wasn't sure, but it was enough to rouse her indignation. 'I don't particularly. But 'twould offend my professional pride if you died in my care.'

'Elizabeth, *please*,' he begged her with a tearing sigh. 'We've not made a very good start, and I know I'm to blame. It's all a haze, but I was at the end of my tether, and . . . Forgive me. *Please?*' She saw him run his tongue around the inside of his mouth. 'And *please* can I have a drink? I'm so parched, I feel like I've got a mouth full of sand.'

Elizabeth was relieved to be able to snap back into her role of efficient nurse. 'Yes, of course. You need to replace all the fluid you sweated out in the night. I'll get you some elderflower cordial from the kitchen.'

She didn't wait for a reply, but hurried down the stairs. She needed to get out of the room, if only for a brief moment. Her emotions were all over the place yet again. She filled the jug and stirred in a couple of pinches of salt. He shouldn't taste it and it would help re-hydrate his body more quickly. When she returned to his bedside, it was somehow with less enmity than before. Once again, she had to help him drink, for he was weaker than ever. She still resented the closeness, his head resting in the crook of her arm, but he gave her no lewd glance as Thomas Arkwright would have done if she'd been leaning over *him*.

'Does your leg feel any better?' she asked, still partially regretting the concern in her voice.

'Not so as I've noticed,' he groaned. 'But I wish to God it did.'

He croaked the words in a tortured whisper, and Elizabeth shied away from the little pull on her innermost sentiments. 'I'll give you some more laudanum. Unless 'tis making you feel queasy. You could have some meadowsweet instead. 'Tis not quite so strong against the pain, though. But Dr Greenwood will probably give you some more morphine when he comes to change the dressing.'

'The meadowsweet sounds good. Thank you. And then you should go and get some sleep. You look all in, being up all night.'

''Tis only my job, sir. And I need to see to your father. I've not been in to him for a few hours.'

'After that, then.'

'Sir,' she told him defiantly. 'I don't think you realize—'

'Do as you're told, Elizabeth. I'll be fine and I'm sure my father will be, too. I'm ordering you. Now, *go*!'

Their eyes clashed, and Elizabeth flicked back a strand of hair that had escaped overnight from the loose ribbon tied at the nape of her neck. Richard Pencarrow must be the most bossy, infuriating man she'd ever met! Even his father could be humoured, poor soul. But if Richard thought he could order her about like that, he would have to think again!

SIXTEEN

'Well, that's looking better,' William Greenwood pronounced with satisfaction some ten days later as he inspected the jagged wound he'd finally stitched together the previous morning. 'We seem to be beating the infection. Your leg's nearly down to its normal size again.'

But Richard fixed the doctor's eyes, his jaw tightly clenched, for the wound was still raw to the slightest touch. 'And what about the tetanus?' he asked grimly.

'Ah, well.' William drew in his chin in the cautious gesture Elizabeth knew so well. 'We can't rule that out for a few weeks yet, I'm afraid. But we did everything possible to prevent it, so let's look on the bright side, shall we? So, Lizzie, do you have anything to assist the healing process now?'

'I do indeed.' She nodded with a little amusement, for William knew full well she did. ''Tis a mixture of lavender oil, hypericum and marigold in a honey base. 'Twill go on fighting off the infection, but 'tis gentle and soothing, too.'

Richard took her by surprise as his mouth lifted in a faint smile. 'There you are, Doctor. You should listen to her more often.'

'Oh, I do, Master Richard, believe me!' William assured him. 'She sent the same thing over to my colleague in

Tavistock a while back. He'd had to amputate a patient's hand. Fellow not much older than yourself. A sea-captain, I believe. He suffered a post-operative infection, and when the worst was over, Lizzie's ointment was invaluable.'

'He lost a hand? Poor man! At least you saved me from losing my leg, and you'll never know how grateful I am for that.'

Dropping his head back on the pillow, Richard caught Elizabeth's eye with a gaze of such intensity that her eyebrows swooped into a frown. What was that look supposed to tell her? That he wasn't as obnoxious as he appeared? That he truly was grateful for what she and Dr Greenwood had done for him, despite his quick temper? Whatever it was meant to say, it unsettled her, and she hurried down to the kitchen to fetch the unguent, thankful to escape Richard's presence, even if only for a minute or two. So, was Richard Pencarrow capable of some humility after all? When she returned to the bedroom and William applied the salve and a fresh dressing to the wound, he bore the discomfort in patient silence.

'There. All done. You can relax now. I don't think I need come again for a few days. Lizzie can change the dressings. It'll help keep your bill down. Not that I expect you can pay it anyway,' William added wryly.

Richard glanced up at him from beneath dark eyebrows. 'And what about my father?' he demanded.

'Ah.' William paused diplomatically. 'I'm sorry to say there's not a great deal I can do for him. It's been two weeks and I'm afraid he hasn't made much progress. We'll just have to leave things to nature. He can't swallow solids yet, but Lizzie's feeding him well on nutritious soups, and she's moving his limbs to keep his circulation going. However, I'm afraid the outlook isn't good.'

'Oh, God.' Richard's torn voice was little more than a whisper. 'This is all my fault. But I had absolutely no idea he was ill,' he groaned in desperation. 'If I'd known, I'd never have . . .'

'Now don't you go blaming yourself,' William reprimanded him. 'It was just waiting to happen. Your father's
always been his own worst enemy with that temper of his.
He brought this on himself by all accounts. Believe you me,
I've been expecting it for some time. What *you* need to do is
concentrate on a full recovery so that you can make the farm
profitable again. You'll be far more use to your father that
way than wallowing in unfounded guilt.'

Richard blinked hard at him and released a long, slow
breath from his puffed cheeks. 'Yes, I suppose you are right.'

'Indeed I am! Now, I'll see myself out, and leave you in
Lizzie's capable hands.'

He left the room with a confident nod of his head, and
Elizabeth began to tidy the bed, smoothing the covers and
collecting the trimmings from the clean dressings.

'Elizabeth, leave that for a minute, would you? Sit down,
and then please tell me what the hell's been going on here. I've
been turning it over in my mind ever since I got back, but all
that morphine and laudanum was clouding my brain. But I
can think straight again now, and I want to know what's been
happening. When I left, the farm was prospering. There were
servants in the house, and now there's only you, and all this
talk about there not being any money. I don't understand.'

Elizabeth hesitated. She'd known he'd want an
explanation at some point, and had been dreading it. He'd
doubtless give vent to his fury at what she had to tell him,
as if it was her fault. Slowly, she sat down in the chair and
clasped her hands nervously in her lap.

She swallowed hard. 'Everyone left,' she began timidly.
'Mainly because they weren't being paid. The farm labourers,
Mr Armitage . . .'

'He was a bloody waste of space anyway.'

The resentment in his voice brought the hint of a smile
to her lips. 'Well, at least we agree on something. Mrs Elliot,
though — she was the cook and housekeeper, but she started
after you left, I believe — anyway, she and her daughter,

153

they left because of me. We couldn't see eye to eye over your father's diet, and he saw it as an economy. Old Henry died, though.'

She dared to glance up, in time to see Richard lower his eyes. 'I'm sorry to hear that. I was very fond of Henry. But *why* wasn't there any money?' he demanded, meeting her gaze again.

Elizabeth took a deep breath, mentally bracing herself. 'As far as I know, soon after you left, your father employed a manager to run the farm. But they never really got on. Eventually, about three year ago, they had a terrible row. There'd been trouble with a wild dog killing the sheep. The manager reckoned as he needed a rifle to shoot it, but your father disagreed. Anyway, the manager went off to Plymouth and managed to buy an American breech-loader, the sort they use to shoot wild buffalo out there. He shot the dog, but of course, he'd landed your father with the bill for the gun. He was so furious, he dismissed him. After that, things went downhill quickly. The manager was never replaced, but your father took little interest in the farm and left the labourers to get on with it. They were good workers but not business-men. Then when what small profit there is in farming fell even further, so did their wages and they all went to work elsewhere. Apart from Mr George, and he's so old now, he can't do much work. Most of the stock was sold, so apart from the rent from the farmsteads, there's been no money coming in for years.'

'But no doubt the old devil went on spending money with his so-called friends!'

'Actually, no. 'Tis said that after you left, he fell out with them all and those . . . those parties stopped.'

Richard's eyebrows arched with bitter irony. 'Just as well. Although I'm surprised. He used to play at cards, only he wasn't very good and ended up owing a great deal of money in gambling debts. To one man in particular. That's how they persuaded him to let them bring their tarts and their mistresses up here, and *then* they'd drink his cellar dry.

Either that, or they'd get legless on the opium they brought with them. I wanted him to pay off his debts, no matter what it cost, and be free of them. But,' he sighed wistfully, 'he was too weak to stand up to them. And he enjoyed their company to a certain degree, although he was probably the most innocent of them all. Oh, he'd get as paralytic on drink as the rest of them. But he never took opium, and he didn't go after the women either, even if he did have an eye for a pretty girl.'

'Oh, but I thought the reason you left was because—' She stopped in mid-sentence, her hand over her mouth as she realized she'd said too much. 'Oh, sir, I'm sorry,' she muttered. ''Tis no business of mine.'

But Richard was adamant. 'No. I want to know what people said.'

Elizabeth stared at him, and had to force the words from her dry mouth. 'The rumour was that you fought over a dairymaid,' she mumbled.

'What?' Richard's expression was incredulous. But then he uttered a derisive grunt and shook his head. 'Oh, that's a good one! We fought *because* of a dairymaid, not *over* one! One of his cronies, the particular one I mentioned just now, had his eye on her, and like a lackey, my father was trying to persuade her. It had been going on for ages. I'd already had . . . an altercation, shall we say, with the wretched fellow over it some time previously, but he kept on about it. And finally, one day, I found my father in the dairy with her, threatening her with dismissal if she didn't do as he said. The poor girl was terrified. I was so ashamed of him, and when I tried to intervene, he threw the butter stamp at me. I've still got the scar.' He paused, raising his hand to a small mark on his forehead just below the hairline. 'It was the last straw. All my life, he'd treated me with contempt, as if I'd deliberately killed my mother when I was born. I was nineteen, and suddenly I just couldn't face living with him a minute longer.' His voice had softened as if he was craving her understanding, but now the rancour in it returned. 'I gather you have a very different view of my father, but that's how *I* see him.'

Elizabeth averted her eyes. Perhaps there was something in what he was saying. 'I'm well aware of your father's shortcomings,' she said stiffly. 'And I know . . . well, that the letters you wrote to him from France, they were always destroyed unopened.' She looked up as Richard uttered a sharp cry. The dejection on his face was unbearable, but her loyalty to Josiah was still strong. 'He wasn't all bad, though, sir,' she insisted. 'He's taken care of me since my mother died, and he always treated both of us with respect. In his own way, of course. And now I can only see him as a sick old man.'

'And you think I don't?' Richard croaked. 'All I ever wanted from him was one word of affection, and now I'll never get it, will I?'

'Oh, come, sir. He could make some recovery yet.'

'Don't try humouring me, Elizabeth. I'm not a fool. And I notice you've only talked about the farm. What about the mine? I suppose that's closed down, too?'

The sharpness of his words made the hairs bristled down the back of Elizabeth's neck. 'Yes, sir. Five year ago. But 'twasn't your father's fault. He tried very hard to keep it going, but the lodes simply ran out.'

She watched as Richard released a ponderous sigh. 'Mines do come to the end of their working lives, I suppose. Look at Wheal Betsy.'

'Oh, Wheal Betsy's open again, sir. Has been for several years. A Scottish company took it over and called it Prince Arthur Consols,' she went on, grateful for the opportunity to turn the conversation away from his relationship with his father. 'They put in some new waterwheels and a new engine house, although the chimneystack was built crooked. But it hasn't fallen down yet and the mine's gone back to being called Wheal Betsy since it changed hands for a second time. 'Tis more profitable than ever. They say they raised five hundred ounces of silver last year, and over a hundred and twenty tons of lead.'

Richard whistled softly. 'And the other mines?'

'Wheal Friendship's still going well, though copper production's falling rapidly, and they're going over to arsenic and pyrite now. 'Tis the same all over. You know Devon Great Consols over at Blanchdown?'

'Of course,' Richard nodded. 'If my father had invested in *that* rather than in his own mine, we'd have been really wealthy.'

'Well, they say that Devon Great Consols produce most of the world's arsenic now. 'Tis that alone that keeps Morwellham Quay alive. Hardly anything goes along Tavistock Canal any more. The railway takes everything. They finished the new track from Tavistock up to Lydford, then 'twas extended up to Launceston. 'Twas just before I came to work here and there's a station at Mary Tavy that serves the mines here now.'

'Yes, I know. And a passenger service. I found that out the day I arrived back. A pity the line doesn't come near Peter Tavy. I could have done with it that day.' His eyebrows lifted ruefully and he contemplated the mound of his leg beneath the bedcovers before suddenly flinging them aside and easing his leg over the edge of the bed.

Elizabeth sprang up. 'Sir, what on earth do you think you're doing?'

'I want to see my father. And then I want to inspect this new-fangled water-closet you keep telling me about at the end of the corridor. Works from rainwater in a tank on the roof, you say?'

'But, sir, Dr Greenwood said you weren't to get out of bed for another week,' she protested, planting herself squarely in front of him.

'No,' he snapped back. 'That could be too late for—' But he broke off as his eyes closed and he staggered as if he was about to faint. Elizabeth stepped forward and caught him by the shoulders just in time.

'You see, sir, 'tis too soon,' she told him. 'You're still too sick.'

'No, I'm all right.' He forced his eyes wide open and took in several steadying breaths before drawing himself up into a standing position. 'And if you won't help me, I'll bloody well manage on my own.'

He went to take a step forward, but as he put his weight on his injured leg, a muted gasp escaped from his lungs and he swayed perilously. Elizabeth's heart skipped a beat and she quickly tucked her shoulder beneath his armpit, for it was the only way she could support his tall frame.

'You don't leave me much choice, do you?' she retorted.

He didn't reply, but leaning heavily on her, took a tentative pace forward. She slipped her arm around his back, her fingers grasping his waist through the light material of his nightshirt, and the length of her body pressed against his. Her stomach had clenched fiercely at their closeness, but when she glanced up, it was as if he was unaware of her presence, his face set with grim determination as he shuffled forward. The few yards to Josiah's room took several minutes. When they reached his bedside, Josiah's head lifted disdainfully, the side of his face which still worked clearly registering his displeasure, and a string of incomprehensible ejaculations spluttered from his uncontrolled lips.

Elizabeth cast a fearful eye in his direction. 'Sir, I don't think this is a very good idea,' she hissed at Richard as he slumped into the chair she'd hastily pulled up behind him.

But Richard growled back at her. 'Let *me* be the judge of that.'

Elizabeth's spine stiffened with contempt. 'Well, don't blame me for any consequences,' she warned under her breath.

'Oh, there won't be any, I promise,' he grated. 'You want to gloat over the mess I've got myself into for as long as possible, don't you, Father?'

Elizabeth recoiled in disgust. The minute Richard Pencarrow showed any signs of humanity, he instantly hurled them aside again. She stalked out of the room, battling to control her anger.

But when she passed the slightly open door some ten minutes later, Richard's broken whisper made her stop to listen.

'Why could you never love me, Father?' she heard him murmur, and realized with disbelief that he was in tears.

SEVENTEEN

'*Il ne faut pas entrer, Eleezabett*,' Chantal cautioned her mysteriously, guarding the door to her father's room. 'You must
not to enter.'

Elizabeth chuckled at the child as she walked along the
landing with an armful of clean bed linen. In the three weeks
she'd been at Rosebank Hall, Chantal's command of English
had expanded rapidly, but Elizabeth found the way she spoke
quite enchanting.

'As you wish, miss.' And with an amused frown, she
opened the heavy door to the linen cupboard.

Chantal disappeared into Richard's room, and moments
later, Elizabeth could hear her muffled giggles. She herself
had been attending to Josiah's toiletry needs, but there'd
been much to-ing and fro-ing along the passageway and up
and down the stairs. Chantal's quick, light footfall, of course,
for although Richard was insisting on hobbling along to the
water-closet, he needed Elizabeth's help to do so. Elizabeth
wondered quite what scheme Chantal was brewing. Having
recovered from whatever traumatic event it was that had led
to her father being shot, the girl had blossomed into quite the
most effervescent little creature Elizabeth had ever known.
She certainly did much to lighten the sombre atmosphere

of the house, as between Richard's sharp temper and his father's senseless gobbling, it was enshrouded in a damning depression.

The child emerged once again and skipped up to Elizabeth's side, her wide grin revealing the gap where one of her front milk-teeth had fallen out two days earlier. '*Papa, il dit* . . . You can enter into ze chamber,' she announced with glee.

Elizabeth smiled brightly at her. 'What *are* you up to?' she teased playfully, and followed her into the bedroom.

She stopped in her tracks, her amber eyes almost translucent with surprise. Richard was sitting in the chair in front of the washstand, studying himself in the small hand-mirror, his head turned sideways as he rubbed his hand along the angle of his clean-shaven jaw. He shot a glance in her direction, then went back to contemplating his reflection.

'*J'avais raison, Papa! Eleezabett ne te reconnaît pas!*'

'In English, Chantal.'

'*Alors, comment on dit reconnaît?*'

'Recognize.'

'*Quoi? C'est trop difficile, ça!*' Chantal shrugged her narrow shoulders. 'Papa is very . . .' She gazed up at the ceiling as she searched for the word. 'Ah, *oui*, pretty . . . *sans la barbe*, you think, Eleezabett?'

Elizabeth laughed softly. 'Handsome,' she corrected the eager child. 'Ladies and little girls are pretty. Men like your father are . . . handsome.'

Her words slowed as she met Richard's gaze across the room and she felt colour flood into her cheeks. Josiah's son was keen-tempered and ungracious, and despite what William had said, Elizabeth couldn't help but blame him for her master's condition. But she had to admit that, beard or no beard, he was the most handsome man she'd ever clapped eyes on. And now, damn him, he knew it!

'I don't usually have a beard,' he mumbled, his voice, much to her surprise, heavy with embarrassment. 'I just hadn't had the chance to shave.'

'I guessed as much,' she heard herself answer, remembering that his jaw had been darkened with no more than a week's growth on the day he'd shattered Josiah's life.

'It's going to be sore, though,' he added somewhat bashfully, as if he was searching for something to say. 'Chantal found that razor in the drawer, but it's as blunt as a butter knife.'

'There's a strop in your father's room. I'd have sharpened it if I'd known.'

'Chantal wanted to surprise you, for some unknown reason.' He smiled affectionately at his daughter and slipped his arm about her shoulders. 'I hope this little game has satisfied you, *chérie*.'

The child looked at him, her nose wrinkled quizzically. '*Eleezabett te plaît, Papa?*'

The smile slid from Richard's face. '*Oui*,' he pronounced guardedly, and Elizabeth wondered why he hadn't replied in English.

'*Alors . . .*' She squinted shyly at Elizabeth, her small, heart-shaped face flushing a deep pink, before she turned her head to whisper in her father's ear.

Richard's shoulders straightening into a rigid line. '*Non! Je te l'ai déjà dit mille fois! J'ai trop aimé ta mère pour ça!*'

His stern reprimand instantly shattered the contented atmosphere in the room, and Chantal, her mouth pouting mutinously, glared angrily at her father. '*C'est que tu ne veux pas que j'aie une mère!*' she squealed back at him, storming out of the room as her face crumpled into tears.

Richard released an exasperated sigh as his eyes rolled towards the ceiling and he muttered something under his breath. Elizabeth's brow furrowed. 'What was that all about?' she demanded accusingly.

'None of your damned business!'

She drew in a seething breath. The man was insufferable. He seemed to possess an unrivalled knack of upsetting everyone in sight, including his own daughter. But Elizabeth was his servant, and he was quite right when he said it was nothing to do with her.

'You should get back into bed now, sir,' she said crisply. 'Dr Greenwood gave strict instructions you were to keep the leg elevated.'

But Richard raised a beseeching eyebrow. 'I was hoping I might be able to have that bath. I wouldn't expect a slip of a thing like you to drag the bath up here, but I reckon I could manage to get downstairs now.'

'No,' she gloated with satisfaction. 'You'll have to wait until Dr Greenwood gives his permission.' Oh, that felt good. Show him he couldn't have everything his own way all the time.

'You're a hard woman, Elizabeth.' He threw her such an enigmatic glance as he got to his feet and struggled back to the bed, that she wasn't at all sure how to interpret it. Was he merely cross with her, or had he guessed her true meaning and was mocking her for being so childish? Either way, she wasn't happy.

'I'll go and fetch the strop,' she announced haughtily.

But when she went into Josiah's room, the old man was dead.

* * *

''Tis good of Dr Greenwood to take you to the church in his trap tomorrow,' Elizabeth said gently, hoping to break the oppressive silence that had blanketed the house for the past few days. They were in the kitchen, Elizabeth clearing away the meal that remained virtually untouched, and Richard sitting with his leg propped up on a second chair.

'I won't be able to help carry the coffin, though.'

'At least you'll be able to walk behind it.'

'Just,' he snorted wryly. 'And no doubt the jungle drums will have been beating, and people will be out to get a glimpse of the prodigal son.'

163

Elizabeth bit her lip. He was probably right. Josiah's tenants had needed to be informed of his death, and doubtless the village grapevine would have spread the news far and wide.

Elizabeth heard Richard clear his throat. 'When you've finished here, you'd better pack your things,' he told her, his expression inscrutable.

She stared at him, senseless with shock, the words taking several moments to sink in. Had she heard right? But she knew she had. She could feel herself trembling and abruptly sat down again.

'Pack my things?' she repeated inanely.

'Well, you can't stay here. Not now.' Richard was looking at her darkly, as if he expected her to obey without question.

'B-but,' she stammered, fighting to find some logic in his words.

'My father is dead and my leg is nearly mended, so your position as nurse effectively no longer exists.'

'But . . . you can't manage without me!' she protested, finally finding her voice. 'I'm not just a nurse. I *run* this house! And what about the vegetable garden we rely on so heavily? And the hens, and the dairy? I know there's only enough for our own consumption, but I still make the butter and cheese.'

'I'm sure Chantal and I can manage perfectly well on our own.'

'But, sir, you can hardly walk . . .'

'I'm getting better every day, and that's part of it. Surely you can see you *can't* stay here any longer.' He leaned forward, his rich mahogany eyes wide and steady as they stared into hers.

Elizabeth felt the whimper die in her throat. 'But Rosebank Hall is my home,' she begged him in a hoarse whisper.

'You have a perfectly good home with your uncle, as I understand it. An uncle who also owes me a great deal of back rent,' he added grimly.

At the mention of Matthew Halse, a black shadow darkened some deep, forgotten recess of Elizabeth's mind. She simply couldn't leave Rosebank Hall. She loved the place, every stone of its walls, every stick of furniture she had polished vigorously over the years.

'But, sir, please . . .'

'Oh, for God's sake, do I have to spell it out?' Richard's voice was harsh now. 'I don't *want* you here.'

Elizabeth's heart dropped like a stone. For several seconds, she sat with her head bowed, hardly able to breathe. If Richard Pencarrow no longer required her services, she knew there'd be no arguing with him. With a supreme effort, she dragged herself to her feet and walked calmly out of the room, all the time fighting the overwhelming desire to break down in tears. For she was damned if she'd let the blackguard see he was destroying her life.

* * *

She fell into step behind him as he followed the coffin out of the church. He was limping painfully and relying heavily on the walking stick, his back nevertheless proud and erect in a good black coat Elizabeth had luckily discovered among a hoard of discarded garments in a trunk in one of the attic rooms, remains of the days before Josiah had gained such colossal weight. Now Richard walked solemnly behind his father's body, the image of a gentleman apart from his hair which was in dire need of a cut. His little daughter, petrified by the staring faces of so many strangers, clung to the beautiful young woman who had devotedly nursed the irascible old man through his final years.

The procession weaved its lugubrious way through the graveyard to where the open trench awaited. A cruel ache raked Elizabeth's throat and she had to bite the inside of her bottom lip to quell the tears that stung her eyes. When Chantal gazed up at her fearfully, she had to force a wan smile to her lips. She'd buried too many people in this churchyard, her aunt, her dearest mother, old Henry and various others she'd known well and to whom her remedies had brought some relief, but mainly miners whose lungs no medicine could save. And now her benefactor who'd given her something to live for when her own life had been torn asunder. Nearly six calm and happy years when her soul had been given the chance to mend, only to be shattered again by the untimely return of his son.

Still holding Chantal's hand, she joined him by the gaping hole in the earth, at his side, but respectfully a foot or so behind. The cold, penetrating drizzle of a damp autumn morning suddenly made her shiver, and she realized she felt chilled to the bone. She noticed the moisture had settled on the fibres of Richard's coat in bright pinpoints, not heavy enough to soak into the material but forming a dewy blanket over his shoulders. She could feel the mist on her own eyelashes. The trees that enclosed the churchyard had already lost their leaves, and when Elizabeth raised her eyes to the open moorland beyond, the high mound that was Dartmoor disappeared into a vaporous shroud. She imagined Josiah's soul soaring high above the clouds, free at last. He'd never been a happy man, not since his wife had died. Elizabeth's gaze alighted on the dead woman's headstone, and she felt peace settle in her heart as Josiah's body was lowered into the ground beside his beloved Rosalind. Died 6 March 1840, she read, the day, or perhaps the day after, Richard Pencarrow was born. That would make him thirty-two on his next birthday, her mind calculated idly. Anything to keep her thoughts from the vicar's droning chant.

She became aware that Richard had turned to her, his eyes glistening, as he offered her a clod of earth. In recognition of what she'd been to Josiah. Not just a servant, but a companion and friend. She nodded, choking on her grief, took the soil in a trembling hand, and let it trickle through her fingers down onto the coffin.

The crowd was quietly dispersing as the rain began to fall, soft as cobwebs, onto the ground. Matthew had been there, of course, desperate to catch sight of the man he'd once scorned as a young upstart, but who was now his landlord. Elizabeth was aware of his presence, and her stomach churned savagely at the prospect of having to tell him she'd been dismissed. For the moment, though, while William was walking Chantal back to his pony and trap, Elizabeth stood alone beside Richard Pencarrow as he bade his ultimate, silent farewell to his father.

'My condolences, Ritchie.'

Neither of them had heard the footfall on the tussocky grass, and Elizabeth turned to discover the owner of the unctuous voice that had broken into her grieving reverie. She searched her memory, but she didn't recognize the fellow, although by the way Richard's face drained of its colour, he was evidently no stranger to *him*. The man was impeccably dressed in a dark, caped Garrick over a black suit, a silk top hat crowning his head. He was almost as tall as Richard, and although somewhat thicker in the girth, he appeared well preserved for his age, which Elizabeth would have judged to be about fifty. He might still have been a handsome man if his attractive looks hadn't been marred by a badly misshapen nose, result of an accident if the thick scar across it was anything to go by. Nevertheless, he cut a distinguished figure, and although she felt piqued that anyone should have interrupted their final moments with Josiah, Elizabeth's curiosity was mildly roused.

'What the hell are *you* doing here?'

Richard's voice was low, like gravel, sending a tense shudder through Elizabeth's body. She gazed up at him, and was appalled to see his face was still ashen. His eyes had narrowed dangerously, his chin tilted at a defiant angle, and Elizabeth wondered who on earth this man could be to have ignited his hostility so instantaneously.

'I heard the old devil was dead, so I thought I'd come and pay my respects. For old times' sake,' the stranger finished with a satirical lift of one eyebrow.

'Well, now you've done so, I suggest you leave before I throw you out.'

Richard's words were mangled from between gritted teeth, but the intruder only flung up his head with a jeering chuckle. 'Oh, yes, you look as though you're capable,' he scoffed. 'Fighting with Josiah again, were you, or was it your mere presence that killed him?'

Elizabeth's heart seemed to stand still, and her shocked eyes darted nervously back to Richard's face. His jaw was set like granite, the muscles working furiously as he evidently battled to control his rage. But it seemed even his lacerating tongue was too numbed to find a suitably cutting response. Instead, he drew in a gulping breath and, as he slowly released it through pursed lips, he shook his head from side to side.

'Just . . . *go* . . . will you,' he grated in a scarcely audible whisper.

But the stranger evidently had no intention of leaving just yet, and swung his walking cane in a jocular fashion as he ambled leisurely around the open grave. 'A churchyard is a public place, Ritchie, and I have as much right to be here as you.'

Elizabeth's chest contracted unbearably at the fellow's insulting attitude. She looked up at Richard again, for once willing him to deliver some scathing retort. But he appeared to rock on his feet, and for one horrible second, she thought he was about to faint. He was still so weak and if it hadn't been for the funeral, would only just be starting to venture from his sickbed. Elizabeth had no idea who the man was, nor why such enmity seemed to exist between them, but there was no way she'd allow the scoundrel to get away with such sacrilegious behaviour.

'A legal right, perhaps,' she said icily, her voice so laced with disdain that the fellow's eyebrows twitched with surprise, and the supercilious grin slipped from his face. 'But anyone with any decency in them would know they don't have the moral right to intrude on someone else's grief in such a despicable manner. You may dress like a gentleman, sir, but you do not behave like one.'

She glared fiercely at him, her eyes glowing like burnished copper, but beneath her composed resolve, her heart beat wildly with anger and frustration. Her scornful rebuke, though, had been enough to unsettle the stranger. The shock of the slighting reprimand from such an unexpected source registered on his face, and his cheeks flushed scarlet. But then his lips lengthened into a mocking sneer that curdled Elizabeth's blood.

'My, my, Ritchie, what a spirited little wife you have!' he purred in an oily tone, clearly delighting in his own gibing taunts. 'What gutter did you find *her* in, eh?'

Elizabeth positively seethed at his continued effrontery, and beside her, she felt Richard draw himself up to his full height and brace his shoulders. 'She isn't my wife . . .' he began defensively.

'Your concubine, then? Oh, even better!' the fellow's foul mouth chortled triumphantly. 'And that little brat is your fly-blow, I take it?'

Boiling fury gripped Elizabeth's chest. How anyone could be so cruel was beyond belief. Much as she resented Richard Pencarrow, he certainly didn't deserve this. But Richard seemed to have taken control of his senses again, and she heard him suck a smouldering breath through his tightly clamped jaw.

'I'm a widower, not that it's any concern of yours,' he growled, his eyes like hardened steel now. 'And my daughter is legitimate, which is none of your business, either.'

'Oh, I should have known!' the stranger conceded, but his top lip twisted into a sarcastic leer. 'Always had to be proper and correct, didn't you, Ritchie boy? Apart from when you did *this* to me, of course!' he added, jabbing a finger at his nose. But then he went on in his former mocking tone, 'I suppose you're going to make an honest woman out of this pretty little vixen, are you? Well, congratulations. I must say, I admire your taste, even if it is a trifle rustic.'

Elizabeth's mouth had dropped open at the idea that it was Richard who'd damaged his nose, but at this further insult a shiver of disgust trembled down her spine as he looked her up and down with piercing eyes. But at that very instant, Richard hobbled forward and valiantly took a hold on the man's arm.

'She was my father's nurse and now she's leaving, which is precisely what you should do if you know what's good for you.'

'Oh, don't worry!' The stranger raised his hands in exaggerated submission. 'You needn't sully your precious reputation on my account. I wouldn't want to spoil the occasion for you.'

'As if you haven't already,' Richard snarled, and shot him a withering glance which, disappointingly, provoked no more response than a derisive bow as the man sauntered towards the churchyard gates with an indolent swagger.

'Bastard,' Elizabeth heard Richard mutter under his breath, and then he turned to her with a wry grimace. 'Thank you for coming to my rescue. I must say I wouldn't want to be on the receiving end of your tongue if I got on the wrong side of you.'

Elizabeth stifled a gasp. The wrong side of her? Good Lord! The times he'd done precisely that in the few short weeks she'd known him, but had been forced to bite her lip because of her position in the household! And was it true what the man had said about his deformed nose? Nevertheless, Elizabeth had never witnessed such vile behaviour as the stranger's just now, and for once her sympathies lay with the man she'd so often cursed.

'Who on earth is he, sir?' her incensed wrath dared her to ask.

Richard's lips compressed into a thin line as he stared after the retreating figure. 'Maurice Brett,' he spat as if the very name burned his tongue. 'One of my father's so-called friends. The one I despised the most. The others weren't quite so bad, but that two-faced bastard . . . ! He was really the one that forced my father into all the goings on at the house.'

'And is it true?' Elizabeth asked without hesitation, since she'd been dismissed anyway. 'Did you really do that to him?'

Richard looked at her sideways, and then gave a half smile. 'I'm afraid so. It was that short temper of mine. But I still reckon he deserved it.'

'I can well believe it,' Elizabeth chipped in, but it seemed Richard's resentment wasn't yet spent.

'You'd be one of the few who would!' he snorted with an ironic grunt. 'He's from one of the most respected families in Tavistock. And he wished to keep it that way, which is precisely why he wanted to keep his nefarious activities as clandestine as possible. Not aristocracy, of course, but a wealthy businessman. The last of the line. The legitimate line, that is. Unless he's married since I've been away.'

His voice rang with bitterness, and Elizabeth instinctively lay a calming hand on his arm. 'Don't upset yourself, sir. 'Tis not the place.'

He met her eyes, and his mouth broke into a faint smile again. 'You're right,' he said quietly. 'But I'm sorry you were drawn into it, Elizabeth.' He turned then, back to the grave. 'Goodbye, Father,' he pronounced solemnly, and bowed his head.

They stood together for a few more moments before making their way in silence to where William was waiting with Chantal by the trap. A few hangers-on were still standing about in the village square, including Matthew Halse, but Elizabeth had been so shaken by the macabre conversation at the graveside that the prospect of speaking to him was somehow far less daunting. He was among those who doffed their caps as Richard walked past, using the walking stick to limp as little as possible, knowing their eyes would be avid with curiosity. When they reached the trap and he turned to Elizabeth, his face was alarmingly pale.

He politely held out his hand. 'Goodbye then, Elizabeth. And . . . I know I haven't been the easiest of patients. God knows, I haven't exactly been at my best. But . . . thank you. For everything.'

Her soft, velvet eyes stared into his rich brown ones, and she felt the knot tighten in her throat as his fingers closed firmly about hers. The contented life she'd known at Rosebank Hall was over, and she was to return to the degradation of her uncle's foul mouth and his drunken abuse. And all because of Richard Pencarrow.

'Goodbye, sir,' she replied tersely, and withdrew her hand.

'I'll bring your belongings over as soon as I've taken Mr Pencarrow home,' William said affably.

'Thank you, Doctor. And the boxes with the remedy jars, if you please. They're all packed up on the kitchen table.'

'And please,' Richard seemed to falter, 'do come whenever you want, and take anything you need from the herb garden. I'll look after it for you.'

'I'll take cuttings when the time comes, and then I won't need to bother you again,' she replied stiffly, and then bent down as Chantal flung her little arms about Elizabeth's waist, sobbing against her skirt. But Richard deftly drew his daughter away and managed to pick her up in his free arm, although he had to take a staggering step sideways to keep his balance.

Elizabeth stood up straight, and turning her back, walked resolutely towards her uncle, unaware that Richard's eyes were following her, and that even as the trap rattled out onto the lane, he turned to catch one final glimpse of her.

Neither did she know that another pair of eyes were also trained upon her. Then the horseman spurred his mount in the direction of the Tavistock road, a pensive smirk on his preoccupied face.

* * *

'Is that the last box, then?'

'It would seem so, Doctor,' Richard replied as he followed William Greenwood out of the kitchen of Rosebank Hall. 'And thank you so much for doing all this. And for taking me to the church.'

'I could hardly allow you to walk, could I?' William smiled affably. 'Now you make sure you keep that leg elevated. Though how you're going to manage without Lizzie, I don't know.'

Richard lifted his chin stubbornly. 'Surely you must understand why I couldn't have her stay on here. For her own sake. Tongues would be wagging in no time, if they're not already.'

'I suppose so,' William conceded. 'But I wish you'd had help for a little longer.'

'I'm sure Chantal and I can get by. She's very capable.'

'Yes, of course. I'll call by in a few days anyway. And heed what I just said about your leg.'

'I will. And thank you again.'

'Goodbye, then. And take care, both of you.'

Richard secured the door to the rear hallway, and stepping back inside the kitchen, paused for a moment with his head bowed. It had seemed a long, hard day, and despite the lift in the trap, his leg was throbbing mercilessly. But there were a few chores he must attend to before he could obey the doctor's orders, the most urgent of which seemed to be to stoke up the range so that he and Chantal could enjoy a soothing cup of tea. The child was standing by the kitchen table, dragging her finger over the surface where Elizabeth's boxes had been stacked. She looked up, her mouth set mutinously, and Richard inwardly sighed. He knew that expression only too well.

'You say *grand-père Pairncarrov* not die!' she rounded on him. 'You . . . you . . .' she struggled, and then shouted angrily, '*menteur!*'

Richard inhaled deeply. He could do without this, but the poor mite had been through so much. 'I'm so sorry, sweetheart,' he said gently. 'I'd prayed he wouldn't, but . . . You must try to say our name the English way now, Pencarrow.'

But his little daughter totally ignored what he realized was a pretty inept reply, and instead she stamped her foot with fiery passion. 'And you say Eleezabett must go! But I want . . . *je veux qu'elle reste ici!*' she cried defiantly, and stomping out of the kitchen, he heard her thump up the stairs and slam the bedroom door.

Richard stood motionless for thirty seconds, and then slowly sitting down in a chair, crossed his forearms on the

173

table and rested his head on them. Dear Christ, everything had turned out so badly. And most of it his own stupid fault. And now he and Chantal would rattle around in this great, isolated house with just a few hens and the two house cows in the barn for company. The place already seemed so empty without Elizabeth.

If only he hadn't had to send her away. He hadn't wanted her to go any more than Chantal did. But there undoubtedly would be gossip, with her such a beautiful young woman, and him of an age to take advantage of her. But he knew very well that as far as he was concerned, it was a convenient excuse. The truth was that he *did* like her, not in the way that everyone would imagine, although she was so lovely. But she was so comforting, so reassuring despite the sharp words that had come between them. He could see himself growing close to her, trusting her, and in an unguarded moment, sharing with her the torment of what had happened in France. And he simply couldn't take that risk. Better that he drove her away, made her hate him, even.

And to his dismay, he felt something in his heart tear at the thought.

EIGHTEEN

Elizabeth stood with her hands on her hips and casting a critical eye over the inside of the farmstead, released a grunt of satisfaction. She'd been back more than a week, and now it was the turn of the house to be knocked into shape as she buried her sorrow and her anger — for she realized that was what her frustrated emotions came down to — in sheer hard toil. Not that she hadn't always worked zealously at the Hall, but now she'd laboured with a frenzied passion which might have offended anyone else but her slow-witted cousin. She felt guilty, for after all Nellie had kept the place going with reasonable success for nigh on six years, but nothing short of perfection would appease Elizabeth. The dairy had been the first to come under her scrutiny, and then the loft over the shippen where the boys now slept. The minute her dear mother had been buried, Uncle Matthew had repossessed the bedroom, and now Elizabeth had returned to sharing Nellie's bed in the attic of the farmhouse.

It was the nights she dreaded most, lying awake beneath the old thatch which still leaked in places, listening to the wind stealing between the worn reeds and Nellie snoring obliviously beside her. She didn't mind the cold, for a hot-water jar or a brick heated in the hearth soon rectified that, but it was the loneliness that was slowly wringing the life from her. She might be surrounded by her uncle and four cousins, but it was their very company that engulfed her in suffocating isolation. It was their ignorance she despised so, the farm and what went into their stomachs being the only topics of their conversation. Apart from Daniel, who sometimes spoke of his work down the mine, but who was so quiet and gentle he rarely got a word in edgeways. How Elizabeth yearned for a newspaper. To take a book from the shelves at Rosebank Hall. To be able to converse about the mass exodus of West Country miners to America, South Africa and Australia as the mines of Devon and Cornwall gradually closed. To discuss the import of cheap wheat from America, wool from Australia and the prospect of developing refrigeration so that lamb could be transported from that faraway place inhabited by strange animals — all matters that should have concerned her uncle but didn't. To question the rights of the white settlers to finally subdue the native American Indians and keep them imprisoned in reservations. To wonder about India and Britain's other colonies, read about other lands she knew she'd never visit. To know what was happening in France now that the war was over and the Prussians had retreated. After all, it lay only the other side of the English Channel! She might not have liked Richard Pencarrow as a person, but he'd been well educated at Tavistock grammar school. He was highly intelligent and would have *talked* to her just as his father had. And he always called her Elizabeth.

She closed her eyes and shook her aching head. Her contented years at Rosebank Hall were over, and she must lock them away in a box and throw away the key. Look forward to . . . to what? William Greenwood's occasional visits? To half an hour's decent conversation once a week, if she was lucky?

Her vigorous exertion of clearing every flake of ash from the hearth and relighting the fire, removing all the blackened cobwebs that hung from the ceiling, washing down the walls and every nook and cranny of the floor, and salt-scrubbing the table so that it almost gleamed white again, had loosened her hair from the string that held it. With a ponderous sigh, she untied the rough cord completely. She suddenly felt weary, the muscles of her slender arms and shoulders protesting. The peat-faggots glowed warmly in the hearth again. If she put some water to heat, she could take it up to the attic, have a good stripped wash, and plait and coil her hair in one of the simple fashions she'd adopted since going to the Hall. Just because she felt raw and empty inside was no excuse to allow her standards to fall.

'There you be, Lizzie! 'Tis good fer see the place spick an' span agin.'

Matthew's voice, so unusually ingratiating, shook her from her melancholy, and she rolled her despondent eyes at the trail of mud his boots had deposited across the stone floor. She hung her head, her spirits drooping dejectedly. Was this what her life had come down to, being no more than a skivvy to these brainless morons? Sadly, though she loved Nellie dearly, she had to include her, for sometimes she wondered if the girl had the wits she was born with. It was only Daniel who seemed to have any spark of intelligence, and that was smothered by his father. Elizabeth's pretty lips straightened into a thin, resolute line. Really, she would have to do something to save her own sanity!

She flicked her head, certain she'd felt her hair move. Matthew had come up beside her, and when she glanced down, she saw his dirty fingers entwining in her shining, honey-coloured locks. Her heart stood still. From somewhere deep in the sepulchre of her memory there arose the demonic ghost of events her soul had buried in the past. But now, as her skin broke out in a slick of sweat, the hideous recollections reared up inside her. She gazed, mesmerized with horror, into Matthew's dark eyes, not the honest, mahogany spheres that somehow flashed across her mind, but a near black that gleamed with lust.

'You'm home now, Lizzie, where you belongs,' Matthew drawled, stroking his hand down her long tresses. 'There be nort fer stop us being wed now, and you can be the lady of the house, just like you deserves.'

Revulsion had scarcely penetrated her mind before he drew her to him and brought his salivating lips down hard on hers. The closeness of him, the stench of his breath, made her stomach heave, and the panic as she began to retch snapped her body into action. She tried to struggle, pushing against him with all her might. But he was twice her size with the strength of a bull, and for once, he wasn't drunk. Her eyes swivelled frantically about her and rested in despair on the broom, still propped against the table where she'd left it. She reached out, her heart bucking wildly in her chest, and her small hand managed to grab the handle. The angle was wrong, and all she succeeded in achieving was a glancing tap across his shoulder. But it was enough to startle him and he released his hold sufficiently for her to wriggle free.

She stood for a moment, stunned with relief, breathing hard and her eyes narrowed into slits. 'I'd sooner marry one of the pigs!' she snarled with scorching sarcasm.

Matthew's face turned a thunderous purple. 'Oh, I suppose you fancies your chances wi' that there pretty-faced bastard up at the Hall, do you?' he scorned with a venomous sneer. 'Well, if I cas'n have you, I'll bloody well make certain no other man'll want you either!'

Before she knew what was happening, he'd wrenched open the drawer in the table and withdrawn the kitchen scissors which he then brandished in front of her nose, his face grim and livid. Elizabeth froze, every muscle paralysed. Dear God, she must *move*! But Matthew stood between her and the door, and there was nowhere else to run to. She had to make herself think. If she could draw him further into the room, and then make a dash around the other side of the table . . . It was her only chance. With a supreme effort, she managed to force her trembling legs to take a step backwards. Slowly. Her feet dragging like lead weights. Another step. Matthew came towards her, wielding the scissors, his expression lurid with a ghoulish grin as he savoured every second. One more step and . . .

She hurled herself sideways across the end of the table and then careered along its opposite side. Matthew let out a maddened roar and she heard him lumber after her. She should make it to the door, and once outside, she could easily outrun him. But it was in that instant that her foot caught in the hem of her skirt. She knew she was falling, but couldn't save herself as her face cracked against the corner of the table.

She didn't feel the pain at first. Shards of brilliant light flashed across her eyes and then her vision blackened into a hellish void. She was sprawled on the cold, hard floor, senseless and yet not. Aware of where she was, unable to move, and yet strangely not caring. Not even when a truss of hair was all but torn from her scalp, and she heard the crisp rasp of the scissor blades somewhere behind her head.

It was Nellie's shriek as she came in from the dairy that brought her to her senses, and she gained the vague impression that the hefty girl launched herself at her father and thrust him away with a raging screech. Elizabeth's groan as she dragged herself up onto her elbows seemed to come from someone else's lips. As she focused on the shanks of golden curls scattered about the floor, it was some seconds before it registered what had happened. But her gaze was oddly restricted, and she realized she was only seeing out of one eye.

It was then that the pain hit her. A violent, sickening agony that screamed across her face and down her neck as if her head was on fire. She wanted to cry out, but a mere whimper quivered from her lungs as she slumped forward again. And then she was being lifted, cradled in strong, gentle arms that rocked her soothingly as she rested against an amply padded shoulder.

'You filthy varmint!' Nellie spat from behind her ear.

And then she shuddered as Matthew's shocked, crawling remorse trembled from somewhere above her. 'Oh, my God! I be that sorry, Lizzie! I didn't mean fer hurt you! I only wanted fer frit you!'

She forced herself to peer up through her one good eye, and the last thing she remembered before she passed out was Matthew's hideous, twisted face.

* * *

179

'There, there, my pet. Now don't try and move.'

It was Nellie's crooning tones she heard first as she moaned softly and realized she was in the bed in the attic, although how she'd got there was a mystery. Her cousin was sitting beside her, her forehead creased with anxiety as she stroked her hand. The torturing pain at once seared through Elizabeth's head, and she shifted in the bed in an attempt to escape the torment. Nellie's concerned, moon-shaped face wavered before her as she tried to remember what had happened.

'My hair,' she whispered hoarsely, as the appalling memory flooded back.

'Now don't you fret none about that,' Nellie told her with firm compassion. ''Twill soon grow back. When you'm feeling better, I can straighten it up so 'twill not look so bad. 'Twill just be like a boy's. With a cap on, no one will notice. 'Tis your face I be more worried about. So soon as Daniel do get back from his shift, I'll send him into town fer fetch the doctor.'

'No!' Elizabeth wailed feebly, and instinctively tried to sit up. But the pain tore across her cheek and she fell back on the pillows with a sharp wince.

'But, Lizzie, 'tis already black as soot, and so swollen your eye be closed. I . . . I think the cheekbone could be broke.'

'Well, if 'tis, there's nothing the doctor can do,' Elizabeth muttered as forcibly as she could, for every word she spoke was agony. 'Just fetch me some laudanum and a rag soaked in witch hazel, and later you can prepare some comfrey. Just do as I tell you, Nellie. Please!' she begged desperately. 'And don't you dare fetch the doctor!'

Fetch Dr Greenwood. It was exactly what she should do, but she mustn't allow him to know what had happened. Poor William would feel responsible for allowing her to return to the farmstead, although her mother had never revealed her secret fears to him. And then he was bound to tell Richard Pencarrow, and that was the last thing she wanted. All her ties with the Hall must be severed. That episode of her life was over. It had never existed. And now she knew she must escape from her uncle for ever. In a few weeks, when she'd recovered. Already a plan was beginning to formulate in her mind.

NINETEEN

Tavistock, November 1871

The grand drawing room was fusty with the bittersweet
fragrance of the cigar smoke that wafted in spirals towards the
high ceiling and then hung in a wispy blanket like dawn mist
over the moor. Maurice Brett stood by the casement window
of his magnificent terraced villa in Tavistock's fashionable
Plymouth Road, gazing down the length of the perfectly
tended front garden and across the wide thoroughfare to
the open meadows beyond. It was the end of November,
not particularly cold, but as usual on the western edge of
Dartmoor, it was raining and thoroughly miserable. The
weather matched his dark mood. Ever since he'd attended
Josiah Pencarrow's funeral, he'd been restless and ill at
ease. In order to calm his spirits, he'd found himself having
recourse to the little pills he kept hidden in the secret drawer
of his desk. They were as precious as stardust since that
ridiculous Poisons Act a few years back, and he endeavoured
to use them only when he was desperate. He didn't relish the
prospect of seeking out that shyster in the Plymouth back
street to replenish his supply, his muffler wrapped around
his face and his hat rammed down over his eyes in the hope

that no one would recognize him. And then he'd have to pay the earth. Extortionist! Still, he himself had held Josiah Pencarrow over a barrel in the first place, writing off the stupid fellow's gambling debts to him in exchange for using his isolated farmhouse as an opium den. Well, that was somewhat of an exaggeration, but it was there that the habit had established itself all those years ago. Not that he was addicted like some he'd known, and whose lives had been shattered by it. He would describe himself as an occasional user, but by God, he craved a dose just now!

Maurice drew deeply on the cigar, tipped his head backwards, and concentrated on releasing a couple of smoke rings into the already choking atmosphere. Damn old Josiah! Or rather, damn that sanctimonious son of his! It hadn't only been when Richard had broken his nose that he'd had a run-in with the milksop when he'd been a mere boy, although that had been the worst, of course. On several occasions, the youth had made an attempt to protect his father, as if the bastard needed it. And his leaving — or rather absconding — had so shocked the old devil, he'd put a stop to their clandestine activities anyway, together with Maurice's chances with the pretty dairymaid. The cursed pup had certainly spurred the dog's conscience, blast him, and now he was back. Maurice was just in the mood to take some spiteful revenge especially when he looked in the mirror and contemplated his blighted good looks. But how? That was the question. He couldn't even use that mettlesome young girl against him, since he didn't seem interested. Bloody hell, he must be insane! She was enough to make any man's blood rise. Exquisite, like some ethereal sprite. Fragile as a snowdrop, braving the weather with a stalwart heart in some wintry crevice, and bowing gracefully in the wind. But inside, she had the courage and nerve of a tigress. And those eyes! The colour of ripe hazelnuts, they'd glowed a translucent gold when she'd sprung to dear Ritchie's defence, yet they'd mellowed to a velvety softness when she'd looked up at him. And the fool had dismissed her! By God, what *he* would give to have her under his roof! His life was so flat. So empty! But how he would relish subduing *her* spirit! And her body.

The thought brought the saliva to the back of his throat and then he shook his head. He didn't even know who she was. Where she came from. She was a nurse, but not one of the drunken gin-sots who put their own lives at risk keeping an eye on victims of highly infectious diseases for the sake of a few shillings; no, she was an intelligent professional. Conversing with and evidently respected by the fellow he knew by sight to be Dr Greenwood. There was something about her that had touched his heart in a way he'd never experienced before. She might even make him a wife, although God knew he was old enough to be her father. Ah, what a pity.

Oh, Jesus Christ, what the blazes did his mother want now? His eyes rolled heavenwards at the thunderous banging on the ceiling above, and he could hear the dreaded, high-pitched cackle through the plasterwork, the robust floorboards and the thick carpet he'd had installed in the front bedroom in a vain attempt to deaden the noise. If only the old witch wouldn't insist on occupying the chamber directly above the drawing room. But every time he tried to move her, she made his life and that of the servants such hell, he'd always surrendered. But her uncontrollable outbursts were becoming more and more frequent and quite frankly, he didn't think he could take much more.

A demanding knock on the door interrupted his chain of thought, and he blew a snarl of exasperation through his fearsomely clamped teeth as his mother's personal maid marched into the room.

'I'm sorry, sir,' she pronounced with irritation, 'but I really can't do anything with the mistress today. Look what she's done to me. Again!' she added pointedly, turning her cheek which was oozing blood along clear scratch marks. 'I've tried to give her the doctor's calming draught, but she just spat it in my face. She's insisting you see her, sir.'

With a roar of fury, Maurice stalked out of the room, bounding up the stairs two at a time. At least he could still do that, he thought grimly, even if he had turned fifty. It was more than Ritchie Pencarrow could manage just now, anyway! Odd, that. Must have had some sort of accident, and quite recently if his gaunt face was anything to go by. Didn't spoil his damnably good looks, mind. He'd matured, broadened while he'd been away. A fine figure of a man. And how he'd love to knock his straight, white teeth out for him!

Maurice flung open the bedroom door and stormed across to where the elderly lady was propped up in bed amongst a sea of white pillows, nightcap askew on her wispy grey hair and her thin, gnarled fingers clutching the walking stick she was thumping relentlessly on the floor.

'Maurice! *Maurice!*' Her shrill squawk hurt his ears, and his teeth clamped hard around the cigar still in his mouth.

'I'm here, Mother!' he growled back, fighting the desire to let his hands fly to her scraggy neck and throttle her. 'For God's sake, will you stop this racket, you old harridan! The whole of Tavistock can hear you!'

'Maurice!' she continued to squeal at him. 'Will you please order that woman back in here this minute! She refuses to get me dressed! The carriage will be here soon, and I won't be ready!'

'You're not going anywhere, you silly old hag. You can't get out of bed on your own, remember? You're incontinent and you smell.'

'But I'm going to the Duke of Bedford's ball!' she insisted.

Maurice sucked in a calming breath around his cigar. Poor old dear couldn't help it, he supposed. And she was his mother, after all. Not that she'd ever shown him maternal affection in any degree. He might as well never have had a mother at all! Brought up by a strict nanny, an even stricter governess and then sent away to boarding school, he was directed straight into the family business. It had suited him well enough, having wealth and respect without having to work too hard for it. His ancestors had originally made their money in the wool trade, but when that had collapsed earlier in the century, his father had expanded into every lucrative enterprise imaginable. Not getting his fingers dirty, of course, but investing his money where he could until he'd died relatively young, leaving Maurice in sole charge of a fortune. Devon Great Consols, that had been the best investment, followed by the railways and the Tavistock Canal in its heyday, although he'd seen the decline in that coming and sold out just in time. The Bedford Iron Works had shut down a few years back. He'd lost a sum over that, but not a great deal as he only had a handful of shares. The other two Tavistock foundries were still profitable, and his investments in Wheal Friendship were producing a steady income. They'd been just for fun, mind, as a goad to Josiah's Wheal Rosalind, small fry by comparison, but Maurice had gloated with joy when it had been forced to close. The thought made him frown darkly. It was his ponderings over how to get even with Josiah's son that had been so rudely interrupted by his mother's tantrum.

Maurice sighed with resignation. 'No, Mother, you're not going to the Duke's ball. It's ten o'clock in the morning. The Duke is in London, and besides, people like us are never invited to Endsleigh. We may have money, but we're not aristocracy.'

'But *you're* going, Maurice! Look at you! All dressed up like a dog's dinner!'

'Mother, I'm in normal morning dress, that's all. With a black waistcoat. See? If I was going to a ball, I'd be wearing an evening suit with a fancy-coloured waistcoat and a white bow tie, wouldn't I?'

'Then you must be going to a funeral,' she decided, her faded, beady eyes scrutinizing him suspiciously. 'Who's dead? Is the Duke dead? What about the ball?'

'No. No one's dead,' Maurice seethed, feeling the flush of impatience rush to his cheeks again. 'I have a business meeting later, that's all.'

'I don't believe you! You're off to meet a woman!' she crowed. 'I'll tell your father when he comes in!'

Maurice scowled malevolently as he fought against the explosion of anger. 'No, you won't. He's been dead over thirty years.'

'Has he? Well, there you are, then. Someone *is* dead!' Her toothless gums worked together, and Maurice felt sick at the loud sucking noise they made. 'And doubtless you're waiting for me to die, too. But who's going to have everything when *you're* dead, Maurice, eh? The family needs an heir. A proper legitimate heir to manage the affairs your grandfather and his father set up, not some bastard you've left somewhere! You need a wife, Maurice! A wife!'

Maurice suddenly thought he would choke on the putrid airlessness of the room. The maids were forever spraying some sickly perfume about the place, but no matter how frequently they changed the soiled sheets, nothing could ever disguise the stink of the cantankerous old crone. God, she was disgusting. He sprang across to the window and, pushing it fully open, gulped at the cold air that swirled in. He'd swing for her one of these days! She'd interfered with his life since he could remember, always telling him what to do even when he was a grown man, even now haranguing him from her festering lair. And what rankled him most at that particular moment was that, on one point, he knew she was right. He *did* need a wife. He didn't *want* one, but he *needed* one. And a son. All his mother's matchmaking efforts had only ever produced empty-headed, unattractive society maids that he wouldn't have wanted as his harlot, let alone his spouse! He'd only once been quite keen on a certain lady, but she'd ruined everything by teasing him about his nose. So the quest had begun again. Any wife of his would have to be . . . refined. No, that wasn't the word. Intelligent. Beautiful, of course. Spirited, not some meek little mouse. Sensuous, yes, that was it! Delicate. Subtle. Creating that feeling of mystery he'd never tire of if he was to remain faithful. And understanding. Yes, quite definitely that. Someone, indeed, like the girl who'd stood so resolutely by Ritchie Pencarrow's side.

'Sir, may I discuss today's menu with the mistress?'

The cook's voice shook him from his daydream and he realized that his cigar was nearly burned through. He quickly threw the stub out of the window so that it landed in the middle of the lawn, where the gardener could dispose of it.

'Be my guest.' He shrugged as he thankfully escaped the room. And then a thought speared his brain like a dagger of lightning. 'When you've finished, will you send your assistant to me in the drawing room?'

'Mrs Elliot, sir?' The cook's white cap flapped up and down as her head bobbed in astonishment.

'Yes. I believe she used to work for a Mr Pencarrow at a farm up on the moor. Rosebank Hall.'

'Yes, sir. I believe she did, if my memory serves me rightly.'

'Good,' Maurice said with a smile that spread into a sly smirk.

TWENTY

'Lizzie Thornton, I be that pleased fer see you! I be that frit about the babby. 'Er be crying all arternoon, and there's nort I can do fer stop 'en.'

Elizabeth slowed her step and reluctantly turned her head to discover who had hailed her so desperately. She was heading down the lane from the busy community of Mary Tavy, which was bursting at the seams with the families of the miners and surface labourers who worked at Wheal Friendship. The numerous shafts and adits, stamps, crushers, waterwheels, tramlines, calciners and flues scattered around the village made it by far the largest and busiest mine on the western side of Dartmoor. But now the damp, penetratingly cold December night was closing in, and everyone who could was hurrying home as the Tavy valley would soon be engulfed in pitch darkness. In the misty glimmer emitting from the open door of one of a row of tumbledown hovels, however, Elizabeth recognized the silhouette of young Susan Penrose. Though it was the last thing she needed, she couldn't ignore the frantic pleas.

'Could you not take him to see Dr Greenwood?' she replied distantly.

'You knows he only has 'is surgery yer twice a week, and 'tiddn till morning.'

Yes. Of course she knew. Twice a week in the sitting room of one of the Station Road houses. And not today. Which was precisely why she'd chosen that time to come into the larger neighbouring village in search of work. It was almost a month since the horrific incident with Matthew, and so far she'd managed to avoid William even on the couple of occasions he'd called at the farmstead. The swelling on her face had at last subsided, although a small lump still protruded over her cheekbone, and her eye socket and cheek were stained a mottled green that William would instantly recognize as the remnants of severe bruising. Even now, as she entered the lowly miners' cottage, the girl gave her an odd look as the dim light from two home-made tallow candles reflected on her face. But Susan had seen the results of a fist aimed in anger or drink often enough, and thought no more about it.

'Ssh!' she said, jerking her head towards the two men asleep on a thin, straw pallet placed on a slatted bed. Why Susan should worry, Elizabeth wasn't sure. The puling of the infant was enough to wake the dead, but apparently wasn't disturbing the miners, exhausted from their long hours in the underground levels. 'They must sleep now. Eddie and Frank'll want the bed when they comes back from their shift.'

Elizabeth nodded. Never a cold bed in a miners' household. Two or three families sometimes shared a cottage, although it would usually be more substantial than this shack, which scarcely kept out the wind and rain. Damp seeped up from the floor, which was nothing more than dried bracken strewn over compacted earth. The walls might have been limewashed at one time, but they now oozed black mould. The humid stench inside was suffocating, probably made worse by the turfs smouldering in the tiny fireplace. The chimney was evidently insufficient, as acrid smoke lingered in the fetid air. Elizabeth wondered how the baby could find enough breath to howl so lustily, for *she* was nearly choking.

She certainly didn't rate its chances of surviving to its first birthday. It was a miracle to her that Susan had gone full term with the pregnancy and come through what had been a difficult labour. The girl was undernourished and no more than seventeen years old; her young husband, dead to the world beside his snoring father, scarcely her senior. That people had to live like this never ceased to appal Elizabeth. At least her own village across the river was inhabited mainly by farmers and farm labourers, who only just scraped a living, perhaps, but worked in the fresh air and fed on the healthy produce of their own labours. No more than a handful of men from Peter Tavy were employed at the mines and most of them, like Daniel, were sons of farmers and so enjoyed the benefits of farming life for at least part of each day. The main workforce for Wheal Friendship was squeezed into Mary Tavy: miners and ore-dressers who worked the rich deposits of copper and sometimes tin and lead that had kept the London adventurers happy for so many years. It was all arsenic production now, of course; and the builders, drafted in to construct the massive lines of calciners, condensing chambers, flues and chimneystacks necessary for its refinement, swelled the already overcrowded population to explosion point.

'Let's see you then, little man.' Elizabeth smiled wearily at the wailing child as she unwrapped his clothing. 'How old is he now, Susan?'

'I baint certain.' The girl shrugged. 'Six month, maybies.'

'And are you still feeding him yourself?'

'Of course. I cas'n afford fer gee 'en proper food, wi' us no longer working at the mine.'

Elizabeth knotted her lips. It was harsh enough work for the men who worked on the dressing floor, exposed to the elements at every season, hands chapped and bleeding from the constant flow of cold water. But for women, or bal maidens as they were called, it must be intolerable. But work there they did — many, like Susan, through eight months of pregnancy. Much of the refining was done by machine in the stamps, vanning tables and buddles, but it was still heavy work. Every time Elizabeth came near the mines, she thanked God she'd been spared such an existence. But, quite simply, girls like Susan needed the money.

'I don't think he's ill,' she said patiently as she examined the baby. 'There's no fever, and he's lively enough. You could try him on the mint and chamomile I gave you before. 'Twill help settle him if he has a touch of colic. But he is a little thin. I reckon as he's hungry.'

'Hungered? I've only just fed 'en!' the young mother groaned. 'Oh, Lizzie, what can I do? There's not a penny fer spare fer buy extra food!'

Elizabeth sighed. Her remedies could cure certain ailments, but poverty wasn't one of them. 'I've got something I can give you to help increase your milk, but he's ready for weaning. Potato mashed so fine 'tis like a thin paste makes a good start and will cost you very little. Just a spoonful at each feed to begin. And you need to change him more often. His bottom's raw, Susan. I'll send you over some cream for that as well.'

The tension on the girl's face visibly faded. 'Oh, I be that relieved. I thought . . . I be thanking you, Lizzie. I cas'n afford fer pay you, mind.'

A wan smile flickered over Elizabeth's features. What difference would a few pennies make to her anyway? At that moment, she really didn't care. Her face was aching again, her head throbbing from the exertion of traipsing all over Mary Tavy in search of a position. She knew she could always go to William — at least she could when her face was healed — and accept his open offer to set her up as nurse and midwife to his wealthier clients in Tavistock. But the truth was she didn't want to leave the upper valley and the people she'd known and helped all her life. The little she could make from her remedies and other services, however, wouldn't allow her to live independently, and Hannah's little nest egg, swelled as it was by her wages from Josiah saved over the first couple of years when he'd been able to pay them, wouldn't go far. She needed a proper position if she wanted to support herself, and Mary Tavy was the only answer. She'd tried the mine-captains' homes first, and the chief agent's, offering her services as a governess. She wasn't needed. And the school mistress already had an assistant. She'd tried the lawyer up the road, but he'd no need of her either, not even as a housemaid. The constable, the station master at the railway, but everyone seemed to have all the help they required, and there were many searching for work who looked a great deal more robust than she did. She'd even called at the Buller's Arms. The innkeeper had looked her up and down, perhaps thinking her pretty face might attract more custom, but he told her he'd prefer a more buxom wench and that she was a bit too hoity-toity in the way she talked. His miners would eat her alive on pay day, that was if there was any money left after settling their bills for powder and candles for their work, let alone food, at the mine shops. And so he, too, had turned her away, for by then she was too exhausted to explain that she was well known to most of his customers already. All the faces she'd seen that day were beginning to waver inside her head, stretching and twisting, grotesquely distorted; her skull pounded with their mingled voices. She closed her eyes tightly, rubbed her hand across her brow as the infant's bawling reverberated in her ears. She shouldn't have come. It was too soon. She suddenly felt stifled in the dank, gloomy cottage and something she recognized as panic took hold of her. She had to get out, draw breath.

'Take him to Dr Greenwood in the morning,' she told the girl brusquely, groping towards the door.

'An' what do I pays 'en with? Chips?' Susan moaned.

'If you must,' she muttered, dragging herself outside and gulping at the cold air. Miners' tokens. Well, it wouldn't be the first time William had been offered them, she was sure. She tipped her head skywards. It was spitting with rain now, sharp, glacial shards that stung her face but were strangely refreshing. She must get home. She'd crawl into bed and allow dear Nellie to take care of her as she had for the past few weeks.

She started down the lane again. Behind her, the thumps and crashes of the building works had ceased as darkness put an end to the day's labour. But the numerous waterwheels that powered the surface works and constantly drained the lower levels of the mines, still creaked and groaned, and men still shouted across at each other through the murky twilight. The ochre-tinted luminosity of oil lamps glimmered from the upper windows of the Count House, all she could see of it, nestled as it was among the spoil heaps on the other side of Cholwell Brook; and the metallic clang from the blacksmith further up the hill still hung on the sodden air. But as she stumbled down the track, the massive stamps and crushers of the vast dressing floor to her right gradually fell silent as the men and women who worked them dispersed for the night and made their weary way to their cramped, humble dwellings in the village. There would still be miners toiling in the bowels of the earth beneath her feet, of course, the inky blackness illuminated only by the candle stuck with clay into the brim of their hats. The last shift wouldn't be finished for another few hours, and until it was over, the roads would be deserted.

So Elizabeth was virtually alone, the deepening dusk becoming hostile as the darkness closed in around her, setting her nerves on edge and making her heart beat faster. The ache in her cheekbone was spreading up through her eye like fire until she felt her head would explode. Her legs came to a stop, and for a few moments she gazed up at Buller's Wheel as she tried to gather her energy for the journey home. The gigantic spokes rotated slowly, silhouetted against the grey, dismal sky like some majestic circular skeleton, powerful and unstoppable as it turned ceaselessly, day and night. She pressed on, her feet trailing like lead as she dragged herself past the church and the cottages that flanked the narrowing pathway. She turned the sharp corner, staggering down the steep, uneven slope towards the river, a desperate whimper in her throat. She could hardly see the ground beneath her feet, tripping on the jutting stones and falling twice onto her knees. When some unknown person suddenly scurried past her from the great barren heap of arsenic waste by the riverbank, her stomach clenched with fright.

She groped her way down the track as it dipped to the river. The roar of gushing water swirled inside her skull as the Tavy, swollen by recent heavy rainfall, hurtled down from the moor, dashing in a raging torrent over the boulders that were strewn in its path. The ford was impassable, so Elizabeth clambered thankfully onto the long wooden bridge, clinging on the handrail and hauling herself across to the other side. The wind was stirring as rain fell more heavily, running down the back of her bonnet and dripping down her neck. She shivered as the dampness soaked into her collar and she wished vehemently that she hadn't chosen that day to go in search of a position. But she had to get away from her uncle. She couldn't possibly go on living in constant fear. So it seemed she'd have to seek William's help, after all. It would be a good life, but the sadness of having to leave the moorland valley was breaking her. To turn her back on her home. Home? And as her eyes moved in the direction of Rosebank Hall — even though she couldn't see it from there — she felt torn by the knowledge that the farmhouse she'd shared with the belligerent old man was the only place she'd ever truly looked upon as home. Now she'd been turned out like some piece of unwanted furniture. Well, she wouldn't let Richard Pencarrow know what he'd done to her. She'd start again, come what may. Only not today. As her determination strengthened, she left the long, narrow lane that climbed between the high banks to the heart of Peter Tavy, and instead cut uphill across the fields and along the track that led onto the moor towards Uncle Matthew's farm.

'Where the divil 'ave you bin?'

A tiny sound squealed from her throat as a familiar outline emerged from the hedgerow. Matthew lumbered towards her, his shoulders hunched menacingly, and Elizabeth recognized his drunken gait at once. She stopped dead in her tracks, her mind blank with shock, as he lurched forward and grasped her arm, his fingers digging cruelly into her flesh.

'I thought as I asked you a question!' he spat, and like a bolt of lightning, his other hand whipped through the air and slammed across her already damaged face.

Her scream of pain and fear was muffled by the deluge of rain that by now was streaming from the indigo sky. Her knees threatened to buckle, but her hatred of her uncle gave her courage and she lifted her head defiantly.

'I've been looking for work, if you must know,' she rasped, wrenching her arm from his hold. 'I'm clearly a burden to you, and 'twill be one less mouth to feed.'

She went to stride on up the hill, but Matthew danced round in front of her, the whites of his eyes glinting luridly in the obscure blur of his face.

'Well, if 'tis work you wants, then you'm in luck,' he chortled, seemingly taking some twisted pleasure from his own words. 'I've just found you a job. In Tavistock. In a posh house that should satisfy even *your* high and mighty ideas,' he added sarcastically. ''Tis what I've bin celebrating.'

'Huh! Well, I can see you're drunk!' she barked at him, but she was nonetheless surprised and intrigued by his announcement. 'What sort of a job?' she dared to ask.

'As nurse to an aud woman. Gentry folk,' he continued gleefully. 'You should be pleased. 'Twould seem you has a reputation. The divil sought *me* out special like. A tidy sum he's offered me fer you!'

'What?' Elizabeth's eyes opened wide with indignation. 'I'm not a slave to be bought and sold, you know!'

'Whilst you'm under my care, you'll do as you'm teld!' he hissed, poking his face close to hers, his beer-reeking breath filling her nostrils. 'You'll be at Mr Brett's house fust thing Friday morning.'

Somewhere at the back of her mind, a terrible anger reared up at the name, and her confused brain struggled to remember where she'd heard it before. And when it came to her, the bitter memory infuriated her.

'No!' she grated. 'I'll not work for anyone of *your* choosing!'

'Oh, I sees!' Matthew bellowed. 'Not good enough for you, eh? And I suppose that handsome bugger up at the Hall *was*! Had his fill of pleasure wi' you, and now he's thrown you out! Well, what you've done fer 'en, you can do fer me! By God, I've waited long enough!'

A ripple of terror pulsed through Elizabeth's body as he gripped her arm again, almost tearing it from its socket, and with his other hand in a strangling vice about her slender neck, swung her viciously into the hedge. The sharp barbs of hawthorn scratched her face, and she was so winded as she landed heavily on her back with Matthew's weight on top of her, that for some moments she could do nothing but lie there as he grappled with the fastenings of her cloak. His huge, brawny hands mauled at her dress until his fingers dug into her bared breasts, but the horror of what he was doing catapulted her muscles back to life. She tried to kick out, but her legs were trapped beneath him, her flailing arms having no effect as she pummelled on his shoulders. His livid face swung tauntingly above her and she managed to rake her fingernails down his cheek. His answer was to slam her head back on the hard ground. Dear God, she could feel herself slipping into some insensible black void as his groping hands fought their way up the inside of her thighs. But she had to fight back! And by some miracle, as her hand scraped at the bare earth around her, her fingers closed about a loose stone.

By pure instinct, she smashed it against his temple. He froze like a statue, and for a horrific few seconds, she thought she'd merely inflamed his rage. But then he rolled sideways, clutching at his head with a fearful groan. She pushed him away, gasping and senseless with relief, and hauled herself to her feet. She staggered backwards, watching for a moment as he writhed on the ground. Not waiting to see what he'd do next, she turned on her heel and fled.

The road back down to the village was long and straight and she'd walked it a thousand times. But the uneven ground was slippery with mud, and in what was now almost total darkness, she kept tripping and stumbling to her knees. She picked herself up and lurched on in blind terror, too petrified to look behind her. The rain was beating down in sheets, lashing into her face so that she could hardly see. The wind licked avidly about her bonnet and finally snatched it away. She didn't dare stop to retrieve it. She reeled on in heedless panic, and coming into the village, drove herself onwards. She had no choice now but to take refuge at William's house in Tavistock and tell him everything. As she passed through Peter Tavy, the doors and shutters of the houses were closed against the wild winter evening. Elizabeth's wheezing lungs forced her to slacken her pace. When she reached the far side of the village, she could do no more than walk briskly beneath the bare, overarching branches of the chestnut trees looming out of the darkness like mocking giants. As she left the village she didn't take the obvious route to Tavistock. If Matthew had guessed where she was heading, he'd doubtless follow the road keeping to the east of the river; and if he managed to catch up with her, well, she mightn't be so lucky as to escape again. So instead she cut down the ill-defined lane across the field towards the old stone bridge over the Tavy at Harford, in the hope of eluding him. And once she was in Tavistock under William's protection, she would be safe.

* * *

Richard Pencarrow turned the horse off the main Tavistock to Okehampton road and, cutting off the corner to the bridge, let the animal have its head across the soft ground. The field was his, after all. A precious parcel of flat, fertile land purchased at great cost by his grandfather and lying idle for God knew how long! Well, it was his and the bank's, he mused ruefully. Or rather the bank's, and hardly his at all. He really couldn't believe what his father had done. Mortgaged just about everything he owned without a hope of repaying the interest, let alone the capital. And now he'd departed this earth leaving Richard to sort out the unholy mess. He'd been numbed with shock in the bank manager's office, and it had taken all his powers of persuasion to sway the man away from repossessing the farmhouse, the land and the four tenant farms there and then. It was beyond Richard how the estate was ever going to have a chance of recovery, but he had to try. If he didn't, Chantal would have nothing. The bank manager had given him six months' grace, and would then review the situation, but the bank could call in the loan at any time. Richard had no choice but to sign the agreement. But at that time of year especially, with the winter starting, virtually no livestock and no fodder crops to feed them on if he had, it was useless. He'd need two years at least before he could make any real difference. He'd then gone on to the family solicitor to see if there was anything at all that could be salvaged, but it seemed virtually everything, bar the contents of the house and the few remaining sheep, was already being used as surety. Josiah's will had left everything to Richard, and he could either sell up to pay off the debts, or accept the gruelling task of attempting to get the farm back on its feet. Either way, he'd be starting from scratch. At least the land tax had been kept up to date, the solicitor had offered optimistically, though there could be some death duties to pay. At this, Richard had stood up abruptly, ashen with agitation as he realized it was getting dark. He'd missed the carrier back to Peter Tavy, and Chantal was alone at the isolated farmhouse. The solicitor had instantly offered him the loan of his own horse which would only be eating its head off in the livery stable, and to be honest, could do with some exercise.

Richard gritted his teeth as the animal's hooves drummed rhythmically over the wet grass. It was years since he'd ridden on the back of anything faster than a plodding carthorse, and his injured leg was aching dreadfully. The mare was young and skittish, and Richard was worried his sore and unaccustomed muscles mightn't allow him to keep his seat if she made any unexpected moves. Added to the crippling anxiety of having left Chantal alone far too long, even if he'd insisted she bolt all the doors, was the relentless, torrential rain that was driving across his face in sheets, dripping from his sodden hair and soaking through to his skin.

He reined in his lively mount and slowed her to a trot as they clattered over the bridge. Just under a mile to the village and then, on horseback, he could cut up the combe, past the old mill and across the moor to Rosebank Hall, a hazardous trail in the dark, but much quicker than following the road. Come on, girl. He clicked his tongue and dug in his heels as they neared the far side of the bridge.

Neither he nor the mare saw until it was too late the shadowy figure that charged recklessly into their path. The petrified animal rolled its eyes, neighing crazily with its ears flat on its head, and prancing wildly, it reared up on its hind legs. Richard tried to grip hard with his knees, but his thigh was already throbbing and as the horse plunged back down onto its forelegs, he was flung forward and shot over its neck. He tried to twist himself and roll into a ball, but the next thing he knew, he'd landed heavily on his right side and the mare was galloping back the way they'd come.

The pain in his leg stunned him, and for some seconds he writhed on the ground as he struggled to stifle his agony. A muted gasp escaped from his mouth and he clamped his jaw fiercely against it as he dragged himself into a sitting position with his back leaning against the wall of the bridge. He glanced fleetingly at the ghostly apparition that had dissolved into a motionless heap, half hidden in the swathes of a cloak. But then he closed his eyes tightly and dropped his head back against the stone wall as he concentrated on nursing his leg. The pain was starting to ease, and as his clearing mind began to take stock of the situation, anger welled up within him. He hauled himself upwards using the wall for support, and tentatively putting his weight on his leg, limped over to the prostrate figure and shook whoever it was vigorously by the shoulders.

'What the hell do you think you're doing?' he yelled above the battering rain, as the picture of Chantal alone at the Hall flashed through his brain again. But as his hands became still, a woman's head lolled to one side. Her eyelids flickered open, and a terrified whimper moaned from her trembling lips.

Richard's jaw dangled open as he stared at the saturated figure. Just then the wind lifted the cloak and the expanse of exposed flesh beneath the ripped bodice of the dress was pale in the darkness.

'*You!*' he cried aloud as realization dawned. 'Dear God! What the—' Anger burned through him as the hideous memory of what had happened in the farmhouse in France seared across his mind, and just as before, he wanted . . . Sweet Christ, surely . . . And then Chantal . . . But he couldn't leave . . . 'Come on,' he shouted as he roughly pulled her to her feet. 'I'll take you home to your uncle.'

'*NO!*' An agonized cry uttered from her lips and she fought desperately to pull away from him. But he swung her round to face him, jerking her forcefully as if he was trying to shake some sense into her.

'*What!* You don't mean . . . it was him?'

She stared back, her throat so taut she couldn't utter a sound. But it was enough. He understood. And muttering a vehement oath, he drew an enraged breath through his nostrils.

'Come home with me, then,' he said gruffly.

She blinked at him, overwhelming relief bringing silent tears to her eyes as her body sagged towards the ground. His hands patted the air uncertainly, but there seemed nothing else for it as his reluctant arms closed about her shoulders. And as he held her, something stirred within him he hadn't felt for a long time. It took him by surprise and he reared away in confusion. No! He couldn't . . . he *mustn't*! But he had no option but to take her home with him, though it was the last thing he wanted.

'Can you ride?' he asked sharply. 'That is, if I can catch that blasted animal.' He didn't wait for an answer, but turned on his heel and hobbled back across the bridge. Elizabeth watched him, and knew that, for now at least, she was safe.

TWENTY-ONE

'Here. Drink this. We might as well make use of what's left. Not that I imagine it's been paid for.'

Richard placed a glass of brandy into Elizabeth's trembling hands as she shivered in the chair next to the kitchen range. The journey back to the Hall had been a nightmare, clinging to Richard Pencarrow for dear life as she sat behind him on the nervous mare, buffeted by the wind and rain that blustered across the moor in angry gusts, petrified that at any minute she'd be thrown off, and all the time glancing fearfully over her shoulder, expecting Matthew to materialize out of the shadows. She'd waited in silence while Richard bedded down the horse, and he'd been obliged to half drag her across to the house, her limbs were so stiff with cold and shock. Even the sight of little Chantal, her ebony eyes huge with alarm to see her dearly missed friend arriving so unexpectedly and in such a sorry state, didn't break through her stupor.

'*Va préparer sa chambre.*' Elizabeth heard Richard's voice as if through a fog, even though he was standing right in front of her. She gazed up at him insensibly, shaking so uncontrollably her teeth were rattling in her head and the brandy was slopping about in the glass. When his strong hand closed about hers to steady it, she flinched away from the human contact. But this was Richard Pencarrow and not her uncle, so she allowed him to bring the glass to her lips. Even though she disliked him, she knew she could trust him and was grateful for his help. The amber liquid burned her throat as she swallowed it, spreading its warmth into her stomach and seeping into her blood.

'Let's get these wet clothes off you before you catch your death.'

His tone was so steady, so in command, that her stunned brain was happy to obey. She stood up on uncertain legs, letting him peel off her sodden garments, hardly noticing his hesitation when she was stripped down to her underclothes and his eyes narrowed at the bruised and scratched flesh that showed beneath her ripped camisole.

'I'll be back in a minute,' he told her gently, whipping a towel from the clothes horse by the range and draping it across her shoulders. 'You get that brandy down you.'

And then she was alone in the kitchen she'd worked in for so many years, servant, housekeeper, and yet virtually mistress of the house. Its familiarity calmed her, bringing her the presence of mind to pull off the rest of her clothes and wrap herself decently in the towel before Richard returned. The alcohol and the warmth of the room gradually penetrated through to her bones and her aching body began to relax.

'Eleezabett!' Chantal came back into the kitchen and rushed over to hug her in her small arms. '*Qu'est-ce que tu as? Et les cheveux!*'

The comfort of the girl's body against hers revived Elizabeth's spirit, and she managed to flash her a wan smile. She hadn't understood Chantal's words, of course, but she knew from the horror on the child's face as she had gazed up at her, that it was to do with the state she was in and doubtless her shorn hair. 'I had a little accident,' she answered, praying Chantal didn't notice the tremor in her voice. 'But I'm fine now. Your father rescued me.'

She glanced up as Richard came back into the room. He'd changed into dry clothes and his damp hair was brushed back from his forehead. 'Put this on,' he said, pushing a bundle into her lap. 'It'll be much too big. You could have had one of my mother's, but they smell somewhat musty after all these years.'

As he deliberately turned his back and made himself busy at the range, Elizabeth was thankful to do as she was told. The nightshirt was one of Josiah's and drowned her in a profusion of blue and white stripes, the sleeves reaching past her knees and the hem dragging several inches on the floor.

'*Que tu me fais rire comme ça!*' Chantal's light giggle broke the silence. 'Oh, it does not please Papa if I speak French.' She grimaced, pulling a mocking face at her father's back. 'You are very funny like zat!'

Richard turned to look over his shoulder, one eyebrow lifted whimsically, and his eyes glinted with a flicker of humour. 'I think we could all do with some hot food inside us,' he suggested, clearly trying to make his voice sound light. 'It's only vegetable stew, and I'm afraid it's nowhere near as good as yours.'

Elizabeth nodded and swivelled round in the chair to face table. She still felt so strange, cocooned in her own misery despite Richard's efforts. She mechanically spooned into her mouth the bowl of food he placed before her, her body warm and comfortable now, but her mind elsewhere.

'Bed, now, Chantal,' she heard Richard command.

'*Mais la vaisselle, Papa?*' the child questioned optimistically, looking at the dirty dishes.

'Leave it.'

'*Alors, bonne nuit, Papa. Et toi, Eleezabett.*'

Richard cocked his head, listening for his daughter's footsteps on the stairs. When he was satisfied she was out of earshot, he sat down sideways in the chair next to Elizabeth's, and taking her hands, obliged her to turn to face him. He fixed her gaze so intently, so searchingly, that she averted her eyes and stared down at her hands, still held firmly in his.

'So, it was your uncle who did this to you?'

His voice was low, calm, and she knew there was no way he'd let her escape his questioning. She opened her mouth twice, but the sound somehow stuck in her throat and instead she moved her head in the indication of a nod.

'And . . . and did he actually . . . I mean . . . Did he rape you, Elizabeth?'

She had to clamp her jaw at the sound of the heinous word and slowly shook her head. 'But . . . I think he might have done,' she answered in a tortured whisper. 'He was drunk. And just so . . . *angry*. He's never gone that far before.'

'*Before?*'

Her heart began to beat even faster and she cursed herself for saying too much, for losing control of what she felt inside. All her life, she'd kept the shame and the hurt of it locked away, and now she was being compelled to confess the truth to this man she didn't even like. 'When I was a child . . .' she muttered, her chin quivering.

'A child? Dear God, Elizabeth . . . !'

'No! I mean he never . . .' she said aloud now, meeting his gaze anxiously, for the savagery in his expression was frightening her. 'He loved his wife, my mother's sister, very much, you see. In his own selfish way, of course. And when she died . . . I look very like her, much more like her than my own mother, and he . . . Well, I think he always . . . He used . . . to kiss me. And then he . . .' Her voice cracked, the crucifying memories closing her throat. 'He touched me,' she managed to croak.

Richard leapt to his feet with such fury that his chair toppled over with a crash. 'Jesus Christ, Elizabeth! Why didn't you say something? You let me send you back there when . . .'

'I thought 'twould be all right!' she moaned defensively. 'I was so young then. I didn't understand. But I do now. I thought 'twouldn't happen again, and if it did, I could handle him. 'Tis always when he's drunk, you see. He . . . he loves me really,' she faltered, her voice dropping to a whisper again. 'He wants me to marry him. But he's never been violent like this before. I didn't expect . . .'

'And is that how you came by your face? And what in God's name happened to your hair?'

She stared at him, not quite sure how to take his appalled anger, and their eyes locked as if in mortal combat. 'He didn't hit me, if that's what you think. I slipped as he was chasing me and banged it on the table.' She paused as he drew a horrified breath through his teeth, and she added, almost as an apology, 'He did chop off my hair, though.'

The ensuing silence seemed interminable as Richard held her gaze, his mouth pressed in a hard line. But then his eyes softened and he exhaled heavily, his head tipped at a slight angle. 'Your hair's not so bad,' he said more calmly. 'I could get used to it, and it'll grow back. But *this*!' He took her completely by surprise by reaching out a hand and brushing his fingers tenderly over her cheek. She flinched even at his feather-light touch, a faint wince catching at the back of her throat. 'The man should be horsewhipped,' he grated as his hand fell to his side. 'It was still his fault that you fell. And there's a fresh hand mark across it. And I don't suppose it was the Dartmoor pixies put those scratches and bruises on . . .' He hesitated, nodding down towards her chest. 'On the rest of you,' he concluded abruptly. 'I'll have the bastard evicted tomorrow.'

'No!' Elizabeth was amazed by her own exclamation. 'There's my cousins, sir. Nathaniel can be very trying, but he's still no more than a child. And Nellie and I are very close. Without her, I'd never have got through these past weeks. And I'm very fond of Daniel. And then there's young David. I couldn't bear to see them thrown out of their home.'

Richard pursed his lips and contemplated her earnest expression as he righted the chair and sat down again, his eyes hardly leaving her face. 'You'll not go back there, though,' he commanded.

'No, sir.' She lowered her eyes, feeling reprimanded.

'What will you do, then?'

'Well,' she stammered, since it was really none of his business. 'I've been looking for work in Mary Tavy. I don't want to leave the area, you see. Only I couldn't find any. William Greenwood has always wanted me to work with him, so maybe . . . But perhaps I should go right away from Tavistock. That man, Mr Brett, approached my uncle wanting me to nurse his elderly mother.'

'What!'

'I was quite interested until I knew who 'twas. And that he'd tried to buy me from my uncle like a piece of meat. 'Twas why Uncle Matthew was so mad. Because I'd refused.'

She paused, waiting for Richard's reaction. His jaw was clenched, his mahogany eyes deepening with rage. But then he rolled his head in frustration and his bottom lip drew back from his teeth.

'I simply can't believe all this,' he croaked. 'I'm . . . so sorry. About your uncle. And not just now. What he . . . And I sent you straight back to him!'

''Twas not your fault, sir . . .'

'But why the hell didn't you *tell* me?'

''Tis . . . 'tis not exactly something you talk about,' she muttered, her head bowed shamefully. 'I've . . . I've never told anyone before.'

She heard him draw in an enormous breath and release it in a long, controlled stream. 'What you need is a good night's sleep,' he said decisively. 'And to make sure you get one, you can take some laudanum.' And when she opened her mouth in protest, he said forcefully, 'That's an order. You bossed *me* about enough when I was in *your* care.'

And despite herself, she returned his hesitant smile.

* * *

The sky was still dark and heavy with rain clouds when she awoke, but dawn had broken some time earlier. She put out a tentative arm, testing her limbs one by one. The ache that had racked every inch of her body the previous evening had gone, and even her cheek was only tender if she touched it. Her eyes swept about the familiar room, and her soul swelled as she gazed at the plastered ceiling with the thought that, come what may, she would never again sleep beneath the leaking thatch of her uncle's roof.

She sprang out of bed, nearly tripping on the hem of the nightshirt. Good heavens, she must look a sight! She hiked it up to her knees as she hurried down the stairs to the warmth of the kitchen.

Richard was in his shirtsleeves, sitting at one end of the table with a sea of papers strewn in front of him, his elbows resting on the wooden surface and his head in his hands. He obviously hadn't heard her pad into the room in her bare feet, and he visibly started when he saw her. His face instantly stiffened, but not before she caught the utter despair etched on his features.

He cleared his throat. 'How are we this morning?' he asked, his voice strange. 'Did you sleep well?'

'Yes, thank you, sir. Surprisingly, I did. May I . . .' she hesitated, 'may I pour myself some tea?' she asked, eyeing the pot.

'Of course. Help yourself.'

He went back to studying the papers, but when she sat down opposite him with the cup of hot, steaming liquid, he pushed his chair back from the table with a ponderous sigh and ran his hand through his hair.

'I've been thinking,' he said pensively. 'You can't go back to your uncle's, and you said you don't really want to go and live in Tavistock. Now . . . Chantal and I have just about muddled through here. But I want her to go to the village school, and now my leg's well on the mend, I've got to start working on the farm. Mending walls, checking the grazing, anything I can do in preparation for bringing in more stock, though God knows how I'm supposed to buy any.'

'How is your leg now, sir?' she asked distantly, for she had a shrewd idea where the conversation was leading.

He raised an ironic eyebrow. 'It wasn't too bad until some idiot made my horse throw me and I landed right on it.'

His gaze seemed to penetrate right through her and she lowered her eyes as colour flushed into her cheeks. 'I'm sorry, sir,' she mumbled.

'Don't be. I'm glad it happened. God knows what would have happened to you if we hadn't bumped into each other. Which brings me back to what I was saying. I need you back here.'

The words had come out as an ungracious command and Elizabeth glanced up, her eyes wide and her heart thudding in her chest. Come back. To Rosebank Hall. To the place she loved. Part of her wanted to cry out for joy, but the other part . . . Did she really want to work for Richard Pencarrow? He'd turned her out once before. His temper was short, and his tongue was so sharp he was in constant danger of cutting himself on it.

'I can't offer you any wages,' he went on stiffly when he saw her hesitation. 'You wouldn't be a servant. It would be a partnership, working together to try to salvage this place. But what I *can* offer you is a roof over your head and protection from your uncle. It's the least I can do. What happened was all my fault, after all.'

So that was it. He felt guilty. Well, she wasn't prepared to . . . 'You said before you didn't want me here,' she reminded him with a proud flick of her head.

Richard drew in a sharp breath. 'That might have been what I said, but it wasn't what I meant,' he answered sheepishly. 'To tell the truth, I didn't really want you to go at all, but . . . It was bad enough you living alone here with my father, but at least he was old and infirm. But with . . . with you and me . . . Surely you can see it wasn't right.'

'And it is now?' she demanded.

'No. No, it isn't. But it seems a good solution to both our problems. I can take the wagging tongues if you can,' he added dryly.

Elizabeth stared at him, her cheeks sucked in stubbornly. She wanted more than anything in the world to say yes, but what if . . . She hardly knew Richard Pencarrow. What if he turned out to be as bad as her uncle? What if he was deliberately deceiving her with his honourable manner? And .
. . and he'd never disclosed why he'd high-tailed it back from

France with a bullet wound in his leg. Something to do with the war, by all accounts, but the war was over, so why . . . ? What if he was a dangerous criminal, a wanted man?

The door that led to the small vestibule and the farm-yard beyond opened quietly and Chantal trotted in with a basket of eggs. Her little face lit up like the sun when she saw Elizabeth. Having deposited her harvest on the table, she danced up to her, grinning broadly so that her two emerging adult front teeth showed clearly in the comical gap.

'*Il y en a douze aujourd'hui,*' she proclaimed triumphantly. 'Zair eez twelve.'

'At least we won't starve today, then,' her father murmured.

'*Eleezabett est d'accord, Papa?*' she asked hopefully.

'Yes. Elizabeth agrees. I think.'

The child at once laced her arms about Elizabeth's neck, and Elizabeth met Richard's arresting eyes across the table. He stood up abruptly.

'Good. That's settled, then. Now, I must take the horse back to Tavistock. But first of all, I'm going to take the opportunity to ride round to some of the other farms. Find out what's what at the moment, and let them know I'm back in business. Might even get some work if I'm lucky,' he snorted wryly. 'But there's no carrier today and I'll have to walk back from Tavistock, so all in all, I'm likely to be out most of the day. Your clothes are dry, Elizabeth,' he added, nodding towards the clothes horse, 'but they are muddy so you may want to wash them. And they need stitching where . . .' He flapped his hand awkwardly across his own chest, his complexion deepening to crimson. 'I'll send a message to your cousin . . . Nellie, didn't you say . . . to bring your other things over. Whatever happens, you're not to go over there yourself. Understood?'

Elizabeth was dumbfounded as she glared at him over Chantal's head. Part of her felt she'd been coerced into staying and she wanted to dig in her heels. But surely anyone who'd single-handedly brought up such a sweet, enchanting child as Chantal couldn't be all bad. 'Yes, sir,' she gulped.

'And can we drop the "sir"?' he commanded. 'We're a partnership now. The name's Richard, in case you hadn't noticed.'

'Now baint this cosy? I might've knawed you'd come running back to 'en!'

Elizabeth's heart stopped beating as the door was flung open and Matthew burst into the kitchen, taking them all off guard. There was blood still matted in his hair from the wound she'd inflicted with the stone, and he looked as if he'd spent the night beneath the hedgerow where she'd left him. But he was sober enough now to take the few strides to where she was sitting, transfixed with dread and with Chantal clinging to her in fear. He took hold of her arm in a vice-like grip and swung her to her feet, sending the petrified child flying.

'You'm coming home, you little varmint!' he snarled, spittle spraying from his loose-lipped mouth.

'No she isn't.' Richard's voice was calm, ice-cold, and Elizabeth felt Matthew stiffen with surprise. 'And I suggest you leave before I fetch the constable. You'd be put away for what you've done to her. I'd have had you arrested last night if it wasn't for your children.'

Matthew's already florid face deepened to a livid puce, his eyes bulging. 'What lies 'ave you bin telling, eh?' he spat, and Elizabeth turned her head away from his stinking breath with a stifled squeal. 'You'm my ward an' you'll do as you'm teld! I've found a good position for you, an' you should be grateful!'

'No!' she shrieked with anger as she struggled to be free of his hold. 'I'll never . . .'

'But she isn't your ward.' Richard's cutting tone was so controlled it brought them both up short, and Elizabeth's frightened eyes quizzed him across the table. 'Not unless you have some legal papers to prove it, which I very much doubt. So she's free to do as she pleases, and just now she pleases to stay here with me. So I suggest you let go of her and take yourself home. And may I remind you that you haven't paid your rent for the last eighteen months. And from this Michaelmas gone, you must pay the full amount. Any deal you had with my father over Elizabeth's services is now terminated. She and I have other arrangements.'

'Oh, yes! I be certain you does! She be your live-in whore now, I suppose!' Matthew sneered viciously, his eyes so inflamed they were like two burning coals in his maddened face. And as he brutally jerked Elizabeth's arm, she gasped with the pain of it. 'Well, you'll not get away wi' it! You'm coming home, maid!'

His brawny hand closed even more tightly around her arm as he began to drag her towards the door. The agony in her shoulder ripped up into her neck, making her feel faint, and for a horrible, sickening moment, she felt she was going to pass out.

She heard rather than saw the punch that smashed across Matthew's jaw, sending him reeling. All at once she found herself crouched on the floor, glancing up just in time to see Richard stumble on his healing leg from the force of the blow he'd dealt her uncle. But he'd hardly recovered his balance when Matthew unexpectedly hurtled across the kitchen and drove his massive fist upwards into his stomach. Richard fell back, his right thigh slamming against the table, and he collapsed with a sharp cry in a shuddering, helpless heap.

Elizabeth held her breath, her heart pounding, as Matthew's thickset figure towered over his victim and he raised his great fist again. She sprang to her feet, ready to launch herself at his back and tear at his hair. But he seemed to hesitate, and thinking better of it, slowly lowered his arm and backed away, panting heavily and wiping his sleeve across his salivating lips.

It was in that moment of stillness that they all heard the distinctive, metallic click of a gun being cocked. At the ominous sound, each one of them turned to stone.

'*Allez-vous-en, ou je tire!*' Chantal's quivering squeak echoed in the large, flag-stoned room.

Elizabeth had no more idea than Matthew what the child was saying, but the meaning was crystal clear as she held the rifle in practised hands and aimed it directly at Matthew's burly chest. His eyes gleamed white with terror and, inch by inch, he lifted his shaking hands in submission.

'God Almighty.' Elizabeth barely caught Richard's muttered oath as he attempted to straighten up and staggered across to his daughter, still bent double. '*Je t'ai dit mille fois de ne jamais le toucher sans moi!*' he spluttered angrily.

'*Mais vous* êtes *ici, Papa!*' she answered, her small face fiercely puckered.

Richard gently took the gun from her hands, carefully de-cocked it and, opening the chamber, tipped out both the cartridges. Elizabeth sighed with relief, and Matthew, still stumbling in his terror, backed towards the door.

'You hit me fust,' he stammered, his fingers feeling for the doorway.

'Just get out!' Richard hissed at him. 'And if you ever lay a hand on Elizabeth again, so help me God, I'll kill you!'

There was something so appalling in the way he ground out the last three words, his face a deathly shade of grey, that Elizabeth felt her hair stand on end. For several seconds, he seemed incarcerated in some ungodly dread of his own, his eyes wild and savage. Matthew took the opportunity to scuttle out through the door, and Elizabeth immediately gazed up into Richard's face.

'Sir?' she mouthed.

He blinked at her, and then rolled his head as if throwing off whatever tormenting memory had gripped him. Then his lips twitched into the shadow of a smile and colour gradually returned to his cheeks.

'And we haven't even had breakfast yet,' he muttered. 'I brought Chantal back here because I thought . . .' He released a weighty sigh and, setting the gun on the table, rubbed his hand across his aching stomach before he turned to Chantal who appeared to be rooted to the spot. 'Don't you *ever* touch those guns again without my permission!' he bellowed at her.

'*Non, Papa. Je suis désolée.*' The girl's chin quivered, her forlorn face crumpling, and Elizabeth frowned with compassion, even though she herself still shook like a leaf.

'Sir, I think she's been frightened enough without you shouting at her,' she dared to whisper.

Richard glanced at her, and his taut features slackened. 'Yes, you're right. As ever. Come here!' he beckoned, and sat down promptly on one of the chairs before Chantal climbed onto his lap and, clinging about his neck, wept against his shoulder. Elizabeth noticed him wince and he shifted the child from his right thigh onto his other leg.

'God, what a brilliant start to the day.' He was stroking Chantal's hair, and her sobs were already quietening to a sniffle. 'It's my fault. I'd noticed there was no lock on the cabinet when I took the guns out and cleaned them the other day. It must have given her the idea. Until then, I'd forgotten what you'd said about my father acquiring a rifle. But I have taught her how to handle a shotgun.'

'Well, she seems to have frightened my uncle off, anyway,' Elizabeth ventured. 'I don't think we'll have any more trouble from him.'

'No, we won't,' Richard snorted in reply. 'I can't possibly have a man like that as a tenant. I'm sorry, Elizabeth, but he'll have to go.'

'Oh, sir, no, *please*!' she protested, although quite why she felt so adamant, she really wasn't sure. And squaring her shoulders, she added courageously, 'I mean, he was right. You *did* hit him first.'

Richard stared at her in disbelief, and then slowly shook his head with a wry grunt. 'True,' he reluctantly agreed. 'But if he ever dares to lay so much as a finger on you . . .'

'Yes, sir.'

'Richard,' he corrected her. And his mouth broke into an amused smile as he contemplated her. 'You know, you really do look very funny in my father's nightshirt,' he observed. He chuckled then, and as his eyes travelled downwards and then back to her face, his shoulders shook as he laughed aloud, a light, soft laugh, and Elizabeth couldn't stop herself from joining in. She was beginning to think there was more to Richard Pencarrow than met the eye.

* * *

Maurice Brett paced irritably up and down the drawing room. The girl hadn't shown up that morning, and his anticipation had turned to a dark frustration. The uncle had assured him she would come, his lips almost drooling at the large sum of money he'd been promised in addition to the tidy salary his niece would receive. But perhaps, after all, the bastard couldn't be bought and wanted to keep her for himself. Poor girl! Something akin to pity touched Maurice's heart. The man was a bully. He could see it in his eyes, in the cocksure way he carried his head on his swarthy neck. Although probably ten years Maurice's junior, he'd let himself go to seed, his thinning hair greasy and unkempt, and his thickset body encumbered by a rotund paunch. The thought of his stained, gargantuan hands on her fragile body, his unwashed flesh against hers, was repulsive. *He*, however . . . Now, he would woo her in a gentlemanly fashion. Bloody hell, he'd need to after the way he'd put her back up at old Josiah's funeral!

She obviously felt . . . well, *some* sort of attachment to Richard Pencarrow, although quite what, he couldn't fathom. And what girl wouldn't, with those blasted good looks? But there was something strained in the relationship between them, so perhaps it was merely loyalty to the family she served. *He* would certainly expect that in the person who was to nurse his mother and who, in time, he prayed would become more than that, if he played his cards right. He was of reasonable height and had kept his figure pretty well. His face was still handsome — apart from his nose, of course — with relatively few lines, and although his hair was beginning to grey, he had plenty of it. And he knew how to behave when it suited him. He'd have to be patient, of course. But

215

there was really no reason why he shouldn't eventually make her his wife.

The Bretts weren't aristocracy at all, just clever businessmen. Mrs Elliot had told him all about the girl's background which, to his delight, was much more elevated than he realized. Lizzie they called her, though he would use her full name, Elizabeth. In addition to all her other attributes, she used to read the newspapers to Josiah, Mrs Elliot had said, discussing all the politics and world affairs that were reported in the *Tavistock Gazette* as well as the local business news. So, all in all, it would be no disgrace if the girl eventually became Mrs Maurice Brett.

She was absolutely everything he'd ever wanted and never found in any of the women he'd known in his life. So alive, so vibrant, he would be the envy of all his acquaintances. She was intelligent, caring, spirited, and still the most beautiful thing he'd ever clapped his eyes on. Surely . . . surely he wasn't actually falling in love with her? But what he felt was so different from the hot fire that engulfed him when, under cover of darkness, he crept into the lowly Fitzford cottage, greedily satisfied his selfish lust with the miner's wife while her husband was on his shift, and then carelessly threw a few shillings on the tumbled bed before stealing away again. No. What he felt for Elizabeth Thornton was beyond his own comprehension.

'Maurice!' The cackling voice rumbled through the ceiling at him, and his head receded with a shudder into his hunched shoulders as the repeated thump from the room above came yet again. Sweet Jesus, when would the testy old shrew give him some peace? If she didn't shut up this minute, he was likely to run up the stairs and hold a pillow over her wrinkled, toothless face until she suffocated. Couldn't she just leave him alone long enough to enjoy his reverie? To imagine what it would be like to hold that ethereal creature in his arms? He shook his head, his eyes screwed tightly, as the vision slipped away from him.

'Yes, Mother!' he sighed, his fists clenching into tight balls as he made for the door.

TWENTY-TWO

In the rear vestibule of the farmhouse, Richard stamped the snow from his boots and shaking the melting flakes from his coat, hung it on one of the hooks before entering the kitchen.

'I wish you'd keep that door locked,' he said gruffly as he padded across the floor in his stockinged feet, and stuffed some old newspaper into his boots, setting them before the range to dry.

'My uncle's not been near the place again.' Elizabeth glanced up from her final preparations for the evening meal.

'That's true. He even went to the bank to pay the rent direct. All the same . . .'

'My door's always open to people who need help. I sold four bottles of cough tincture today.'

'Before this blizzard set in, I imagine.'

'Oh, Papa, you 'ave cold!' Chantal shrieked, flying into her father's arms as he warmed his hands in the heat from the range. '*Ah, non!* You *are* cold!' she corrected herself.

'So would you be if you'd been up on the moor all day,' he grunted. 'I took the last of the mangolds up to Mr Widcock's wethers for him. Had to dig a couple of them out of a snowdrift. A fair exchange for having his bull cover our two house cows, I'd say!'

'They won't calve till the autumn, though, sir. And their present milk will dry up about the end of March, I reckon.'

'Just have to go without then, won't we? At least both their present calves are heifers. And stop calling me "sir",' he complained irritably.

'We'll have no milk to sell. Or make into butter. Richard,' she added, his Christian name sounding uneasily on her tongue.

But he seemed not to notice her embarrassment as he went on, 'We'll have some ewes' milk in the spring, though. Which reminds me. Mr Widcock wants to take me on for the lambing, but what about our own ewes? Poor old George isn't up to it on his own. His legs have been so bad these last weeks he can hardly walk. He only just about managed putting the ram in with the ewes in the first place.'

'Oh, I can take care of the lambing,' Elizabeth shrugged. 'I helped Uncle Matthew every year from when I was four year old.'

Richard arched an eyebrow at her. 'Do you think you could? Then I could work for Mr Widcock. We really do need the money. Hmm. Is there no end to your talents?' he teased her now, his eyes dancing roguishly. 'You know, I didn't realize quite what a gem you were when I asked you to come back.'

'*Asked!*' Her face flushed with indignation as she took courage from his relaxed attitude. 'As I do mind, you more or less ordered me!'

'Well . . .' He pulled a mocking grimace. 'It hasn't been so bad, has it? We seem to get along well enough. I'll tell Mr Widcock yes then, when I go up the day after tomorrow. I think I'll go into Tavistock in the morning, if we're not snowed in. Try to sell a couple of my grandfather's clocks. That French one in the drawing room should be worth a fair sum. Then maybe I can buy some more ewes. I'll keep an eye out at any auctions. You never know, I might pick up some bargains.'

'D'you think we could possibly order some more coal?' Elizabeth dared to ask him. 'Even just living in the kitchen, we're nearly out.'

Richard exhaled heavily as he pumped some water into the stone sink to wash his hands. 'Yes, I know. But unless I can pay off my father's bill at the coal merchants . . . So let's hope I can get a good price for that clock. Otherwise, I'll be starting work on the hedgerows soon, and we could try burning the brushwood from that on the range. Depends how green it is, really. I reckon there's a couple of dead trees to come down, but that won't solve our immediate problem. And I reckon it'll be up on the moor to cut peat in the summer.'

Elizabeth chewed on her lip as what she'd been thinking all day passed through her mind again. 'Sir . . . I mean, Richard,' she began hesitantly, 'I have a little money. My mother left it to me, and I added to it whenever I could . . .'

'No.' Richard's shoulders tensed. 'I wouldn't hear of it. If I fail in this, you'll need it. But . . . thank you for the offer. Now then,' he turned round, leaning backwards against the sink as he dried his hands on the towel. 'I'm famished, and, as ever, your cooking smells delicious, Beth. And don't tell me it's the herbs, because I know it is. And I also know that without your vegetable garden, we'd have starved.'

His face creased into such an appreciative smile that her heart quite definitely missed a beat. He'd taken to calling her Beth since Elizabeth was, he said, too formal, yet Lizzie in his opinion was too plain for her abilities. He thought Beth was more suitable if she didn't mind. She'd been astonished, and yet she found she rather liked it. There was something both friendly and respectful about it, and she'd begun to wonder if she hadn't misjudged Richard Pencarrow. In the month she'd been living back at Rosebank Hall, a quiet contentment had slowly crept over her, soothing away the injuries her uncle had inflicted upon her. Richard could often slip into a dark depression that easily quickened his sharp tongue, but she'd come to realize it was born out of worry. And he could equally well display such a keen sense of humour that she couldn't help but laugh at him. At moments like these, she prayed that nothing in her life would change.

* * *

Maurice Brett slammed the front door behind him, his jaw clenched with such brutal anger, the veins in his neck stood out in thick cords. Dear God, the old hag would be the death of him! He could still hear her now, ranting at him from the pulpit of her bed and threatening him with the cane when his father returned. He felt he would suffocate if he spent another minute in the house, and had pulled on his overcoat and silk top hat without the least thought of where he would go. And now as he strode down the long front path, wrapping his scarf around his mouth and nose against the stinging cold of the February night, he yearned desperately for the comforting curves of the miner's wife who lived in one of the Fitzford cottages. He couldn't go there, of course, for he wasn't sure if her husband was working or not, but either way, he wouldn't be going anywhere near the place for the time being. An outbreak of smallpox had been reported there in the paper last week and it appeared to be spreading. There was no way Maurice would put himself at risk. He wondered vaguely about the woman he'd frequented for a couple of years now. He'd be sad if she died, he supposed. He'd been quite fond of her at first and it had been a convenient arrangement. But there were plenty more where she'd come from, and he *was* getting a trifle bored with her. Though if he could only find someone who matched up to Elizabeth Thornton, who might become his wife, there would be no need for these sordid dalliances. And it would put an end to his mother's raving at him to get married. It was ridiculous, but he simply couldn't put the girl out of his mind.

Maurice turned in the opposite direction from the Fitzford cottages and sauntered along Plymouth Road, taking care not to slip on the icy pavement. He could call in at the

Bedford Hotel and see if any of his business acquaintances were drinking in the opulent lounge. But his mind was restless, his body pumping with pent-up energy. A cab drew up alongside him, depositing its passengers at the front door of the hotel, the handsome grey that pulled it breathing wreaths of white vapour into the frosty night.

'Mary Tavy. The Buller's Arms,' Maurice commanded, and leaping inside, rapped the handle of his cane urgently on the roof.

He sat back, amazed at himself. There was still snow blanketing the moor from the blizzard back in January, but as far as he knew, the main road to Mary Tavy was clear. The mining village was very familiar to him, for he had fingers in many pies, including shares in the railway which passed through Mary Tavy. He'd never sought company there, though, and certainly not of the sort he craved just now. But no one would recognize him. Many miners would have flocked to such a thriving mining community for work, leaving their wives and sweethearts many miles away at home for months on end. So were there not those other women in the village who earned their living by stepping into the breach?

* * *

Matthew Halse had to calm the spring in his step as he crossed the long wooden clam over the river. The wooden bridge was perilously slippery in the glacial temperatures that had gripped the region for several weeks, and he didn't want to end up in the freezing water! His way was lit by the hurricane lamp that swung from his thick fist, the glow transforming the smile on his face into a lurid grin. Just a pint at the Buller's Arms and then on to Widow Silverlock's humble but cosy abode. Her pension from the miners' club was shortly to expire after the statutory six months following the death of her husband — silly beggar had been careless when blasting at a low level and blown himself up — and she was looking for a replacement to support her. And he was looking for a new wife who was willing to give him what he wanted every night — unless he was too drunk to perform. Which was less often now, and he preened himself on being a new man. Now that little bitch was quite definitely beyond his reach, tucked up with that good-looking bastard at the Hall, he'd had to do something, hadn't he? And Widow Silverlock suited him very well. A comely woman and a not very strict Methodist, she was a plain speaker, and he'd found himself quite willing to smarten up his appearance, taking a wash now and then, and shaking the moths from his Sunday best, which hadn't seen the light of day for years. He even *felt* different, curbing his blasphemous tongue quite naturally. To his surprise, she'd allowed his roaming hands free range, apparently welcoming his attentions to her ample bosom and wobbling thighs. Somewhat unlike the slenderness of his dear departed Margaret or that fairylike cheel of a niece — and he almost salivated at the idea of what she was getting up to in Richard Pencarrow's bed — but the change was new and exciting, and he hadn't had 'it' for so long now! When Widow Silverlock would actually let him have 'it' he wasn't sure. But he had the feeling that even if she had to become the second Mrs Halse, it would be well worth it.

When he finally reached the comfort of the Buller's Arms, he sat down at a table with a glass of his favourite ale, aware of the jeering eyes upon him at seeing him spruced up to the nines, and delicately wiped the froth from his upper lip with a clean handkerchief that Nellie had pressed for him. He was quietly anticipating the pleasures that were to come when, to his surprise, a gentleman sat down opposite him with the clear intention of engaging him in conversation. He tipped his head in curiosity, but drew back sharply when the fellow unwrapped the scarf from his face, and he recognized who it was.

'What happened to your niece, then?' Maurice barked, fixing him with steel-grey eyes. 'She never turned up after our agreement.'

Matthew gulped, feeling the heat prickle beneath his tight collar, and his gaze darted towards the door. But he could hardly make a dash for it, could he? ''Twould seem her knawed you, an' refused,' he answered accusingly in an effort to hide his nervousness. 'I tried my best but I cuddn't force her.'

'You could have threatened to throw her out,' Maurice snarled, 'then she'd have had no choice.'

'That be the trouble, Mr Brett, sir. Her be back wi' that divil Pencarrow.'

Maurice's face, already flushed with a double brandy, turned an ominous black, and his fingers closed so tightly around the glass, which held a second measure, that he was in danger of crushing it. Pencarrow! That . . . that bloody sanctimonious pup who, when it came to it, was probably no better than his father! Well! His mouth opened and shut several times like a goldfish, his eyes bulging out of their sockets so that from the other side of the table, Matthew was afraid he might take his wrath out on *him*!

'Er . . . Yes, I knaws!' Matthew stammered, trying to pacify him. 'I be that angered, like! Turned down *my* offer of marriage back along, her did! Think her were so white as snow, you wud, an' then her do go an' live back with 'en!'

He stopped abruptly, his fear subsiding as Maurice's tense face slowly relaxed and he appeared to have recovered himself. Matthew picked up his tankard. He couldn't get out of the place quick enough, but he was damned if he was going to leave the best part of a pint! He gulped it down in one draught, ale dribbling down his chin which he wiped on the back of his sleeve when he had finished.

'Goodnight to you, then,' he muttered, and shot out through the door.

Maurice didn't bother to watch him go, but swirled the brandy round in the glass before downing it in one. By God, he'd need several more of those to quell his boiling fury! It was bad enough that the girl had slipped through his fingers and dashed his plans to persuade her to become his wife. But to think of her living with Richard Pencarrow! It was nearly three months since she'd failed to turn up on his doorstep, and he'd tried hard to put the galling frustration to the back of his mind, but now . . . ! The yearning burned inside him, fanned by the anger that had been simmering in his heart for years. Richard Pencarrow had ruined his face, while the bastard himself was still young, in his early thirties at most. Tall, straight backed and broad shouldered with strong, chiselled good looks that would turn any girl's head. How long would it be before . . . Hell. His teeth ground dangerously at the vision of the pair of them rolling between the sheets . . . How he *hated* Richard Pencarrow! He'd bloody well make sure he got back at him somehow!

Maurice got to his feet, still trembling with anger, and went up to the bar. He had to shoulder in between two young lads, miners by the looks of them. One of them winked at the other, shifting an openly mocking eye at Maurice's fancy attire, and Maurice drew a seething breath through his nostrils. Local boys, clearly the cocky sort who'd know no doubt where he could find the sort of woman he was looking for. And then the thought struck him like a bolt from the blue.

'Fancy a brandy, boys?'

He saw them exchange a wary glance. What did the stranger want? It took all sorts, they supposed, but there was a limit to what even *they* would do for a few shillings. But what harm could a brandy apiece do?

''Tis mortal kindly of you this snipey weather,' one of them replied cautiously.

'Good.' Maurice secretly smiled. 'Two more for these gentlemen, please,' he ordered, noting but choosing to ignore their sniggers. 'Now tell me, does either of you know someone by the name of Lizzie Thornton? Pretty girl, I've heard. Knows about herbal remedies and such.'

Thomas Arkwright almost choked as he spluttered into his brandy.

* * *

'Once zree is zree, twice zree is six, zree times zree is nine, four times zree is twelve. *Voilà!*' Chantal chortled proudly. 'I commence to be very good, *n'est-ce pas?*'

'You do indeed!' Elizabeth laughed in reply. 'But "I'm getting very good" would be more normal. Commence is very formal, like in a business letter.'

'Oh, Eleezabett!' The child released a dejected sigh. 'I 'ave so much to learn.'

'But you're doing very well!' Elizabeth put down the knife with which she was chopping the parsnips, and placed an encouraging arm about Chantal's shoulders. 'Most children of your age can't write their own name, let alone say their tables in two different languages. *I* can't do that! Now, you do *like* school, don't you?'

'Oh, yes!' Her eyes beamed with enthusiasm. 'I like to be wiz ze uzer children! In France, zair was no school. It is Papa 'oo teach me, and my gran'parents.'

'Your grandparents?' Elizabeth's eyebrows lifted in curiosity.

The little girl's face instantly shut down, her jaw clamped and her eyes like two fierce globes. 'But zay is dead,' she almost snarled.

Elizabeth snatched in her breath. There was something horrifying in the way the child had spoken that shocked her deeply. It reminded her of when Richard had threatened to kill her uncle if he ever interfered with her again, and his words had seemed to hold some horrific hidden meaning for him. But just then, a strong draught gusted across the kitchen as the door to the outer hall rattled on its latch. They heard the outer door being locked and bolted, and Richard elbowed his way into the room, unusually still wearing his boots and evidently carrying something beneath his coat.

'Talk about March winds.' He frowned, but his lips were wriggling as if he was trying not to break into a smile. Then a harsh cough overtook him and he sniffed hard. 'I think I'm getting a cold,' he grumbled. 'I haven't had one for years, and I have to catch one just now with lambing about to start. And there's the oats to sow at the end of the month.'

'Well, 'tis lucky I've some cold remedies you can take,' Elizabeth said coming towards him. 'I think I've some elderberry syrup left, and I can easily make up some rosemary, sage and thyme . . . Ooh!'

It was then that she noticed the little black nose snuffling out from beneath his coat, followed by a black and white snout and two round, searching eyes. Her mouth stretched in delight, and when she looked at Richard's face, he was grinning broadly as he held out the squirming ball of fluff and deposited it in Chantal's eager arms.

'*Oh, Papa! Comme il est mignon!*' She squealed with glee as the puppy cocked its head up at her, one ear comically lifted. '*Comment il s'appelle?*'

'It's a she, actually.' Richard chuckled at his daughter as he stooped to unlace his boots. 'And you can choose a name for her.'

'Oh, but I do not know a good name, not in English,' Chantal pouted, but then her face exploded with joy as the animal's rough pink tongue licked her chin.

'I've only blackberry syrup left,' Elizabeth said over her shoulder as she reached up to her shelf of remedies. 'But 'tis still very good. Oh, I know!' she cried, surprised at her own flash of inspiration. 'What about Bramble as a name?'

'Bramble?' Chantal's forehead corrugated into a frown.

'*Mûrier sauvage,*' Richard translated. 'Sounds a lot better in English.'

'Bramble it is! Do you like, Papa?'

'Oh, yes.' But he was looking at Elizabeth, his expression inscrutable as his eyes remained fixed on her face. 'But she's not a pet, Chantal. She'll be a working dog, so you mustn't spoil her.'

'*Quoi? Je ne comprends . . .*'

'*Ce n'est pas un animal domestique,*' Richard translated again. '*C'est pour travailler. J'en ai besoin.*'

But Chantal evidently wasn't paying too much attention as she dropped on all fours in pursuit of the young animal, and Richard rolled his eyes in exasperation. 'Mr Widcock gave her to me as an extra for all the work I've done for him. She's the runt of the litter and no one wanted her. But I don't mind how small she is if she does her job.'

'How old is she?'

'Four months, despite her size. She seems pretty obedient already, so I'll be able to start training her as a work dog before long. I just hope *mademoiselle* here doesn't ruin her chances by mollycoddling her.' He nodded briefly at the antics of the two young creatures who'd clearly become instant friends. 'Perhaps we can find some old blankets to make a bed for her, but she's to come no further into the house than the kitchen. I'll really need an obedient dog if my plans succeed.'

''Twas good of Mr Widcock to give her to you.'

'I've worked damned hard for him, mind.' He dropped down heavily in one of the kitchen chairs, his long legs stretched in front of him as weariness pulsed down his limbs. 'And I'll probably be up there for three solid weeks once lambing starts. Are you sure you and George can manage our ewes on your own? There's nearly fifty with the ones I bought at auction. Some of them are quite old ladies. Thankfully, they've been mainly pasture fed, so their teeth are good and they should have a few years left in them yet.'

'I do realize how precious they are,' Elizabeth assured him. 'But I've been lambing since I was four year old, and George has a lifetime of experience. I'm sure we can manage between us. I can't do the ear-marking, mind.'

'Not done that myself since I was nineteen. If George can't do it and the neutering, I'll have to get old Joe in, if he's still around. But it's not until a month after lambing, so . . .' He stifled an irritated cough. 'I never thought I'd see the day I had to be a labourer on someone else's farm, leastways not back here.'

'Pride, sir?' she suggested softly.

He met her gaze, and his mouth screwed awkwardly. 'Probably,' he admitted.

She bit on her lip, colour flooding to her cheeks. 'Everyone's entitled to a little pride, you know. You've made a good start on the farm. You should be proud of that.'

He stole a furtive glance at her. 'I couldn't have achieved what little I have without you, Beth. We've one hell of a struggle ahead, but I hope you'll stay here.'

'Oh, I think so,' she answered lightly, but she was aware of the flutter in her heartbeat. 'I think Chantal would be upset if I left.'

Richard mumbled something she didn't catch, and then jerked his head towards the week's *Tavistock Gazette* on the table. 'I'll have a look through the paper after we've eaten. See if there's any more auctions coming up. I might've earned enough to buy another weaned calf or two. Heifers, of course. One went for fourteen shillings when I bought the sheep. The farm could just about support a dozen dairy cows, and I've plenty of grazing. But what I'd really like is a pair of horses, if only I could afford to feed them.'

'Talking of the paper, 'tis reported the smallpox is spreading in Tavistock. They're advising revaccination for older children and adults. I think we should pay a visit to the Vaccination Officer. The surgery times are in the paper.'

'Yes, I agree,' Richard nodded. 'And the sooner the better.'

And then both their heads turned at Chantal's shrieks of merriment as she followed the prancing puppy as it explored its new home.

* * *

When Chantal entered the kitchen the next morning, her eyes were gleaming black with excitement as they eagerly searched for the new puppy. 'Where is Bramble?' she asked, dancing up to the table.

'Your father's taken her with him. He was going to check the new ewes in the top field. He wants her to get used to being with sheep from the start.'

'Oh.' Chantal's face fell with disappointment.

'And you, young lady, have school. So hurry up and eat your breakfast, or you'll be late. You'll see Bramble again this evening.'

'But I can tell ze uzer children about 'er, *n'est-ce pas?*'

'Of course!' Elizabeth smiled as she wrapped a chunk of bread and some cheese in a cloth for her. 'But the children are all from local farms, and I'm afraid they won't find another puppy very interesting. Did you not have a dog in France?'

'*Non,*' Chantal replied between mouthfuls. 'We only grow zings in ze ground. But we share two 'orses wiz anuzer farmer, so we 'ave to leave zem be'ind.'

Elizabeth softly pursed her lips. The child said more than her father, but it was clear neither of them was going to divulge very readily the reason for their flight from France. A shadow darkened Elizabeth's heart, as she still didn't know if it was wise for her to be living under the same roof as a possible criminal.

'Chantal, you must try to say "th" instead of "z",' she chided, glad of something to change her train of thought. 'Put the tip of your tongue out between your teeth and blow. Look, like this — "th".'

The child obediently copied her, her young brow pleated in concentration. She blew so hard, her cheeks puffed out like two ripe peaches. In an instant they were both laughing so raucously they scarcely noticed Richard burst in through the back door with Bramble bouncing around his heels. Without a word, he strode across the kitchen and out into the hall.

The levity slid from Elizabeth's face. 'Richard?' she called after him. But before she'd reached the door, he stormed back in, the rifle slung over his shoulder by its leather strap as he stuffed a handful of cartridges into his jacket pocket. Elizabeth stared at him, slack-jawed, as she took in his grim face. 'Whatever's the matter?' she hardly dared to ask.

He glared at her, his mouth tight and his lips almost white as he growled viciously between clenched teeth. 'Some bloody idiot left the gate open and the new ewes have got out onto the moor!' he exploded. 'They managed to get on top of the tor and half of them went over the edge! Those that aren't dead need putting out of their misery!'

'What!' A cold horror trickled down Elizabeth's spine as she stared at him in disbelief. He'd worked incredibly hard to earn the money for those ewes, struggling at the same time to have his own land ready for bringing in more stock and pushing himself so hard when he should have still been convalescing. He had every right to be so vexed. 'But . . . I don't understand,' she stammered.

'Do I have to repeat myself?' he yelled, and swiftly spinning on his heel, poked his face down towards his daughter. 'It was you, wasn't it?' he bawled. 'You keep going up to look at them, don't you, and then you sauntered onto the moor, which I've forbidden you to do anyway, and left the damned gate open!'

Elizabeth's neck stretched with fury and indignation as Chantal gazed at him, teeth chattering as she tried to speak. '*Je . . . je ne comprends pas,*' she finally stuttered.

'*C'était toi! Tu as laissé la barrière ouverte!*'

'*Mais non, Papa!*' she protested, cowering beneath him.

A grunt of exasperation rasped at the back of his throat. 'Oh, what the hell does it matter *who* left it open,' he muttered under his breath as he made for the door.

Elizabeth's lips screwed into a seething knot as she stepped boldly into his path. 'You shouldn't talk to her like that! Look at her! You've terrified her!'

For a hideous moment she thought he might strike her as he drew in a furious breath, his eyes narrowed with menace. But then he simply strode past her and made for the farmyard. 'And keep an eye on that damned dog!' he called over his shoulder as he slammed the door behind him.

* * *

Ten minutes later as she hurried down the track to take Chantal to school, Elizabeth shuddered as a rifle shot echoed down from the moor. Then another. And another, until she lost count. Ten, eleven, was it? And with every one, another hope for their future was dashed. But perhaps she shouldn't care? After Richard's display of temper just now, she questioned her own sanity at staying on at the Hall.

Neither Richard nor the two girls saw the figures crouching behind the stone wall, their hands over their mouths to smother their chortling sniggers of glee. They'd have to lie low for a while so that Pencarrow wouldn't see them congratulating themselves on the night's work. They might even miss the beginning of their shift, but that wouldn't be unusual for Thomas Arkwright and Samuel Grainger. What did it matter anyway? The stranger would pay them handsomely for their troubles, and if they kept it up, they might never need go down the stinking mine again! And it felt mortal good to get their own back on old Josiah's son! There were no guesses who warmed his bed at night, and they'd both been itching to get in her drawers for years and pay her back for that wretched trick she'd played on them, giving them both the skits for days on end. And though Tom had never breathed a word of it to another living soul, the jealousy that riddled his mind was two-fold. No one else knew that before Richard Pencarrow it had been her uncle as well. Yet he, Thomas Arkwright, who was irresistible to any other woman, had never had a look in.

* * *

Maurice Brett amicably doffed his cap at his neighbour as he tripped jauntily along Plymouth Road in the direction of Tavistock's centre. A brisk wind overnight had chased away the heavy, rain-sodden mist that had enshrouded the Tavy valley for days. Now no more than a clutch of small, cotton-wool clouds scuttled across a sparkling blue sky. It was cold despite the sunshine, but then it was still March. There was little sign of any buds on the trees, although daffodils were breaking out in sheltered corners in the long front gardens of the elegant villas.

Life was looking up. Or, somewhat ironically, he mused, the hand of the Grim Reaper was gradually creeping nearer his mother's neck. What a relief it would be when it finally had her in its grasp. She was his mother and he knew it was an evil thought, but she was driving him insane. And she, poor soul, what sort of life did she have — bed-ridden, incontinent, confused, when once she'd been so absorbed in her society life that she'd virtually abandoned her small son? The situation was even worse now she'd suffered a mild stroke. It hadn't curbed her speech though, more was the pity, and her haranguing of him — every hour of the day it seemed — never let up. Driven from his own home, he'd spent more time than ever looking after his business interests, and joining his acquaintances at the Bedford Hotel. He didn't even have the distraction of the woman from the Fitzford cottage any longer, since she'd succumbed to the horrible death from smallpox. He was sorry for that. But it was time to move on.

Perhaps he'd call in at the bank to see what profits he'd made in the last few days. The thought set him rubbing together his finely gloved hands and brought a satisfied smirk to his lips.

But suddenly his face hardened into a grim mask and his heart began leaping about inside him. There she was. Standing at the end of the queue outside the Vaccination Officer's and holding the hand of the dark little girl he recognized as Richard Pencarrow's daughter. Jesus Christ! The sight of her quite took his breath away. It was madness, he knew. He was more than old enough to be her father, and yet the desire to possess her, to have her as his own, was driving him out of his senses.

He was powerless to resist the need to speak to her and his feet seemed to make their own path towards her. Elizabeth looked up as he approached, the smile from her conversation with the child slipping from her face when she saw who it was, and her golden eyes glinting with animosity.

'Good day, Miss Thornton.'

She said nothing, but stared at him with open hostility, her small chin tilted with defiance. Dear God, what a mettlesome little thing she was, but tempered with refined composure. It made his pulse beat even harder. He cleared his throat.

'Vaccination. Ah, very wise.' He nodded his head with slow deliberation, trying to make himself as amiable as possible. 'I called in my own physician a week or so ago. Attended my entire household, servants, everyone. But then I pride myself on caring for my workers. So much better than queuing here with any Tom, Dick and Harry. But I suppose you can't afford a physician's fees.' He stopped himself adding that he'd heard Richard had suffered bad luck over some sheep, as she might question him on how he knew. Instead, he managed a casual lift of his eyebrows. 'And what about Ritchie? Or is he of the opinion the smallpox is of no consequence?'

Elizabeth straightened her shoulders, her jaw clenched with contempt and her eyes boldly meeting his from beneath the brim of her battered felt bonnet. 'Mr Pencarrow has a heavy cold and 'twas considered appropriate to wait until he's better. Not that 'tis any concern of yours.' She stared back at him, her expression so scathing that Maurice was torn between anger and delight at her spirit.

'Then I wish him a speedy recovery. Please give him my regards.' He raised his hat, but his expression was stiff, his grey eyes cold as he spun on his heel and sauntered on his way with deliberate calm. Inside the hard outer shell of his body, his flesh was trembling. He could just imagine Ritchie Pencarrow tucked up in bed with that glorious creature tenderly mopping his fevered brow. Just as a loving mother should care for her child, but as Patience Brett never had done for him! What an irony her name was! She'd never kissed her son goodnight, never looked after him when he was ill. Elizabeth Thornton, now, she would nurse Ritchie devotedly, tending to his every need — whatever that might be! What had begun as a tiny rosebud of envy somewhere deep inside Maurice was blossoming into a tangle of jealous briars whose cruel barbs were tightening around his soul. He'd always managed to obtain everything he wanted, trifling things that didn't really matter. And now, because of Ritchie Pencarrow, the one thing that would bring him contentment, that was consuming him with passion, was out of his grasp. He had tried to forget her. Put her out of his mind. But it seemed that fate kept placing her in his path, torturing him.

Maurice Brett's hands were clenched into fists inside their straining leather gloves, his jaw rigid with frustration. There was nothing else for it. He would have to brave the trip to the back streets of Plymouth and pray the opium dealer was still in business. With his mother squawking at him every waking minute and the girl gnawing away at him like a cancer, it was the only way he could survive.

Elizabeth had watched him go, her eyes boring into his back. He was cunning. Richard disliked him, but she . . . she distrusted him. There was something about him that set the hairs bristling down the back of her neck. She could have told him that William Greenwood had offered to vaccinate them free of charge, but it seemed unfair on the good doctor; that despite his cold, Richard was working just as hard as ever and that neither of them would give up the fight to save Rosebank Hall. That although they didn't always see eye to eye, some invisible thread seemed to be drawing them closer and closer together.

TWENTY-THREE

May 1872

Elizabeth paused as she dried the dishes from the evening meal. The low whistle whispered in her ears once again, only this time it quavered on a different level and with a differing intonation. Her heart breathed a mellow sigh; at least something was going well on the farm. Small though she was, Bramble was proving to possess not only a steadfast courage, but a sharp and willing intelligence. The natural instinct of a working dog gleamed in her brilliant eyes as she gazed up at her master, ready and eager to learn. A smile tugged at Elizabeth's lips as she thought of the sleek, soft-flanked animal that was unfurling from the black and white bundle of fluff Richard had carried home nearly three months earlier.

Elizabeth went on with her mundane task. There were buckets of elderflowers she'd gathered that day waiting to be turned into preparations for sunburn, coughs, colds and the like, bruises and sprains. But first she must make sure the kitchen was spotlessly clean and tidy. Richard would be off out to his own fields after Bramble's training session, as having toiled all day for Mr Widcock — who thankfully still needed his labour — he would have to continue sowing the mangolds and turnips that, together with the swedes and flatpoles he'd be planting in a month or so, would feed his little flock during the following winter. But the crop would be hard-earned. The hiring of a pair of horses was quite simply beyond their means, and every furrow in the neglected earth had been turned by hand, each seed buried in the soil until Richard's back ached miserably every night as he forced himself to work on until darkness fell. Old George did his best, teetering on his swollen, knotted legs, to keep a watchful eye on the surviving ewes and to coax a little milk from their teats before their lambs sucked them dry. But it was Elizabeth who ran the household. She washed, ironed, mended and sewed. She cleaned the house, black-leaded the range and kept it swept. The very heart of their existence, it was essential to keep it in working order. Elizabeth created their meals from her vegetable garden and the hens' eggs, supplemented by the rabbits Richard sometimes snared or shot on his own land, and the meagre supplies they could afford at the village shop. She made cheese from the ewes' milk, a soft, pungent slab for their own consumption, since there wasn't enough to sell at market. With Chantal's help, she saw to the hens and the two rapidly growing piglets they'd acquired. She gathered herbs, roots and flowers to turn into healing lotions and concoctions to sell for pennies to the local workers, especially the miners who lacked knowledge of the hedgerows. She took Chantal to school in the village each day and fetched her home. She made tangy, refreshing lemonade for when Richard returned, parched, from his labours. As soon as the summer began to yield her fruits, she'd be busy with jams and preserves; as the ingredients became available, she'd prepare more remedies to store through the winter. In August, there'd be plump whortleberries to collect up in Tavy Cleave, which she'd sell to the townsfolk at Tavistock market. There was never a minute to spare, from the moment she rose at six until she fell into bed in an exhausted stupor at the end of the day.

Even so, Richard had always gone by the time she awoke, striding across the moor to Mr Widcock's land as the sun stole into the lightening sky. It was often a poor, colourless disc, translucent as it edged between the banks of grey cloud or battled valiantly through the vaporous layers of mist. Generally, the weather had been kind throughout May, making their outdoor labours more pleasurable and giving the seeds Richard had shrewdly purchased at auction a good chance to germinate in the warm, damp earth. Even when Elizabeth simply couldn't wring another ounce of energy from her lifeless muscles, Richard somehow managed to draw on some hidden reserve. By the end of the day, the shadow of a limp sometimes crept into his gait. He never mentioned it, but Elizabeth noticed, and would catch him easing his leg as he sank into the welcome comfort of the armchair they'd dragged into the kitchen for the winter. It was mild enough again now to use the unheated drawing room, but somehow they never did. The kitchen, with its gleaming green and white tiles, had become the undisputed centre of the house.

Elizabeth cast a critical eye over its surfaces and was filled with the satisfaction of a job well done — even if another was to be performed before she could climb the stairs to bed. She stood for a moment, hands on hips, mentally listing the utensils she'd need. Then she turned her head with a joyous grin as a black snout snuffled its way through a small gap between the door and its frame, quickly followed by the elegant dome of the young collie's head, one slack and one comically cocked ear, and finally the wriggling, smooth-coated body from which the longer fringes were just beginning to emerge. Bramble trotted into the kitchen, searching for one of the kind humans who fed her. She at once came and sat at Elizabeth's feet, her swishing tail sweeping the floor, as her shining round eyes expectantly asked for her dinner.

Elizabeth laughed aloud at the animal's antics and bent to ruffle her hand in the thick, silky hair around Bramble's ears. 'There, my sweet!' she crooned, relishing the feel of the creature's soft, warm body. 'Now, paw!' she commanded firmly, and the young dog instantly lifted one front leg, her head tilting to one side. Elizabeth's heart swelled. When she was a child, she'd never managed to teach old Spot, her uncle's dog, to perform the trick, but Bramble had picked it up in days. And now Elizabeth shook the proffered paw with a deep chuckle. 'There's a lovely girl!'

'And a damned clever one, too!'

Elizabeth glanced up. Richard was leaning indolently in the doorway, a rare smile smoothing the habitual grimace from his stern face. It reminded her so much of his father, accentuating the wide, square jawline and revealing the even set of his strong, white teeth, that Elizabeth was sure her heart stood still. It was his eyes that were so different. They didn't share Josiah's pale, penetrating stare, but were blessed with a pensive, mahogany clarity that seemed to portray mysterious, hidden depths. Elizabeth averted her gaze, turning her attention back to the playful young dog. Richard still had her walking on eggshells after six months of living back under the same roof. She never felt sure of him, she supposed that was it. He discussed the farm with her, but little else, as if he were perpetually on his guard. He remained a stranger she sat with for twenty minutes as they consumed their meal each evening, his occasional flashes of humour so rare, she could count them on the fingers of one hand.

She placed Bramble's bowl on the floor and the animal wolfed down her dinner. When Elizabeth looked up again, the moment of understanding, of shared emotion, had gone as Richard's smile faded.

'She'll make a good sheepdog,' he announced brusquely, 'if only I had a decent flock for her to look after.'

Elizabeth frowned, her lips softly pursed. 'You have twenty-seven ewes and over thirty lambs. We didn't lose one.'

'Thanks to your efforts.'

She felt a surge of pride and grateful recognition tingle down to her toes, but she also flushed with embarrassment. She'd done no more than carry out the task she'd been schooled in since she was knee-high to a grasshopper, and she'd been assisted by George with his lifetime of experience. Elizabeth brushed Richard's comment aside and continued as if he hadn't spoken. 'Most of them are female, and you've said yourself there's one particularly promising-looking male you might keep as a serving ram to swap with another flock.'

'Huh!' Richard grunted sullenly. 'You just make sure he doesn't get castrated with the others when old Joe comes next week!'

Elizabeth's eyes flashed. Why was it whenever Richard relaxed his usual rigidity for just one minute, his caustic sharpness always returned two-fold as if to make up for the lapse in his churlishness? 'I'm sure I'm capable of keeping one lamb separate from the others,' she answered tersely. 'And of seeing he marks all their ears properly and keeps the instruments clean. And I'll be up at dawn collecting pennywort leaves to put on the wounds.'

Richard blinked at her, astounded. Had she not prickled with such anger, she might have laughed at his expression. 'Good God, am I to be the only farmer on Dartmoor with sheep running around with little green flags on their ears?' he groaned.

'If 'twill prevent infection, then why not?' she retorted. 'You peel back the top layer of the leaf and then fold it over the ear. 'Twill stay in place for but a few minutes, then a lotion of marigold and St John's Wort should do the trick.'

'As you put on my leg.'

'Exactly. And which wouldn't have been necessary if you hadn't been fool enough to travel hundreds of miles instead of having it properly tended.'

She regretted the words before they'd even left her lips. She snatched in her breath and held it until her lungs were fit to burst. Richard's face had turned to granite, his eyes darkening to ebony pools of fury. But somewhere in their depths was something Elizabeth was sure resembled fear, and his mouth clamped into a pale line.

'How dare you!' he growled, his eyes glinting with shards of anger. 'You know nothing of the circumstances . . . For God's sake, not even Chantal knows the . . .'

'Then I suggest you keep your voice down before you wake her up!'

Their eyes locked across the room, and Elizabeth thrust out her chin to conceal the trembling that had taken hold of her. But then Richard's broad shoulders seemed to sag wearily and he rubbed his hand over his forehead.

'I'd best get on,' he murmured as he turned to the door. 'I must get the drilling finished so I can get the shearing done next week.'

Elizabeth stared after him, her stomach turning cartwheels. She lowered herself into a chair, and sat, stock-still, waiting for the tide of bitterness to subside, overwhelmed by the silence of the thick-walled house. Bramble sensed her unease and resting her silky snout on Elizabeth's knee, whined softly. Elizabeth smiled and stroked her hand along the young dog's smooth head, instantly feeling more relaxed. For two pins, she'd be out of that door and away to find a new life for herself. If it wasn't for Chantal, she'd pack her bags this instant.

Bramble twisted her head and her rough, pink tongue darted out to lick Elizabeth's fingers. It tickled, and the tension drained from Elizabeth's stiff limbs. She sighed deeply, feeling the rush of air through her nostrils. Would she? Would she really leave if it were just herself and Richard Pencarrow living at Rosebank Hall? She'd tried once before, and look where it had got her! Even if she went to work in association with William and held a position of respect, she'd still be treated in most households as an employee. At least here she was virtually mistress of the house. She worked every hour God sent, but no one told her what to do. Richard never once criticized the way she ran the house. Rather, in his own curt way, he showed his appreciation. But then why . . . *Why* did they so often lock horns? She wasn't *afraid* of him. She *wanted* to be friends. Sometimes, when she caught him off guard, laughing with his daughter, her heart turned a complete, lurching somersault . . .

Elizabeth stood up abruptly, shaking her head vigorously from side to side. No! No matter how he talked of partnership and equality, he was still her lord and master! And yet . . . He was desperately worried over the massive debts his father had saddled him with, working himself into the ground to have the farm up and running again. Elizabeth had to admit to some admiration for the determined way in which he toiled for sixteen strenuous hours each and every day. So if his temper had a short fuse, he at least had the excuse of both anxiety and exhaustion. But there was more to it than that. On the rare occasion he'd mentioned his wife, Elizabeth had noticed his eyes glisten with unshed tears, and he'd brusquely turned away to hide them. And it wasn't the only thing she sensed he was hiding. It was as if he was deliberately distancing himself from her. All to do with whatever had happened in France, she was sure. If only she knew the truth! And then perhaps . . . perhaps everything would be different.

* * *

It was one of those rare days on Dartmoor when not a whisper stirred the motionless air. Even the birds were stilled by the heartless sun that seared down from a cloudless sky. The third week of June had been hot and sunny, perfect for cutting the tall hay and gathering it into long, straight windrows one day, turning it after the dew had dissipated the next morning, and stacking it into ricks at sunset. But the heat was becoming oppressive, the temperatures soaring to the high eighties. Miners were happy to be swallowed up by the cool underground adits, those that didn't reach the insufferable warmth of the deepest levels. Children splashed amongst the boulders on the edge of the Tavy, its waters placid during the summer months, or in the brooks and streams that tinkled down the sides of the valley. For the farmer, though, it was a race against time. The fine spell might not last, and heat such as this was bound to end in a battering storm that would flatten all his endeavours.

Today, however, was Sunday, and despite the demands of haymaking, many farmers, the Methodists especially, refused to work. Richard had been accepted into the local farming fraternity again, and during the week they banded together, going from one farm to the next and helping each other, for a mowing team was far more efficient than individual efforts. It was gruelling labour, but the camaraderie was greatly enjoyed, and other family members would join in whenever possible. The area had resisted the introduction of the relatively new horse-drawn mowing machines, and provided the weather was good, haymaking with scythes and hand rakes was looked upon as a happy interlude. Their attentions, however, had yet to be turned to Rosebank Hall, and Richard wasn't prepared to waste a whole day when the weather might so easily break. He'd been out since the crack of dawn, making a start on the sloping fields behind the Hall. Unlike his neighbours, *he* would have used a mowing machine if he had one — or the horses to pull it. Why resist a machine that saved so much time and, ultimately, money? It seemed to Richard no different from the plough and the drill that everyone used. His own had been left to decay in the barn, and he could well have done with them earlier in the spring if they hadn't been unusable. It was his plan to restore the machinery during the long, dark evenings when winter returned, and hopefully he'd be able to afford a team of horses by the following year. Mr Widcock had indicated he'd require Richard's services as long as possible to work on his extensive land, so at least they were assured of that income for some time to come.

Richard made the final sweep of the scythe as he reached the top of the field once again, and propping the implement into the ground, leaned on its handle to take the few moments' rest he allowed himself at the end of each row. His sleeves were rolled up to his elbows, and he turned his head into the crook of his raised arm to wipe the sweat from his forehead.

His shirt was glued to his back, sticking uncomfortably to his skin, and he wondered if he shouldn't remove it altogether. The fields behind the isolated farmhouse were at the highest level one could expect to gather hay from, and he was alone apart from Elizabeth, who'd joined him in his labours after morning church, Chantal having stayed on at Sunday School. Elizabeth had seen him unclothed often enough during those long weeks she'd nursed him, and he'd feel much better stripped to the waist. What he could imagine just now was plunging into the cool, refreshing waters of the Tavy where it formed a pool high up in Tavy Cleave, miles beyond the point where the leat led off to serve the local mines. He'd done just that so many times as a boy, stripping off every stitch of clothing and not caring if anyone might wander by. Not that anyone ever did, for who had the time to take such leisure in a community that only ever worked or slept? He'd been privileged then, not required by his father to do anything during the school holidays, totally ignored by him, in fact. It was only his uncle who paid him any attention on the rare occasions he was home on leave from the army, relating exotic and exciting tales of faraway places. Richard had dreamed, then, of joining up himself. It wasn't until his uncle had died from his wounds at Sebastopol that it dawned on him that, as a soldier, you were expected to kill people, to drive your sword through the entrails of another human being. Besides, Richard had always hung on the coat-tails of George, young and spritely then, and the other farm labourers, learning as he went, leaning over a gate in the evening as they discussed the day's work while sucking on their pipes, and he chewed a length of straw in imitation. And then there'd been the mine, of course, named for the mother he'd deliberately killed with his own entry into the world, or so his father insisted. When other men might have battled to keep their sons from being devoured by the ground, Josiah never batted an eyelid when the small heir to the estate was dragged out of the mine by an irate captain, only to sneak back at the next available opportunity. In the end, the mine-captain had solved the situation by taking the boy under his wing and had then discovered an astute student in him.

Richard exhaled ruefully and shook his head at the thoughts that had wandered, unbidden, through his brain. All that was in the past. Now he had a rundown farm to build up again and a massive debt to repay. The loss of those ewes back in March had been a severe blow. The money their carcasses had fetched at the abattoir hadn't covered what he'd paid for them. If all had gone to plan, he should have made a reasonable profit from their lambs at whatever point he decided to sell them, and should still have been able to breed from the mothers for another year or two. Still, overall, he was keeping his head above water. What with working flat out for Mr Widcock up until haymaking, selling his fleeces direct to the woollen mills at Buckfastleigh, and the rental from the small tenant farms, he'd managed to keep pace with the interest payments on his father's mortgages and loans, and pay off all other outstanding bills. He'd also been able to purchase the flatpole seedlings from Tavistock market, as well as the seeds that, together with the hay, would eventually provide his winter fodder.

But he was well aware that he could never have managed it without Elizabeth.

He squinted through the dazzling sunshine at the figure toiling at the bottom end of the field, raking into neat, loose windrows the hay he had felled, so that it would dry in the scorching heat. She wore a simple peasant's frock of drab grey cotton with a battered straw boater on her head to protect her face from the burning sun. But Elizabeth would look beautiful wearing a sack.

Pain crashed into Richard's chest just below his heart. She was nothing like Madeleine. His wife had been tall. Willowy, but with a deep bosom. Attractive rather than pretty, with dazzling poppy lips in a sallow face out of which her ebony eyes had smouldered mysteriously like hot coals. She'd captivated his soul the instant he'd clapped eyes on her,

her laughing sensuality spurring his male ardour to tearing frustration, as he knew at once that he wanted her in his bed as his wife. They seemed made for each other in the glorious heady nights after their marriage, which were crowned only a few months later with the discovery that Madeleine was with child. Richard bit his lip, his eyes staring blindly as the image of her stone-hard face as she lay in her coffin swam in his mind. Elizabeth couldn't be more different. So how could his affection for her possibly be growing so strong when he was still grieving for his wife?

Richard took up the scythe again, but as he went to make the first swing he saw that Elizabeth had evidently seen him looking towards her and so was now waving in response. He waved back, and paused to watch a moment longer as she began to drag the rake through the long-cut grass again, so graceful as she worked. Richard felt angry at himself for thinking of her in that way. But as his arms made another sweep with the scythe, he saw her suddenly fall to the ground. And his heart thudded with fear as he raced towards her.

* * *

'Beth?'

It was Richard's softly spoken, anxious voice she heard first. She wasn't sure where she was, and it was some moments before she opened her eyes. The top three buttons of her dress were unfastened, the material drawn back from her skin, and the distorted face that swam above her was Uncle Matthew's. Her mouth stretched in a startled cry, her eyes wide with terror. But as the features fell into place, she realized it was Richard who was kneeling over her, and she fell back in relief. She was no longer exposed to the blistering heat in the middle of the field, but lying in the narrow strip of shade created by the stunted oaks beside the stone wall. Richard must have carried her there, and having loosened her clothing, he was fanning her vigorously with her hat, his brow folded with concern.

'I'm sorry,' she murmured, and went to lift herself upwards.

But Richard put a restraining hand on her shoulder. 'You stay there until you feel better, and then I'll take you back to the house.'

'But what about the hay?' she moaned.

'George can give me a hand when he gets back from checking the sheep. His legs aren't too bad at the moment. Anyway, the team will be coming here the day after tomorrow. I just wanted to make a start. I shouldn't have let you help me.'

'Oh, I'm fine normally. 'Tis just that . . .' She stopped abruptly, realizing she was about to say something that was quite unmentionable. She could hardly tell him it was her time of the month, could she?

But Richard's mouth broadened into a gentle smile. 'Yes, I've a shrewd idea. I've noticed you looking peaky for a few days once a month, and I thought this morning . . . I do know about such things, you know. And in this heat and working as hard as you were, you fainted. Well, from now on, I must take more care of you.' Elizabeth was amazed at the easy way he spoke of such a delicate subject, so that she didn't feel the least embarrassed herself. And then he tipped his head as he looked at her askew. 'You know, Beth, I really am very grateful for everything you do on the farm.'

Their eyes met, surprising each other, the moment natural despite its strangeness. Elizabeth shook her head. They shared a common cause, didn't they? The farm. So it was only logical they should be drawn together in spite of their differences . . .

'Ah, Richard, lad, I be glad I've found you. Oh . . .'

They both glanced up at the burly figure lumbering towards the field from the farmhouse. Mr Widcock still wore his usual tweed jacket, and his face was scarlet and bedewed with great globules of perspiration beneath the brim of his hat. But the colour in his cheeks deepened even further when he espied Richard Pencarrow bent over the pretty girl lying on her back in the grass with some of her buttons unfastened. He took off his hat and fingered it awkwardly in his hands.

Richard cleared his throat, flushing himself as he guessed the older man's thoughts. 'Stand back, would you, Mr Widcock? Poor Beth just fainted in the heat,' he mumbled.

Mr Widcock nodded, and his mouth dropped open in a long 'Aaah'. But then he turned to Richard, his expression recovered and quite serious now. ''Tis bad news. There be foot and mouth on this part of the moor. You'd best get your sheep down afore they get infected. And get any you want to sell off to market. There'll be movement restrictions within the fortnight, mark my words. I thought as I'd better warn you.'

Elizabeth sat up slowly and glanced warily in Richard's direction. His back was rigid, his jaw like chiselled marble as he stared at Mr Widcock. 'Yes. Thank you,' he gulped at last through pale lips.

'Well, I'd best be off,' the farmer flustered. 'I've others to tell. If you come to my farm, you'll find disinfectant at the start of the lane, and more by the yard gate. I suggest you do the same.'

He turned, and seemed relieved to hurry back to where he'd tethered his horse in the shade. They watched him go, stunned by the appalling news he'd delivered. Richard sank back on his heels, leaving a smear of dirt as he ran his hand over his face.

He gazed down at his tightly clasped hands, not moving a muscle for a full minute before his mouth twisted into a bitter grimace. 'I think someone up there must have a grudge against me,' he finally muttered, dropping his head back on his shoulders with a dejected groan. 'It's just one thing after another. It seems no matter how hard I work . . . Perhaps I should give up,' he snorted, his eyebrows lifting with supreme irony. 'Go and work for someone else. In a shipping office or something in Plymouth. I've got a brain, although sometimes I wonder . . . I could make a decent life for Chantal and myself without flogging my guts out.'

He hung his head again, his shoulders slumped with desperation. Something stirred in Elizabeth's heart as his words filtered into her brain. For Chantal and himself. What about *her*? Where did *she* come into the picture? She didn't, did she? After everything she'd done to help him! Well, damn Richard Pencarrow! She wouldn't let him give up! Not now! She'd put her trust in him, despite the massive question mark that hung over his past and had never been answered. Fury bubbled up inside her. She was fighting for her future now, a future she didn't want to face . . . alone.

'But . . . you'd hate it,' she rounded on him, swallowing down the crack in her voice. 'You love the farm. 'Tis in your blood. You *can't* give up now. Not after all you've done. I . . . I won't let you! This . . . this foot and mouth outbreak may come to nothing.'

'Or we may lose everything, the entire flock, even the house cows,' he croaked in defeat. 'I don't think you quite realize, Beth, just how bad my debts are. If that happened, I just simply couldn't recover from it.'

'But you don't *know* anything will happen,' she said pointedly, her conviction growing as she spoke. ''Twas good of Mr Widcock to come all this way to warn you. Do as he says. Forget the hay for now. Bring the sheep down off the leer. Now. Today. You're luckier than others. You've plenty of enclosed fields to graze them on. And,' she added with a flash of inspiration, 'we'll give them regular doses of sage, rosemary and thyme decoction. I've never tried it on animals before, but it helps resist infection in humans. We can keep a constant eye on them, separate any that show any signs. And if any do get it, I've plenty of soothing balms that might help get them through it, so that they can still eat. That's the main problem, after all, isn't it?'

She stared at him, her eyes glowing with consternation as she waited for his reply. He turned to her at last, his expression incredulous beneath his deeply furrowed brow. 'Good God, Beth! Have you got an answer for everything?'

'Of course not. But we must try. I know . . . I know it must be hard after everything . . . with your father and . . . But you can't give up!'

She watched, every nerve tense, as he chewed on his bottom lip. 'All right,' he said, holding up his hands as if in submission. 'We'll do our level best to survive. But this isn't going to make life any easier.'

'But what would life be without a challenge?' she asked, her eyes wide as she awaited his reaction.

But he blinked at her then, and grinned. 'Just don't you go fainting on me again,' he chided with a short laugh.

'I'll do my best,' she promised as he hauled her to her feet.

TWENTY-FOUR

Tavistock, October 1872

'Now, Maurice, you go along and play,' the toothless, dribbling mouth lisped at him, and a gnarled, bony hand patted the fine worsted sleeve of his frockcoat. 'But don't spoil your clothes, or your father will take the strap to you when he comes in.'

'Yes, Mother.' Maurice shuddered with revulsion as he brushed the back of his hand across his other arm where her fingers had touched him, as if he were flicking off some vile contamination. She was totally incontinent now, as the stench in the room confirmed. No matter how clean the personal maid tried to keep her, God knew what was on her hands.

He cast a sideways glance at the buxom woman he'd at last found to care for his mother, not the sort he normally liked to employ and disdained by the other servants for her uncouth ways, but beggars couldn't be choosers. Anyway, she spent most of her time in this stinking room, even sleeping in what had once been the spacious dressing room with the door propped ajar in case her services were required during the night. That's what he'd wanted and it eased his conscience somewhat.

Maurice couldn't get out of the room quick enough, and tripped lightly down the stairs to pick up his scarf and hat.

There'd be no work done at the offices and foundries and other small industries in the town today. It was the October Goose Fair. Unless you were involved in some trade which made money out of the thousands of revellers who swarmed into Tavistock for the day, you would lock up your business securely and either barricade yourself securely indoors, or join in. Maurice had no qualms about choosing the latter. He'd meet up for lunch with his business acquaintances at the Bedford Hotel, which kept out the raucous riff-raff simply by being far beyond the reach of their pockets. But first he would spend what remained of the morning, for it was already nearing eleven o'clock, in the pleasant pursuit of watching the world go by.

Overnight, Plymouth Road had turned from the fashionable avenue it normally was, to a bustling thoroughfare. From well before daybreak, as with all the major routes into the town's centre, farmers had been driving their animals towards the pens, ready for the opening of the market. There were, of course, hundreds of geese — thousands perhaps. But the market wasn't just confined to the long-necked honkers. Livestock of all sorts would be bought and sold: sheep, cattle, hens, cockerels, the occasional goat, sometimes pups of working breeds, and kittens. You had to watch where you put your feet, Maurice reminded himself, disdainfully wrinkling his nose, but it was worth it for the free entertainment the day would offer. The noise the droves of animals made hadn't disturbed his sleep, as his room was at the back of the opulent villa, and he felt refreshed and invigorated to enjoy the day which, this year, had dawned dry and bright, instead of pouring with rain as it usually did.

Maurice joined the human mass converging on Tavistock's elegantly redeveloped centre, and he smiled complacently. Living where he did, he could arrive on foot and so avoid the jumble of traps, wagonettes and other conveyances caught up in a tangled standstill in the road, the flags that adorned them for the day dangling limply while the drivers shouted at each other, irately waving their arms in wild gesticulations of impatience. People flocked from all over, miners and farm labourers from the directions of Gunnislake, the Bere Peninsula, Dartmoor and beyond, and the belching trains spilled forth in their multitudes the human cargoes from Plymouth, Devonport and Launceston. Maurice shouldered his way through the jostling, boisterous throng. He stopped to watch a dancing bear put through its paces by its evil-looking owner brandishing a thick leather truncheon, but once he glimpsed the bolt through the creature's nose, he smartly walked on. Sweet Jesus! It was barbaric! But what could *he* do to rescue the poor beast? A conjuror, a juggler, oh, and look at that, a fire-eater, now that was better. And if the fellow burned his lips, it was his own fault. He deserved the silver threepence Maurice flipped into his begging bowl. A small crowd screamed and gasped, then loudly applauded with whistles and clapping hands, and when Maurice stretched up on tiptoe to look over the top of their heads, he saw a group of players taking their bow, one still holding aloft a dagger, and another with something red stained over the front of his costume. The streets were lined with small, striped booths with signs inviting you to pay your sixpence and come inside to see the fat lady, the bearded lady, the dwarf, the giant, and the man covered in tattoos. There were street-singers passing round the hat, young girls daring to expose a shapely calf beneath their skirts as they danced to the music of a barrel-organ — until the constable moved them on — gipsies selling crocheted doilies and wooden pegs, saveloy and pasty stalls, pedlars punting their trinkets, and the inevitable Punch and Judy show. Maurice was happy to weave amongst them all, winking at a pretty woman here and there, but always with his hand firmly in his pocket, for no one was going to lift *his* wallet from his possession. And when he had sufficiently enjoyed the surging company of the common crowd, it took his fancy to wander along to the livestock market and listen to the auctioneer's lightning-quick tongue.

'Any more offers? Do I hear any advance? Going, going, gone!' the booming voice announced. 'Sold to Mr Pencarrow, thank you, sir. Now then, lot number . . .'

The rest of his words were lost to Maurice's thunder-struck ears. Richard Pencarrow, whom he hated with a vengeance, was in the position to *buy* stock! Even after the trick the Arkwright boy had played on him, and the foot and mouth outbreak that had decimated various farms in the area! It was over now, the restriction orders having only recently been removed after a difficult summer. Maurice's mouth tightened into a venomous knot as he edged as near as he dared to the clerk who was in the process of taking Richard's payment and issuing a docket. He cocked his head, straining to catch a snippet of their conversation.

'You've done well today, sir,' the clerk was congratulating his client. 'They young wethers of yourn fetched a good price. And you'd already had a first fleece from them. Mind you, they were a good healthy lot compared with some. They ewes you've just bought, mind, might've been cheap but they look a bit scraggy to me. Got some sort of secret way of revitalizing them, have you?'

'You might say that,' came the enigmatic reply, and Richard walked away, threading his steps towards the Pannier Market.

Maurice stood and fumed, his fists clenched and the pleasures of the morning forgotten. Where was the bugger going now, he wondered viciously, and without another thought, followed him across Bedford Square, under the Town Hall archway, and into the pretty colonnaded cloisters of the little market.

She took the breath from his body.

There she was, packing spotless, chequered cloths upon which she must have displayed her produce into the baskets which would have contained them. Everything sold, it would seem, eggs, cheese probably, and maybe butter. She looked up and smiled as Richard approached, a radiant brilliance that made Maurice's heart jerk in his chest. The two spoke for a moment, and then a dark-haired child he hadn't noticed before darted forward with a young but obedient dog on a lead. Richard placed an affectionate hand on the girl's shoulder and then, taking up one empty basket while Elizabeth Thornton carried the other, steered her in a most gentlemanly fashion towards the rows of sideshows and booths in Duke Street.

Maurice's feet moved like two drawn magnets. It was easy to pursue them from a distance, since Richard stood half a head taller than most others in the street. They stopped at various stalls, and then Maurice had to pull back sharply, as two arguing revellers, obviously the worse for drink, stumbled into their way and started a bout of fisticuffs. Richard had whisked Elizabeth and his daughter out of danger and Maurice remained where he was as they moved off again. His pulse was reverberating in his skull, his senses dulled with the image of Ritchie Pencarrow and the lovely young woman. She should have been *his*! Maurice Brett's! Somehow — and he didn't know quite how — he would have to prise them apart! For if *he* couldn't have her, he would make sure Ritchie didn't either!

Perhaps it was time he saw the Arkwright boy again.

* * *

Elizabeth had taken Chantal to school down in Peter Tavy and now she was on her way home. She hurried up the long straight track that led up to Rosebank Hall, having cut across from the combe, her feet nimble on the uneven path. She'd only gone as far as the cottages above the old mill. Children lived there who also attended the village school, so Chantal would have company for the rest of the way. There were plenty who roamed the moor alone from that age — Elizabeth herself had done so, or at least within a certain radius of the village as specified by her mother. But Chantal still felt uneasy on the lonely walk from the isolated farmhouse, and Elizabeth was happy to accompany her.

It had rained heavily overnight, and dampness hung in the air like an opaque veil. Elizabeth could feel the occasional spit of moisture on her cheek, as in the rush to leave on time, she'd forgotten her old felt bonnet. At any minute, it could start again, a constant, steady drizzle that would soon penetrate through her shawl to her dress. She wished she'd worn her coat. She'd considered it, but the day was mild for late October, with no wind, and she didn't have far to go. Now she quickened her step, so intent upon watching where she placed her feet in order to avoid the puddles and the worst of the mud that she didn't see Thomas Arkwright until she all but bumped into him.

The shock of meeting someone on the lonely path, followed by the dubious relief that it was only Tom, rippled into her belly in an uneasy knot. He'd been an irritating nuisance to her all her life, but she'd always managed to get the better of him. She hadn't seen him for some while, and suddenly felt wary. In that time, the hard toil of working down the mine had turned the skinny youth into a bulky, solid man.

'Morning, Tom,' she said cautiously. 'Shouldn't you be at work?'

''Tiddn my shift, not till this arternoon. Me and Sam,' and caution tingled down Elizabeth's spine as she saw his swarthy companion emerge from behind a boulder in the process of fastening his trousers, 'we thought as we'd take a little walk. Fer see the whore of Rosebank Hall.'

'What!' Elizabeth's voice sparked first with disbelief and then outraged offence, her eyes glinting like the flash of the sun on polished copper.

'Hmm.' The sardonic grunt gurgled somewhere in the back of Thomas's throat, and his mouth stretched in a warped grin. He was biding his time, taunting her, and it set her nerves on edge. Thomas Arkwright had never before had the wit to do anything in so calculated a manner as he was now. ''Tis so plain as the nose on your face,' he scoffed. 'Living up yere wi' that there Pencarrow divil! Pretend fer be some sort o' saint, when all the while you'm earning your keep on your back! Fust 'twere the aud man, an' now 'tis the son! I wonders which one you prefers?' And then drawing level with her, he whispered in her ear, 'Or were your uncle the best?'

Elizabeth stopped dead. He knew. Dear God. Thomas Arkwright *knew*! But . . . how? The blood seemed to rush from her head, but as Sam Grainger came to stand shoulder to shoulder with his comrade, forming an impenetrable wall across her path, the instinct for self-preservation took command and she forced herself to think clearly. Old George was laid up with his arthritis again, probably in an armchair in his cottage further on up the track beyond the farmhouse. Richard had been out since daybreak down in the fields he owned near the village, digging up mangolds and storing them in clamps before the first frosts came. She was all alone. No one would hear her screams, come to her rescue. But this was only Thomas Arkwright, and she'd dealt with him often enough before. This time, though, it was different. Her only chance was to hide her fear and treat Tom with the same contempt she always did.

So she squared her slim shoulders, her rigid chin lifted scornfully. 'I might've known your grubby little mind would believe anything it hears! Not exactly the brightest star in the sky, are you? As for Richard, he be a perfect gentleman . . .'

'Oh, 'tis Richard now!' Tom jeered derisively. 'Wouldn't call 'en that if there were nort gwain on atween you! An' who says he be a gentleman, eh? Claims fer be a widower? Huh! How can us be certain there ever *were* a Mrs Pencarrow? P'raps that cheel be nort but a fly-blow! An' p'raps he'll be filling *your* belly an' all afore too long! Unless I does fust!'

Utter disgust at his obscene words mingled with her terror and galvanized her into action. She launched herself at Tom so swiftly that by dint of surprise rather than strength, she pushed him aside and, hoisting up her skirt, began to run, splashing straight through the puddles, Tom and Sam's lusty brays of laughter ringing in her ears.

''Tis a sin what you'm doing!' Tom shouted triumphantly at her back. 'Us good Methodists doesn't hold with it! Folk be talkin' 'bout you! And does you mind what happened to Annie Simpkin?'

She put twenty yards between them, and dared to glance over her shoulder. They weren't following her, but she was so petrified, she knew she wouldn't stop running until she reached the safety of the house.

The first stone hit her squarely between the shoulder blades. She gasped with the shock of it, but scarcely hesitated in her flight. She could only think of Annie Simpkin, the unmarried, pregnant girl who'd been driven out of the village by local Methodist disgust when Elizabeth had been but a child. Her terror was interrupted by the next missile that struck her hard on the fleshy muscle between her neck and her shoulder, and a third that glanced off her bare head, cutting the taut skin beneath her hair. It brought her up short. Incensed anger rampaged through her body, for it was well known that Thomas Arkwright dipped his wick at every available opportunity. She turned to tell him so, but before she had a chance to open her mouth, what must have been a sharp flint slammed into her forehead just above her temple.

She really wasn't sure what happened after that. The next thing she knew, she was sprawled across the track, her neck, her shoulders, her head throbbing pitilessly. She tentatively fingered her forehead and drew back at the tenderness of it. There was blood down the front of her dress.

She drew herself up, taking her time, and staggered to her feet. She was all alone, not a sign of Tom or his companion. Other than the rain pattering gently on the dying ferns, there wasn't a sound to be heard. The farmhouse seemed but a blur in the distance, and slowly she dragged herself towards it.

It seemed to take for ever, but when she finally lurched into the kitchen, the familiar room seemed to swim in front of her eyes. She stumbled across to the stone sink, supporting herself on it for a few moments while she gathered the strength to pump up some water from the spring deep beneath the house. The cool, refreshing liquid spluttered noisily into the enamel bowl, and cupping her shaking hands into it, she splashed it repeatedly over her face. The wound on her forehead stung viciously, but her senses were gradually reviving.

Her golden hair, which had grown down about her shoulders again, had come loose from the ribbon she'd hastily tied it in that morning, and fell forward into the bowl. She paused to hook it back behind her ears. As she did so, her heart stood still as she heard the back door open.

'Beth! I'm back!'

She slumped forward in relief at Richard's voice, the life force suddenly draining from her limbs. She knew he'd be removing his boots and hanging up his jacket in the back hallway, and then she heard him pad into the kitchen in his stockinged feet. She stiffened, turning to stone, as she stared at the red-stained water in the bowl, for some inexplicable reason not wanting him to see her face.

'Well, I finished that quicker than I thought,' he was saying. 'I'm gasping for a cup of tea, and then I'll dig over that patch in the vegetable garden for you before I go and fetch the ram from Mr Widcock. And I'll check on the . . .' Silence then, and Elizabeth inwardly shrank. 'Beth?' he said quietly. 'Beth, what's the matter?'

She couldn't move, rooted to the spot, as he came up behind her and put his hands lightly on her shoulders. She shuddered at his touch, pulling away with a wincing squeal.

'Beth?' he breathed, swiftly lifting his hands. 'What on earth's happened? There's . . . blood in your hair. Beth, will you please turn round and look at me!'

But her muscles were paralysed, and it wasn't until he took hold of her arms and guided her round to face him that she was able to move at all. She knew she couldn't resist, but her head remained bowed and hidden in the thick tangle of hair, until he placed a finger under her chin and gently tilted it upwards. She looked up at him then, staring into the clear depths of his appalled eyes.

'Jesus Christ,' he rasped, his gaze travelling in bewildered horror over her face. 'Is this . . . is this your uncle's handiwork again?'

Elizabeth's jaw juddered up and down as she tried to speak. 'N-n-no. 'Tw-'twas . . .'

'Oh, don't tell me, Thomas Arkwright, and that witless moron who hangs on his coat-tails,' Richard groaned, narrowing his eyes as he bent his head to scrutinize her more closely. 'I passed them in the village, and they both legged it in the opposite direction when they saw me. I thought it was strange, the bastards. But . . .' He frowned anxiously. 'But *why*, Beth?'

Her eyebrows arched, her resolve gone as his concern melted her shock and she started shaking. 'He . . . he said . . . I was a whore,' she choked, her teeth chattering out of control. 'Living alone . . . here with you. He said . . . people are talking . . .'

She was losing the fight. Her throat closed up, and she simply couldn't force out the words. It was so unjust, so untrue, it was unbearable. And then there was that other hideous degradation . . . She felt so ashamed, so defiled, she couldn't look at Richard any more and turned her head away, swaying perilously. He caught her, and held her close against him, tucking her head under his chin as she wept in great, wrenching sobs.

'Oh, God, this was what I was afraid of all along,' he whispered softly into her hair. She could feel the strength of him, the steel in his arms, and sagged against his chest, taking comfort from the warm closeness of his body. She felt . . . an intimacy that seemed to soothe her soul. The pain began to ease, and she wondered how she could discover such solace with this man she'd once so bitterly resented.

He sensed her tears subsiding, and like a malleable child, she allowed him to sit her down in one of the kitchen chairs. All at once, she missed him, but then he was back, setting a bowl filled with fresh water on the table. He carefully moistened a clean tea towel and dabbed it deftly over the wound on her forehead. She winced, but his touch was so caring and delicate, she somehow didn't really mind.

'Did he *hit* you?' he asked softly.

'No. They threw stones,' she was able to answer more calmly. She heard him suck his breath sharply through his teeth, and his gaze fleetingly met hers. 'He mentioned the Methodists. As if 'twere some sort of religious retribution. And . . . and . . . he knows about my uncle.'

'What!' Richard cried, and she saw the colour drain from his face before it flushed with anger. 'Well, he certainly didn't hear it from me! But I'll damned well find out where he did! But . . .' He took a deep breath and smiled encouragingly at her. 'Don't you worry about it. I think I can deal with the likes of Thomas Arkwright. Now put your head up and let me finish cleaning this cut.' She instantly obeyed, studying the concentration on his face as he worked. His brown eyes were deep pools of concern fringed with long, dark lashes, the wide brow above lightly furrowed, and his well-shaped mouth closed in a firm line. She'd always thought him handsome even when she'd detested him, but his hard exterior was mellowing as he dragged the farm back into business. They had weathered the storm of the foot and mouth outbreak, their stock unaffected except by the movement restrictions. A less grim Richard Pencarrow, even with a mild sense of humour, was emerging from the worry-worn ogre. And now it was as if he'd swept the horror of Tom's revelation clean away from her.

'There,' he announced at last. 'I think that'll heal nicely. And it's just a nick on the back of your head. Now, was there anywhere else?'

'Here,' she replied, indicating the side of her neck, lulled by the comfort of his gentleness. 'And between my shoulder blades, but that's all.'

Her body rippled with nervousness as he began to unfasten the buttons of her dress, just a few, enough to slip the bodice over her shoulders and expose the wound on her back. She noticed a slight tremor in his hands, but she was ready to trust him, though her breath fluttered at the back of her throat. He drew her tumbling mass of curls to one side, his touch as tender as gossamer as he fingered her injured flesh.

'The skin isn't broken,' he said thickly, the awkwardness of the situation clearly not lost on him, either. 'But the bruising's coming out already. We could put some witch hazel on it, unless you have some other fabulous concoction you prefer to use.'

His voice was serious, but when she glanced up, she caught the mildly teasing light in his eyes, and her mouth answered with a soft smile. And she felt so very glad he was there.

TWENTY-FIVE

Elizabeth glanced up as Richard came back downstairs and into the kitchen that evening after kissing Chantal goodnight.

'Are you going to work on the plough?' Elizabeth questioned him. After they'd eaten and Chantal had gone to bed, that was what he'd been doing during the dark autumn evenings, wrestling with the rusted metal by the glow of two storm-lamps in the barn.

'No. Not tonight, Beth.' His tone was hesitant, and she shot him a sideways glance. 'Come and sit down.' He beckoned her towards the easy chair that was drawn up to the warmth of the range. She did as he commanded, drying her hands on the towel as she came. The bruises had developed as the day had worn on, and she'd taken a little laudanum, not sufficient to induce sleep, but enough to lessen her discomfort and make her feel more relaxed. She lowered herself into the chair, frowning as she noticed Richard flexing his hand, not for the first time that evening.

'Have you done something to your hand?' she ventured.

His face hardened for a moment, but then he allowed himself a wistful smile. 'I carried out a little retribution of my own,' he admitted somewhat sheepishly. 'And I made him tell me how he knew about what your uncle . . . I'm sorry,

Beth, but he saw it all.' He paused, his voice softening as she lowered her eyes. 'He said you'd had words, and that you'd tricked him or something, and he followed you back to your uncle's farm to have his revenge. Instead he saw . . . through the dairy window . . . He swears he's never told anyone, and after today . . . Well, let's say I persuaded him he never will. So, I don't think as you'll be having any more trouble from Master Arkwright.'

Elizabeth's eyes widened. 'Oh, Richard, thank you. But d'you think you should have done that? I mean . . .'

'Physical violence?' he finished for her. 'It seemed the only way. And I didn't hurt him nearly as much as I'd have liked to. Besides, he deserved it. And that's what I want to talk to you about.' He sat forward earnestly in one of the kitchen chairs, balancing his elbows on his knees and meeting her enquiring gaze. 'Unfortunately, part of what he said was true. Tongues *are* wagging. But from that point of view, there is a way we can stop anything like this morning ever happening again.' He seemed to hesitate, and Elizabeth tipped her head to one side. But she wasn't prepared for the bombshell he was about to drop. 'Marry me, Beth. That'll put a stop to their ugly gossip.'

Elizabeth's mouth dropped open, her lungs held in mid-breath as she stared at him in disbelief. Had she *heard* right? But it seemed she had!

'It would make sense, Beth,' Richard was saying from some planet the other side of the universe. 'I mean, nothing would change. It would only be a marriage on paper. There'd be no . . . physical side to it. I think you know me well enough to trust me on that score. But it would give you respectability. Put you out of reach of the Thomas Arkwrights of this world. And your uncle, not that we've had any problem with him since he remarried. And . . . and to be quite honest, Chantal needs a mother.'

'I can be as good a mother to Chantal without being married to you!' The cutting response was automatic, coming from some other part of her brain as the feeling slowly trickled back to her senses. Marry him. *Marry him!* It was true he'd been far more even-tempered of late, and this morning wasn't the first time he'd revealed the tender side of his nature. And she did trust him, there was no doubt of that. But, *marry* him! That was a different kettle of fish!

'I think it would help her,' he murmured, his head bowed and his eyes gazing down at his hands which dangled limply between his spread knees. 'It would give her some stability after all she's been through. And . . . and you would be mistress of Rosebank Hall. Officially.'

Her mind was turning circles now, and she stared at him, mesmerized with shock. Mistress of the Hall. Never had she imagined . . . But she was virtually that already! But . . . it could be taken away from her . . . But as Mrs Pencarrow, it would be hers for ever. And the security that came with it, that was if Richard didn't lose the farm after all, despite all his efforts. And yet even so, wasn't there some small part of her that was beginning to feel more than just affection for him? No, it was madness! All he really wanted was a mother for Chantal, and she was as good as that already.

'I'm flattered, sir,' she answered, her voice dull and expressionless as the distance between them swiftly returned. 'But I can't marry you. For all you say, I'm no more than a servant. And what if you ever met someone of your own class that you *really* loved? I'd just be . . .'

'My own class?' Richard leapt to his feet, and there was fire in his eyes as he paced the room. 'Dear God, Beth, I thought you'd know better than that. I'm a yeoman farmer. My family are no more than farm labourers who've worked hard and used their brains. I had the best education of them all, and that only at the local grammar school. But *you*, Beth!' He sat down again abruptly, surprising her even further by grasping her hands in a firm grip. 'Your grandfather was a parson! Poor, maybe, but educated. And look at *you*! I've never met such an intelligent woman! Look at all your remedies! You know almost as much as William. It was *you* who saved my life, Beth, not him! And as for finding anyone else,

I loved my wife. Who, for the record, was of peasant stock, if such a term must be used. I'll . . . I'll never love anyone like that again!'

His eyes were boring into hers with crystal brilliance and she could hardly dare to hold his gaze. She didn't know why, but his last sentence had ripped into her heart. Her breath seemed to have become trapped in her throat. She felt her chin begin to tremble and for some reason she wanted to cry as if her very soul was being torn to shreds.

But then he inhaled deeply and cast down his eyes. 'Of course,' he muttered. 'How could I have been so stupid? There's someone else, isn't there? I should have known. Someone as lovely as you must . . . I'm sorry. I didn't think . . .'

'No. There isn't.' Her hand moved forward of its own volition and rested on his arm. She couldn't believe it, or the words that were coming from her lips as though someone else was speaking. He looked so dejected. So lost. A spark of growing sympathy flickered deep in her breast, and she found it in her to smile. 'Where would I find the time to harbour some secret lover, eh?' she sighed softly. 'Besides, I know everyone for miles about, and I've never met anyone else who—'

She stopped. Anyone else who . . . who what? Intrigued her, attracted her? Made her heart quicken, as he frequently did, usually with vexation but more recently with something warm and glowing? He was looking at her with raised eyebrows, his face grave and suddenly bloodless, so that she blinked at him in anxious anticipation.

'But . . . before you even think about it,' he croaked, his voice catching in his throat as tiny beads of perspiration began to glisten on his forehead, 'there's something I must tell you. The reason I came back from France in such a state when, as you've quite rightly pointed out on numerous occasions, I should have been in bed under the care of a physician.' He was looking directly at her again, and her heart gave a sickening lurch as she saw the fear in his eyes. An oppressive, suffocating silence rang in her ears as she waited for him to continue. But she wasn't sure she wanted to hear whatever it was he had to say, and he evidently wasn't sure he wanted to tell her. Elizabeth glanced down at his hands. They were shaking. As her own heart hammered out of control, she knew she was about to hear something appalling.

He swallowed hard. 'No one else knows what happened,' he began, his voice so low she could barely hear him. 'Except the few people who were directly involved, of course. The . . . the thing is, Beth, I . . . Oh, God!' He rolled his head, his face torn in an agony of despair. Elizabeth waited, holding her breath, aware of the seconds ticking away until he appeared to take a grip on himself and ran his hand hard over his mouth. 'I killed a man,' he finally grated in a tearing whisper.

Elizabeth gasped, recoiling in the chair, and felt the blood drain from her head. Killed a man. Oh, no. She thought he might have done something wrong, driven on by his quick temper. Take what had happened today with Thomas Arkwright, though she had to agree that a good hiding was the only sort of lesson Tom would understand! But if she thought back to Josiah's funeral, Richard had controlled his anger at Maurice Brett so admirably, so . . . But . . . killed a man. Oh, God, no!

'Beth, please don't judge me until you've heard the whole story,' Richard begged, his tortured face a leaden grey. 'It . . . it was all to do with the war. I never meant to become involved, but—' He broke off, biting hard on his bottom lip, and Elizabeth stared at him, willing him to say something that would exonerate him in her eyes.

'I remember you said you followed the events of the war in the newspapers . . . with my father,' he faltered, finding his tongue at last. 'So you probably know about the battle at Sedan. In the September.' Elizabeth frowned, dragging her mind back two years to when Josiah was still alive and she had no premonition that her life would change so dramatically. She nodded silently, for though she tried, she found she couldn't utter a sound. 'Apparently, it was a blood bath,'

Richard went on, his brow knitted in earnest. 'The Prussians had the French army trapped, and . . . well, virtually all those that weren't killed were taken prisoner. It wasn't the only battle, of course, but it was the major disaster. And I'm sure you know there was fighting all over the north-east, so we were in the middle of it. Anyway, all through the winter, French troops were trying to regroup at Arras, in dribs and drabs, and our village was only seven miles away, to the south-east. A place called Fontaine-lès-Croisilles. Just a poor farming area. By chance, I'd stopped there on my way home. I'd gone down to the south at first, to the Mediterranean, working my way as I went. I spent a few years working in a vineyard, and then I decided to come home. But by the time I got back up north, I was running out of money and I found work on this small farm. For an older couple who were beginning to find it hard to cope. When they took me on, I didn't know they had a beautiful daughter. Madeleine.' A sad smile flickered over his features, and for a moment he seemed lost in his own bittersweet memories before he shook his head sharply. 'You know what happened then,' he forced himself onwards with a heartfelt sigh. 'After she died, I naturally stayed on. I couldn't leave Chantal, and neither could I take her away from her grandparents. Maddy's death really aged them. Xavier could hardly work any longer, so they needed me to work the farm for them. And then eventually the war came along.'

His face hardened again, his jaw clamped fiercely. Elizabeth found herself listening intently, the initial shock subsiding, though she knew the worst, what she was dreading, was yet to come.

'After Sedan, the Prussians flooded the entire area,' Richard continued. 'You can't imagine what it's like to live in an occupied country. You can't sneeze without them knowing. There were troops everywhere. They were looking for French soldiers, of course, any that had escaped from Sedan and then, later, for any who might be trying to join forces at Arras. There was a local network, a sort of underground resistance, secretly helping any French soldier. I vowed not to become involved. I saw it as my role to protect Chantal and her grandparents. Anyone who was remotely suspected of harbouring a French soldier was taken out and shot, no questions asked.' His words faltered again, his eyes shutting briefly at some terrible memory, and Elizabeth's face tightened with horror. 'Not only that,' Richard went on, his tone hard with resentment, 'the Prussians took everything they wanted, food, money. It's surprising what you'll hand over when you're staring down the barrel of a rifle. But there were the French partisans as well. Small groups, working independently, picking off the odd Prussian soldier, setting ambushes for patrols, that sort of thing. They were genuine in the main, doing whatever they could to fight for their country. But there were others who saw it as a licence to run riot. They became undisciplined, expecting local people to consider them as heroes, and demanding food and shelter just like the Prussians, except they were often worse. Anyway, by the spring, the situation in Paris was really building up. You'll probably know from the papers that the French were at each other's throats, different factions fighting and killing each other while the Prussians were laying siege to the city?' He looked up, bitter lines about his mouth, and Elizabeth nodded. Yes, she had read about it, and the news had appalled her at the time. But Paris had seemed a long way off. She realized now it wasn't.

Richard seemed to hesitate. He sucked in his lean cheeks, the expression on his face crucifying as he wrung his hands. Elizabeth watched him, motionless, her chest crippled with dread as she realized he was coming to his own part of the story, to the murder he had committed. He started to speak again, but the sound died on his lips. He had to clear his throat, and even then his voice was strange and husky. 'By May,' he croaked, 'the Prussians were concentrating their forces around Paris in the final push towards its fall. Because of that, their presence in our area was vastly diminished, much to our relief. All everyone wanted was surrender and for our lives to return to normal. Mine . . . didn't.' He paused, dropping his head into his hands, his words almost too terrible to utter. 'I was out working in the fields. I heard a couple of shots, but we were used to gunfire. But something told me . . . I ran to the farmhouse. And then . . . I went inside.'

His shoulders heaved in a violent, strangling sob, and Elizabeth snatched in her breath.

'Go on,' she prompted, though her heart was thundering.

He didn't lift his head. 'I'll . . . never forget . . .' he breathed in a distraught whisper. 'Marie and Xavier . . . they were . . . huddled together on the floor. Sitting . . . arms still about each other.' And then, strangely, his voice became cold as he said, 'Both of them shot clean through the head. The wall behind them was . . .'

Elizabeth's senses reeled, her mind hearing but somehow blocking out his horrific, vivid description. She simply didn't want to hear any more, but Richard was talking freely now as if, having broken the barrier, his thoughts were flowing out unchecked, and Elizabeth had to force herself to listen.

'One of them was eating straight out of the pot, with his fingers, just like an animal. The other one had . . . had little Aurélie over the table . . . The girl from the village who helped Marie in the house . . . twelve years old . . . and . . . and . . .' His handsome mouth drew wide in a stricken grimace, and Elizabeth could see he was fighting off desperate tears. 'No one moved,' he choked brokenly. 'They were just as shocked as I was. They were French partisans, not even Prussians. I . . .' He pushed his clenched fist against his mouth so that the words came out muffled. 'I went berserk. Totally lost my reason. They'd left their rifles propped up by the door. I grabbed one, and used the butt to hit the one who was . . . He fell off the table, and I went to hit him again. But then I was hit myself from behind. I swung round. The other chap was wielding the other gun, using the butt the same as I had. I'd been used to shotguns all my life, and with the war, I'd observed a lot as well. In that split second, I realized it was an old muzzleloader he had, so I guess he knew it would take too long to load it and shoot me with it.

And thank God, the bayonet was missing. But the one *I* was holding was a chassepot. The French army rifle. So whether one or the other of them had deserted and turned partisan instead, I don't know. Anyway, they both went for me, but I was determined to hold on to that rifle, no matter what. The one without the gun, he drew a knife instead, but I knocked it out of his hand with the rifle butt. It went under the dresser, and from the way he hollered I think I must have broken some bones in his hand or wrist or something. Then the other fellow made one last effort and swung the barrel of the other rifle at me. I managed to duck so that it only caught me on the shoulder. Even so, I nearly blacked out and he tried again to take the chassepot from me. But,' Richard sighed, talking slowly as he recalled every detail, 'I suppose when you're in a situation like that, you find some strength within you. All I know is that one of them was screaming in pain, and the other realized I was stronger than he was and I also had the better weapon. He gave up and they both ran off while they could. It took me a minute or two to come to my senses properly, and then . . . I checked if the rifle was loaded. So automatically. I remember I could smell it had only just been fired. He must have used it to shoot . . . well, probably Xavier first . . . and then reloaded to kill Marie. It only takes a second or two to reload, you see, and I remembered there was a short gap between . . . The chamber was empty. I was mad with anger. And then I noticed an ammunition pouch on the floor. It must have slid from one of their belts as they took their trousers down to . . . It was full of the special cartridges you need for a chassepot. It's what's called a needle-gun. So I loaded it and ran outside. They were already at the far side of the field, but with such an accurate gun, and . . . well, you know I'm a fairly good shot. I fired. And one of them fell. The other one stopped, but I reloaded and fired again. That time I missed, but it frightened him off. He left his comrade on the ground. When I got to him, he was dead.'

Richard was gazing at her, his face ashen. Elizabeth stared back, not knowing what to say, what to feel, her brain numbed. She shivered, and her hand reached out to open the door of the firebox, although she could have sworn she hadn't moved a muscle. The heat spilled out, putting spots of crimson in her cheeks. Richard watched her, his brow furrowed in some hellish agony as he waited silently for her condemnation.

But she couldn't . . . How could she . . . 'Was there . . . was there nothing else you could have done?' her lips trembled.

He slowly shook his head, closing his eyes so that the lashes fanned out darkly on his cheeks. 'You couldn't just go and fetch a constable,' he rasped bitterly. 'The Prussians had turned everything upside down. And anyway, I just didn't think until it was too late. And by then, I was in real trouble. If anyone had found out . . . I was an Englishman who'd shot a brave French partisan. Oh yes! That's how people would have seen it. I'd have been lynched.'

'Even after what they'd done?'

'Oh, Beth, I don't *know*! I've been over and over it a million times in my mind! I don't think I'll ever know if what I did was right or wrong!' His cry was hysterical, heart-rending as he bit down hard on his knuckles. 'I just . . . keep seeing their faces, Xavier and Marie, clinging to each other . . . And Aurélie, just a child! I was too late . . . She'd already been . . . They'd probably have killed her afterwards as well if I hadn't got there when I did.'

He hung his head, his shoulders shaking in violent spasms. Elizabeth felt her heart bleeding as she absorbed the horror of his story. No wonder he'd kept it to himself for so long. But the strain of it must have been unbearable. To keep such wretchedness locked inside . . . And yet, he'd done such a terrible thing. But . . . if she'd been there, witnessed what he had seen . . . But she knew there was no evil in Richard Pencarrow. That his actions had been spurred by grief and anger. That he had suffered such intolerable guilt . . .

Elizabeth's hand closed firmly about his wrist, and his eyes lifted to hers. 'You did,' she whispered hoarsely, 'what any decent man would have done. No one could blame you. And in the heat of the moment . . .'

'But that's just it, Beth. I was totally calm. I knew exactly what I was doing. I could have aimed to wound him, but I didn't. I aimed to kill. And I'd have killed the other one as well if I'd been able to.'

'And he'd have deserved it.' She caught her breath, meeting his startled gaze. In that moment, she suddenly knew that she believed what she was saying. 'They'd . . . violated a young girl, and killed a defenceless elderly couple. In England, they'd have hanged for that! You did the only thing you could, and I think none the less of you because of it. I just . . . I just wish you'd told me before.'

Her eyes stared hard into his, but the pain only seemed to deepen in his haggard face. 'How could I? You'd have hated me even more than you did already. And it's hardly something you blurt out to a stranger. As it is, only Aurélie and her parents, and the village priest know what happened.' He paused, dashing his hand over his eyes. 'Her parents helped me bury the dead man. He was so young, not much more than twenty, which somehow made it all worse. It seemed the only thing to do, bury the body where it would never be found. The priest buried Xavier and Marie, of course. He put about the story that Xavier had dropped dead with a heart attack, and Marie was so distraught, she followed him within hours. They *were* both very frail. They'd had Maddy late in life, and her death had broken them. I'd always felt guilty about that, too. As if it was my fault. Anyway, nobody suspected anything, at least, not that we know.'

'But . . . what happened then? I mean, your leg . . . ?'

His eyebrows lifted in a rueful arch. 'A few days later, Paris fell,' he went on. 'They say there were terrible recriminations in the city. But no one bothered about what was going on in a country hamlet. The Prussians left and we picked up our lives again. I thought about coming home to England. But I'd been the official tenant of the farm for some time with the rent paid well in advance. And far more than that, it was Chantal's home, and after losing both her grandparents . . . And,' his mouth twisted sadly, 'I didn't want to leave Maddy's grave. The summer came and went. And then, one day, I was out ploughing. Aurélie came rushing hell for leather across the fields to warn me some madman was running amok in the village with a rifle. In the chaos that followed the fall of Paris, many weapons were never handed in, you see. And this devil was demanding to know where the Englishman was. Some poor sod was so frightened, he'd told him. And by then, I could see him coming. As you might imagine, I ran!' He paused for a moment and his eyes flashed at her. 'My instinct was to double back to a small wood behind the village, to a secret arbour no stranger would ever find. But until you get there, it's all open fields. He got within range and opened fire. The first shot missed, but . . . well . . .' He wet his lips and swallowed. 'I was almost at the wood, when something stung into my leg. I knew I'd been hit, but I *had* to get to the arbour. Fortunately, my trousers were soaking up the blood, or I'd have left a trail a blind man could follow. It wasn't until I was safely hidden that the pain hit me. I wanted to scream, but he came within three feet of me and I had to keep as still as a mouse. But by then I'd lost so much blood, I passed out anyway and . . . The next thing I knew, I was in Father André's house. After hearing what had happened, he'd put two and two together and the arbour was the first place he'd looked, thank God. The man who'd shot me had gone off shouting that he'd be back to finish me off. That he'd learned I had a daughter and he'd kill her first, so that I'd know what it was like to lose a child. He was obviously the father of the boy I'd killed,' he continued, his voice low and uncertain. 'Like a fool, I'd shouted at them in English, and I suppose the other fellow must have told him. It made me pretty easy to find. Only I don't suppose he'd told him what they'd done between them. But . . . the decision to leave was instantaneous. Chantal's life was in danger as well as my own, and if the truth had come out . . . I'd probably have been hanged by a lynch-mob if not by whatever authority was eventually re-established. The best thing seemed to be to spirit Chantal and me away during the night. Poor child didn't know what was going on. I just thanked God she hadn't been at the farmhouse when they'd . . . Or even out ploughing with me that day. It was sheer luck . . . Amazingly, it turned out Father André had been part of the secret network. We'd had no idea. In the middle of the night, he took us in his trap to a woman a couple of parishes away. I should think she was eighty if she was a day. She was used to patching up wounds, and . . . well, all things considered, we decided not to fetch a doctor. *She* didn't ask any questions, but someone else might. The trouble was, I think her eyesight was failing, and all she had in the way of anaesthetic or antiseptic was a bottle of brandy.'

Elizabeth shuddered. 'Yes, I remember you saying. But I must confess, I wasn't so sympathetic then.'

The hint of a wry smile tugged at Richard's lips. 'No, I don't suppose you were. I must have been pretty obnoxious when I crashed in through the door. But I was in such a state by then, I really didn't know what I was doing. You know what a mess the old woman made. Thank God, I was only semi-conscious at the time. But after a couple of days, I'd recovered enough to be hidden in a farm-cart that got us to the other side of Arras. From then on, we were on our own, but I felt better by then. Father André had been back to our farmhouse for a change of clothes for me, and burned all the bloodstained ones. He'd fetched all the money I had, and gave me all he could spare, too. I owe him my life and yet it'd be too dangerous to contact him again. Anyway, it was just enough for the fare to the coast, and then I managed to talk our way onto a British merchant ship to get across the Channel. That took a day and a half, and by then I knew something was seriously wrong. I felt so ill, Beth, I can't tell you, and the pain was just getting worse and worse. I had with me the watch my uncle had given me before he went to the Crimea. As soon as we landed, I pawned it. I wonder what he'd have thought if he'd known it would help save my life twenty years later. We got a train to London, spent the night on the streets, and caught the morning train to Plymouth, then another up to Tavistock. Those nine hours on the train were the longest I've ever known. Every minute was torture. I hired a cab at the station, but I only had enough money left to take us to the village. How I walked up here, I honestly don't know. Just the will to be here, I suppose. To see Chantal safe. And . . . the rest you know.'

He finished speaking, and Elizabeth sank back in the armchair, her index fingers pressed hard against her pursed lips. She felt drained. The laudanum had muddled her senses, and yet her neck and head still throbbed with a dull ache. She sat immobile for what seemed an eternity, trying to take in the details of Richard's harrowing story, and acutely aware of his presence. Her heart was locked in a tangled web — horror, shock, disbelief, interlaced with sorrow and even admiration. It explained so much. Little things Chantal had said. Richard's fever-ridden nightmares, his reaction when the child had aimed the rifle at Uncle Matthew. His general behaviour, the sullen reticence that was gradually mellowing.

'No one must ever know.' She realized Richard had spoken again, his tone weary as if his emotional endurance, too, was spent. 'Especially Chantal. She believes her grandparents died because they were old, and that I was shot by some madman. She'll forget in time. The war, the Prussian occupation, it was all so confusing for a child. She can build now on the security *you've* given her. I trust . . . I *beg* you, Beth,' his voice cracked, 'never to tell a living soul. I know what I did was terrible, but I live with that guilt every day of my life.'

'Then you shouldn't.' Her eyes looked into his, clear and steady with resolve. 'I believe you did the only thing you could. But you should have told me before now.'

Richard bowed his head. 'It wasn't easy,' he murmured, his jaw set like a rock. 'And I apologize for unburdening myself on you, especially after the day you've had.'

Elizabeth shivered as she suddenly remembered how the conversation had started, and his proposal of marriage. It paled into insignificance after the story he'd told. It would take some time for her to absorb the full horror of it, but at least now *she knew*. And she was already beginning to feel they could build on the trust he had placed in her.

'I'll . . . think about it,' she said, her voice little more than a whisper. 'About . . . getting married. But now . . . I think I'll go to bed.'

And she felt Richard's eyes on her as she walked out of the room.

* * *

Tavistock, December 1872

'Shall I deal?' The neat little man sat back in his chair and drew deeply on his cigar. His rotund belly sprawled incongruously above his trousers like a lump of clay slapped on by a potter with a facetious sense of humour. If it hadn't been for the sharp expression on his face, he might have appeared comical.

'No, I don't think so, Bruce,' Maurice Brett replied somewhat irritably, and glanced at his companions around the gaming table. They nodded in agreement and Maurice smiled congenially. 'Just because you're on a winning streak! You've cleaned me out, and I didn't bring any cheques with me. I'll just finish my drink and I'll be off home.'

'Oh, come now, Maurice, gentlemen.' The fellow's porcine eyes glinted through the haze of cigar smoke. 'The night is young. It's Christmas Eve. You can't go home yet. You can always write an IOU.'

Maurice hesitated. It would be good to have the chance to win back his money. It was a paltry amount for someone of his financial status, but he was convinced the devil was cheating and he wanted to prove it. Maurice didn't hold with cheating. You used your skill at cards and your brain to outwit your opponent, and the element of luck was exciting, but you didn't cheat.

'If you're happy to accept.'

'I'll accept IOUs from the present company.' The man called Bruce grinned like a fox. 'I wouldn't from just anyone, mind. Remember Josiah Pencarrow? Lost a tidy sum to me, but never paid up. And now the old sod's dead, I'll never get the money.'

The hairs bristled at the back of Maurice's neck. His collar suddenly felt tight, and he ran his finger inside it to loosen its stiffness. The Arkwright boy had come to him sporting a black eye and walking a little strangely, babbling that he wouldn't do any more 'tricks' for him. Maurice had been furious, but his supply of little pills had been helping him to forget the exquisite young woman with the amber eyes whom he longed to possess. But at the mention of the Pencarrow name, his pulse accelerated and his damned fingers trembled.

'Same with me,' he managed to grumble quite casually. 'The son's back, though. Completely debt-ridden, of course, so there's no use presenting him with any IOUs even if I still had them, and I wouldn't know how legal they'd be, anyway.'

'Yes, I heard he was back. Over a year now. And making a go of the place again, by all accounts. Mind you, he always was a worker as I remember, even as a lad. And have you heard, he was married a few weeks back? To some sort of servant girl. Used to look after the old man. Pretty wench, they say.'

They all turned their heads as Maurice spluttered into his drink.

TWENTY-SIX

March 1873

It was early March, and there were signs that spring was on its way. Snow had fallen high on the moor during the winter and had been driven by vicious winds into deep drifts from which farmers needed to extricate the older wethers that had been left to roam free. They always had to be checked regularly and extra fodder provided when necessary, but the snow was an added difficulty and Farmer Widcock was more than grateful to be able to call on Richard when he needed an extra pair of hands. The rushing water in the mine-leats had never frozen, though, so the massive wheels in Mary Tavy trundled on, keeping the mines productive; only the surface-workers grumbled as the biting cold made their chapped hands bleed. But it was a job and it put food in the mouths of their children. And Lizzie Thornton, or Lizzie Pencarrow as she was now, would always have some soothing unguent to rub into their stinging skin, and she only charged a penny or two in exchange.

But for Maurice Brett, the winter meant succulent hot meals, a new overcoat and two new pairs of gloves, evenings spent toasting himself before a blazing fire, cocooned in a warm cradle of content. Or so his colleagues imagined, although they noticed he socialized less these days. He kept a strict eye on his business investments, in which he was apt to be more ruthless, attending meetings and dinners, but he rarely appeared at their private gambling sessions and other dubious entertainments. No one missed him. He'd become surly, no longer the dominant force behind their activities. And he was looking thinner, so perhaps his health wasn't what it used to be.

Maurice's hand hesitated on the handle of the drawer. He'd reached towards it instinctively as he did every evening when he felt cold and shivering, though his flesh sweated and his muscles ached with unease. The tiny pills always worked, but now he needed two or three instead of just one. The supplier in Plymouth grinned and rubbed his hands as Maurice's custom became more frequent, while Maurice grimaced at the wad of cash he had to part with. Still, without the opium he felt as if he was permanently suffering from a vicious bout of influenza; but as he reached again for the drawer, he realized with a shock that it was only nine o'clock in the morning. Good God! He wasn't becoming addicted, was he? The thought dumbfounded him, and he sat down abruptly on the edge of the bed. That was why the stuff had been made illegal, of course, except when prescribed by a physician. But surely he, Maurice Brett, couldn't succumb to its powers? Surely he was stronger than that! Mind you, the old hell-hag in the stinking room across the landing was enough to drive a man to drink, or any other solace he could find. He never ventured through the door unless it was strictly necessary. If he did, she'd instantly harangue him about his duty to produce a legitimate heir, and her ranting could be heard through the entire house. Jesus Christ, the old crow was insufferable!

Yes, he knew he needed a wife. But there was only one woman who could ever fulfil that role in his heart, and now because of that bastard Pencarrow, he could never have her. Maurice closed his eyes and she danced before him, her tiny waist, her slender arms swaying gracefully in a way that set his heart racing and tightened the pit of his belly. Elizabeth was like a rosebud just blossoming into the full flower of womanhood, sweet and tender, yet full of desire. She would run the tip of her pink tongue between her pretty bowed lips, her golden eyes brilliant with teasing, her springing, radiant hair loosened from its pins and cascading down her back in a shining, waving curtain. And then she would . . . slowly . . .

His eyes snapped open and he had to stifle a wounded cry. She would never do that for him. But she would be doing it now for Ritchie Pencarrow! That bloody clever, handsome pup whom he'd hated as a child with his strait-laced, moralistic attitude. Not only had he spoilt Maurice's face for life, but now he'd taken the one woman Maurice had ever really felt any true emotion for. The strength of his own longing astounded him, but it was there, day and night. It was wrong, he recognized that, an obsession fuelled by his jealousy. But he was helpless, and there was nothing he could do about it.

Or was there . . . ?

He was a shareholder in Wheal Friendship. There was no reason why he shouldn't occasion a visit. And while he was there, he might come across the Arkwright boy. Ten pounds should change the devil's mind. Besides, the mine wasn't far from Peter Tavy and he might catch a glimpse of her, talk to her even, politely and amiably, and ease the pain in his heart.

* * *

'Goûtons voir, oui, oui, oui,
'Goûtons voir, non, non, non,
Goûtons voir si le vin est bon!
Goûtons voir, oui, oui, oui,
Goûtons voir, non, non, non,
Goûtons voir si le vin est bon!'

The snow had finally melted from the high moorland, swelling the rivers into dangerous, swirling eddies, but this morning a chillsome wind was driving a fine drizzle against their faces like sharp barbs of ice. Chantal, though, hardly seemed to notice as she skipped along the track to the jaunty rhythm of the song she chanted lustily at the top of her voice. Her joyful enthusiasm brought a smile to Elizabeth's face as she found herself joining in the easy part of the chorus.

Chantal turned to her with a giggle, her two new front teeth looking enormous in her child's mouth. '*Papa est très méchant à m'enseigner cette chanson, tu sais,*' she confided, her eyes twinkling roguishly. '*Oh, pardon!* Papa is very naughty to teach me this song. It is an old drinking song, about a man who want to be buried in a wine cellar with 'is 'ead under the tap of the — 'ow you say — ah, *oui*, barrel. And 'e want to be writed on 'is tomb that 'e is the king of the drinkers! So it is not really a good song to teach a little girl, but Papa can be very funny sometime. 'E is not always . . .' She pulled a long face, and to emphasize her expression, ran her index fingers down her cheeks. 'We drink always much wine in France, you know, Elizabett,' she added wisely.

'So I believe.' Elizabeth concealed her amusement with a grave frown. 'Your father complains that your grandfather filled the cellar with good wine when he had no money to pay for it, but I notice he enjoys drinking the occasional bottle. And I quite like a glass myself to keep him company,' she admitted.

The merriment slid from Chantal's face as they walked on in silence for some minutes. 'You and Papa, why do you not sleep in the same room? It is what you do when you are married, *n'est-ce pas?*'

Elizabeth's palms were suddenly clammy with sweat. The child's question had sliced through her contentment, driving a cruel wedge of doubt into her heart. However deeply she dug into her soul, she still wasn't sure quite why she'd agreed to marry Richard. A grim understanding had developed between them since the terrible evening he'd made his broken confession to her. Elizabeth had been shocked to the core, although not by what Richard had done so much as by the horrifying effect that war could have on ordinary people's lives. For several days afterwards, they'd tiptoed politely around each other, fearful of the other's reaction, until Elizabeth could stand the tension no longer, and had summoned the courage to broach the matter once more. It seemed it was all Richard needed. He began to talk, going over every detail, the agony etched deep in his drawn, anguished face as he poured out to her the desperate guilt that had been torturing him for so long. But opening up his heart to her had provided such a release that the real Richard Pencarrow, the strong, kind, hard-working man whose face could light like a beacon when he smiled, was growing more apparent with every day that passed. And when, on a sudden impulse, she'd said yes, she would marry him, they'd both been so astounded, neither of them had spoken for several minutes.

Richard had certainly been right on one score. In the weeks between his proposal and her acceptance, she'd realized that people had been cooler in their attitude to her, whispering behind her back, their conversations patently interrupted as she entered the village shop. But the moment the first banns had been read, she'd been regaled with congratulations, welcomed back to the fold, as it were. It was meant to be a quiet wedding with no invited guests, just William to give her away, dear old George acting as best man, Chantal as bridesmaid and George's wife as the congregation. But the church had been crowded with well-wishers, even though there was to be no wedding breakfast. There'd been an awkward moment when Richard had been given permission to kiss the bride and, thankfully, he'd merely brushed a peck onto her cheek. But that night, and every night since, he'd kept to his word and retired to his own room as if nothing had changed.

And now little Chantal, with her innocent question, had opened up the uncertainties Elizabeth had been trying to bury in the back of her mind. She was bound to Richard Pencarrow for life, and she envisaged the years stretching ahead, secure in the home she loved so dearly, safe now from her uncle and Thomas Arkwright, and happy with her lot.

But, just sometimes, she wondered if she hadn't made the most horrendous mistake.

She chewed on her lip. She could answer the child's question, but not her own. 'Your father and I both work so hard,' she said cautiously. 'We need a good night's sleep and wouldn't want to disturb each other.'

Chantal shrugged in that odd, indolent way she had, and skipped on, her tight curls bouncing about her head, as they came down the combe, to the little row of cottages where her friends were waiting. This morning, Elizabeth had a patient to visit in the village and was armed with a basket of remedies, so she waved to the other mothers on their doorsteps — for she counted herself among their number now — and followed the chattering group of children down to the school. Chantal was like a magnet, she mused, her young peers flocking about her, eager to hear her charming, faltering accent, and she was delighted to oblige.

It was as Elizabeth walked away from the school that she spotted the two familiar figures coming down the lane, Mr Widcock's rotund torso lumbering on his bandy legs, and Richard's striding gait, all sign of a limp now disappeared, his gun slung over his shoulder by its leather strap. Elizabeth waited for them, surprised as several people hurried past behind her. Their haste struck her as unusual, but she paid little heed. Richard had been out all night, helping Mr Widcock hunt down a troublesome fox that had been worrying his ewes. They would be exhausted, and she wondered if the venture had been a success.

She returned Richard's enigmatic smile as the two men drew level with her. 'Did you catch him?' she asked warily.

'We did that!' Mr Widcock nodded, his round head bobbing on his thick neck. 'This husband of yourn be a crack shot! I could've peppered old foxy with my shotgun, but when I lured the old devil with the lanterns, Richard yere got him clean between the eyes with that rifle of his!'

Elizabeth caught Richard's eye and the look that passed between them spoke secret volumes. Beneath the dark shadow of overnight stubble, Richard's jaw was set. He took no pleasure in killing any animal, and Elizabeth alone knew how he detested having to use a gun for whatever reason.

'The poor thing didn't suffer then?' she said with compassion, and saw Richard raise a surprised but appreciative eyebrow. 'Oh, well, 'tis for the best. We can't have a rogue fox on the loose with lambing about to start.'

Mr Widcock's kindly face seemed somewhat nonplussed at her words, and he looked about him in bewilderment as several more villagers scurried by, heading in the direction of the river. He shook his head, mumbled something incomprehensible under his breath, and evidently went off to question someone on the unexpected activity.

Richard bent his head as he spoke to her, keeping his voice low. 'Thank you. It wasn't exactly easy shooting the wretched creature.'

'I know.' Her fingers intuitively squeezed his arm as her soft, velvet eyes gazed into his dark, troubled ones. The taut muscles of his strained face relaxed and his mouth moved into the shadow of a smile.

'Been an accident down Wheal Anne!' Mr Widcock's animated voice broke into their conversation. 'Men trapped or summat! Serious, they say!'

'That's impossible. Wheal Anne's been abandoned for nearly twenty years.'

Elizabeth felt Richard stiffen beside her. Minor accidents were almost a daily occurrence underground, the occasional fatality accepted with stoicism, but a defunct mine could present untold dangers. The small mine along the riverbank had been idle ever since she could remember, the entrances sealed against any foolhardy explorer, so how . . .

'Come on. Let's find out what's going on.' Richard took her elbow and propelled her towards the lane that led down beside the inn. 'We may be able to help.'

They found themselves virtually running down the long, steep track, Richard taking the basket so that Elizabeth could hitch up the hem of her skirt. There were others, both behind and in front of them, as the news spread, all with faces creased with dread. When they reached the wooden bridge that spanned the gushing river on stout stone pillars, the desperation that hovered in the dank air was palpable. The riverbank was a treeless muddle of derelict mine buildings, overgrown wheel-pits, their wheels long gone, rusted kibbles and a rotting stamp, all latticed with leats and escaping water that had formed into trickling rivulets. The distant clatter of machinery and shouting voices from Wheal Friendship on the opposite side of the river echoed eerily as the crowd that had gathered huddled together in small, silent groups, shoulders hunched as each one gathered his or her terror inside as they waited to hear exactly who was involved, hardly daring to breathe, let alone utter a word. Women with worn shawls wrapped tightly about them in a vain attempt to shut out the shivering cold of shock, small children clinging to their mothers' skirts, and bleary-eyed men waking from their sleep after yesterday's late shift and anxious to help whoever it was had ventured down the old mine.

Elizabeth held her breath. So many people moving about soundlessly in an unreal world, desperate for news of a husband, father, brother, son, so certain they were at work down on one of the levels of Wheal Friendship, and wouldn't have been reckless enough to go down the disused shafts, and yet dreading to hear those ultimate, fatal words. Elizabeth glanced up at Richard, seeking his reassurance, but his eyes met hers with equal solemnity.

'You stay here,' Richard whispered, instinctively joining the muted shroud that enveloped the sea of dejected faces. 'I'll be back as soon as I find out what's happening.'

He weaved away from her through the crowd. Elizabeth stood for several minutes, feeling strangely alone, surrounded as she was by people she'd known all her life, but who were all incarcerated in personal agony as they feared the worst. Mr Widcock had wandered over to some other acquaintance, his natural geniality respectfully subdued. Elizabeth followed his example, floating noiselessly between the white-faced statues, offering a comforting smile here, a hand squeezed in sympathy there, for there was no magic cure for this ailment among the remedies in her basket. She passed Susan Penrose, another sleeping babe in her arms, eyes wide as she sought news of her young husband. Safe, or among those involved in the accident?

'Good day to you, Miss Thornton, or should I say, Mrs Pencarrow? I understand congratulations are in order?'

Elizabeth jerked up her head at the unctuous voice that slashed through the tense atmosphere all about her. Who did she possibly know who'd be so callous as to speak aloud in such a glib, insidious tone? And yet some recollection was triggered in the depths of her memory. Her eyes flashed with reproach, and Maurice Brett felt his heart lurch. She was so glorious when she was vexed.

'What are *you* doing here?' she hissed. She'd recognized him the instant she saw him, even though she'd only ever clapped eyes on him twice in her life. His despicable behaviour at Josiah's funeral mingled with her anger at how he'd then attempted to buy her from her uncle, and the vicious attack on her it had provoked. Not that Matthew's drunken assault had been his fault, but the fellow's obnoxious presence at this terrible time was outrageous.

'I happen to be a shareholder in Wheal Friendship.' Maurice's words were more subdued this time. 'I was merely paying a visit, but didn't expect to find such a catastrophe.'

It was true. He'd come in search of Thomas Arkwright, hoping he could persuade the knave to perform some perfidious act that would ruin all the effort Ritchie Pencarrow had put into rebuilding his farm — and drive his lovely young wife away from him. Instead, he'd found the mining community in the throes of a horrendous disaster which was touching even his outsider's heart.

'Well, perhaps you could have the decency to show some respect for those whose lives are in danger,' Elizabeth spat.

Oh, she was magnificent! Married life had given her even more confidence! But married life with Ritchie Pencarrow!

How he'd love to tear that bloody bastard apart, limb from limb.

'Please, forgive me, Mrs Pencarrow,' Maurice purred, swallowing his jealousy with acrid resentment. 'It's just that I've known your husband,' and he nearly choked on the word, 'since he was a child, and I've not yet had the chance to say how pleased I am for him. I meant no disrespect to these poor people. I just wish there was something I could do to help.'

'Put your hand in your pocket for the widows,' she grated implacably.

Maurice blinked at her, his chest swelling with admiration. Her mettlesome spirit took his breath away, such undaunted defiance quite mesmerizing in someone so delicately beautiful. 'Of course,' he managed to answer levelly. 'I'm not a miserly man, you know. I was the one who persuaded the board of Wheal Friendship into higher percentages for the miners, and various extra safety measures.'

Elizabeth pursed her lips. Yes, she'd heard something about it, and it peeved her that Maurice Brett had been the instigator of such philanthropy. But she had no time to ponder further as the crowd suddenly surged forward as one of the mine-captains and other officials from Wheal Friendship, followed by a team of grim-faced tributers, made their way to the centre of the throng to make an announcement. Elizabeth could see Richard coming towards her, his expression grave and forbidding. When he saw Maurice Brett standing beside her, he threw him such a disparaging glance that the ingratiating smirk slipped from Maurice's lips. Not a word passed between the two men, and though her heart cried out to hear the announcement, Elizabeth allowed Richard to lead her aside.

'What the devil is *he* doing here?' he muttered sourly.

'I'm not sure,' Elizabeth whispered back, her voice a confused murmur. 'Said he was just visiting. He's a shareholder in Wheal Friendship, you know.'

Richard lifted his eyebrows. 'That's true enough. But we could do without him today.' He paused, and as his dark, steady eyes fixed hers, Elizabeth felt her heart drop down inside her like a lead weight. 'Apparently, some London adventurers are interested in re-opening Wheal Anne,' Richard told her, 'and as men were arriving for the early shift this morning, they offered any willing tributers from Wheal Friendship a good sum of money to go down and make some initial explorations. They had a mining engineer with them so it should have been relatively safe, but one of the volunteers was Thomas Arkwright. The one chap who managed to escape in the nick of time saw him, but it was too late for the others. He'd already lit the fuse. The bloody idiot took it upon himself to blast out what he thought might be a rich vein, I suppose. They were on an upper level that hadn't flooded, but it didn't dawn on the half-wit that he was at the far end abutting right against an old adit of Wheal Rosalind. The fool used so much explosive, he blasted right through. And of course, the whole of Wheal Rosalind is further downstream, and I remember the problems we used to have with drainage.'

Elizabeth felt a vile, cold sweat moisten her back. 'Oh, no,' she moaned piteously. 'Then they've all drowned?'

'Not necessarily. It would depend on the level of water. The explosion caused a massive rockfall that's completely blocked the level from the Wheal Anne end. They're already working to clear it, but it could take days.' His brow furrowed as his hands tightened about her upper arms. 'The others who went down . . . One of them . . . was your cousin Daniel.'

Elizabeth's head swam sickeningly and she was unaware of Richard holding her as she swayed on her feet. Young Daniel, so meek and inoffensive. It was unbearable.

'Elizabeth,' Richard was saying urgently now, 'I've got to leave you. There's a possibility we can reach them better from the other side. From Wheal Rosalind.'

She gazed at him, immobile, as the full, terrifying meaning of his words sank into her brain. Oh, no. She couldn't take that, too.

'I've given the gun to Mr Widcock to look after,' Richard told her, his face tight. 'And the rest of the cartridges. Obviously I can't take them down with me.'

'Mr Pencarrow, sir . . .' an entreating voice behind him pressed.

'Beth, I must go.'

'No, Richard, please!' She must stop him, and she clung frenziedly to his arm. 'You can't!' she wailed miserably. 'You've been up on the moor all night. You must be exhausted already.'

'I've got to, Beth.' But his eyes were questioning the strength of her feelings as he frowned at her. 'No one knows Wheal Rosalind like I do. The miners we employed are all long gone. Now don't worry. I promise I won't take any stupid risks. There'll be no heroics. And we're well prepared.'

'Promise, Richard?' The tiny whisper squealed from her lungs.

'Promise.' And his eyes smiled with an intensity she'd never seen in them before.

She watched him go, joining the team of rescuers armed with ropes, pickaxes, levers and jacks, and any other equipment they expected to need. She was empty, sick with dread as the gathered assembly walked past her, following the rescue team along the riverbank where it flattened out to allow the great rock of Longtimber Tor to rise up like a majestic tower, and then along to the boarded-up entrances of Wheal Rosalind, all surface machinery dismantled long ago, and the small mine building already disappearing beneath a jungle of ivy. Her eyes were blinded to the figures that shuffled past. The only image her jangled mind would focus upon was of Richard risking his own life in the pitch-black, water-engulfed abyss of hell somewhere in the belly of the earth deep beneath her feet.

* * *

Minutes turned into hours. Eternity became a reality. It took some time to prise the boards from the main mine entrance which was evidently where Richard wanted to try first. There were so many preparations, ropes to be tied, drawings and diagrams of the underground workings to be studied, grim discussions, and Richard in the thick of it. William Greenwood had arrived from Tavistock and begun organizing makeshift stretchers. Matthew Halse had been fetched from his farm, and stumbled unsteadily towards the derelict mine, supported by his daughter, Nellie, and his new wife. Matthew's head was muddled not with drink, but with the awful fear of losing his son — most precious son, if the truth be told; the only one of his four offspring to resemble his beloved Margaret, God rest her soul. Matthew looked frail, a shadow of the hectoring bully who'd dominated all their lives, his face a ghoulish grey and tears in his eyes. His wife led him away like a malleable child as he began babbling to Elizabeth that he was so mortal sorry, over and over again — though sorry for what, Widow Silverlock, as by local tradition she was still often known, had no idea. Nellie fell on Elizabeth's neck, almost crushing her, as she wept inconsolably, and Elizabeth tried to comfort her, while at the same time suffering her own dreadful nightmare.

Finally, Elizabeth managed to free herself and scramble up the slope towards the lane, away from the sinisterly silent crowd that milled aimlessly below her. From her lonely vantage point, she could clearly see the group of men by the mine entrance, suddenly still as it seemed all preparations were complete. And then she saw Richard, his head crowned with a hardhat, a candle fixed to the brim in time-honoured fashion, pause by the narrow, irregular fissure in the hillside. He looked about him, searching, but didn't spot her, and as he disappeared from view, swallowed up by the hungry earth, something inside her died. Slowly Elizabeth sank to her knees. The contentment that she realized now had cradled her since her marriage to Richard Pencarrow had fragmented into splinters of despair.

Richard's swift, agitated gaze hadn't found her, but someone else's had. Maurice Brett felt the life go out of him as he watched Elizabeth from a distance. She was distraught. Composed and dignified as he knew she would be, but frantic with worry over her husband. He'd hoped against hope that there might be some chink between them, that even now he could somehow make her his. But it was as clear as day that she loved him. Maurice shut his eyes at the vile thought that came into his head. May God forgive him, but he prayed Ritchie Pencarrow would never emerge from the mine alive.

* * *

It had rained while they waited, but no one really noticed. Heavy, fat drops that plopped onto the surface of the rapidly growing puddles, making little circular ripples. The sodden ground was churned beneath so many feet and horribly muddy by the time the first anxious shout echoed from the mine entrance. A macabre hush settled over the assembled company, although a heart thudded painfully inside every ribcage. The interminable, excruciating hours of waiting were over. The men who'd sat, torn with the feeling of uselessness, by the mine entrance, now sprang into action to assist their comrades and disappeared into the adit. A minute or two later, the first figure emerged and staggered to his knees in exhaustion, followed by another, and another. They collapsed together on the wet ground in varying poses, each one wearied beyond imagining from their long, treacherous struggle in the dark, waterlogged passages. And all to no avail.

Maurice Brett's face blanched. He'd never seen a corpse before, let alone that of a child, for really Daniel Halse was no more than that. The boy's open eyes stared sightlessly from his muddied, blood-smeared face at the young woman who knelt over him. She looked so calm and yet her cheeks had taken on a frosted transparency that spoke of grief too deep to bear. Elizabeth took a handkerchief from somewhere in the folds of her skirt and did her best to clean the boy's face before his father saw him. He was there now, hunched with misery, shrivelled beside his large-framed, weeping daughter, and the stout woman who had taken the place of the boy's beloved mother. Slowly, he took off his coat and spread it over his son's mangled body, and then dissolving onto his knees, gathered Daniel into his arms.

"'Tis my punishment,' he said clearly, peering through his misted eyes at the young woman whose own face was like marble. And then he began to rock back and forth as an unearthly howl gurgled in the back of his throat.

Elizabeth rose to her feet like a spectre. There would be time enough to grieve for Daniel later, but other men were being brought out of the mine and she might be able to help. Survivors. But the dejected silence that had blanketed the riverside all day was now shattered by mournful wails and stifled groans of sorrow. Everywhere little groups were clustered about a motionless heap that only hours earlier had been a vibrant, active man. Someone began to sing, in a man's deep, faltering tone, the sober requiem that would be heard again in the twin churches of St Peter's and St Mary's in the days to come. Elizabeth's throat closed so that she couldn't speak. She caught sight of William administering to an unrecognizable face prostrate on the ground. He came over to her only briefly. There'd been no need for him to confirm that young Daniel was dead.

He tipped his head over his shoulder at her expectant look. 'No,' he whispered. 'It'll be over for that poor soul, too, in a minute. That means all of them who originally went down are dead. Apart from the one who escaped and raised the alarm, of course. So they're all accounted for. Eight in all.'

He left her again, and she stood, a motionless, sagging marionette. Seven people she knew, her young cousin among them, all dead, for the pig-headed stupidity of Thomas Arkwright. He was gone now, and she even felt some sorrow for him, too. Not one rescued alive. All that effort. For nothing.

And where was Richard? She raced across to where the rescuers were grouped on the ground by the mine entrance, endeavouring to collect enough energy for the weary trek home. She darted between them, their dirtied faces gazing up at her unseeing. Richard was not among them.

Elizabeth's stomach gripped with dread as the entrance to the mine behind her beckoned with a greedy leer. Richard must still be inside, but so many other men had already come out. What if something had happened behind them and they hadn't realized? What if Richard was trapped, hurt, or even . . . She had to find him! But she'd never been down a mine before and a sheen of icy sweat slicked her skin as the narrow, uneven tunnel swallowed her into its inky obscurity. The tons of rock above her head deadened every sound but the steady drip of water and the wild pounding of her own heartbeat in her ears. She rounded a bend in the winding labyrinth and was instantly eclipsed in such darkness, it was as if someone had put out her eyes. Panic squeezed her lungs and she crazily thrust out her hands. They met with nothing. She squealed in terror, turned, felt a solid wall of wet, unyielding rock in front of her. She turned again but met more rock. She was trapped, disorientated. Dear God, which way should she go?

'No, miss! Thee mustn't come in yere.'

The voice from close by made Elizabeth's body jerk violently. A man stood beside her, his face grotesque in the candlelight that flickered from the brim of his hat. Even so, she could scarcely see the rocky walls that glistened with running water.

''Tis a maze down yere. Only your husband knows 'en, and *he* were testing his memory. He'll be along in a minute, don't thee fret none. He and that there mine-captain were just putting back they boards over the shaft. You just come back wi' me. Fine man, your husband. Would've made a proper mine-captain hissel'.'

Elizabeth's shoulders drooped with relief. If she hadn't been so driven by the need to escape the impregnable, blinding darkness, her knees might have given way beneath her. She whimpered a tremulous reply, not sure what exactly she said, and then teetered along behind the fellow. In a matter of seconds, the faint ray of light from the entrance glimmered along the narrow, twisting adit, illuminating their way to the grey world outside. The miner, who back in the daylight she recognized as someone she'd once treated for a chest infection, patted her shoulder paternally, and installed her on a large boulder near the tunnel mouth before he went in search of his own anxious family.

Elizabeth sat and waited. As if she hadn't done enough waiting that day. The miserable, murky light was already beginning to fade, and soon the children would be dismissed from school. How could she possibly break it to Chantal, after all the poor girl had been through, that her father had gone down the mine to retrieve the dead, but hadn't returned himself? She couldn't bear it if . . . The thought of Richard being entombed, perhaps for ever, in the myriad black, sightless entrails of the mine was past enduring. Elizabeth felt so helpless, perched up on the rock out of the mud, her jaw clenched in an effort to fight back her tears of frustration and fear.

It wasn't until they'd almost reached the entrance that she heard the scrape of their boots on the stony floor of the adit, splashing through the steady trickle of water that drained away from the tunnel hewn into the hillside. The mine-captain emerged first, followed by Richard, bent low as the mine wasn't built for men of his height. He staggered slightly, stretching his back and flexing his shoulders painfully, his eyes screwed shut against the poor light that was enough to dazzle the vision after such long exposure to the pitch dark. Before he could open his eyes again, Elizabeth was pressed against him, her arms laced about his neck, sobbing with tears of relief.

Richard squinted down at her. 'What's all this?' he murmured hoarsely, his throat parched after so many hours of strenuous toil without a drop of liquid to pass his lips.

'I've been worried sick,' she groaned, looking up at him, her tear-stained face distraught and her eyes glittering with moisture.

Richard blinked at her, his brow pleated with surprise as his vision adjusted to the light. 'I'm so sorry about your cousin,' he croaked. 'He didn't drown like some of the other poor sods. He was caught in the rockfall. He'd have died instantly, if it's any comfort.'

Richard instinctively held Elizabeth to him, though every muscle of his body ached with cold and fatigue. He'd been working in one way or the other for the past thirty-six hours, with nothing in his stomach for the last twenty. All he wanted was to get home to the comfort of a hot drink, some food and his bed. Not that he could enjoy the latter luxury until he'd attended to all the livestock. He prayed George had realized he wasn't there and had at least managed to take care of the essentials. Elizabeth still wept against him, her tangled agonies erupting in an unfettered flow. She could feel the vigorous strength of his hard body against hers, and to think she'd come so close to losing him. She pulled away from him at last, though, realizing that if her own clothes were damp from the rain, his were saturated and the water, in which she later learned he'd been working up to his waist for hours, was dripping from him. He was coated in mud, his face smeared with dirt, and his filth-encrusted hands torn and bleeding from scraping at the fallen rocks. The other miners, in an equally sorry state, had gone, and the small, forlorn groups were dispersing, carrying their dead on makeshift stretchers.

'Come on. Let's fetch Chantal from school and go home,' Elizabeth rasped, exhausted now her emotions were spent, and dreading the long walk back to Rosebank Hall.

Maurice Brett's conscience was torn with remorse as he observed Richard and Elizabeth from the other side of the bridge. Arms about each other's waist, neither of them steady on their feet, but supporting each other as best they could, they clambered up the slope to the lane that led back to the village. Maurice bit his lip as they disappeared from view. She was lost to him. She belonged to Richard Pencarrow, heart and soul. How could he possibly have wished the fellow dead, when it would have broken her heart, just as his was breaking now. He would just have to learn to live with the emptiness of it for the rest of his life.

But . . . could he?

TWENTY-SEVEN

May 1873

Richard was whistling softly to himself as he pumped some water into the stone sink to wash his hands, and Elizabeth threw him an enquiring, sideways glance. She lifted the earthenware teapot and poured out three mugs of the steaming liquid, pushing one across the table to where Chantal sat, biting lustily into a slice of freshly baked bread spread with their own home-made butter.

'You sound happy,' Elizabeth observed, cutting into the crusty, mouth-watering loaf once more. ''Twas not as bad as you thought at the bank, then?' She turned her head as Richard sat down beside her. It was strange to see him smartly dressed in the black tailcoat that had once been Josiah's before he'd gained such mammoth weight. The garment had served Richard well for their marriage ceremony and for Daniel's funeral, as well as the other tragic services they'd attended back in March. It had been a harrowing few months, the spirit of the two villages in tatters, and yet united in sorrow. But life moved on, the fight for survival for those who remained overshadowing the memory of those who had departed. Inevitably, Richard's struggle to rescue the farm continued. Wool prices were a fraction of what they would have fetched at the start of the century, but Richard had sold his fleeces direct to the only surviving mills in the area over the far side of Dartmoor, and so achieved the best possible price. But towns would always need meat, and Richard's flock was slowly but steadily increasing, and in a year or two, he would reap the benefit of his labours. With shearing over, the ewes and their new lambs were about to be released onto the moor for the summer, together with the year-old lambs that Richard had recently brought back from being over-wintered in the milder climes of a farm on the Bere Peninsula. Already he'd begun once more the backbreaking task of sowing mangolds and turnips by hand, returning muddied and filthy from the fields each evening. So to see him so well groomed, his jaw closely shaven, and presented as a true gentleman to answer his summons to the bank, was quite a change.

'Not too bad, no.' Richard's face was straight, although Elizabeth noticed that the corners of his mouth kept twitching upwards. 'Mmm! That smells delicious. I haven't eaten all day. Everything all right here?'

'Of course. I *can* manage without you for a few hours!' Elizabeth laughed lightly, for there was something about Richard's mood that was infectious.

'I wouldn't have expected any different,' his bantering tone replied as he sipped his tea. *'Et toi, ma petite, tu as bien travaillé à l'école aujourd'hui?'*

'Naturellement,' Chantal giggled through a mouthful of food.

'So, why did the bank want to see you?' Elizabeth insisted.

'Oh, nothing really.' Richard shook his head, but his eyes were twinkling merrily. 'I'll tell you later.'

Elizabeth frowned at him, quite baffled. The weeks following the accident at Wheal Anne had been hard, and the adventurers had decided not to pursue their explorations. Daniel's death had been devastating, and in addition to coping with her grief, Elizabeth had been obliged to associate with her uncle. Although he was a changed, broken man, and it was all in the past, the obscene memories had flooded back. Richard had been a tower of strength to her, and the whole incident had brought them closer together. But he was teasing her now, she was sure of it.

'Richard Pencarrow, you can be the most exasperating devil!' she cried, and picking up a tea towel, began flicking it about his head. He put up his hands in mock fear, laughing aloud now, his mouth wide with amusement and revealing his even, white teeth. Elizabeth grinned back, her heart stopping as his handsome face beamed across at her.

'All right, I give in!' he chuckled. His eyebrows were raised as if he would delight in tantalizing her further. But then he swivelled round in his chair to face her, and took her hands firmly in his. 'I have had the most extraordinary day,' he began, 'but it's quite a long story, so you must be quiet and listen carefully,' he ordered with feigned authority.

'Yes, sir.' Elizabeth dipped her head obediently, but she was all ears to hear what he had to say.

Richard wet his lips and swallowed. 'You know I had an uncle, my father's younger brother. My grandparents both died before I was born, and my father inherited the estate. As you know, he wasn't a natural farmer or a businessman come to that, but it's traditional for the elder son to inherit any land. But Uncle James was left a considerable sum of money, some of which he used to buy himself a commission in the army. He did very well and became a high-ranking officer. I was only fourteen when he was killed. But I do remember him visiting when I was about seven to find Wheal Rosalind had been opened in his absence. All hell broke loose. He said my father should have invested in Devon Great Consols rather than sink all he had *and* a substantial loan into his own mine. And he was quite right. You know more than I do how Wheal Rosalind closed in heavy debt.' Elizabeth nodded, her eyes watching him intently. 'And you also know that Devon Great Consols is still productive, with arsenic now rather than copper, but it's keeping Morwellham Quay alive. Most of the ore from Wheal Rosalind used to be shipped along the Tavistock Canal to Morwellham, as well, which is ironic when you hear the rest of what I have to tell you. Anyway,' he paused for breath, pulling in his chin, 'my uncle was home on leave shortly before his regiment was to join in the Crimean War. He and I were great friends. I lived for his visits. He must have realized there was a strong chance he wouldn't come back, and apparently on his way back to his regiment, he invested all he had in some shares in a schooner called the *Swallow* that was being built in Plymouth. Nobody knew apart from a Plymouth solicitor, who was to hold the shares in secret, accumulating any dividends until I was twenty-one. Of course, when the time came, I was in France and my father couldn't have said exactly where I was even if he'd wanted to. The solicitor made periodic enquiries, but it seemed I'd disappeared, so my case was filed away and forgotten about. Now, this is where it gets really interesting.'

He shifted in the chair, rubbing his hands together, and a suppressed smile on his lips. Watching him, a tingle of glee slithered down Elizabeth's spine, and her heart somehow thrilled as, after eighteen months of strenuous toil, at the start of which he shouldn't have been working at all, his usually drawn face was lit with excitement.

'Oh, do go on, Richard, and stop keeping me in suspense!'

He gave an infuriating laugh, blinking at her with deliberately irritating slowness before grinning broadly. 'All right. But it's worth waiting for. Well, you know how worried I was at being summoned by the bank manager. Anyone whose finances are in the state mine are, would be! When I went into his office, there was someone else there as well as my solicitor. A chap, very well dressed, just a year or two older than myself, at a guess. Very polite. Stood up immediately and shook my hand. He was introduced to me as Captain Bradley. Of course, I had no idea who he was, and my heart was in my mouth. Now, going back to my uncle, the *Swallow* came to be owned by a Captain Farthingay. Well, I say owned, but there were certain shareholders in it, including Uncle James. When Farthingay died about six years ago, Captain Bradley bought his three ships, including th *Swallow*. He had his own ship already, and he'd also recently inherited his father's wine merchant business in London. He still owns it, but he was so upset by his father's death — must have been a deal closer to him than I was to mine — that he sold the family house in London in order to make a fresh start, and came to live in Morwellham, which he'd got to know through Farthingay's little fleet. Evidently, he then had a lot of problems — he didn't say what, but I gather it took him some years to sort out — but everything's settled down now, and going through the *Swallow's* accounts, he became curious that all the dividends, right from the beginning, about twenty years in all, had been paid into the same account without a word of communication. So he traced the trustees, that is, the solicitors in Plymouth, and his visit prompted them to update their enquiries. And of course, this time they found I was back. So now, here I am with a lump sum in my pocket, and shares in a ship!'

Elizabeth stared back at him, dumbfounded, as the news filtered into her brain. It was like a dream. A small miracle! Jubilation bubbled up inside her and an ecstatic grin split her face. 'Oh, Richard, I'm so pleased for you!'

'For *us*, you mean.' His eyes had crinkled into a smile, though his mouth was merely closed in a soft curve. 'It doesn't mean the struggle's over,' he said, his tone sober again. 'But I've now paid off the whole of the back interest my father had accumulated, with a substantial sum left over. I could use it to reduce the loan, but I think in the long run, it'll be better to invest in the farm, a certain amount, anyway. I'm definitely going to buy a pair of horses. There's an auction at a farm near Bridestowe next week, and they've got two cobs up for sale.'

Chantal's huge eyes gleamed like ebony. 'Oh, Papa, we are going to 'ave some 'orses?'

Her exultant expression brought the smile back to Richard's face. 'Well, I hope so. It would certainly save my poor old back, and I could produce twice as much fodder. Then I could increase the flock, and maybe think about more cattle, too,' he replied thoughtfully, chewing on his bottom lip. 'Anyway,' he went on, cocking his head to one side, 'to celebrate, and to make up for the delay in the money getting to me, Captain Bradley has invited us to dine with him and his wife at the Bedford Hotel tomorrow evening, and to spend the night there, all at his expense. He's a fairly wealthy man, I gather. Perhaps George and Kate could stay here to look after Chantal.'

Elizabeth's shoulders jerked as she gazed at him, her cheeks suddenly pale. 'I . . . I can't,' she stuttered, her chin trembling. 'I've never been anywhere like that in my life. All those knives and forks! All those *people*!' she wailed, desperate as she could see Richard was trying not to laugh at her. 'Besides,' she nodded her head emphatically, 'I've nothing to wear.'

'And *I* have?' His eyebrows lifted almost to his hairline. 'I've only this, unless I can find an evening suit to fit me amongst my father's old clothes. And you can wear the dress you were married in.'

''Tis hardly suitable.' She got to her feet, her chin tilted haughtily. 'I'm not going, and there's an end to it.'

'Oh, yes, you are.' Richard stood up to face her, his eyes narrowed curiously. 'You looked stunning that day. As if you don't every day, whatever you're wearing.'

She blinked at him in shocked amazement. She opened her mouth, but before she could think of the protesting words she wanted to utter, Richard had stepped forward and, cupping her face between his hands, placed his lips tenderly over hers. Soft. Warm and sensitive. A tiny squeal died in her throat and her heart stood still as every mesmerized fibre of her body seemed to tingle.

'*Oh, là! Enfin!*' she heard Chantal chortle with joy and then clap her hands.

Richard pulled back sharply. '*Allez, va-t'en!*' he snapped over his shoulder, and Chantal obediently skipped out of the door with a cheeky laugh.

Their eyes met, hers totally stilled and his dark and rueful as colour flooded into his cheeks.

'I'm sorry,' he muttered awkwardly. 'I shouldn't . . . I'll just go and change out of this straitjacket.' And so saying, he sidled out into the hall.

Elizabeth didn't move, her brain, every muscle, her entire being transfixed by the delicious sensation that wreathed itself about her. Slowly, she drew up her hand and tentatively fingered her quivering lips, reliving that brief, sensuous moment. And knowing she hadn't wanted it to end.

TWENTY-EIGHT

Captain Bradley was tall, even though Richard topped him by perhaps half an inch. He was clearly a man of some physical prowess, the muscles of his broad shoulders straining beneath his well-cut evening coat that tailored to his trim waist. He held himself so straight, his natural bearing so commanding, that Elizabeth immediately felt in awe of him and wished vehemently that Richard hadn't talked her into coming. But then, as the captain shook her hand, his chestnut-hued eyes smiled congenially at her and she began to feel more at ease.

It was Mrs Bradley's presence, though, that was more unnerving. Considerably younger than her husband, she was resplendent in an evening dress of cornflower silk that reflected the deep sapphire of her lovely, almond-shaped eyes. No taller than Elizabeth, her figure was a little rounder, but then, she'd only recently given birth to her second child. Her sleek brown hair was entwined in a complicated arrangement down the back of her head, and Elizabeth felt ashamed of the rustic, plaited knot she'd struggled to achieve with her own bouncing curls, and the wayward, spiralling wisps that had loosened about her face during the journey between Rosebank Hall and Tavistock, in a trap borrowed from Mr Widcock. She saw Richard swiftly conceal the widening of his eyes as he was introduced to the beautiful young woman, and a strange pang . . . was it of jealousy . . . pierced Elizabeth's heart.

'A pleasure to meet you,' Captain Bradley was saying in his cultured London accent. 'Did you have a good journey?'

'Yes, thank you, Captain.' Richard's slight Devonshire lilt suddenly seemed more perceptible by comparison. 'It is only two or three miles.'

'Oh, please, call me Adam.' A warm smile crinkled the captain's handsome face. 'Rebecca and I don't like to stand on ceremony.'

'Neither do we,' Richard assured him with an encouraging glance in Elizabeth's direction. 'I'm Richard. And my wife is Elizabeth.'

Elizabeth forced a smile to her lips. His wife. It seemed incongruous to be introduced as his wife. If only they knew . . .

She was grateful when Adam took charge of the proceedings again. 'I've ordered a little champagne before we go through to the dining room.'

Elizabeth found herself swept up in a whirlwind. The spacious, high-ceilinged rooms, the opulent furnishings, the brilliance of the gas lamps that were just being lit as the evening closed in. Uniformed waiters ready to fall on their every whim, and Adam Bradley, in a kindly and polite manner, ensuring they were properly attended. They were ushered into an elegant lounge and even before they'd sat down, a silver tray set with four lead-crystal glasses charged with pale effervescent champagne was delivered to the graceful, occasional table that was placed before them.

'Your good health!' Adam pronounced with vigour, and savouring the drink critically, nodded his head in approval.

'And yours!' Richard replied.

Elizabeth took a sip of the light, sparkling liquid. She'd never tasted champagne before and the bubbles tickled her nose. She might have giggled had she been alone with Richard, and not in such awesome company that she was overwhelmed with nervousness.

''Twas such a delight to discover who that money belonged to!' Rebecca Bradley unexpectedly burst into speech, her generous mouth broadening merrily. 'And especially to someone who really needed it.'

'Rebecca!'

Adam's reprimand was so sharp that Elizabeth and Richard exchanged glances. But Rebecca merely waved her hand. 'Oh, stuff and nonsense, Adam! You shouldn't have told me if you didn't want me to talk about it! Besides, how can we be friends if we don't talk the truth? We've known financial difficulty ourselves before now, you know.' She nodded energetically. ''Tis all in the past, but I'll not forget it. And Adam, well . . . You've always worked so hard, haven't you?' She patted his arm so lovingly Elizabeth felt a twinge of envy. 'Adam's father were a wealthy merchant, but mine were a humble miner. Worked his way up till he became Chief Assaying Officer at Morwellham, *and* Harbour Master. So I never take anything for granted.'

Adam threw up his right hand in a gesture of exasperation. 'I do apologize. My wife is of an irrepressible nature.' But then he turned to Rebecca with such a tender softness in his eyes that Elizabeth's heart lurched. 'It's why I love her so much,' he concluded almost under his breath as if his words were only for her.

'My father was a miner, too.' Elizabeth found her tongue for the first time, warming to the lively Mrs Bradley who raised her fine eyebrows with genuine interest. Encouraged, Elizabeth seized their common ground and went on, 'He was in line for captain, but he died in a mine accident.'

'Oh, I'm so sorry,' Adam and Rebecca answered as one.

Elizabeth smiled wistfully, not wanting to spoil the evening which, to her relief, seemed to be going well. 'Oh, I hardly remember him. I was a very small child at the time.'

'And your mother?' Rebecca enquired with eager innocence.

Elizabeth lowered her eyes. 'She died when I was fifteen. 'Twas a cancer.'

Rebecca Bradley stretched out to squeeze her hand with such feeling that Elizabeth knew she was going to like this young woman, who only ten minutes earlier had inspired her with dismay.

'I'm so lucky,' Rebecca breathed fervently. 'I understand you have no family, either, Richard, so I'm the only one amongst us who still has both parents living.'

'And do they still live at Morwellham?'

'Yes, they do. My father's still Harbour Master, though there's far less shipping nowadays. But 'tis probably just as well. My father's not as young as he was.'

'And you still live in Morwellham yourselves?' Elizabeth asked.

'Most of the time,' Adam put in. 'I've taken some rooms in London, just a modest affair. Much of my business is still in the capital, you see. Rebecca comes with me occasionally, although not since Charlotte was born. And I . . .' his face stiffened strangely, 'last year, I inherited a large country estate in Herefordshire from a distant relative. We spend time there as well. It's very beautiful.'

'And as well as having a huge dairy herd, the estate produces vast amounts of cider, which of course is more than interesting for him!' Rebecca added. 'Mind you, I wonder sometimes if we shouldn't move there permanently. I worry so much about the children's health. Since they opened the arsenic works at Gawton, the vegetation's dying off all along the river. It can't be good. But 'twould be such a wrench to leave Morwellham. 'Tis part of me,' she groaned, throwing a wistful, sideways glance at her husband. 'So much . . . happened in our lives there. And with my parents . . . My sister's moved away to Plymouth now. Her husband, Misha's a sea-captain, too. He's mastered the *Emily* for Adam since . . . so 'tis easier for her to see him when he's in port. Adam only captains the *Emily* a few times a year now, to give Misha a rest. Sarah hasn't had a child yet, and she never will if Misha's away all the time.'

Adam cleared his throat, casting a warning glare in her direction. Rebecca's eyelids batted in a comical pretence of remorse, the merriment instantly returning to her expression. 'Honestly, Adam, you'd think . . . Do you have children, Elizabeth?'

Elizabeth's heart contracted. Children. A child. She'd never considered it. Or had she? Driving it to the back of her mind, because she knew what you had to do to have a child. Uncle Matthew had destroyed any feelings she might have had in that direction. But . . . surely that was years ago. And when it was with someone you loved . . . That was what her mother had said, wasn't it? And look at Adam and Rebecca now. The love between them was palpable. And when she thought of the few occasions that Richard had held her in his arms, after Thomas Arkwright's attack on her, or when poor Daniel had died, for instance, a feeling so deep had entangled itself in her heart. But she had reared away from it.

'We've only been married six months,' Richard answered for her. 'But I do have a daughter, Chantal. She's nearly eight. I was both married and widowed when I was away in France, you see.'

Elizabeth's thoughts came back into focus and she smiled gratefully at Richard. His eyes lingered on hers, as if he'd read every thought that had raced through her head.

'Your table is ready, Captain Bradley, sir.'

'Ah, thank you,' Adam smiled amiably. 'Shall we go through?'

As they rose to their feet, Richard offered Elizabeth his arm, and she slipped her hand into the crook of his elbow, her fingers gripping tightly. He must have felt her unease as his other hand closed reassuringly over her tense hold as they followed Adam and Rebecca through to the dining room. Elizabeth felt so conspicuous in her simple dress that boasted no bustle or train as every other lady at the hotel seemed to sport, and couldn't wait to be seated and conceal her rustic attire. The dining room was just as dazzling as the lounge, with an array of gleaming cut glass and sparkling, polished silverware on snowy white tablecloths. Starched napkins folded into fans stood like sentinels between lined-up armies of cutlery, and vases of early carnations graced every table. Elizabeth was spellbound as she clung to Richard's arm. He drew out the chair for her, and she gracefully lowered herself onto it, copying Rebecca's example. Adam had stood back, allowing the waiter to perform the honour, and Elizabeth wondered why. But the room was so beautiful, her eyes kept sweeping across it in admiration. Smart gentlemen in evening dress, elegant ladies with gloved hands eating daintily. She noted with relief as she sipped at the light consommé that Rebecca's hands were bare apart from her wedding band and an exquisite diamond ring. The fish course followed, salmon from the Tamar caught that morning and poached in a creamy sauce, all served with wine chosen carefully by Captain Bradley.

'Can you manage?' Rebecca's lowered voice was so soft and natural as she turned affectionately to her husband.

'I think so.' Elizabeth noticed that he picked up the fish fork in his right hand and used it sideways to slice down into the pink flesh of the salmon. She must have frowned curiously, for he caught her eye across the table and, his face breaking into a wry smile, lifted his left hand which she noticed for the first time was motionless and clothed in a fine kid glove. 'I lost my hand in an accident at sea,' he said simply. 'This contraption isn't very useful, but it does look rather better than an empty cuff.'

Elizabeth realized then why he'd been unable to draw out Rebecca's chair, and felt herself blush, but the compassion was clear in her shocked voice. 'Oh, I'm sorry. I had no idea. Please forgive me.'

Adam lifted an eyebrow, but Elizabeth could see the pain in his eyes. 'I've learned to live with it,' he murmured. 'With Rebecca's help. I felt my life was in ruins when it happened. But she showed me that it wasn't.'

He turned to his wife, and a look of such ineffable devotion melted between them that Elizabeth was caught up in its enchantment. If only something like that could exist between her and Richard.

'Forgive me for asking,' Richard's hesitant words broke the spell, 'but did your physician provide a herbal ointment to help heal the wound?'

Rebecca twisted her head, her astonished eyes glowing a peacock blue. 'How did you know?' she gasped. 'Yes, Dr Seaton got it from another doctor, who knew a good herbalist.'

'That was Beth here!' Richard announced, looking at her with a pride that made her heart swell. 'I remember William . . . Dr Greenwood . . . once mentioning that Beth had helped cure a sea-captain who'd suffered such a terrible misfortune.'

'Oh, yes, I remember,' Elizabeth nodded. 'The wound wasn't healing properly, and your doctor had discussed the case with William.'

'Good Lord!' Adam's face stretched in amazement. And then he lifted his glass. 'Then I must propose a toast to my secret healer! And, I hope, to a lasting friendship.'

Elizabeth began to relax. She felt accepted on her own merit, and the wine eased the tension that had initially gripped her, allowing her to enjoy the company of the two strangers. By the time the sumptuous dessert arrived — although heaven alone knew how she was to squeeze it into her already bursting stomach — she felt as if she'd known them all her life.

'Excuse me, madam, but I have a note from your maid.'

The waiter bowed politely as Rebecca took the folded paper from the silver tray. Her eyes scanned the writing and she looked up with an angelic smile. 'Charlotte's crying. I'm feeding her myself so we had to bring her with us. Come, my dear Elizabeth. You shall meet our beautiful daughter.' Rising to her feet, she linked her arm through Elizabeth's. 'Amy will be quite amused at being called my maid,' she chatted on as they swept out of the dining room and up the staircase. 'She used to keep house for Adam when he first came to Morwellham. But now she's one of the family. Worth her weight in gold. I just couldn't do without her.'

Elizabeth smiled back at the vivacious young woman she somehow sensed was to become an integral part of her life.

The sort of friend, equal in intellect and social standing — despite her initial misgivings — she had so often yearned for. As they reached the door, she could hear the familiar wailing of an infant and experienced, as she frequently did, the desire to rock the suffering babe in her arms. She never could, of course. She was there to heal, usually colic or a fever, or a raw and torturing bottom caused by a mother's neglect or ignorance. Charlotte Bradley, though, she was sure was cared for to the point of pampering, and wanted nothing more than the comfort of her mother's breast.

'Elizabeth, this is Amy.' Rebecca took her fretting daughter from the wizened woman who was pacing the room and who then, to Elizabeth's amazement, bobbed a curtsy at her.

'Pleased to meet you . . . er . . . Amy,' she stammered in surprise.

'Likewise, ma'am.'

'Oh, Amy, do undo the back of my dress, please. 'Tisn't designed for feeding babies.'

''Tis very beautiful, mind.' Elizabeth looked on enviously.

Rebecca settled herself in an upright but finely upholstered chair drawn up to the fire, and as the loyal Amy slid the gown over her shoulders, she unfastened the front of her fine corset and the pretty camisole beneath. 'Just fripperies, my dear. And I hate wearing stays, but I have to with this gown. At home, I never wear anything so fancy. You know, in London, the ladies wear fashionable clothes all the time, but I couldn't be doing with that. Now, you sit down beside me and we can talk while I feed little miss.'

She expertly squeezed her full marbled breast so that the minuscule mouth could take in the entire protruding nipple, something Elizabeth had so often been at pains to teach a first-time mother. But she'd never experienced the sensation herself, and now, suddenly and inexplicably, she felt a strange longing in her heart.

'Did Toby behave after we went downstairs?' Rebecca whispered over her shoulder.

'Oh, yes, the little lamb! I read him his favourite story and he went to sleep straightaways. 'Tis little miss who wouldn't settle.'

Elizabeth glanced about the room. The gas lights had been turned down low, and in the resulting gloom she hadn't noticed the small figure sleeping in one of the beds. 'May I?' she asked, keeping her voice low.

Rebecca raised her head from gazing down rapturously at her baby daughter, her face calm and serene. 'Of course,' she purred contentedly.

Elizabeth tiptoed over to the bed. Lost in an ocean of pure white sheets, a small boy of about five years old was slumbering peacefully, his thick raven curls matted about his slender face and his black eyelashes fanned out on his dusky skin. Elizabeth smiled with admiration. The child reminded her of Chantal.

'He's a handsome little lad,' she whispered as she resumed her seat. 'He's not the least like Charlotte, is he?' she asked in all innocence.

Rebecca looked up sharply. The lovely sparkle went out of her eyes and a deep shadow seemed to darken her face. 'Toby . . . isn't Adam's son,' she confessed in a hesitant whisper as she solemnly lowered her gaze. 'It were before I married Adam. Toby's father . . .' she faltered, and Elizabeth was acutely aware of the emotion in her voice, 'died before he were born. I was broken-hearted. When I first met Adam, I thought he were an arrogant pig, I were so blinded by my grief.' She broke off, and for some moments, seemed lost in some other world Elizabeth didn't dare to intrude upon. But then she smiled wistfully. ''Tis a long story. I'll tell you some time. But now I know a finer man never walked this earth, and I love him so much it hurts. But I'm sure you know what I mean. With Richard. He seems a good man. I . . . I don't mind you telling him, but I trust 'twill go no further.'

'No. Of course not,' Elizabeth murmured, stunned by the unexpected revelation and the sudden sadness on Rebecca's face.

'We all have our crosses to bear, our secrets to keep,' Rebecca went on distantly as she stroked the soft, pink cheek of the now sleeping infant. 'Let me slide this little one back into her crib, and then we can go back downstairs.'

Elizabeth waited, staring into the fire, her thoughts entirely engaged by Rebecca's words. What was *her* secret? Uncle Matthew, of course. The way he'd touched her unknowing, child's flesh, even though she knew now how much worse it might have been. Had she forgiven him? No. Never that. But perhaps she understood more now. It was behind her. In the past. She could get on with her life. She had a far graver secret to bury in her heart now. Richard, and what had happened in a country torn apart by war against an occupying force. She'd been horrified, but she didn't blame him. Some part of her even admired what he'd done. He'd acted with the instincts of a courageous man, defending his family and delivering punishment for a heinous crime when there was no proper authority to do it for him. He would live with the guilt of it for the rest of his life, and she . . . she would support him in every way she could.

* * *

'You go on up,' Richard said casually as he pressed the key into her hand. 'It's such a pleasant evening, I think I'll take a turn around the square before I come to bed. Would you mind showing Beth to the room, please, Adam? And thank you once again for a splendid evening.'

'It's been a real pleasure. We must keep in touch. But perhaps we'll see you at breakfast?'

Rebecca's face creased into its beautiful smile and she linked her arm through Elizabeth's again as they mounted the staircase. Adam politely opened the door for her, and wished her goodnight, and then she was alone in the bedroom, the sumptuous meal, the brightly shining lights, the dazzling company of Rebecca Bradley whirling dizzily in her head. Elizabeth felt so happy as she walked a little unsteadily towards the huge bed, for the wine had flowed freely and she'd never before imbibed so much in one evening. It was a lovely room, tastefully and richly decorated, and she marvelled at its luxury through her wavering vision. The small valise they'd brought with them had been placed on a special stand, and it wasn't until she opened it and took out her nightdress that it dawned on her why Richard had sent her ahead of him. Of course! In all the excitement, it hadn't crossed her mind that Adam would automatically have booked them into the same room. Oh, dear Lord! Richard was allowing her time to get undressed and into bed without his being there.

She sat down on the edge of the bed, the wonder of the evening totally dissipated. Her heart dropped down inside her like a stone and she pressed the back of her hand against her mouth. Richard had done the gentlemanly thing in the circumstances. But then he always had. Of course, she'd been uncertain of him at the beginning, but she'd very soon come to trust him, even before the real Richard Pencarrow — who was strong and kind and sensitive, and could sometimes be so amusing — had emerged from the sullen, quick-tempered ruffian who'd staggered over the threshold of Rosebank Hall. And when he'd risked his life attempting to save others down the mine, she'd known that if he hadn't returned, her own life would have been shattered. If that wasn't love, what was?

Elizabeth lightly stroked her lips. When Richard had kissed her yesterday, it had merely been the expression of his jubilation and relief, she was sure. He'd buried the wife he loved back in France. He would never love again; he'd said so quite distinctly. Elizabeth was a wife on paper only. Richard was *fond* of her, but that was all. The love between Adam and Rebecca Bradley was almost tangible. It had fluttered about them all evening, a touch of the hand, a twist of the head, an enraptured gaze. That was what *she* wanted with Richard . . .

The need to cry raked her throat but she mustn't give in to it. She stood up abruptly. Richard would be back in a minute and she must be tucked up in bed. She flung off her clothes, not caring that they were the best she possessed, and

313

pulled the nightdress over her head just as a gentle knock came at the door. She went to unlock it, and as Richard entered the room, an embarrassed smile flickered over his face.

'I'm sorry about this,' he mumbled. 'I hope it won't spoil your evening. I'll sleep in the chair, of course.'

Elizabeth nodded and pulled the pins from her hair. It tumbled about her shoulders, still not quite as long as it had been before Matthew had hacked it off in a rage, but nevertheless rioting down her back in a cascade of glossy, lustrous waves that shimmered like spun gold in the lamplight. She hurriedly clambered into the bed, pulling the sheets up to her chin and watching, with ardent regret, as Richard began to undress. He stripped down to the waist, his back deliberately turned towards her, and his strong muscles rippling beneath his amber skin. Elizabeth felt a tightening deep in the pit of her belly, and her pulse quickened.

''Tis silly, though, when there's so much room in this huge bed. 'Twill be so uncomfortable in the chair. You won't sleep well, and 'tis back to work tomorrow.'

Richard stopped and turned to her, his hand still outstretched as he reached for his nightshirt. He blinked at her, and she stared back in confusion, her heart hammering in her chest. She was sure someone else had spoken the words that had been articulated by her lips. Richard shook his head slowly, his eyes dark and brooding, and she saw his broad chest expand as he drew in a deep breath.

'Don't . . . ask that of me,' he grated.

Elizabeth lifted her chin. Paused. Frowned. 'I . . . don't understand. I do trust you,' she assured him.

There it was again, that voice that wasn't hers but was coming from her mouth. But . . . it hadn't faltered. It was strong and resolute, though deep inside she was terrified by what she recognized was a yearning desire. But Richard had bowed his head, arms dangling limply by his sides, and Elizabeth's eyes filled with moisture as she averted her gaze to stare into the fire that still crackled in the grate, a pathetic glimmer now as neither of them had thought to add any more coal from the polished copper scuttle. The dying flames set apricot shadows dancing on the pale walls, and Elizabeth's misted vision followed them, mesmerized by her own dejection. He mustn't see. Mustn't know that his closeness, his presence in the room, was tearing her apart.

'But . . . I don't trust myself,' she heard him breathe thickly.

She stiffened, and her eyes flew wide open as she looked back at him. He was standing stock-still, his expression tortured and ardour flaming in his eyes.

'Damn it, Beth, I love you,' he croaked.

She stared at him, drowning in the smouldering brilliance of his eyes, her heart soaring like a bird as the wretched misery was extinguished. In its place, a spark of hope, of joy, was waiting to be kindled, and yet it flickered with fear and uncertainty. Richard continued to hold her gaze, and she felt her stomach churn with a nervous need as she rose up in the bed. His eyes were stilled, dark and intense as he scrutinized her face, and then, stepping forward, he bent down until his mouth brushed tenderly against hers. She could smell the warm fragrance of brandy that lingered on his breath as it softly fanned her cheek, intoxicating her senses as a tidal wave flushed down to her loins.

'I'm sorry, Beth. Forgive me.'

Richard pulled away, his features contracted with anguish. But Elizabeth's hands were about his neck, her fingers entwining in his thick, wavy hair as they guided him back towards her. His mouth met hers again, more passionately this time, the warm moistness sending shockwaves down her spine as her lips parted to yield to his passion. Her pulse throbbed, every nerve of her body on edge and waiting, needing to be coaxed, caressed. Their lips clung hungrily for minutes, and then Elizabeth held her breath as Richard began unfastening the buttons of her nightgown. He was kissing the creamy smoothness at her throat, drawing his tongue lightly over her skin as his fingertips, their touch enticingly deft despite their work-worn roughness, crept downwards and gently cupped the soft roundness of her trembling breast.

'Is this . . . really what you want?' he whispered into the glorious tangle of her hair.

Elizabeth stared at him, unblinking. She knew now what it was to love, to be lost to this strange force, more powerful than herself, that whipped every fibre of her being to fever pitch. Her throat closed so that she couldn't speak, so instead she nodded in silent, joyous consent.

Richard disentangled himself from her arms, crossing the room to poke the fire back into life and add more coal. Then he was back beside her, his trousers and underdrawers discarded in a heap wherever he'd let them fall, his hand held out to her, his mouth faintly smiling. Questioning. Her eyes wandered over his nakedness, feasting on his muscled shoulders, the firmness of his trim waist, his flesh mellow and glowing in the building flames. The lean strength of his limbs. The ugly, jagged scar on his thigh, half hidden in the dark hairs.

She took his proffered hand and let him lead her to the thick, luxurious rug in front of the fire. The now leaping flames soothed her quivering limbs and she stood, motionless and trusting, as Richard peeled off her nightgown. She shuddered then, the breath fluttering in her lungs, and, sensitive to her shyness, he encompassed her small frame in the comforting circle of his arms, the hard length of his body pressing against hers. Their closeness lit a fire deep down in Elizabeth's soul. Richard tilted her chin and as he kissed her again, she found herself responding with eager need. His arms tightened, and lifting her off her feet, he laid her tenderly on the rug. Her hair fanned about her in a gilded mantle, her skin a warm honey in the firelight as he delicately played his lips over the well at her throat, running his hands over her shoulders with feather-light touch. Her velvet eyes deepened to a rich topaz, shocked by the painful yearning that plunged down to her loins, and yet ready to yield to its demands. Richard moved downwards, his tongue tracing the contours of her breasts, taking his time as he leisurely explored every inch of her, stroking, tantalizing. Elizabeth whimpered softly and, as her small hands reached out to his arms of steel, to his powerful shoulders, she began to move against him, wanting to please, not quite knowing how but following some glorious instinct she hadn't known she possessed. Richard's breath quickened, matching her own growing urgency. She didn't notice her own tiny squeal as he finally slipped inside her. He was so gentle, so calming, so deep in his loving, and suddenly a sensation she could never have imagined exploded within her, sending exquisite ripples through her being as Richard cried out his triumph. Elizabeth clung to him, amazed by the moment of frenzied wonderment as the rapturous tension slowly eased.

Richard rolled away onto his back and Elizabeth suddenly felt ashamed of her nakedness, and alone. Silent tears brimmed beneath her eyelids and began to trickle down her peach-hued cheeks. But all at once, she was enfolded in Richard's loving embrace as he kissed and stroked her hair.

'Oh, my darling,' he murmured, his voice ragged and quavering with emotion. 'I love you so much. Are you . . . are you all right?' He lifted her chin, and made her look into the intensity of his eyes. 'I . . . I didn't hurt you, did I?'

His brow was so wrinkled with concern, she had to smile, her doubt fleeing for ever. She couldn't find any words, but answered him with another soft, lingering kiss. He drew her to him again, burying her head against his chest, their bodies moulded together.

'I've been such a bloody fool,' he muttered into her hair. 'I've loved you for so long. I *knew* I did, but I just wouldn't admit it to myself. I felt . . . I felt I was betraying Maddy. Every time we got close . . . I shied away from it. And I was so afraid of frightening you, after what your uncle . . . So I made myself believe I didn't love you. But now I know . . .'

Elizabeth raised her head and placed a forefinger gently on his handsome mouth. 'And *I* love *you*,' she uttered reverently. And then, with a gleeful laugh, she cried exultantly, 'I love you, I love you, I love you!'

'Well, it's taken us both bloody long enough to realize it!' Richard's mouth stretched into a rakish grin, his eyes sparking playfully. 'You know, I think I fell in love with you that very first night. When I was half delirious. You came into my room in the middle of the night like some ethereal angel, and you were carrying a lamp. Do you remember?'

'Yes?' she frowned quizzically.

'Well, you put it down on the table behind you, and I'm sure you didn't realize, but I could see right through your nightdress. Every inch of that lovely lithesome body! What with that, and this glorious mass of hair!' he teased, stroking her golden tresses that were spread across his chest. 'It stirred something in me I hadn't felt since Maddy died. Only I was so angry with myself, I believe I was unforgivably rude to you.'

'Well, I forgive you now.' And with growing confidence, she trailed her hand across his bare flesh and down over his flank.

'Good God.' His eyes widened with shocked delight. 'I think I'm going to enjoy being married to you, Mrs Pencarrow.'

And she melted into his arms once more . . .

TWENTY-NINE

July 1874

Maurice Brett scowled at his reflection in the mirror. He was looking old. His full head of hair, of which he'd been so proud, was rapidly thinning, and what was left was fading to an iron grey. His misshapen, crooked nose with its ugly scar seemed even more prominent than ever. He'd lost weight, the smooth skin of his face falling into deep creases as the flesh beneath disappeared, leaving him gaunt and haggard with dark pouches beneath his dull, lifeless eyes. It was those damned pills, of course. He couldn't manage without them for one day now. Without them, he felt sick, shivered and ached. His supplier had been cunningly suggesting he should start injecting himself, but though Maurice had considered it, he'd decided against the idea. He'd thought everything would be put to rights when the old she-devil died. He'd almost danced on her grave with delirious joy. But it had been short-lived. In some strange, incomprehensible way, he missed her. The house seemed so silent, so empty, and Maurice realized he was just a lonely, unloved man.

Yesterday he'd seen the girl again and the agony had flooded back.

It was well over a year since the disaster at the mine, for that had been March, and now it was July. The summer heat made him feel as if he was running a constant temperature. He'd accepted on that terrible day that she loved Ritchie Pencarrow. Her husband. And that she was lost to him for ever. He'd been devastated, but he'd witnessed such scenes of grief that day, that his lust had been severely sobered. Since then he'd deliberately avoided all the places he might have seen her, in the market selling her produce or by Ritchie's side at the auctions. The bastard was doing well for himself, clawing his way out of debt as he expanded the farm. But yesterday, Maurice had literally bumped into her as she studied some swatches of material in a shop window. He'd lifted his hat in apology, not recognizing her at once. And his heart had plummeted as he realized she was expecting. Nowhere near the end of her term, but definitely with child.

It was proof. Distinct, ultimate proof of her love for her husband. And what went on between them in their marital bed.

Was Ritchie a good lover? The answer was most probably yes, damn him! He would be caring, considerate, and with those bloody good looks . . . ! Any woman would be captivated. *He* now, he was losing his touch. No decent woman seemed interested in him nowadays, even though he'd tried to socialize more. With the burning passion rekindled inside him, he'd been obliged to take the train into Plymouth the previous evening to find a house of ill-repute. Up in a cheaply luxurious room, a voluptuous girl had freely displayed her wares to him, but when it came to it, he simply couldn't 'get it up'. It was a crude, revolting expression, but it described his inadequacy well enough. His head had been too full of his vision of loveliness, a quick-witted intelligence, a deep compassion, a refined dignity . . . The girl before him had been none of those, and her thrusting nakedness had disgusted him. He'd thrown a pile of money on the bed — enough for the slut to set herself up in a decent trade, if she had the desire and determination, which she probably didn't — and left.

Maurice sighed wretchedly. He was a vastly wealthy man, and yet all his riches couldn't buy him happiness. Or could they? The idea struck him like a swift, penetrating arrow. At least he could wreak revenge on Ritchie for destroying his good looks and subsequently his life, ruin him, which would be satisfaction in itself! The bastard had never apologized, not even now, and Maurice felt quite justified. If he could manipulate the situation successfully, he might be the only person who, considering her condition, might offer Elizabeth Pencarrow employment.

Maurice stepped back from the mirror, preening himself, his brain spinning with insane elation. Vengeance! And if he killed two birds with the one stone, brought Elizabeth to live in his house and fill his home with love, oh, what sweet joy! He wouldn't need those bloody pills today! He would need a clear head. What luck the bloody sod banked with the same establishment as he did, where he was by far the richest client and had more than a little influence. And Mr Gaskell, the manager, why, wasn't he, Maurice, party to a little 'indiscretion' of the fellow's, and Mr Gaskell married — above his station, of course — to the sister of the bank's owner?

* * *

'There, come along, my lovely,' Elizabeth muttered into the mare's ear. 'Your master'll be back from town shortly, and he'll be wanting you hitched to the cart for the afternoon. You're going to fetch ferns for the hayricks.'

The corners of her mouth were lifted in contentment as she took hold of Briar's halter and led her from the field and into the stable. The pretty dappled cob was a willing animal, easy to catch, relishing human company as much as that of her lifelong friend, Lug, that Richard had ridden into Tavistock earlier to answer a summons to the bank. The horses had been worked as a team for years when Richard had bought them the previous summer, both strong and hard-working, and with the advantage that either could be ridden. Briar also liked to draw the old trap, which Richard had bought cheaply and renovated himself during the long winter evenings. The two cobs had been a godsend. Ploughing, muck spreading, drilling, harrowing, just about every task on the farm had been made so much easier and therefore more efficient, so that now almost all the suitable land Richard owned was in production. Not only could he grow so much more fodder and hence expand his livestock, but he no longer had to work himself into the ground. He still laboured from dawn till dusk, but now spent what Elizabeth considered more sufficient hours asleep in his bed. Their bed. And not always asleep, she mused with an impish smile as her eyes rested on her growing belly. Richard had opened up for her a secret, glorious world that was theirs alone, the love between them as intimate and trusting as that of Adam and Rebecca Bradley, who had become their dearest friends.

Elizabeth removed Briar's halter but the huge padded draught collar would be too heavy for her to lift. She could manage the cart saddle though, and had just secured the girth and was feeding Briar's tail through the crupper, when she heard Lug's heavy hooves in the yard, clattering at an unusual pace and coming to an abrupt halt. Briar noisily whickered her greeting as Richard dragged the surprised, stolid gelding into the stable, and Elizabeth looked across at him, open-mouthed. A white line had formed about his compressed lips, his face like hewn granite as he hauled the saddle from Lug's back.

'Richard? Whatever's the matter?'

Richard shot her a glance as dark as thunder, his jaw clamped, as he withdrew a letter from his inside jacket pocket. '*This* is what's the matter!' he snapped, and thrust the paper into her hand.

Her fine brow corrugated. Richard met her gaze, his mahogany eyes glinting with anger before he expanded his lungs to capacity and then blew out the breath in a furious blast. 'I'm sorry,' he grated. 'But just . . . read that!' he ordered as if it burned his tongue to speak.

Elizabeth stared at him, her heart scudding as she realized something was horribly wrong. He was scowling fiercely, his face ashen beneath its sun-browned skin as he turned Lug into his box. Elizabeth scanned the first few lines of the letter, the words becoming jumbled on the page.

'I . . . I don't understand,' she finally managed to stutter.

'It's not exactly complicated,' Richard growled, his normally soft voice like gravel. 'The bank has foreclosed on the loan. What part of that don't you understand?'

She blinked at him, dumbfounded. 'But they can't do that,' she spluttered. 'Not after . . .'

'Oh, yes, they bloody well can! They've every legal right, as Mr Gaskell was at pains to remind me!'

Their eyes locked over the partition that separated the two loose-boxes, Richard's dark and foreboding, hers shocked and tearful. Elizabeth stood transfixed as Richard spun round, slamming the bolt across the door of the loose-box and pacing the stable twice before storming out across the yard to the house.

Elizabeth watched him, numb with horror. They couldn't. Not now! Richard had paid off every penny of the interest and even some of the capital. By sheer hard work and the sweat of his brow, the farm was becoming profitable. The time was approaching when all his exhausting labour would come to fruition and he could reduce the loan further. It was the nature of farming to need time to establish itself. Surely the bank knew that? It was madness to call in the loan now.

Elizabeth buried her face in Briar's hairy neck, the gentle creature turning her head and affectionately nuzzling at her mistress, somehow sensing her distress. Even Bramble, ever playful when she wasn't hard at work, lay flat on her stomach, nose flattened on outstretched paws, her eyes raised dolefully to Elizabeth's face. The dusty stable with its familiar smells was warm and still in the afternoon sunshine, yet it held no consolation for Elizabeth's anger and despair.

At length, she followed Richard into the house, her feet dragging. She found him sitting in the kitchen, his elbows on the table and his head in his hands. A bottle of fine malt whisky that Adam had given him at Christmas was by his side with an empty glass — evidence that he had already tossed a good measure down his throat. He didn't move until she sat down opposite him. He lifted his head then, rubbed his hand hard over his forehead, the taut muscles of his jaw slackening.

'What am I to do, Beth?' he croaked in a hoarse whisper, his liquid eyes wide, like a lost child.

Elizabeth bit on her lip, her heart bleeding to see him reduced to such agonized desperation. 'But . . . surely they can't take the entire farm?' she dared to murmur, 'not when you've repaid some of the capital?'

But he shook his head with a tremulous, bitter sigh. 'It's what the farm is actually worth *now* that counts, and it's only worth what someone is willing to pay for it. People simply don't buy farms of this size anymore. They've had an offer, though, that they're happy to accept. It . . . it leaves a shortfall, so there's going to be an auction in a few weeks, to get what they can for my goods and chattels to make up the difference. And before you ask, I have no say in the matter.'

Richard reached for the bottle again, half refilled the glass and gulped it down. Elizabeth looked on, thoughts spun frenziedly in her head. 'What about the stock? And you'll still have the rent from the tenant farms, surely?'

'Huh!' He threw up his head with a cruel, sarcastic laugh. 'I never told you, but they're mortgaged, too. So, my dear Beth, I've lost everything. Even most of the stock, probably, and what good is any stock when you've no bloody land to keep it on? Mind you,' his voice rang with scornful irony, 'they have, most magnanimously, offered me the lease of Moor Top Farm. On my own bloody land, would you believe! The grazing's so damned poor up there, no one's wanted to rent it for years, and as for growing fodder, you can forget it! The whole place is derelict. I can't have our child born into that!' he groaned wretchedly. 'I went straight out and bought a newspaper to see if there's anywhere else decent up for rent, but there isn't. And then I went to the auctioneers to see if anything's coming on the market to buy, but there's nothing at the moment, and besides, they said they couldn't accept any bid of mine until the exact state of my bankruptcy is known. Oh, yes! News travels fast. Bankruptcy! That's the word he used. When I think how I've bloody near killed myself the last couple of years, and now I'm right back where I started! Only worse, because the buggers are going to take *everything* this time!' He slammed his fist forcefully on the table, but then, with a deep sigh, he raised his eyes to Elizabeth, his eyebrows knitted in misery. 'I've let you down, Beth,' he choked, wringing the words from his throat. 'And I'm *so* sorry. After all *your* hard work as well. And you know, the bastards are even throwing George and Kate out of their cottage. I pleaded with them, but they just wouldn't listen. How the hell am I supposed to tell old George? I'll not see them end their days in Tavistock work-house! George was born in that cottage, damn it! It's been his home all his life.'

Richard's eyes were wild and deranged, and Elizabeth's lips tightened into a pensive knot. She'd listened to his embittered tirade with appalled sympathy. After everything he'd overcome, the devastating events that had brought him back from France, his valiant efforts to rebuild the farm, this cruel twist of fate seemed to have wrecked his morale in one fell swoop; destroyed the masculine independence that made him what he was. She knew just how he felt, falling through some bottomless chasm. But he was blaming himself when he'd done everything in his power to save Rosebank Hall. His eyes were riveted on her, despair engraved in his pallid face. Elizabeth couldn't bear to witness his torment, and drooped her head from her sagging shoulders.

'I'll write to Becky,' she muttered, her own voice no more than a thin trail. 'I know Adam was to sail a few days ago and she was taking the children to Herefordshire, but she'll know how to reach him. Send a telegraph. She may not even need to. She may have some sort of power of attorney in his absence. I'll ask her—'

'What?' Richard interrupted flatly. 'To bail me out because I'm too damned useless to stand on my own two feet?'

Elizabeth chewed on her fingernail. She knew he wouldn't like the idea. 'It makes sense. Adam's a wealthy man. And he knows what 'tis to get into financial difficulty through no fault of one's own. You know their story as well as I do. They'd be only too happy to help. They *are* our best friends . . .'

'Exactly!' he roared, so sizzling with anger, she shrank from him at the opposite side of the table. 'I'll not take advantage of their friendship! I'm not a bloody charity case yet!'

Elizabeth's thrust out her chin with challenging defiance. She hadn't heard his razor-edged tongue for so long it was as if Josiah had risen up from his grave. She straightened her back, eyes snapping. ''Twould be a business arrangement with fixed terms and interest, just as if you'd transferred the loan to another bank. Adam would see the sense of it. He'd look upon it as an investment. And may I remind you, 'tis not just yourself we're talking of here! 'Tis Chantal and myself, and the baby.'

'You think I haven't considered that?' his voice crackled accusingly. But then he lowered his eyes, his breath torn and ragged. 'I'm sure Adam would be only too willing to offer his generosity, although even *he* may not have sufficient spare capital . . . But I couldn't accept it. You have to understand that,' he whispered brokenly. 'I just couldn't.'

His lean face had turned grey, and Elizabeth contemplated his bowed head. Richard was her whole world now, and she was being rent asunder by his despondency. He'd simply reached the end of his tether. It could happen to the best of men, and she counted him amongst them. He'd been so strong for her in the past; now it was time for her to help him.

'All right,' she said, spreading her hands on the table. 'If you're so proud and stubborn that you refuse to accept the logical solution, I'll support you. But not if you sit there wallowing in self-pity. If we're to move out of here, there's work to be done. I'll box up all the things like the silver and the rest of your grandfather's clocks this afternoon and take them to William to look after for us. Then we must decide what we can sell. There's plenty of good furniture in the house that we won't need and could fetch a good price. And what about the livestock? I assume Moor Top has Commoners' Rights? But you're only allowed to graze on its leer what the farm itself can support, so how many's that? And if the land's as poor as you say, we'll need as much fodder as possible, so I suggest you get yourself back to work this minute!'

Richard's gaze had been drawn back to her, his narrowed eyes crinkled at the corners, and his well-shaped mouth spreading into that beguiling smile she knew and loved so deeply.

'Dear God, I'd be lost without you, Beth,' he murmured thickly. 'Under that meek exterior, you're a little fighter! Come here,' he invited her with an almost unnoticeable beckoning jerk of his head.

Elizabeth obeyed eagerly, letting Richard pull her down onto his lap. He rested one hand lovingly on the growing mound of her stomach, and then, entwining the other in the hair which tumbled down her back in glorious abandon, brought his lips, warm and moist, against hers. 'Bugger the work,' he articulated somewhere at the back of his throat. 'What I really want before that cheeky daughter of mine comes home from school, is to take you upstairs and slowly peel off every stitch of your clothes and . . .'

He whispered the rest of the sentence into her ear. Elizabeth chuckled softly in response, her stomach tightening deliciously, for he had the strange power to light the beacon of desire inside her at the slightest touch. She forced herself to pull away.

'*Work*, Richard!' she ordered firmly.

He sighed, a deep reluctant grunt. 'You're a hard taskmaster! But you're absolutely right. If we're to . . . It'll take a lot of work to make the place habitable again,' he warned her. 'It's an old single-storey house. Shippen on one side, house on the other. Just two rooms, as I remember. No ceiling, just open to the roof. And only an open hearth to cook on.'

'I'm used to that. At my uncle's, remember. Richard,' she said, looking deep into his eyes, 'we can do this. We started from scratch before, and we can do it again. And this time, we have each other. Properly.'

'Yes. I know. It was just for a moment, I . . . Moor Top will only be temporary. We'll save every penny and by next year, we'll have somewhere better. But I *promise* you, if things become too bad, I'll go cap in hand to Adam. I won't let you or the children suffer.'

'You'll have lost Rosebank Hall, though.'

'Yes, I know,' he barely breathed. 'But I think even Adam would be hard pressed to raise enough capital . . . I'm sorry, Beth. I really am.'

'But we have each other, Richard. And that's enough for me.'

THIRTY

Elizabeth stopped for a moment to catch her breath, her gaze feasting on the desolate beauty of the high moorland and filling her lungs with the clean fragrance of the ferns and swathes of furze and heather that stretched in every direction. It was early September, and so much had happened since that dreadful day they'd learned they'd have to leave Rosebank Hall. Richard had slaved like a madman to make the house at Moor Top relatively habitable, limewashing the stone walls inside and out, removing the moss that was growing between the flagstones of the two small rooms, repointing them with mortar, and scrubbing them clean; sweeping the chimneys; replacing rotten wood and broken glass in the tiny windows in the thick walls, and mending the leaking roof. But despite this — and a layer of slate in the stonework — the building was still damp. They could only hope the repairs and continuous fires in the two grates would keep the problem at bay. Richard had been in a dark mood the day he'd paid the rent up until Michaelmas. Two pounds and ten shillings was the annual rent for the thirty-five acres of poor land and the decaying hovel, the whole of which would have fitted in the kitchen at Rosebank Hall, and which was a slum compared with the cosy cottage George and Kate had been forced to vacate. The elderly couple had no family with whom they could lodge, and Richard had rented an empty miner's cottage for them in the village. George had served the Pencarrow family for nearly seventy years, and Richard wasn't about to see him homeless in his old age, even if it meant he had to work himself into the ground to pay for it.

Who had bought Rosebank Hall, they had no idea. It stood empty, the furniture that hadn't sold in the auction and was of no use to them in their cramped new home, gathering dust as the weeks passed. Only the semi-feral cats lived on in the deserted farmyard, surviving on the mice and rats that had moved into the empty barns and stables. Mr Widcock, bidding a deliberately high price, had bought Briar and Lug, pronouncing them available for Richard's use whenever required. He admitted to being pleased that Richard had returned to his employment, although he wished it had been for other reasons. They'd managed to retain one of the house cows and her calf, two pigs, some hens, half a barnful of hay and a small flock. Richard had released the latter onto the leer or stretch of common allocated to the farm, but the creatures were confused by the move and kept wandering from the unfenced boundary, trying to return to their usual territory. Every morning and evening, as dawn broke or as dusk descended, Richard and Bramble had to go in search of his sheep and drive them back. In the meantime, he was preparing the enclosed grazing ready for the winter, clearing it of all poisonous plants, and mending the walls. He'd sown some rye, and bending as well as her protruding belly allowed, Elizabeth had helped him to transplant cabbage seedlings, swedes, potatoes and any other vegetables that might possibly succeed at such an advanced time of the year and on such poor soil. She'd taken cuttings and, where possible, seeds from her garden of healing herbs in case the plants she'd brought with her didn't survive the move. Now, just as she should be putting her feet up and preparing for the final stages of her pregnancy, she was busier than ever.

It was a long trek up to the peat ties in the warm, late summer sunshine, dragging the empty wheelbarrow behind her. Elizabeth sat down on its rough edge, resting her arm on her jutting stomach. It contracted fiercely beneath her touch, preparing for the birth in two months' time. She'd begun taking raspberry leaf tea to facilitate the baby's entry into the world, and was eating the most nutritious food they could obtain under the circumstances. But she couldn't sit back and watch Richard exhausting himself yet again. His naturally lean face had taken on that gaunt, haunted look she'd known before, and his good nature had been lost in the sullen silence of utter fatigue. He did try to pamper her, but the more he demonstrated his love for her when he was clearly dropping where he stood, the more guilty she felt. And there wasn't a farthing to spare. Every penny had to be saved so that the moment a suitable farm came on the market, Richard could make a reasonable bid for it. The only concession he'd agreed to, was to allow Adam to buy his shares in the *Swallow* at what he realized was a more than generous price. But buying coal when the farm possessed peat rights wasn't an option. Richard had felled the one pedunculate oak on the farm, which had been dead for some years, but the resulting logs wouldn't last long, so he'd been cutting turfs from the allocated peat tie high on the moor. They'd be perfect for storing just now, dry but not over-dry. Richard would have a fit if he knew what she was about, but her spirit was restless and the long walk would do her good, if nothing else.

Elizabeth wiped the back of her sleeve across her sweat-bedewed brow and got to her feet again. The previous year, the military had begun periodically using certain areas of Dartmoor for training, and sometimes the distant explosion of a shell could be heard from the firing ranges, but today all was silent. High up on the moor, the only sounds were the mewing of a circling buzzard, the song of a mountain blackbird, and the chat-chat of a stonechat searching for insects. She had seen many a tiny, delicate wheatear flitting amongst the outcrops of rock, and even glimpsed a ring ouzel. The high moorland bathed in sunshine on a beautiful warm day, oh yes, Dartmoor at its very best, and it brought a sublime peace to her heart. But this part of the moor was dangerous with peat bogs, and Elizabeth kept rigidly to the familiar path.

Others were working on the peat ties when she finally arrived, her back and her swollen legs already aching. Among them was Matthew Halse.

Her heart bounced in her chest as he came towards her, his perspiring face grim as he glanced sternly at her. 'You cas'n be doing that,' he growled as he cast a deprecating eye over the few turfs she'd heaved into the barrow. 'Not in your condition. You needs a horse wi' a wooden crook on its back fer carry turf. You knows that! What do that husband o' yourn be thinking of, sending you up yere?'

'He . . . doesn't know,' she stammered unsurely. 'I was just trying to help him.'

'Hmm,' Matthew frowned, rubbing his fat lips between his fingers. 'You've fallen on hard times, I've yerd tell. An' I've a new landlord, though I doesn't know who. Well, sit yersel doon, cheel, an' take a rest. And if you've any sense, you'll leave yon barrow yere an' get yersel home.'

Elizabeth blinked at him through the brilliant sunlight. 'Yes, you're right,' she muttered, ruefully lowering herself onto the ledge formed by Richard's last journey or row of cutting, and feeling the relief drain through her limbs.

''Tis a fool you be,' Matthew grunted. 'I've learned my lesson from losing my Daniel. There be nort so precious as family.'

Elizabeth pursed her lips, but she didn't have the energy to examine Matthew's motives. 'How's Nellie?' she asked, ignoring his comments.

'Walking out wi' a young miner from Wheal Betsy. An' Nathaniel's like to wed a cheel he met at market. From over Lamerton way.'

'Oh, yes?' She smiled, though she'd pity anyone married to her cousin. 'Tell Nellie to come and visit me when she can.'

'Well, you shuddn't be walking all the way to *us*, let alone fetching turfs.' He poked his head at her. 'Now you take care, an' I'll not see you up yere again. Now get yersel going.'

Elizabeth rose awkwardly to her feet. She might have sat there all day, if the truth be told, but she was only too eager to be away from Matthew's company. She eyed the barrow, reluctant to leave it up on the moor. But then a sharp twinge that plunged down into her protruding belly took her breath away, and she stood for several seconds, unable to move, as it held her in a vice-like grip.

'Don't forget to tell Nellie!' she called over her shoulder, forcing a smile to her face, since she wasn't going to let Matthew see she was in trouble. The smarting spasm was easing, and this time she braced herself to strike out down the track. For some stretch, it was easy going and she made steady progress as the peat pass sloped gently downhill. But then the way became rutted, deep, dried gouges in the earth, and she wondered quite how she'd managed to haul the barrow through them on the way up. But she hadn't been in any discomfort then, and now she began to utter silent curses as tears pricked her eyes. It came again, the pain that stabbed deep inside, as she dragged herself onwards, sweat slicking her entire body as the sun gathered strength and beat down on her back. Elizabeth threw off her wide-brimmed straw hat. It was supposed to keep the sun from her face but it was making her head unbearably hot and now she blinked into the blinding sunshine. Matthew's words echoed in her head. What had she been thinking of? But when she'd set out, the contractions had only been of the practising kind. Now they were so strong, she was sure she must have been mistaken.

By the time Elizabeth left the main track and branched off towards the isolated farmstead, the stabbing cramps of labour were striking her every five minutes, racking her hardened abdomen. She struggled on over the rough, stony path, the need to get home to safety driving her onwards. She couldn't think straight, and it wasn't until she felt something rupture inside her, and a warm sticky substance began to trickle down her legs, that she seemed to come to her senses. Dear God, her waters had broken. It wasn't just raking pain that gripped her now, but a crucifying panic as well. Sick with fear, she lifted her skirt. Her thighs were glistening with flowing liquid, and it was bloodstained.

Elizabeth swayed as a suffocating wave of dizziness pulsed through her body. She staggered about in a full circle, the moorland, the spiky furze, reaching to infinity, spinning around her, empty but for a group of unperturbed sheep cropping the sweet grass. She screamed for help, at least she thought she did, not aware that she merely whimpered at the back of her throat, and no one was there to hear her cries. The pain came again, tighter, stronger, bringing her to her knees, and she waited for it to pass. It didn't. Hardly had the spearing contraction eased than it exploded again, but Elizabeth drew herself upwards, her head still spinning nauseously. She *had* to get home. Each step a savage effort as the agony bore deeper into her flesh. She stumbled to her knees again, crawling along the ground, the only way to reach home . . .

* * *

Richard trotted into the yard and swinging his leg over Briar's bare back, dropped neatly onto his feet. Mr Widcock was acutely aware of his desperate financial situation, and had insisted he took the willing animal for the afternoon to bring down the cut and dried turfs while the weather held. The generous fellow had said he considered he was merely fostering Briar and Lug until they could be returned to Richard's ownership.

'Beth!' Richard called as he left the mare to drink from the bucket he filled for her, but there was no reply.

His forehead furrowed. She was always there to greet him, running into his arms, her chin tilted to receive his warm, tender kiss and make him wish he could take her straight to bed instead of having to toil like a slave. She must be resting as he'd told her she should every afternoon. He'd just pop his head around the door to tell her what he was about.

But the place was so quiet and his frown deepened. All was still and dusty in the September sunshine, but for the occasional cluck of one of the hens. Bramble, who as ever had padded along at his feet, had disappeared through the cross passage to the farmhouse, and now re-emerged, slinking timorously and whining.

For one vile, horrible moment Richard's heart stood still and then it kicked hard in his chest. Something was wrong, he knew intuitively. He catapulted forward, crying out Elizabeth's name, flying over the threshold and across the few feet to the bedroom door.

'Oh, no.' The whispered words quivered in his throat. 'Oh, sweet Jesus Christ, no.'

Richard stood, trembling, not daring, not able, to breathe. His dearest, beloved Beth, who'd salvaged the tatters of his life, was lying motionless on the bed. She was curled up on her side, her skirt around her thighs, her legs and the coverlet soaked in blood. And at the foot of the bed, still attached by a long cord, a tiny, grey, lifeless form.

He couldn't . . . No, it wasn't . . . Oh, God . . . ! Bramble cocked one ear at his broken cry, her eyes dolefully on her master, for though she had smelled death and was afraid, her loyal heart made her follow him into the silent room. Slowly, as if in a nightmare, Richard dragged himself across the flagstones and kneeling beside the bed, gathered his wife into his arms.

* * *

William Greenwood paused as he contemplated the hunched figure of Richard Pencarrow sitting slumped forward in the chair, his head buried in his hands so that his dark, wavy hair stood on end. He looked up sharply as the doctor entered the room, his eyes still red-rimmed and his pallid cheeks streaked with the tears that had washed unashamedly down his face. He was shivering despite the warmth of the sunny afternoon, and William knew he had not one, but two patients to care for.

'She's sleeping peacefully now,' he said gently, rolling down his sleeves. 'The womb's contracting nicely now after the manual stimulation I gave her, just like *you* would a cow or a ewe,' he explained, knowing that as a farmer, Richard would understand such matters. 'She's had some ergot and also some laudanum, so she'll sleep for some time.' He hesitated before he came and sat opposite the husband of the girl he looked upon as another daughter. 'I'm sorry about the baby, Richard,' he attempted to console him. 'I'd say it had been dead for a couple of days, so you know as well as I do, it's best she aborted spontaneously.'

Richard didn't answer. He'd gone back to staring at some invisible spot on the floor. His shoulders heaved, the breath shuddering in and out of his lungs as he fought to stifle his suffocating tears. Watching him, William drew in his lips. He'd seen many a grieving man in his time, but Richard's crushing sorrow was a deep, brooding melancholy that brought a constriction to William's own throat.

'This was how it was with Maddy,' Richard croaked at length, his voice no more than a choked whisper. 'Chantal was safe. She was full term, but . . .' He lifted his head, his eyes screwed shut and his lips twisted with despair. 'Maddy . . . the bleeding never stopped. We never . . . We were never man and wife again. And now . . . Oh, this is all my fault!' he groaned pitiably, his eyes staring wildly at the bare rafters. 'If it wasn't for me, she wouldn't have been . . . And she went through all that agony all alone. Oh, God! I couldn't bear to lose her, too!'

Richard broke down again, weeping great wrenching sobs that seemed to tear him apart. William's heart gripped with helplessness as he patted Richard's arm. There was no point assuring him Elizabeth wouldn't die. But he would do everything within his power to make sure she didn't.

THIRTY-ONE

Maurice couldn't believe his eyes. His lips curled in a furious snarl, his nostrils flaring like some savage beast. He knew Ritchie hadn't as yet been able to move from the dilapidated hovel Maurice's machinations had reduced him to, as he'd just paid the rent for the next six months while Rosebank Hall stood empty. All done through the bank, of course, for Maurice wanted to choose his moment to reveal who the new owner was. It had cost him a great deal of money with no return for his investment except his warped pleasure, which at that moment had been shattered into a million pieces. For Ritchie was buying half a dozen sheep before his very eyes at Tavistock's annual Goose Fair. How could he do it, Maurice fumed maliciously. Not being a farmer, he little realized that Richard had already drafted out for slaughter those elderly ewes whose teeth were too far gone for them to be able to feed properly, and that he was simply replacing them with younger stock. Besides which, he'd flung himself into even more exhausting work than ever in order to assuage his guilt and make sure nothing ever happened to Elizabeth again. She was gaining strength, and William was of the opinion that there was no reason why she shouldn't bear a child in the future. But not yet, and so Richard must be content to lie with his wife wrapped round him at night, and nothing more. It was enough for him that she was alive, and if his frustrations tortured him, it was merely the punishment he deserved.

Elizabeth was with him now, of course. The Goose Fair was the one occasion in the year, apart from Christmas Day, when no work except the bare necessities was achieved in the entire area, and everyone flocked to the town to enjoy the festivities. For some, it was just another market, as usual, and that was why Richard Pencarrow was there. Treating his wife like a piece of precious porcelain, Maurice noted with jealous resentment, sitting her down safely and making sure she was comfortable before he went about his business at the auction. She looked fragile, her clear complexion pale beneath her simple hat, and her waist tinier than ever. What had happened to the child, Maurice mused disinterestedly. There was no sign of it, only the dark, curly headed girl Ritchie had brought back with him from France, fussing about her stepmother like a brood hen. Well, if she'd lost the baby, all well and good! It would be one less Pencarrow brat in the world, Maurice sniggered with chortling delight. But then he was overcome with guilt, as she must have been devastated. But never mind! *He* would give her a dozen children, and provide for her in a way Ritchie could never hope to in his wildest dreams! If he could only have a chance he would woo her as only a true gentleman could, with the little delicacies every woman appreciated. And then, when the time was right . . . His mouth filled with saliva at the thought of what he would do to her delicate body. It would be nothing outrageous, for that would offend her. He'd left all that behind in the tumbled bed of the miner's wife in the Fitzford cottage. Elizabeth Pencarrow's silken skin, her graceful limbs, would be so exquisite he would have no need of that.

Huh! He grunted viciously, shaking his head. She'd never come to him. Not in a million years. And certainly not while Ritchie was alive.

Maurice was sure his heart had ceased to beat and for one petrifying moment, he thought he might be about to be struck dead. Surely he couldn't have sunk so low? But how could his soul ever find peace until she was his? The pain of his longing was unbearable, and only Ritchie stood in his way, Ritchie, whom he'd hated for more than a dozen long years. If only . . . The Arkwright boy was gone now, thanks to his own stupidity. And the great lummox who always used to hang about with him had even less brain than his departed companion. So Maurice had only himself to rely upon. An accident. Yes, it would have to be that, for he couldn't risk discovery. And then he'd offer her comfort, a shoulder to cry on, a home. He'd even take on Ritchie's brat, prove to Elizabeth that he was a good man and not the monster she thought he was. With his devoted affection, she would, in time, get over her widowhood, and come to love him instead. He'd treat her like a princess, and she'd be a wonderful mother to their children, and if ever he were unwell, she'd care for him as his own mother never had. She would outlive him, of course, and so he'd have a reason to make that will his solicitor was always badgering him about. He'd leave everything to her, of course, and their children. At long last, there would be some meaning in his life.

The plan both elated and calmed him. He'd enjoy a few hours at the fair, observing her at a distance, without pain because he knew now she would be his. And then go home, lock the door of his study, take out the small phial and the syringe he'd recently learned to use, roll up his sleeve, and soon he would be dreaming blissfully of her . . .

* * *

Bramble lifted her beautifully domed head from her paws, one ear cocked attentively. She was lying stretched out on her belly before the hissing peat fire, the long day's work done. She'd been out on the moors, obeying her master's every command as he drove his remaining ewes down to the pens to receive the services of the hired ram which was due to arrive the following day. Only the older wethers would be left on the leer for the winter, and Richard would have his work cut out to keep his stock well fed. The turnips he'd planted so carefully at the end of May and which he'd normally be starting to feed to his animals at this time of year were not his to harvest, and were rotting in the ground in the fields he used to own, together with the mangolds that should be dug up and stored in clamps before the frosts. The only winter fodder he had were the hastily planted swedes which had yet to develop to a respectable size, and the hay he'd brought from Rosebank Hall and stored in the small barn, whose roof he'd recently discovered was leaking. He was in the throes of replacing the broken slates with new ones they could ill afford, one ladder propped up to the eaves of the low building, and another lashed by ropes over the roof to the apex. But with the ram due next day he'd been obliged to interrupt the work to fetch in the ewes, the few first-year lambs he possessed having already been taken down to the milder climes of Bere Alston for the winter.

Now Bramble cautiously stirred, got to her feet and padded over to the door, her hackles raised so that Richard arched a questioning eyebrow. The animal snuffled her snout along the foot of the door, and a growl rumbled deep in her throat as she began scratching at the flagstones.

Elizabeth looked across at Richard as he stood up, slipped into his coat and reached for a storm-lamp, lighting it with a taper from the fire. 'I'd better take a look. I don't want anything scaring the ewes when they're about to go to tup. Will you be all right for a few minutes?'

'Of course.' She smiled, reaching up to catch his sleeve. 'There's no need to fuss over me so much. I'm better now.'

Richard softly pursed his lips. She was vastly improved since that terrible day seven weeks ago, but she was still pale and lacking in energy, and he worried about her every waking minute. He reluctantly left her now, sitting in the armchair by the fire. She sank back contentedly as he went outside, the cold blast of air from the open door soon dissipating in the warm atmosphere. She'd been devastated at losing the child. But she'd suffered such agony and had been so weak afterwards that for some time there'd been no place in her heart for grief. It had hit her later, like running full pelt into a brick wall. She'd wept for days on end. But she was over it now and relieved that she and Richard and Chantal could get on with their lives. They were together, and that was all that mattered. There would be other years, other children, William had assured her, and with winter on its way, there were other problems to contemplate.

'Nothing,' Richard announced, shaking his head as he came back in. 'The ewes are quite happy. Bramble's still uneasy, so I've left her outside. She'll go and sleep in the barn once she's settled down.'

'Mmm.' Elizabeth nodded, and then she stretched languidly. 'I think I'll go to bed. It's been nice, just sitting here by the fire.' She stood up and laced her arms about Richard's neck. She brought her lips so amorously against his that he held his breath, his eyes screwed tightly as longing he knew he shouldn't entertain invaded his loins. The smell of her was so sweet, her flushed cheek so warm against his cold one. 'Will you come, too?' she murmured, her voice low and thick as she traced her finger around the open neck of his shirt. 'William called today. He said . . . it should be all right now.'

Richard frowned, his eyebrows fiercely knitted as he rested his gaze on her lovely face once more. 'Are . . . you sure? I suppose if I'm gentle . . .'

'You always are,' she purred, her eyes smouldering as she led him into the little room beyond, past where his daughter was sleeping soundly, to the heavily curtained bed that was their secret sanctuary. And from which they were totally oblivious to what was happening outside.

* * *

Richard poked his head around the door so that he had no need to remove his muddy boots. 'Right, that's all done,' he told her. 'I'm going to get on with the barn roof before Mr Widcock arrives with the ram. I don't know what's the matter with Bramble, though. She seems almost asleep.'

Elizabeth's eyebrows shot up in alarm. 'Oh, dear, I hope she's not ill.'

'No, I don't think so. Come and see for yourself. She's in the barn.'

Elizabeth flung her worn shawl about her shoulders and followed Richard across the yard. She put her hand on his arm as he picked up a slate from the neatly stacked pile and placed one foot on the first rung of the ladder.

'You mind yourself up there,' she warned him.

He smiled down at her, his rich brown eyes melting at the memory of their rapturous love-making the night before. He pulled her to him with his free hand and pressed a light, sensuous kiss on her mouth which left Elizabeth's lips tingling with excitement. Her heart fluttered deliciously in her breast, waiting for the moment when the day's work was over and Chantal was asleep, and she could entwine herself around him again, her slender flesh pressed against the hard length of his strong body.

Bramble was curled up in the straw, her nose softly poised on her flexed paws. She opened one eye and her furry tail brushed the barn floor as her mistress knelt down beside her. She yawned then, revealing the long line of her large white teeth, and settled down again. As Richard had said, she didn't appear ill, just mysteriously sleepy.

The rattling slither from somewhere above them jerked up Elizabeth's head. Her eyes widened with fear as her ears followed the resounding clatter down the roof of the barn and then the splintering crash before an ominous thud on the compacted earth of the yard. Then sickening silence.

Oh, God! Oh, dear God in heaven, NO! She shot out of the barn and skidding round the corner, came to an abrupt halt. Oh, please God, no. Let this not be true. But it was. Richard lying face down on the ground. Motionless. One of his arms twisted out at a strange angle. The broken slate lay in fragments beside him.

Elizabeth shrank away, her hands over her bloodless face. A shriek of horror echoed from her throat as she stepped forward slowly, not wanting . . . And yet . . . she had . . . to . . . *know* . . .

Richard moaned faintly as she dropped on her knees at his side. His eyes flickered open but instantly screwed shut as awareness of the pain flooded his senses.

'Richard, don't move,' Elizabeth instructed automatically as her instincts, her years of experience, mercifully took over. 'I'll get help.'

But he was already pulling himself up on all fours, though his left arm dangled awkwardly from his shoulder and he let out a tortured cry as his body stiffened to stone. Elizabeth flew to support him, waiting as he struggled to catch his breath and then slowly, excruciatingly slowly, inched himself upwards.

'My God, how . . . how did it happen?' she croaked as he leaned heavily on her.

'I . . . I don't know,' he rasped through gritted teeth, his face colourless as he fought to snatch short, trembling gasps of air. 'It just seemed . . . to give way beneath me.'

And as Elizabeth raised her eyes to the barn roof, she saw the broken rungs of the ladder.

* * *

William rubbed his chin in the kindly way he'd had since he was a medical student in London. He was well into his fifties now, his thinning hair threaded with silver and enhancing the trust his calm confidence had always inspired.

'I'd say you have the luck of the devil.' He nodded, his eyes stretched beneath his bushy grey eyebrows. 'A dislocated shoulder and a few either badly bruised or cracked ribs are nothing to the injuries you might have sustained falling from that height.'

Richard dropped his head back, his breathing short and shallow through his clenched jaw. 'I did try to break my fall by grabbing on to whatever I could. I knew . . . if I landed head first—'

'Well, let's not think about that,' William interrupted him. 'First of all, I need to put that shoulder back in. I warn you, it's going to hurt, and it'll be somewhat sore for a while. And I'll be strapping your ribs up for the next few days at least. You must have total bed rest until I say so. If you put any pressure on your chest and one of those damaged ribs were to snap and puncture your lung . . . well, I'm sure you don't need me to tell you how serious it could be. If the pain gets worse at all, or you feel unwell, I must be fetched at once. But no doubt Lizzie will be giving you comfrey so the bones will heal quickly if they are broken.'

'Oh, Christ, what about the farm?' Richard groaned and then winced painfully, bringing his right arm across his chest. 'And the ram's coming this afternoon.'

'Oh, I'm sure Mr Widcock would stain the ram and put it in the field for us, and then I can keep an eye on things.'

'Yes, but what about everything else? Beth can't do any work on the farm, can she, Will? I mean . . . after . . .'

'No.' William drew in his chin emphatically. 'I'm afraid you'll have to hire some help. And now I suppose you're going to say you can't afford it.'

Elizabeth lowered her eyes. 'We'll just have to. Adam bought Richard's shares in the *Swallow*. We were saving the money to buy a new farm but we'll just have to use some of that. They've been so good to us, Adam and Rebecca.'

'It's what friends are for. And *this* friend won't be charging for his visits. No, I insist!' He lifted his hand at Richard's protest. 'And when I've done here, I'm sending the constable from Mary Tavy. I've looked at that ladder. The rungs didn't break. They were sawn part way through. And Bramble. I reckon she was doped. I don't believe this was an accident, Richard. I believe someone tried to kill you.'

344

THIRTY-TWO

Maurice stared at the headline on the front of that week's *Tavistock Gazette*. 'Attempt on Life of Local Farmer.' He simply couldn't believe it, and such a violent shaking took hold of him that the paper danced in his hands and he had difficulty in reading the remainder of the article. After all that . . . after all his efforts . . . observing the lowly farmstead for days on end to decide what to do, then hiding in the pitch of night, shivering in the penetrating damp he wasn't used to, his heart in his mouth when Richard had emerged with his confounded dog, then dealing with the cur which fortunately he'd anticipated. He'd nearly broken his own neck up that ladder in the dark. He'd never been up a ladder in his life, and the climb had petrified him. But he was a man incensed. No matter what he did, bloody Ritchie managed to bounce back. And now, even after what he himself recognized as a crazed, reckless act, the bastard was still alive! Injured, and suffering, but still alive. Well, he hoped he was in agony.

But . . . attempt on his life! They *knew*! He'd never used a saw before, had 'borrowed' the thing from the box of tools he provided for his handyman. The fellow insisted on working with quality instruments and had put in a bill for a new blade only days before. It was what had given Maurice the idea when he'd been spying on the farm and saw Richard working on the barn roof. Perhaps the tool had been too damned sharp! It had certainly sliced through the wood with surprisingly little effort, and in the dark, he'd found it hard to know when to stop. He just wanted the rungs to be weakened enough so that they gave way under Ritchie's weight, leaving a jagged break that looked natural.

So they were on to him, were they? No. Of course not. And his lips curved into a complacent smirk. His avid eyes scanned the article more calmly this time. There appeared to be no motive, and all enquiries had drawn a blank. Well, they would, wouldn't they? He chortled with a venomous sneer. Who would suspect *him*, a highly respected businessman in Tavistock? Even the bank manager was unlikely to put two and two together, and even if he did, he wouldn't come forward with his suspicions, for that's all they would be. And would the blackguard risk losing one of his best customers, maybe his reputation, his job, his whole life? But just think, what if his conscience overtook him and he did?

The thought brought Maurice out in a clammy sweat that oozed onto his forehead and upper lip like glistening pearls. He was beginning to feel ill again, shivering, his eyes watering. Time for another injection before anyone noticed. That Mrs Elliot, now she'd been elevated to housekeeper, had eyes like a shrew and saw everything. It was so wrong, he knew, the supply of the drug illegal — as his wallet was all too aware — but he could afford it, and it brought him such comfort. So he unlocked the drawer of his desk and reached for the box. It wasn't there. He started to rummage more and more dementedly among the papers, bills and pens, throwing them out and scattering them in every direction all over the study floor until he finally discovered the container he was looking for. His trembling fingers fumbled to open it, and he took a deep breath to calm himself. He couldn't do it if he was shaking so much. Ah, that was better. He drew off the required amount and set the syringe aside while he brought up a vein. And then — he sat back in the chair and waited.

Come on, come on, *work*, damnable stuff! If he was arrested for his attempt on Ritchie Pencarrow's life, it would be too late! He'd never have her, that divine creature who'd enslaved his heart the moment he'd set eyes on her! All that money he had, all that bloody fortune, was worth *nothing* without happiness, and only she could give him that. Every plan he'd made to win Elizabeth's love, to prove his worthiness, had been thwarted by that sanctimonious bastard! And now the devil had even survived a fall that should have killed him! A black surge of anger flooded through Maurice's veins; a maddened, strangling need to satisfy his frustrations; a determination to quench his seething jealousy, come what may. And what did it matter if he swung for it, for what was his life without her?

If only he could have her. Just once. Feel that slender, lithesome body against his, wrapped around him in the act of love. Run his fingers through that flowing ocean of golden hair, feel himself floating on a heavenly cloud in a way that even this damned drug couldn't achieve. That one moment of ecstasy would last him the rest of his days. It would have to. She'd never be his wife. But he would hold the memory of it in his heart for ever, would dream of it at night, and when the needle allowed him to escape his loneliness.

But how? The answer came to him through the fog of his drugged mind. There was only one way she was sure to come to him. And willingly. He closed his eyes, and let his soul drift away on a cloud of tranquillity . . .

* * *

Richard rubbed his hand over his strong jaw and sighed. 'I can't just sit here doing nothing,' he grumbled. 'Can't I help you with that?'

'The ironing?' Elizabeth lifted her head in amazement, and a broad grin illuminated her face. 'You can't *iron*! 'Tis women's—'

'I could learn. I'd have had to in France, if I hadn't had poor Aurélie to help in the house.'

'No,' she answered firmly. 'You have to twist your body and 'twould do your ribs no good at all. 'Tis little over two weeks. William said you could get out of bed and sit in the chair for a while, no more, and there you are up and dressed, and wanting to get back to work.'

'But my shoulder's mended now, so it's only my ribs, and they . . .' But as he got to his feet, a pained wince caught him by surprise and he failed to stifle the sharp intake of breath.

'There, you see!' Elizabeth glowered at him, her hands squarely on her hips. 'David's doing a perfectly good job looking after the sheep, so you've no need to worry. All the other jobs can wait till you're better.'

Richard grunted with discontent and bent his head to look out of the small window. 'I couldn't believe it when your uncle lent him to us free of charge,' he said distantly. 'He's a good lad. He's been well trained.'

'For all his faults, Uncle Matthew's a good farmer, especially when he's sober, which is all the time these days.' She put down the flat iron and contemplated the folded sheet before her. 'You know, I think I can understand him now. He loved my aunt passionately in his own way, lusty and selfish though 'twas. I looked so much like her, and he loved me, too, so when he was drunk, he just transferred his feelings. And I was fond of him in many other ways. 'Twas why I never said anything — *that*, and being so confused. But I think he just couldn't help himself, even though 'twas so wrong.'

'Wrong! I'd knock his bloody teeth out for him, if you'd let me.'

'You'll do no such thing, Richard Pencarrow! But, maybe, if 'twill stop you pacing up and down like some caged beast, you could walk down and meet Chantal from school. If you promise to go slowly. She'll be halfway home by the time you get there but 'twill make her day. William would have a blue fit, mind, if he knew.'

She hadn't finished speaking before Richard had wriggled into his coat and was frowning at his outdoor boots, refusing to admit he couldn't bend down to his feet. Elizabeth gave a knowing laugh and knelt down to lace them for him. With a swift kiss dropped onto her hair, he was off into the fresh air he craved, Bramble, as frustrated as he was, at his heels.

Elizabeth went on with the ironing. It could have been so different. Richard could so easily have been killed in the fall. She forced the unbearable thought from her mind and worked on to finish the neatly folded pile of laundry. Whatever task she had to perform at Moor Top, the lack of facilities meant that it took twice as long. There was no pump inside the house, just a wooden launder in the yard that flowed with water diverted from a stream; no luxurious water-closet as at Rosebank Hall, but an outside earth and ash privy. Although Elizabeth could cook on an open fire, it was limiting and took so much longer. With no range boiler, there was no constant supply of hot water, which meant they had to wait for anything from making a cup of tea to having a good stripped wash, a proper bath being out of the question. Even the ironing took for ever, setting the flat iron with the base towards the heat rather than directly on the hot surface of a range. Still, at least they had a roof over their heads. Nothing but the slates between them and the outside world, though, so it would be freezing cold in the months to come if they had a bad winter. If they were still living there, which looked likely. It was already very near the end of October, and there was no sign of any other farm becoming available either for sale or to rent in a ten-mile radius. And this setback of Richard's fall, however it had happened, hadn't helped. But they had each other, and they had Chantal. Elizabeth had tried to put the memory of their tiny son behind her, but sometimes she felt she would choke on her grief. They'd buried him next to her mother, without a name. He'd never drawn breath, never lived outside the womb. They'd agreed it was better that way. Next time, it would be different.

Elizabeth wiped her fingers over her wet cheeks and hung the kettle over the open fire, ready for a cup of tea when her husband and stepdaughter returned.

The quick, laboured footfall of someone running across the yard lifted Elizabeth's head. It was only moments before the door was flung open and Richard stood there, clinging to the doorpost and gasping for breath, his deathly pale face torn in agony and one arm clutched across his ribs. Elizabeth came towards him, her pulse racing. Something was terribly, unthinkably wrong, and she gazed up at him in horror.

Richard was panting in short, trembling gasps. 'Chantal,' he finally managed to splutter. 'The bastard's got Chantal.' He strode the few feet to where his two shotguns and the rifle were hooked high up on the wall, and reached up for the latter, wincing at the stretch to his chest. And then, laying the weapon on the table, he removed the key from its secret hiding place and opened the ammunition box on the shelf.

Elizabeth watched him in appalled silence as he checked the gun. 'I don't understand. *Who's* got Chantal?'

Richard's wild eyes flashed her a menacing, deeply foreboding glance. 'Bloody Maurice Brett, that's who!' he cried, snarling at the very name. 'Why in God's name didn't I think of him before! It's been him all along!' And when Elizabeth inclined her head in confusion, he jammed his hand into his pocket and withdrew a crumpled sheet of paper. 'I met her little schoolfriend, Brian,' he wheezed, for he still hadn't caught his breath. 'He was running towards me like a bat out of hell. He said they'd met a man. He spoke to Chantal in a strange language. Must have been French. Brett's the only person I know who could . . . and she went with him. And the man gave Brian that letter . . . and told him to bring it to me straight away. I read it and told Brian to run to the constable in Mary Tavy and tell him to come . . . to White Tor, at once.'

Elizabeth blinked first at him and then at the paper. Her stunned mind refused to take in the words properly, and she had to piece their meaning together.

You always did get in the way, didn't you, Ritchie? Always spoilt the fun. But your father owed me money, lots of it, and he never paid me back. So now you owe me. And I'll never forgive you for what you did to my face. Some years ago, it stopped me from marrying the only girl I'd ever fancied as a wife, and now you've taken Elizabeth from me as well. You just couldn't keep your hands off what I wanted, could you?

Elizabeth should have been mine, but you had to have her. You ruined my life all along, so now I want you to know it's been me ruining yours. Oh, yes! I own Rosebank Hall and the hovel you're living in now. So how does it feel to have the tables turned, eh? And who do you think tampered with the ladder? I just wish you'd broken your neck, but I'll teach you! Vengeance is so sweet! I have your daughter, Ritchie, but it's not her I want. It's your wife. And I'm sure you know what I want from her. So, if you want to see your daughter alive again, tell Elizabeth to come to White Tor alone. I'll be waiting.

Maurice Brett

For some seconds Elizabeth couldn't move. Maurice Brett wanted *her*. His evil words rattled in her skull, filling her with a terror greater than anything she'd ever known before. But he had Chantal and was threatening her young life! The horror of it snapped Elizabeth to her senses and she sprang to Richard's side as he slung the rifle over his shoulder by its leather strap. Their eyes met. She knew what they had to do. They both knew. And if she'd ever doubted Richard's need to do what he had done in France, that doubt now fled. She understood.

For . . . dear God . . . a child, this time, Richard's own daughter, was in terrible danger. It was happening again.

* * *

Richard and Elizabeth snaked through the tall, dying ferns on their bellies, Bramble beside them, her hairy body flattened into the damp earth. They hadn't taken the direct route to the tor, but had skirted it at a distance in order to approach

351

from an unexpected direction, one which would afford the greatest cover and hopefully fool Maurice Brett from his vantage point on the highest outcrop of rock. They'd seen him from way off, a black outline silhouetted against a clear coral sky as the late October sun began to sink over Cornwall. And held against him, the figure of a little girl.

They'd half run, both breathless and bent low so that he wouldn't spot them. Once Richard had collapsed onto his hands and knees, struggling for breath, and Elizabeth had been terrified. But after a minute or two's respite, he seemed to recover and they moved on. The instant he spied his daughter, Richard slackened his pace. Movement could give them away and if they could see Maurice, it was possible Maurice might catch sight of them. From different cusps of the tor, there was an uninterrupted view in every direction. But he couldn't look everywhere at once, and he would have to clamber across from one outbreak of rock to another, dragging Chantal with him.

Richard crept forward with the stealth of a cat stalking its prey, constantly checking Maurice's whereabouts. Elizabeth stole along behind him, obeying his every silent hand command. Her face was streaked with mud, her hair pulled loose, and stuck with dead leaves and fragments of the brittle, russet bracken. The chilling damp of the air invaded the very marrow of her bones, and yet she had to lie inert on the ground whenever Richard commanded. Her mouth was dry from fear, the need to awake from this nightmare desperate, but she mustn't give in.

Richard slunk nearer, seeking the cover of the boulders that in ages past had broken away from the tor and rolled down the steep slope. He needed to get within range, but not too close. The rock formations were deceptive, and once amongst them, one obscured the other. It would be better to lie in wait and be ready for the moment when Maurice presented himself as a sitting target.

'I know you're out there, Ritchie!' The sudden bellow from not so far away boomed eerily across the silence of the moor. 'Wouldn't stay away, would you? But you can see I have your little brat here! And I have a knife at her throat. If you don't believe me, she'll tell you herself.'

Lying beside him hidden in the bracken, Elizabeth saw Richard start as if he would leap up there and then, and she put a cautioning hand on his arm.

'Oui, Papa, c'est vrai!'

Chantal's shrill squeal shrieked through their ears and Elizabeth shivered, closing her eyes to the horror that surrounded her. Richard's fingers clawed at the earth, the muscles of his clenched jaw working frenziedly. But then he seemed to take hold of himself and pointed across the jumble of smaller rocks to another large boulder. Elizabeth followed him on hands and knees across the gap, praying at every moment that Maurice wouldn't see them.

'Just send up your wife, and I'll let the child go!'

Richard shut his eyes as if blocking out the hideous, ghoulish voice, and then reached into his pocket for the cartridges, dropping one into each of the two chambers of the rifle and closing the breech. As he settled the muzzle on the top of the rock, Elizabeth heard the ominous double click as he pulled back the hammers. She held her breath, burying her head in the ground, waiting for the resounding bang.

'Jesus Christ, Chantal, get away from him!' she heard Richard hiss.

Elizabeth looked up. Maurice had changed his position, standing like some demonic icon on the very apex of a rocky buttress, fearless and triumphant. He'd made himself the perfect target. Except that he had Chantal clasped against him, and was turning in circles as he searched the moorland with eyes unaccustomed to the camouflaging hues of the furze and bracken.

Richard gave a groan and turned his head into his shoulder to wipe the sweat from his forehead before squinting down the length of the barrel once more. Elizabeth heard him draw in a trembling breath in an effort to calm himself, but then he lifted his head and dashed his hand across his mouth.

'Oh, dear God,' he murmured in an agony of frustration, and she read the unutterable terror in his eyes as he glanced at her again. If he got it wrong, he could hit Chantal. He could kill his own daughter!

Richard lined his jaw against the rifle butt yet again, his finger on the first of the two triggers, motionless as he trained his keen eye on the figures on the rock. Elizabeth gazed on him, knowing his soul was tortured with the need to rescue his daughter. The man she'd come to love with a burning, consuming passion. His wavy, ebony hair curling over his collar, the length of his beloved body stretched out among the dying ferns. Her heart swelled with a love that surpassed anything else she'd ever known.

A love she was willing to die for.

As Richard concentrated desperately on his aim, Elizabeth silently backed away, the only sound the rustling of the bracken. She'd deliberately moved twenty, thirty yards away to draw Maurice's attention from Richard's position, before she got to her feet, her head held high, her chin set resolutely, and began the climb to the tor. She heard Richard's hoarse, strangulated whisper as he called her back, but nothing would stop her, though her heart battered out of control and she had to force aside her panic as she placed one foot in front of the other. How many times in her life had she scrambled to the summit of this tor to enjoy the stunning views, drink in the air of the valley that was the very substance of her being? This was no different, she told herself. She must concentrate on the puling of the scavenging buzzard, the strident call of the raven. If she had to die, she could think of no better place, and suddenly she was no longer afraid. And what would he do to her, anyway? No more than her uncle had wanted from her, perhaps. If Richard could face the past that haunted him, then so could she. And she thought of the love they shared, and her lips parted in a smile.

'I'm here, Maurice.' Her voice steady, unflinching. But the lovely golden light was gone from her eyes, leaving a dull, muddy glimmer. Tendrils of her billowing hair drifting across her pale, impassive face. She didn't dare look at the stiffened, terrified child, but instead stared at some unseen point in the distance.

Maurice turned, and his teeth flashed white as he saw her. He stood, still as a statue, his head to one side as his eyes travelled slowly over her body. A sheen of sweat broke out over her skin under his unnerving gaze, and it took every fragment of her courage not to turn and run.

'Take off your clothes and let me see you properly,' he ordered, his nostrils flaring and his eyes gleaming with a savage lust.

Elizabeth shuddered. The moment had come. Somehow, her deadened limbs obeyed, dropping her shawl onto the unyielding rock surface, followed by her simple dress. Then she unlaced her boots, removing those, too, until she stood in nothing but her chemise and petticoat, her bare feet on the cold granite of the tor.

'Let the child go now.'

But Maurice's once handsome face twisted into a lurid smile as it caught the amber glow from the setting sun, the lines on his sallow skin hewn out in deep slashes. 'I'm not a fool, Elizabeth,' he snorted, his tone ringing with sarcasm. 'Come here, and we'll do an exchange, you for the brat.'

Elizabeth stared into his eyes, and swallowed. She was ready to sink onto her knees, but she *must* save Chantal. As she edged forward, the image of Matthew as he fumbled at her child's innocent body, flashed across her mind. But she had put all that behind her, and all because of one man, the man she loved, and who now lay in wait, his rifle poised and aimed to save his child.

Elizabeth came to within a few feet of Chantal, and smiled reassuringly at her white, blank little face. And then she straightened her back, squaring her slim shoulders, and looked Maurice challengingly in the eye. He faltered at the closeness of the exquisite beauty that had unhinged his mind, her scantily dressed body, her graceful arms, her slender throat. And he released his hold on the petrified child.

Chantal couldn't move. For God's sake, MOVE! Elizabeth silently screamed at her. But she stood, frozen into a pillar of ice.

Elizabeth reached out, grasped her arm and tugged her forward. Then she pushed her away towards safety. 'RUN!' The whispered shriek cracked in her throat as she hissed in Chantal's ear. And in that instant, she felt herself dragged into Maurice's grip and the cold steel of the blade against her own neck.

Maurice laughed, his head pressed against hers, an unearthly, disembodied cackle. 'You can't escape so easily, my dear,' he purred. And then he hollered so thunderously, her ears rang, 'You see now, Ritchie! I have her! I have your wife! And now you can see what I'm going to do with her!'

Elizabeth shuddered. Maurice was obviously crazed, possessed. Her wild, desperate gaze focused on Chantal. The child was coming to her senses, slithering backwards over the rocks. She was safe, free, and Elizabeth felt her courage soar.

'Never mind about Richard,' she soothed, turning her head over her shoulder. Feeling Maurice's hot breath fanning her cheek. 'I never realized what you felt for me, or I'd never have married him. You just never said. I'd have come, Maurice, if I'd known.'

She felt his body slacken and recognized confusion in his eyes. She was able to twist within the circle of his arms then, and raised herself on tiptoe, bringing her lips, sweet and delicate, onto his, her body pressing against him. Her stomach heaved, but somehow she managed to control it. She closed her eyes. Tried to pretend it was Richard she was kissing.

Elizabeth heard the clink as the knife slipped from Maurice's fingers and landed on the rock, but she didn't want to risk moving too fast. His hands entwined in her thick, curling hair, squeezing her tighter, his hungry mouth bruising her lips. She wanted to squeal and fight him off, but she knew she mustn't. She must be submissive, like the bewildered child who had once allowed her uncle to maul her ignorant body.

'Maurice, I'm so cold,' she scarcely had the voice to mutter. 'There's a sheltered spot,' she paused to kiss his neck, 'among the rocks. 'Tis soft and grassy.' She smiled at him, lovingly, but saw his hesitation. 'I'd be . . . *good* to you there . . .'

Her left hand found his right and she moved as if to lead him somewhere, taking three slow paces away from him, stretching both their arms to full length. Still smiling at his surprised expression, she turned him . . . so that his body was exposed to Richard's direct line of fire, and she herself, dear sweet Jesus, she *prayed*, was far enough away.

For God's sake, *shoot*, Richard, damn you, she screamed in her head. *SHOOT before it's too late!*

Her ears had been deaf to the low whistles and she was taken off guard when, at that second, a blur of black and white streaked past her feet and sunk its teeth into Maurice's ankle. He cried out and let go of Elizabeth's hand. She flung herself away, landing heavily on the stone surface of the tor, just as a reverberating explosion cracked through the air, scattering the peacefully grazing sheep. The echo of the gunshot died away, leaving a hollow, sepulchral silence.

When Elizabeth dared to lift her head, Maurice was gone, and Bramble was pacing along the sheer edge of the tor, growling, her ears flat against her head.

Elizabeth dragged herself into a sitting position. She could hear voices, anxious and muted. One was wheezing, agonized, calling her name. And then Richard's head, followed by his shoulders and body, appeared as he climbed the other side of the tor, one arm clutched across his ribs as he scrambled frantically towards her with Chantal close behind him. Within seconds, both she and Elizabeth were encompassed in the powerful circle of his arms. 'You shouldn't have done that, Beth,' he whispered hoarsely. 'I could have lost you both.'

Other voices followed then, voices she knew, all around them. She learned later that the constable had alerted others whose presence he deemed necessary, and in doing so, word had spread through the village in no time.

Richard looked up into William's stalwart face. 'Better see to him,' he croaked, jerking his head towards the ridge.

'I already have.' William's tone was grave. 'He's dead.'

'What!' Elizabeth felt Richard stiffen as she leaned against him. 'But I only winged him!'

'Yes, I know. It was the fall that killed him. It's only a short drop, but he cracked his head on a rock.'

'Oh, Christ,' Richard breathed, and dropped his head against Elizabeth's shoulder. 'Heaven knows what'll happen now,' he murmured. 'But thank God you're all right.'

She clung to him like a child, her bare, frail limbs drawing warmth and comfort from his strong body, the masculine scent of him she knew and loved. 'I'm so sorry. But I had to save Chantal,' she groaned miserably.

'And *you* were hardly supposed to be out of bed!' William reprimanded Richard, as he considered what dose of sleeping draught he should administer to the silent little girl who was clearly traumatized out of her wits.

'For God's sake, Will, he'd kidnapped my daughter!' Richard cried in anguish. 'It was him all along, you know. The ladder. Driving us out of the Hall. It's all in his note back at the farm. He was totally insane.'

'You don't deny shooting him then, sir?'

Elizabeth looked up at the constable from Mary Tavy who was standing between William and, amazingly, her uncle.

'No.' But Richard's voice was suddenly wary, and Elizabeth felt an insidious fear creep into her veins.

'You should have waited for me, sir.'

'What, and have him kill either my wife or my daughter, or both!'

The constable frowned, and taking off his hat, scratched his head before replacing it. 'I'm sorry, sir, but I think I'm going to have to arrest you for the murder of this . . . this gentleman.'

Elizabeth stared at him from the protective cradle of Richard's embrace as an utter, inexorable terror took hold of her. Slowly she and Richard rose as one to their feet, Chantal clinging to her father's leg.

'You can't do that, Constable,' William commanded. 'Mr Pencarrow was only defending his family.'

''Tis true, I saw it all!' This from Uncle Matthew. 'Had that there kitchen knife at the cheel's throat!'

But the constable grimaced with embarrassment. ''Tis not for me to decide, I'm afraid. I be obliged to take him into custody.'

'But you can't!' William protested again. 'He has several damaged ribs because of that blackguard, and God knows what damage chasing round out here has done!'

'You'll be free to attend him, Doctor, I assure you, and I'll make sure he's made comfortable in the cell. 'Twill not be for too long, though I believe the coroner be away at present. 'Tis his decision as to whether any prosecution will proceed. So, come along, sir, if you please.'

'I don't think *those* are necessary!' William railed at him, and Elizabeth caught sight of the cold steel of handcuffs.

She raised her glittering eyes as Richard took her cheeks between his strong hands and gazed deep and meaningfully into her tear-ravaged face. His lips closed in a knot and he gave an almost imperceptible shake of his head that only she understood, before pressing her quivering body against him and bringing his mouth down tenderly on hers. She returned his kiss, her hands around his neck, in his hair, holding him desperately to her, their mouths locked, her soul racked in agonized grief. They couldn't take him away! Not now! After everything they'd been through!

But Richard pulled away. They had to fight to tear her hands from him and hold her back. She stared up at him, her eyes wild and unseeing, blind to everything but the beloved face that swam before her. She saw his prominent Adam's apple move up and down his neck as he swallowed hard, and his eyebrows dipped excruciatingly.

'I must go,' he mouthed, for no sound came from his throat.

He kissed her hands then, and slowly let them fall. Then he backed away, his eyes trained on her, yearning, longing — until he was out of sight.

Elizabeth screamed and went to hurtle after him, but William's restraining arms closed about her. She lashed out, clawed and kicked, until her senses reeled away and she sank onto her knees.

EPILOGUE

The two young women sat patiently in the hired carriage as it waited in Tavistock's Bedford Square. They kept their voices low so as not to disturb the tall man who was slumped in the corner next to one of them. His eyes were closed, his gaunt face ashen behind the strong, dark stubble on his jaw. The women, too, looked tired and drained, though there was an air of relief about them.

'I do wish Adam would hurry up,' the more elegantly dressed of them whispered fervently. 'I don't know what he's doing.'

The golden-headed girl smiled wanly in response. It had been the longest few weeks of her life, she had hardly slept and now she was exhausted with the anxiety of it all. The constable from Mary Tavy had been right. Tavistock's coroner had been away, and they'd had to await his return. In the meantime, Dr Seaton, the most senior physician in the town, had carried out the post-mortem on Maurice Brett, confirming it was the fall and not Richard's bullet in his shoulder that had killed him. Curiously, the examination had revealed that this apparently upright man had been a user of opiates, and both Dr Seaton and William agreed that this could have gone a long way towards clouding his judgement and fuelling what must have been a bitter obsession. When the coroner finally returned, he immediately opened the initial inquest and then, as expected, adjourned it again while the police sergeant from Tavistock completed his enquiries. And all this time, Richard had been held in the grim, damp cells beneath the Magistrate's Court, despite both William and Adam's attempts to have him released on bail.

'You've been wonderful, both of you,' Elizabeth answered at length. 'Having Chantal and me to stay with you. And everything else. I . . . I don't know how I'd have got through it without you,' she faltered as a tear slid down her cheek.

'Stuff and nonsense. 'Twas the least we could do. And Dr Greenwood were a tower of strength to you, too. He visited Richard every day, didn't he, to check on his ribs, and he were there throughout the inquest, same as us.'

'Yes, he was. Oh, Becky, I'll never forget how you've all supported us.'

It was true. Everyone had been so kind during those appalling weeks and at the Coroner's Court, when Elizabeth's heart had continuously pounded in her chest. The case had aroused so much public interest that the inquest was held in the Magistrate's Court to accommodate everyone, and the room was filled with villagers from both Peter and Mary Tavy, people whom Elizabeth had helped in the past and who wanted to show the coroner and the jury that they were solidly behind her and her husband. When she had been in the witness-box, reliving the ordeal all over again, she had felt shamed, though it was none of her fault. But she had had to do it, for Richard's liberty — even his life — was at stake. And the sea of encouraging faces had given her strength. Then Matthew Halse had told how he had seen everything that had happened at White Tor that day, and Mr Widcock had testified that Richard was a crack shot, and although one could never be sure, his aim was so good and the American rifle so accurate, that he would have been reasonably confident of wounding rather than killing Maurice Brett. It seemed that everyone from the Tavy valley was willing the case to be dismissed, and finally, that morning — on the third day — the jury had given their verdict, and the coroner had ruled that Richard's actions in defence of his wife and daughter had been reasonable, and that he was free to go.

Elizabeth had almost fainted as she sat on the bench beside Adam and Rebecca, and between them they had managed to revive her. The room had burst out in a riotous clamour of celebration, people shouting and cheering, jumping up and down with excitement, so that Elizabeth's view of the prisoner's stand was blocked as she regained her senses. It had taken some minutes for Richard to force his way through the crowd, so many wanting to shake his hand or clap him on the shoulder. And then he was standing before her, the strain of the last weeks engraved alarmingly on his haggard face, and she was folded in his arms, her cheek against his chest and her head tucked beneath his chin as the joy unfurled in her breast.

And now the crowds had dispersed and they were waiting in the carriage Adam had hired to take them all back to Lavender Cottage, his and Rebecca's home at Morwellham. Richard stirred as Adam finally climbed inside and took his place beside his wife.

'Sorry to wake you,' he apologized.

But Richard shook his head. 'I wasn't really asleep, just resting my eyes. Everything keeps going round in my head. I can't imagine I'll ever sleep again.'

Elizabeth met his gaze and smiled as he squeezed her hand. 'Yes. I know how you feel.'

'Well, I've got something that might help.' And Adam's chestnut eyes shone as he held out a metal object in his hand.

Elizabeth and Richard both sat forward in disbelief. 'That's . . . the key to Rosebank Hall,' Richard stammered.

Adam grinned. 'It certainly is. And it's yours.'

Elizabeth turned her head and looked at the equal astonishment on Richard's face before she glanced back at Adam. 'I . . . I don't understand,' she mumbled.

'It's quite simple, really,' Adam shrugged. 'I persuaded the bank that they should buy the Hall back from Brett's estate for you, and reinstate your mortgage on it. The manager seemed only too willing to do so, which I thought was a little odd. But still, we had to agree it with Brett's solicitors, of course, but it seems he died intestate as he had no one to leave his wealth to. So his estate should go to the Crown, so they'd only sell the Hall anyway. And if some distant relative did emerge from somewhere, they'd still have the value of it. There'll be some paperwork, of course. But Rosebank Hall is yours again.'

'So that's where you've kept disappearing to so mysteriously!' Rebecca beamed, her face aglow with pleasure and surprise — and not a little pride in her beloved husband.

Elizabeth and Richard stared at each other open-mouthed, and then Richard shook his head with that soft laugh Elizabeth had thought she would never hear again. 'I can hardly believe it!' he finally spluttered.

'Well, if you prefer, I need a new farm manager for our estate in Hereford,' Adam said more seriously now. 'The job's yours if you want it. The estate lodge goes with it. You'd have none of the financial worry, and Beth could be a lady of leisure instead of having to work so hard.'

Elizabeth and Richard's eyes met steadily, but there was no need for any word to pass between them. ''Tis proper kind of you, Adam, but I don't think there's any question,' Elizabeth answered as her hand found Richard's again. 'Peter Tavy, the valley, 'tis our home. 'Twill be hard work, but I reckon as we can do it, can't we, Richard? Get Rosebank Hall back as it should be?'

'Of course,' Richard replied, though he still seemed stunned. 'But how can we ever thank you?'

Adam waved a dismissive hand. 'No need. But where shall I tell the driver to take us? You're coming back home with us so we can look after you both until you're properly recovered from all this, but we could go up to the Hall first if you like.'

'Do you feel up to it, Richard?' A soft, caressing light came into Elizabeth's eyes as she turned to him.

He smiled, his eyebrows arched ruefully. 'I think I can manage that. In fact, I can't think of anything I'd like more.'

They held hands, shifting closer together, as the carriage moved along narrow Duke Street and then out through Parkwood on the road to Okehampton. After a couple of miles, they turned off, clattering over the bridge where once Richard had rescued the traumatized girl escaping from her uncle, then through the village and out to the track that led to the Hall. It was late November, and up on the high back of Dartmoor snow had already fallen inches deep, but here on the side of the valley it had merely wafted in the air in a powdery dust. But it was bitterly cold even inside the carriage, and the iron-grey sky threatened more snowfall before the day was through.

They finally drew up outside the Hall, and Richard and Elizabeth alighted from the carriage while Adam and Rebecca remained inside, not wanting to intrude. Their feet crunched on the frozen ground, and Richard paused for a moment to draw in a lungful of the pure, glacial air.

'I can't tell you how good it is to be free,' he murmured as the cutting north wind grasped at his coat. 'Those bloody cells were awful. We were allowed an hour a day in the exercise yard, but that was hardly any better. You know, there was a chap . . . He was waiting to go before the magistrate. Accused of a violent robbery, but he swore he'd only stopped to help the victim after he was attacked in the street. I was inclined to believe him. I can't help wondering what happened to him.'

Elizabeth turned to this man who was so good, and patted the lapels of his coat as she shivered with cold. 'Poor fellow. But you can't worry about *everyone*, Richard,' she said gently. 'Come on. Let's go inside. We shouldn't keep Adam and Becky waiting too long.'

Richard nodded, and a moment later the heavy front door groaned open and they stood in the hallway of the house that they loved. Their home. It seemed cold and echoing, most of the furniture and carpets gone. They would have to start again, but they had each other and Chantal and Bramble, and soon the place would ring with contentment again.

Elizabeth gazed about her, and then realized Richard's narrowed eyes were smiling at her as he took her in his arms. She lifted her hand to brush his lean jaw, lost in the rapturous depths of his liquid eyes as the courageous spirit that had always been hers swelled her heart. He kissed her then, long and deep and passionate, the first time they had been alone together during all those anguished weeks.

'Oh, God, I love you,' he breathed thickly, scarcely moving his lips from hers. 'We'll never be apart again, I promise you. Never.'

'I know. I couldn't bear it.' Moisture misted her vision and she felt her tears welling again as the appalling memories of the past weeks flooded back. But Richard's dark eyes bore into hers, shining pools of ardent, tender passion, his love for her so deep it glowed from him like the sun. He dipped his head, and when his mouth found hers again, moist and sweet, a joyous ecstasy tingled deliciously down her spine. Richard pulled away, and she reluctantly opened her eyes, gazing breathlessly up at his familiar, handsome, smiling face, her heart full.

'Shall we take a look around, Mrs Pencarrow?'

'Why not, Mr Pencarrow?' she replied with a grin. And took his hand.

THE END

ACKNOWLEDGEMENTS

With very many thanks to all the local people who have contributed information for this novel. My heartfelt gratitude must go, in particular, to my good friend Paul Rendell, Dartmoor guide and historian, and editor of *Dartmoor News*, who has sought out all manner of obscure detail for me. Also to the Abel family who have farmed in Peter Tavy for generations, and who gave me the benefit of such broad knowledge of the history of farming in the area. I must also mention Marjorie Sherrell, who was brought up in the village and is now a farmer's wife not so far away; Geoffrey Weymouth, a farmer in another part of Dartmoor but who kindly gave me some basic farming instruction; the late Gerry Woodcock, a Tavistock historian who generously filled me in on various details of the town's history; Graham K. Cook, the Adjutant at www.clash-of-steel, for his advice on small firearms; my dear friend, Anne-Marie, who polished my somewhat rusty French; and last but not least, Simon Dell, MBE, of the Devon and Cornwall Constabulary, for advising me on the history of policing in the Tavistock area in the relevant period.

Thank you for reading this book.

If you enjoyed it please leave feedback on Amazon or Goodreads, and if there is anything we missed or you have a question about, then please get in touch. We appreciate you choosing our book.

Founded in 2014 in Shoreditch, London, we at Joffe Books pride ourselves on our history of innovative publishing. We were thrilled to be shortlisted for Independent Publisher of the Year at the British Book Awards.

www.joffebooks.com

We're very grateful to eagle-eyed readers who take the time to contact us. Please send any errors you find to corrections@joffebooks.com. We'll get them fixed ASAP.

Made in the USA
Columbia, SC
12 May 2023